A ^slight Change of Plans

A *slight* Change of Plans

by John Zobel

Goodfellow Press
Redmond, Washington

ISBN: 1-891761-C1-3
Library of Congress Catalog Card #: 98-074115

Edited by Pamela R. Goodfellow
Cover illustration by Barbara Levine
Cover photography by Jeff Pruett
Cover design by CJ Wyckoff and Matt Buchman
Book design by Matt Buchman

Printed on recycled paper in Canada

This book is principally set in Garamand Normal Condensed, 12.5pt with a 14.6pt leading. Drop Caps are Black Chancery & various fonts were used for titles, newspaper clippings, etc.

For Eric Hart, to read another day

— 1 —

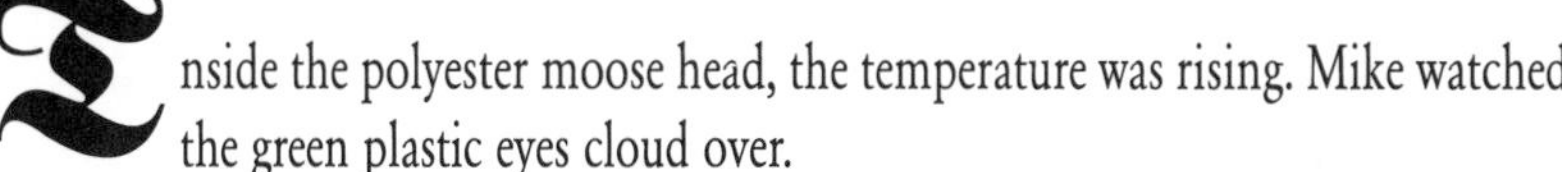

nside the polyester moose head, the temperature was rising. Mike watched the green plastic eyes cloud over.

"Three minutes!" Carl's muffled voice came from somewhere beyond the dressing room.

Condensation of breath, Mike told himself, nothing to panic over. All the same, he had the feeling of having burrowed into a plastic bag, the clingy, suffocating, keep-away-from-children kind.

The moose costume, of course, was not designed to repel children. On the contrary, from the tips of its goofy antlers to the ends of its oversized feet, it had one purpose: to keep the munchkins enthralled, gumming on the cheesy rubber discs that Pizzazzip somehow passed off as non-toxic. Anesthetize the tots, ran the theory, and the parents would stay in the Grownup Garden, washing down underfilled pitchers of overpriced, watery beer.

Mike wriggled, hoping for a more comfortable fit. How nice it would be to chalk up the sense of confinement to the brutal humidity of a summer evening in Our Nation's Capital and not to a cloud of lethal carbon dioxide. Had anyone ever smothered in a moose? The thing was a coffin with feet. Some epitaph: DIED WITH HIS HOOVES ON.

The green eyes dripped and streaked, not that the moisture blocked any fabulous views. The cramped dressing room, with its cracked paint and concrete floor, boasted all the luxuries of a broom closet. To take his mind off the steam, Mike began to inventory, by feel alone, the bruises on one thigh. He closed his eyes. One more show, just one, and things would be better.

Every Monday and Thursday night for the past four weeks, from five to nine, on the hour and again on the half, the ritual had unfolded with grim precision. Music, curtain, and onto the stage wedged in a corner of the pizza so-called palace stumbled Michael T. Archer, the bundle of nerves inside huggable, lovable, loathsome Morty Moose.

He didn't have to sing, didn't have to lip-synch, didn't really have to dance. All he did was spasm around the miniature stage for two minutes and thirty-seven seconds in time to a perky little ditty with lyrics that would justify homicide: *Why, howdy kids, it's just no use / For me to be a silly goose / I've gotta let my feets run loose / For I'm that wacky Morty Moose . . .*

Caroming about the stage, Mike had plenty of time to work out further rhymes, which seemed to center on 'abuse.' He had grown over the years to realize that each job, even when it turned out not to be the job, held its nugget of wisdom. 'Why did the last guy quit?' he now knew, would be a good thing to ask at the next job interview. If he lived that long.

"Nine o'clock." Carl loomed on the other side of the streaky plastic, his prematurely shiny scalp rendered a nauseating green. He rubbed his hands like some Martian Napoleon. "It's almost nine on a Thursday, and you know what that means."

Mike took a last stab at convincing his manager that beer, at night, in a children's pizza place, was a bad idea. "Here's the thing," he said borrowing one of the guy's own expressions. Vigor, logic, passion. That was what Char preached, and that was what Mike planned to give. He sensed the antlers swinging, but communication was stymied by the absence of an opening in the polyester head.

Carl put on his Patient Face. "Mike." It was his standard argument. As if struck by the beauty of the logic, he repeated it before slapping the padded back. "Mike. Give 'em a good show, kid. Two minutes!" He wandered toward the kitchen, waving an upraised hand.

Bad idea, staying in costume. Mike released himself from the sweaty shell.

"Hey!"

Carl turned, the light on his scalp now day-glo yellow. Mike sucked in cool oxygen. Damp hair hung in his eyes.

"I'm sorry, Carl, but I'm not going on tonight."

"I say you are, bub."

"I am not." He maneuvered the antlers into a headlock. "It's crazy. This costume's for children. You could lob grenades out there now without hitting a kid. The last family left an hour ago. There's no point in my going on this late, without any kids out there. Hardly anyone at all. Just those same . . . who am I supposed to be singing to?"

"Well." Carl tried an indulgent look. "Here's the thing. It's in your contract. What can I do? Come on, ace, we've had this talk three weeks in a row. Every Thursday." He shook his head. "You know why you gotta go out there. You gotta go out . . . because it's in your contract."

"Wait." Mike raised a hand and the moose head dropped to the floor. "Damn. You know I don't have a contract."

"Your deal, then. And a deal's a deal. Anyhow, it's good for business."

Mike retrieved the head, wondering about the 'it' Carl found so terrific. "Yeah, but they're out there."

"Who's out there?" Carl was all innocence. "Who is? What do you mean?"

Mike dusted the polyester nose. "We reserve the right to refuse service, don't we?"

"It's a right. We don't gotta exercise it."

"Still," Mike nearly made eye contact, "you can't . . . force me out there."

The bogus sympathy melted away. "Let's make it simple, college man. You don't have that furry ass on stage ten short seconds after the music starts, you hit the pavement."

"Hang on, Carl. You don't get to–"

"Dad'll back me on this, bet on it. He thinks you're lazy. Or tell you what." Carl laughed. "Take it up with your friend on the Hill. Dad never wanted to hire you in the first place. He only did it for Uncle Steve."

Carl Handley. A nothing, a petty tyrant. Easy to defy, in theory. Mike reached behind himself and felt for his spine.

"Ten." Carl spread the fingers of both hands. "Ten seconds. Got it?" He flexed his shoulders and, hiking up his pants, ambled toward the kitchen.

Great. Lose the job, she thinks you're a failure. Keep the job, you know you're a corpse. Mike jammed his tongue against his teeth. Maybe those guys wouldn't come tonight. Maybe.

He tugged off a moose mitt and pushed the sleeve from his watch. No time to debate. He bent and yanked the leggings closer to his feet. Pizzazzip costumes were designed to the specs of franchisors who must have found it difficult to picture anyone six feet tall in the role of Morty Moose. Mike used his only pair of dress socks to bridge the gaps. Carl's voice snickered down the hallway, the words unintelligible.

Mike forced the head past his ears, turned, and promptly strode into something solid. He doubled over and his fingers brushed a fire extinguisher. Clutching his stomach with one hand, he used the other to feel his way to the door. He worked his fingers under the neck of the costume and smeared steam from the plastic eyes. On impulse he grabbed the fire extinguisher. They'd never expect that. But already the moment was on him, unavoidable, a freeway pileup in fog. He crossed the hall as the music began, a grating crescendo and a riot of trumpets. He zippered the head to the body. A disembodied voice, his own, echoed in the polyester shell: ". . . four, five, six," and he could hear a sound from the dining room, beyond the stage curtain, a raspy roar: "LET'S MESS WITH THE MOOSE!"

It was what Carl had waited all week to hear.

". . . nine, ten, damn," and Mike dove onstage, clutching his weapon. On each of the past two Thursdays he'd tried to survive by mimicking the carefree critter every survey said the kids wanted. At least when they were present, which they weren't. Mike switched tactics by taking up a defensive position with his back to the curtain and aiming the nozzle toward the room.

The music washed over him. He tried to keep his breathing minimal as he leaned to one side, peering through the bottom half of an eyehole. The dining room appeared to be empty, and for a moment it was worth believing. He lowered the nozzle but then leather and chains and reflector sunglasses and two-day stubble engulfed him, all nine circles of hell at once, and here came their chant again, "LET'S MESS . . ."

The extinguisher was torn from his mitts. Visualize calm. There must be a reason this is happening. Beyond the noise of ragged breathing, the tinny recording pattered on: *Why, howdy, kids . . .*

The goons pummeled him and tossed him like a ball in a rugby match. Surely they had better places to hang out. Fate or bad karma?

Four weeks of practice, and they'd become pretty good, to give them credit. With coordinated lifting and heaving, they caught him after a dizzying drop. Panting breaths filled the moose head. The costume tugged at his throat. Someone had the antlers as the routine began in earnest.

. . . that wacky Morty . . .

They spun him, two guys gripping the polyester head, building up momentum as if in a collective hammer throw. Mike's jaw pressed against the throat of the costume as he scrabbled at the zipper. Maybe the antlers would tear. Who bothered to reinforce antlers?

He felt the nausea of centrifugal force. Too late to fight back, too late to do anything but hang on. Each breath took a conscious effort. Fur heels brushed the stage as he spun. Faster. Faster. His hands grew so heavy he could hardly feel anything in his fingertips.

His feet rose without bidding, slaves to one of Newton's laws and through the steamy eyeholes he caught flashes of his toes as around he whirled, and again, the blood rushing to his ankles with the blurry, beery faces howling, or was it Kepler, and once every rotation he could see Carl backstage, doubled over, hand clamped on the phone in case anyone thought of calling for help.

". . . two, one, LAUNCH," and for the first time all night Mike was free, weightless, arcing across the room feet first. A false respite. Fire in the capsule!

He slammed against a table, skipped off it like a stone on a pond, and came to rest supine in a corner of the foam-covered PlayLand. His breath came in shredded gasps. Impossibly far away, high fives and shouts exploded like fireworks.

His head wouldn't move. One of the antlers, or maybe it was an arm this time, had twisted under his body. Ceiling cracks chased one another in endless circles. His breath came hard, sealed into the head as he was, but the air seemed a shade fresher as the music came to the end: *. . . that wonderful, funderful Mo-o-orty Moose!*

He lifted his free hand without significant pain and clenched the paw in a victory fist. It should have been obvious. Things had a way of working out in the end.

▼ ▼ ▼

A swirl of muggy air followed Liz into the house, and she slammed the front door closed on June. Another month conquered. If only the humidity, the District of Columbia, the whole irritating world in fact, would simply leave her alone. Inside was little better. The alarm wailed and the telephone rang. Hell of a price for privacy. She ignored the phone and concentrated on disarming the system.

"And stay off," she told the keypad.

The phone wouldn't give up. She kicked her shoes across the hall and walked through to the kitchen. No reason to run. It was far too late for anyone civilized to be calling. And it was her house, damn it. In the kitchen, she dumped briefcase and purse and yanked the antenna of the cordless with her teeth, just to have something to punish.

"Yes?"

"Geez, you took long enough. You got Hillton-Tanner wrapped for me?"

"I'm fine, Bud, nice of you to ask." Thank heaven for kitchens. Not that she ever had time to cook, but what a spot for pacing.

"Yeah, yeah, now what's wrong?"

"Just a long day. Nothing you'd understand." She stared at the ceiling, willing herself to relax. She rubbed her foot over the cool floor, enjoying the tingle through the sole of her nylons.

Bud nattered on. ". . . and even then I made it to work by eight."

"Hooray for you. I had a dozen crises before seven." She flicked the switch on the popcorn machine and let him listen to the roar, but the blast was too hot to stand near very long. She turned it off.

"Anyway." He made a choking noise, no doubt fighting off that famous L.A. smog.

She propped herself against the counter and examined her fist. "Let me tell you a story. Once upon a time there was a man who ran across a brilliant master's thesis on computer viruses. He found it so impressive he hired the author sight unseen. She was thrilled. Four years went by and she realized her boss took an awful lot of things for granted."

"Nice story. What about this H-T mess? All tidied up?"

"Just about." She spun the combination lock on one side of her briefcase, feeling the click of the tumblers. Company policy said the case should have been locked before it left the office. For that matter, company policy said work went home only in emergencies. She realized her first response hadn't been reassuring enough. "There's nothing to worry about." The man was a professional neurotic.

"I knew it. I knew it. Tell all."

"Come on, Bud, it's almost ten on this coast." She ran a thumb over the metal numbers. "Call me tomorrow. At the office, even."

"Yeah, right. Guess what?" He coughed.

"What?" She could picture him welcoming the sunset from the ramparts of his Santa Monica castle and gagging on his drink. She held the cordless to her ear with her shoulder and headed for the bedroom. Along the way, she pushed against the front door. Closed. She stooped to retrieve her shoes and tapped the heels together for luck. No place like home.

His voice came back, weak. "I lined up your next project."

"Swell." She imagined his deck sliding into the ocean.

"You're gonna love this."

She flipped on lights in the hall and bedroom. Everything under control.

"I hope it can wait. As you know, I'm leaving in two days. Remember? I have an island lined up without phones, faxes or beepers, for two well-deserved weeks of vacation. And that last part's a quote."

"Oh, sure. The mysterious island you won't name. I don't believe it exists."

"You can afford to let me have that much privacy."

"Knock it off. Anyway, who goes to the Caribbean in July?"

"Bingo." She stood in the walk-in closet and unfastened her skirt. The pumps went into their space in a short line along the wall.

"Sorry." He didn't sound it. "Critical path here. They need you ASAP."

"They don't, Bud. It's Fourth of July weekend. Send Joey."

"Can't do that."

"Why not?" She juggled the phone as she unbuttoned her blouse.

He coughed.

"Geez," she said. "Back on the cocaine, or what?"

"That's not funny." The coughing stopped abruptly. "Don't even joke about that kind of stuff on an open wire."

"All right, calm down." She leaned against the closet wall and stared at her thighs. Back to the running program tomorrow morning, no excuses.

"I can't send Joey." Bud blew his nose. "Besides, they need the best. They even asked . . . look, they need the best."

"Don't give me that." She tossed the blouse toward the wicker basket. A shower would be nice. She lifted the hair from the back of her neck.

"It's the truth. Anyhow, this Westfield job is a high pay, very high pay, quick turnaround kind of deal. Perfectly straightforward. Plenty of, I don't know, stuff you like. Plus, it's almost in your backyard, but very remote, this little place. Hartigan Gap, Virginia."

"Hartigan Gap?" Allie's image flashed before her like a poke in the eye.

"Yeah," she barely heard him say. "Nice little spot. Not an hour's drive. Shoot down, take care of their problem, you're back to Hillton-Tanner on Monday, snorkeling by mid-week."

"Monday's a holiday in this country. For humans."

"Tuesday, then."

"I don't know." It had been a long time since she'd thought about Allie, about what had happened that last day. High in one corner of the closet she spotted a cobweb. Too many things had slid for too long.

"Look," he said, "the place is a mansion. I'm telling you it's cushy duty."

She unfastened her bra, wondering whether the man had any idea he was talking to a practically naked employee. Revolting thought. He controlled enough aspects of her life.

She hugged an arm across her chest. "How cushy, exactly?"

"Cushy cushy. Your contact can give you details. Look, we'd better not talk about this on the phone." Funny, the way he'd always pull that out after he'd babbled for ten minutes. "You might get an idea what's involved if you look at today's *Post.*"

"I don't take the paper."

"So grab a copy somewhere tomorrow." Naturally he'd seized on her lame response, sensing her weakening. "Do this for me, Liz. You'll get an extra day off. I mean that. An extra day."

"You are all heart." All bypass.

"Two days, then. You're gonna love this."

"Hold it right there." She rested her head against the wall. "I haven't said yes. I'll think about it, that's all, okay? Hang on." It couldn't be considered weakness if she made a conscious decision to do it.

"Oh, yeah. Sure." She hadn't realized until then how nervous he was that she'd turn him down. She pulled a baggy t-shirt from the top shelf and shook it loose. The Holyoke seal had faded, but in what remained of it she could see Allie's face, the eyes unwilling to meet hers, looking toward . . . what?

She tossed the phone on the quilt and pulled the shirt over her head, letting the cotton drop to her knees. When she picked up the handset again, Bud's breathing was harsh, in a way she didn't like, even coming from a guy with asthma. She found paper and pen and dropped into an armchair. Better. She swung her legs across the upholstery.

Bud switched to tuneless humming. She gritted her teeth and almost hung up. But there'd be time enough later. Let him pay for the vacation first. Besides, she wasn't sure she wanted the new assignment. He still had some grovelling to do. She tucked her hair back.

"Okay." She took a good, slow breath. "Tell me everything you can. What's the big crisis in Hartigan Gap?"

▼ ▼ ▼

In his limping retreat toward the changing room, Mike heard boisterous laughter from the kitchen. He separated the moose head from his own and shouldered his way through the swinging doors.

Carl perched on a three-legged stool, holding forth on the aerodynamic capabilities of the human body. His audience was Bill the pizza master and the dishwasher, a new kid, all elbows and teeth. As Mike entered, Carl burst into cascading guffaws.

"Oh, that was great." He swiveled toward Bill. "Pow! The way he bounced off the table? Outstanding. Wish I'd got it on film. I'm bringing my camera next week."

"Glad you enjoyed it." Mike rubbed his back.

"Enjoyed, are you kidding? I'd pay to see a show like that."

"Oh?" Even Char couldn't have scripted it so well. "Does that mean you'll give me a raise?"

"Give you a . . ." Carl lost it again.

Bill reached into the freezer. The kid at the sink raised gloved hands in a helpless gesture. Mike nodded thanks for the support, such as it was.

"Sure." Carl sucked in a breath. "Yeah, I'll give you a raise. You wanna perform on a high wire? That enough raise for you?"

The door to the dining room flew open.

"Order in." Christi, on solo waitress duty, shoved past and jammed a ticket in the wheel, spinning it to face the cook. "Hi," she said to Mike.

"Hi." The tormentors must have worked up an appetite.

Carl tugged her arm. "Whaddya think, hon, put the guy on a high wire?"

"Heights, Carl." She pulled away, smoothing her uniform. "He doesn't like heights. Leave him alone." She stomped out to the dining room.

"Oh, yeah." Carl smacked his forehead. "I knew it was something. Afraid of heights. How come?"

Mike wiped his face with a dish towel. Might as well get it over with. He spoke from under the towel.

"Say, Carl, could I see you a minute?"

"Here I am."

He pulled the towel from his face. "In private, I meant."

Not quite stifling a giggle, Carl slid from his perch.

"Oh, sure, sure, step into my big old office." With a laugh, he ushered Mike through a door marked 'Exit.'

They stood in the alley between Pizzazzip and Barry's Big 'n Tall. A floodlight threw a beam across a large dumpster.

Mike had never worn the costume outdoors before. It seemed wrong, as if the alley were somehow less private than a restaurant stage. An exhaust fan blew hot, tomato sauce-scented air across his face, drying his mouth.

"Well?" Carl blocked the door, arms folded.

Mike pried his lips apart and gave Char's speech. "You know, I was serious about that raise. I mean, I've been here a month. So I've earned it, really, getting tossed around and all. Thursday nights."

"Nope." Carl shook his head. "Don't remember promising any raises."

"You didn't, technically, but . . ."

"Tell you what, smart boy." Carl patted his longest strand of hair into place. "Maybe you deserve a little bonus after all. Let's see, let's see . . . oh, I know. You can have the leftover pepperoni-mushroom that just came back. Half a good pizza there." He grinned. "Don't say I can't spot good work."

Mike felt his shoulders droop. "That's not exactly what . . ."

"Hey, don't be taking advantage of me."

"Well, I wasn't."

"You think I can't tell the way you treat company property, I see that rip in the leg." Carl pointed. "Fix it by tomorrow night, bub, or it's out of your pay. Have it here by four-thirty."

Mike opened his mouth, but Carl was quicker.

"Don't piss me off, cowboy. I got a guy coming over I need to impress. Some of us are trying to make something of our lives, not just sitting around waiting for it to happen." He spat. "Ripped costumes. Unbelievable."

Mike examined the slit in the fabric. Blood welled from a gash near his knee. The door to the kitchen thudded shut, and he heard a definite click.

"Oh, come on." He rattled the knob.

From inside came a muffled voice. "You're off shift. Use the front."

"I need my clothes, Carl." What a jerk.

"I said, the front." His laughter receded, fading into the restaurant.

The front. Where the moose-tossers waited.

Mike tried his farewell speech aloud. "I quit. Guess what, Carl, I quit." It sounded good, echoing off the bricks. "Hey, I quit. Give me back my clothes."

Damn. Damn Char, and her damned connections.

The frosted window of the washroom creaked open, and a bundle flew out, landing at his feet. The window banged down again. A dishtowel lay wadded on the ground, the corners knotted into a sack. He patted at it and felt his keys and wallet. Maybe shoes, shirt and pants would take the same flight path. He stared at the small window. Nothing followed.

Punching something would be nice, something that wouldn't hurt too much. He thought about knocking over the row of motorcycles parked out front, but the brief pleasure wasn't worth the pain that would surely follow.

To hell with Carl anyway, and his stupid games. Mike lifted the dumpster lid and slammed it, producing a satisfying crash. He slouched toward the street, clutching bundle in one hand, antler in the other. Okay, funny guy, you want your costume fixed, you can wait.

The broad sidewalk was mostly deserted. No one he knew anyway. Mike took a hesitant step into the light. Dragging Morty Moose along the pavement, a caveman with his kill, he steered for the nearest Metro entrance. He'd figured all along Pizzazzip wasn't the place he was supposed to end up. His next stop was bound to be better.

▼ ▼ ▼

Liz swung her legs down from the chair arm. Bud's explanation had been sketchy, but he hadn't lied. It was right up her alley. A riddle in a computer.

She headed for the kitchen. Into the popcorn maker she tossed a handful of kernels. The lone beer in the fridge was tempting, just a bit tempting, left over from the highly forgettable Colin era. She went with juice.

Her briefcase lay on the table. She worked the tumblers, set this month out of sheer laziness to the simplest Fibonacci sequence: 112 358. In the main compartment was a disk, labeled 'spellcheck etc.' to discourage the curious. She made a nest for her juice glass in the bowl of popcorn and padded across the carpet toward the study. The house was too quiet. She detoured past the front door and reset the alarm. It occurred to her, not for the first time, that it might be nice to have a cat around.

"At least I wouldn't be talking to myself," she told the alarm panel.

In the act of sliding one of the usual CDs into the player, she changed her mind and chose her only jazz recording, a recommendation from Allie five years earlier. She'd never liked it much, but perhaps now was the time to give it another chance.

Her computer skittered through a self-diagnostic before deciding it was awake. Red letters filled light blue background: 'MEMO TO SELF: GET A LIFE.' She made a face at it and opened a new file, RUNLOG.630. A diversion in case anyone broke into her system. She stared at the file name. The suffix made her think she'd forgotten something. Something about June 30th.

The sax hit the heartbreaking section, the one part she did care for, and she paused to let it flow through her. The things she didn't know about jazz theory could have kept a graduate seminar busy for years. Strange, because music was math, and math was her bread and butter. But classical music defined her boundaries. Jazz lacked sufficient structure.

Her finger stroked the 'Exit' key. Instead she called up the fifth listing on the 'Errands' directory. She hadn't been wholly candid with Bud about Hillton-Tanner. Saying it was just about wrapped up really meant she had finished yesterday but wanted to admire the scheme a little longer before she turned the results over to the client.

The H-T execs had known for some time that they had a problem. What they'd initially dismissed as a software glitch, however, soon revealed itself to be much more. Several times a month, the whole system unaccountably crashed. At first, the shutdowns had been merely irritating. But the vendor had no explanation, and that was frightening. The H-T guys called Bud. And he called Liz.

It had taken her longer than average to discover what was happening, which meant someone knew a thing or two. A bug in the system, obviously, but this was no virus. Rather than destroying or deleting files, the renegade program created some and altered others, using the crashes as smokescreens. She'd needed a week to piece it together. Whenever Accounting recorded a customer payment in excess of $50,000, the program shut everything down, created a new 'Miscellaneous' account, transferred 10% of the payment, set up a phantom 'loan payable' in the same amount, and rewrote the receivable at 90%. The books balanced, while management tore out its collective hair wondering why sales were off ten percent.

It was a cute trick. The beauty of the plan though, lay in where the skimmed funds went. Liz would have expected a bogus vendor or a fictitious employee, but every one of those entries checked out. She hadn't even been able to match outgoing payments with the missing amounts. Not until she'd gone back to the crashes themselves had she stumbled on the answer. Each subsequent dump swept the 'Miscellaneous' account, made an automatic deposit to a Hillton-Tanner bank account, and deleted the loan payable. She'd asked, discreetly, about that bank account. No one knew anything. So the bug artist not only waited to make sure his skim hadn't been detected, he sent the money to what looked like a company account. No paper trail. Poof.

There wasn't, strictly speaking, any reason for Liz to pursue the matter further. She had a good idea what H-T would find in the end: a signature card with a name no one had ever heard of, and a series of wire transfers to an offshore numbered bank account. She leaned back in her chair and closed her eyes. The witch hunt at Hillton-Tanner she could skip. Embezzlers were the worst and cleanups anti-climactic. The challenge was to figure out the puzzle in the first place.

▼ ▼ ▼

As Mike hurried past a diner, the door swung open and a disheveled figure barreled into him.

"Bloody hell, watch where you mope."

Mike took a step away, gripping wallet and keys. "Sorry, I . . . distracted."

In the shadows, the figure resolved itself into a rumpled man who fumbled with thick glasses and squinted.

"Cripes, fella can't half take a step round here without being run over by a . . . by a flipping . . . by a . . . Mikey?"

Mike had always hated the diminutive. He drew himself to full height and peered at the stranger.

"Do I know you?"

"Know me? 'Know you,' he says. I should think, slick. Know me? It's Gray." The man jabbed himself in the chest. "Westfield!"

"Gray?"

An emphatic nod. He pushed the hair off his forehead.

As Mike took another step back, he teetered on the edge of the sidewalk.

"Gray! Well, I'll . . . you let your hair go. And where did you get that appalling accent?"

"London. Three smashing months. Just back. Ain't it a cracker?"

"Three months?" Mike recovered. "Three months, you old phony, and that's the best you could do? What happened to Oxford and Cambridge? What happened to upper class? The accent's not permanent, is it, like a tattoo?"

"Ha ha. There's the old Mikey." Gray landed a soft shoulder punch. "Come on, Guv, now what was you expecting, Margaret bleeding Thatcher?" He squinted. "You . . . you are wearing a moose suit."

"Yeah, thanks for the warning."

"The mind leaps to ask, why?"

"I'm coming from work." Mike saw Gray's mouth opening. "Look, I'd rather not talk about it."

"Righty-o." A shrug. "Well, come inside and have a cup."

"I'd just as soon not." Mike gestured toward the moose head.

"Probably best." Gray pointed at a huddle of trees across the street. "Shall we pip over to yon park for a chat?"

While Mike sought a plausible excuse, Gray stepped from the curb, looking to his right. Mike had to yank him from the path of a bus.

"Oops, thanks. Haven't got back the hang of the bloody traffic."

And that about summed up their relationship. In college, Gray had tossed out ideas like life rings and towed his friends behind a canoe toward what sounded suspiciously like waterfalls. The result for Mike had been much swimming for shore.

When they were safely across the street in Washington Circle, Gray dropped onto a bench. "What's it been, Mikey, four years?"

"Nearer five. Since graduation." Same body, different person. There must be a specific moment when two people stopped being friends, best friends, without any intervening event. If only one could see the moment coming. If only one had a second chance to stop it.

Gray wiped his glasses. "Last I remember, you were off to get a visa."

"VISTA. I volunteered for VISTA."

"Right." Gray didn't sound interested. "How was it?"

"Fine. I had to leave after two years."

Gray perked up. "Oh? Some sort of scandal?"

"They make everyone leave. Kind of like shoving baby birds from the nest. They don't want you to get too dependent."

"Makes sense." Gray failed to suppress a smile. "Where did you land?"

Mike watched the traffic, wondering why it should be obvious that he hadn't learned to fly.

"I guess I'm still searching for a good landing site. I thought VISTA was a choice in itself. It turned out to be a deferral. To tell you the truth, I haven't figured out where I've ended up. Or if I have."

"In other words, nothing's changed."

More cars passed. Mike caught himself fiddling with an antler. Some people came so close to your life, they hurt you without trying. An odd way to recognize friendship.

"Still seeing what's-her-name?"

"No." Mike tried to guess which what's-her-name Gray was remembering. "For the past few months I've been with a woman named Char." That sounded too intimate. "Lotte," he appended.

"Really, now. You might say that with a splash of enthusiasm."

"What do you mean?"

"Oh, hang on. Is this one of those, you know, tectonic relationships?"

"Those what? You mean platonic."

"Right, right. Knew it was something to do with continents."

"No," Mike said. "Definitely not."

"Ah. I see. So what's the attraction?"

"We help each other out." Mike picked an acorn off the bench. "She's a smart, attractive woman, and she puts up with me."

"Sorry. Hadn't realized that was it. We're meant to be looking for someone who'll put up with us, is that it? That's the goal? How hugely depressing."

"Don't push it." There was no point in disclosing Char's own take on the relationship, which was that he didn't have the nerve to leave her. She was wrong. It wasn't a question of nerve.

"Right," Gray said. "Well, then. Not to pry. The thing is, the moose suit. I mean, what?"

"It's just a job."

"Sure. Been at it long? Start as a fish, work your way along the chain?"

Mike pressed his spine against the bench. "I've been doing it a month." He felt the need to come up with something more impressive. "That is, I had been. I just quit."

"Did you? Brilliant. Couldn't be better." Gray slid closer. "Tell you what. Ditch the suit, pack your case, hop the train with me to Briarwood tomorrow."

"Briarwood." Somewhere in Virginia. "Is your father still there?"

"Right. Well, for today, anyway. But that's another story. Look, there's a bunch of his friends coming for the holiday weekend. He loves to have a dance party, fireworks in the back yard, all that rot. You'd be quite welcome. See, I'm supposed to be out there, to get a job and whatnot, and bring money in. A job. Isn't that just Dad?" Gray gripped Mike's arm with both hands. "Here I have the perfect plan to shower self with riches, and the man wants me to work. At least you don't have that kind of parental pressure."

"I don't want to hear your theory about my father."

"Jolly good. In that case I won't ask after your brother, either."

A couple of young women passed in the darkness. At the sight of Mike's costume, one of them pointed.

"Fur is murder! Fur is murder!" Her companion pulled her away.

"I need to take care of something first," said Gray. "But I tell you what."

"You'll lose that sorry accent?"

"Not a bit of it. We'll go partners. Me and you. And maybe one other. This is your thing, spot on."

"People tell me that all the time." Mike stood. "It never is."

"This will be."

"What will be?"

"Your next job. My plan."

Planning. It had been the most impressive thing about Gray in college. He was always moving toward a goal, never mind that the world continually knocked him off course. Too smart for his own good maybe, but at least he had a strategy. And job prospects.

"This is the best plan yet." Gray dropped his voice to a raspy whisper and made the disclosure behind one hand. "Vid-Za."

"Vid-Za?"

"Not so loud. Vid-Za. Combination video store, pizza delivery. Here's how it works." In his excitement, he let the accent slip. "Customers have our menu at home, and a list of movies. They call and order the pizza and the film they want. We bring them to the house together, pick up the movie next day, outside the door if you request. No muss, no fuss. Perfect."

"It's been done."

"Sure, but not like this. See, we get our delivery guys to dress up in costumes. Like . . . well, like your moose suit. It's a natural."

Mike hefted Morty's head. Danger, that was the snag in Gray's plans, the distillery in the dorm room a prime example. Danger, ultimately, to Mike.

"Excuse me, Gray. Were we once friends?"

"Still are, surely."

"And you want me to go partners . . . in a pizza place? With costumes?"

"Well, sort of." Gray looked less certain. "Yeah, sure."

Mike swung the head back and forth. "I'm going to kill you now."

"Come to Briarwood." Gray waved off the threatened attack. "You'll see."

"No, I won't see. I most certainly will not see. Because I'm leaving now. Don't try to follow me. I've got . . . antlers." He brandished one. "Nice to see you again. Lots of luck."

At the entrance to the Metro, he turned and looked back. Gray sat hunched on the end of the bench, polishing his glasses, gazing at the stars. Mike opened his mouth to call 'good luck' again, but he changed his mind and walked away. He might not know what he wanted from life, but he most certainly knew what he did not want.

It was progress, of sorts.

▼ ▼ ▼

The desk phone rang. Liz kept an unlisted number, and Bud wasn't likely to push his luck so soon, which narrowed the odds considerably.

"Hello, Mother."

The cheap shot hit its mark. "I won't call if you don't want me to."

"No, it's fine." She could see it coming: another impossible conversation, unapologetically one-sided.

From the other end came the sound of papers being shuffled. "You said this wasn't too late."

"No." She checked her watch. "It isn't."

"Am I interrupting something?"

"Of course not. Just . . . work." She saved the file.

"You're by yourself?"

"Well, except for the usual crowd I invite over to watch me work." She regretted it before the words were out. The line crackled.

"I only meant you might be working with someone."

"It's not that sort of job." It wasn't worth explaining, again. Much of what she did was confidential and the woman refused to understand computers.

But on came the march. "So. Is there . . . anyone with potential?"

Potential what? Major-league fastball? Ability to fly?

"No, Mother. You'll be the first to hear."

A clucking sound. "You know, dear, I sentenced a woman your age today. For car theft. She has two children."

"Quite the role model."

"You know what I mean. It's not that I'm worried about who you spend time with. I'm concerned about you."

Sure you are. "Hang on a minute, let me turn off the computer."

With the machine stilled, the room grew darker, gloomier. Liz stared out the window as the static on the line became almost palpable. She shifted her focus to the stereo speakers, and the bookshelves. Both needed straightening.

"I'm driving to the cabin this weekend."

"Great." Liz waited.

"I don't suppose there's a chance of your coming up?"

"I'd love to," she lied, "but I have to go to Virginia. For work."

"Where in Virginia?"

"Nowhere." Liz wondered when she'd decided to go. "A little place called Hartigan . . . nowhere." She began to doodle.

"Hartigan Gap? Didn't you have a friend from school who lived there?"

Give the woman credit, memory like a death grip. "That's right." Liz put down her pen. "Allie Harper."

"Of course. She was always falling in love. What was your little joke?"

" 'Lost her Hartigan.' I didn't make it up."

"That's it. How nice. Will you stay with her?"

"No, I told you, it's for work. I'm not sure she still lives there."

"Did you have a fight?"

"Not really." Liz touched the end of her nose. Not growing yet. "She turned out not to be the person I thought she was."

"That's true of most people, dear."

"Well, we drifted." Liz shrugged, dislodging the phone from her shoulder. "It happens." Yeah, it does. It happens when someone is dishonest. When she betrays you. You don't just drift then. You throttle up the outboard.

More unsolicited maternal advice poured from the phone: ". . . good to keep up friendships, sweetheart. They aren't easy to find."

Liz covered her eyes. The conversation was spiraling into a familiar purgatory. There was no way she planned to rehash the Allie meltdown. You didn't 'keep up friendships' with people who . . . who treated you as Allie had. She stood and began to pace.

A colossal sigh meant the end of the call. "Have a nice weekend, dear."

"'Night. You, too." She hung up. And instantly she saw the big yellow tent, where the high school mortarboards had flown like a flock of blackbirds before a self-absorbed graduate even noticed the empty folding chair. She clutched the pages of the speech that had seemed so important minutes before.

"Didn't Dad make it?"

"I don't know where he is, dear." For once, Mother seemed to be paying enough attention to worry.

"But where is he? How could he miss my graduation?" And how selfish it had been to voice that thought.

"I'm sure there's a good reason."

But there wasn't. There was no good reason. Three hours later, the call had come from the hospital: Dr. Halloran dead of massive trauma. Not a mile from the graduation tent, hurrying from his patients, he'd rounded a curve head-on into a pickup that had strayed to the wrong side of the road.

Oh God, Liz had thought. Oh, God. It's my fault. I should have skipped a grade the way he wanted. I'd have been in college now. This wouldn't be happening. Please, please, can I catch up to that life?

And that was why the .630 file had touched a responsive chord. Today would have been their, hell, their thirty-fifth. She scooped up the phone and stabbed at the buttons.

The ringing was interminable. She squeezed her eyes shut, picturing a small house in Vermont where the phone cord had been disconnected, as it was every night. Trees falling in a forest. The only ringing was in her ear.

—2—

At the entrance to the subway, the machine scanned Mike's ticket, scrawled electronic graffiti across its face, and spat it out. An antler snagged as the barrier closed behind him. The Metro offered comforting, subterranean protection and didn't usually make him feel vulnerable. But that was when he was, well, furless. We have nothing to fur . . . we're losing it.

A dozen people loitered in the station and all looked dangerous. Not quite the leather and chain collection on display at Pizzazzip. Here they tended more toward improbably placed earrings. Circular lights embedded in the platform began to flash in synchronized warning though there was no sound of any train. Mike stared at the hypnotic flashing. He eyed his fellow travelers.

A rushing sound from one end of the tunnel heralded the arrival of the train. He drew well back, half afraid of succumbing to some lemming-like urge to abandon safety by jumping off the platform.

The train slid to a stop. Doors opened before him on heavy rubber wheels. A couple of preadolescents ran out, off for a night of rioting no doubt. Mike stepped over the crack between the platform and the train.

Inside the nearly empty car he sat alone by the window. A newspaper had been tossed on the floor. The only other passengers were an old guy sleeping at the far end and two middle-aged women who stopped talking when Mike boarded. They watched as he plopped the moose head on the seat next to him. When they kept staring, he draped the dishtowel over it.

The train pulled out of the station and jostled through tunnels. He let his head rock with the motion. Gray. Trust Gray to bring up Dad and Bob.

A page of the newspaper caught his attention. He pulled it toward him with a fuzzy foot. The women spoke in hushed voices, casting nervous glances. He tried to give a reassuring grin.

"Kid's party." He gestured toward the moose head. They looked at each other, rose, and made their way toward where the old man snored.

Mike picked up the paper and found the local section of the *Post.* Someone had given up on the crossword. He solved the final handful of clues in his head. The paper offered little else in the way of guidance. A West Coast coffee shop planned to open new stores . . . possible job opportunities. No one had claimed a ten million dollar lottery prize and the half-year deadline was next Monday. Twenty-seven percent of those polled favored putting a Nixon Memorial by the Watergate complex. He pondered the editorial page. 'Freedom of expression,' he eventually worked out, could be converted into POOF, MODERN SEX IS FREE. He was starting on MOOSE FIRED when the train reached his stop.

At the head of the station steps, he paused. A few automobiles moved along the street just fast enough to discourage anyone from hassling them. On the sidewalk, a news vendor muttered as he eyed the stack of papers he hadn't unloaded. Mike dug money from his wallet and paid for the same news he'd just read.

▼ ▼ ▼

Liz tipped back in the swivel chair. The clock now read well past ten, a long day made longer by Mother and Bud. She had the computer on again, but it was pure procrastination. Her popcorn bowl was empty. On her desk was the official photograph of Mother, robed and grim, and next to it Dad at the lake, a snapshot taken by Liz at fifteen. He strained on the oars of the rowboat. Her camera had caught his wide grin, sunlight turning his hair golden. Behind him was a blue expanse of lake and a cloudless sky. Over one of his shoulders, in the distance, a sailboat raced away. When the glossy print had come back from the drugstore, he'd pointed at the sails. 'Your ship, I see. And a poor swabby breaking his back to get the captain aboard.' She wished the photo didn't show the toes of her tennis shoes propped on the thwart.

The music, that was why she felt crummy. It was too mournful, too melancholy. In the darkened living room, she cut off the CD in mid-number, folded out the doors of the oak cabinet and clicked the TV to life. A quick surf through the channels, with a pause for weather and the score of the Red Sox game, was all it took to confirm there was nothing worth watching. The image dwindled to a speck.

She went back to the study and hit the space bar. Water lilies blinked out of existence, replaced by a mouse pointer that hovered over the desktop icon, Ariel. On an impulse, she clicked on the icon and sat back to wait. A window appeared and began to fill with his text. She shivered. It was like watching a player piano without knowing the tune, keys pressed by invisible fingers.

ariel: YOU'RE UP LATE, MIRANDA.

She used two fingers of each hand to type.

miranda: FOR ALL YOU KNOW I'M WATCHING THE DAWN IN ISTANBUL.

ariel: ISTANBUL? NOT CONSTANTINOPLE?

So, if you've a date . . . She smiled.

miranda: WHERE ARE YOU THESE DAYS?

Had she truly wanted to know, she could have tried to trace him. But she enjoyed the sense of mystery. 'The guy's okay,' Bud had assured her. It was good to respect the man's privacy.

ariel: ANYTHING THE MATTER?

She hated the way he could tell.

miranda: NO. NOT AT ALL. NOTHING. I WANTED SOMEONE TO TALK TO.

On screen, it looked like the lie it was. It was hard to believe they'd met a year ago, if it could be called meeting when you never saw each other, never heard a voice, never corresponded except electronically. Ariel the sprite, formless. He was one of TekSekure's 'masked' clients. Liz tried not to pass judgment as long as no one expected her to break the law.

The computer problem for which Ariel had first come to TekSekure was nothing more exotic than a crashed disk, fairly mundane, the opposite of his personality. Or, at any rate, his persona. He intrigued her, although not in a romantic attraction, not one of those seedy cyberaffairs. In fact, she had the notion, never confirmed, that he was twenty years her senior. She just enjoyed talking with him. The cursor flashed below his last response.

ariel: HERE I AM. TALK AWAY.

Bud had him down as 'Nemo,' which Liz found rather pedestrian. A year ago she'd started off with 'Cindy Rella,' but Nemo soon told her the name was beneath her. So, if she felt a sense of coming to the ball, it must be more the wonder of discovery. 'Miranda,' he christened her, and when she shot back, wanting to prove she'd read a book or two, 'Does that make you Prospero?' he said he'd never be so presumptuous. They'd compromised on 'Ariel.'

Now, on an impulse, she typed:

miranda: WERE YOU AN ENGLISH MAJOR?

ariel: SORRY. A MERE WELSH MINER.

miranda: HA. WHERE DID YOU GO TO COLLEGE?

ariel: WHAT MAKES YOU THINK I DID?

In the soft semi-darkness, she waited. New text skittered across the screen.

ariel: DID I MENTION I HAVE A NEPHEW YOU SHOULD MEET?

She leaned her cheek on her fist.

miranda: ONLY ABOUT A DOZEN TIMES. AND YOU CAN STOP NOW. I GET ENOUGH CATASTROPHIC PARENTAL MATCHMAKING.

Mother seemed to have an endless supply. After Roger, Liz had imposed a moratorium.

ariel: SO, YOU RANG. WHAT'S THE TOPIC?

miranda: ADVICE, I THINK.

ariel: ABOUT MEN?

miranda: DON'T BE A JERK.

ariel: WOMEN?

miranda: NO, BUT I APPRECIATE THE OPEN MIND.

ariel: THEN WE'VE EXHAUSTED MY AREAS OF EXPERTISE.

miranda: I DOUBT IT. REMEMBER, I'M ON VACATION NEXT WEEK?

ariel: AHA, YOUR ISLAND. MY ADVICE: USE A GOOD SUNSCREEN.

From a holder on her desk she shook out a handful of pencils and arranged them by levels of softness. His words looked the same as always. But these felt different, more dismissive.

miranda: YOU'RE A HOWL TONIGHT. PROBLEM IS, POO-BAH JUST CALLED WITH A RUSH JOB.

She glanced at the airline tickets and hotel forms stacked on the desk.

ariel: TESTING YOUR LOYALTY?

Liz picked at the lead on one of the pencils. No, that wasn't it. Bud was beyond testing her loyalty, of all things.

miranda: I'D TELL HIM TO STUFF IT, BUT THIS ONE SOUNDS INTERESTING.

ariel: AND?

He had a marvelous ability not to ask the obvious.

miranda: AND I'M LIKELY TO RUN INTO SOMEONE THERE. I'M AFRAID OF OPENING OLD WOUNDS.

ariel: WHERE IS 'THERE?'

She pushed herself from the terminal. How disappointing. Bud would go nuclear if he learned she was leaking his precious secrets.

miranda: A LITTLE PLACE IN VIRGINIA.

No response. She tapped the keys.

miranda: YOU THERE?

ariel: SORRY. INTERRUPTION. YOU REALLY WANT MY ADVICE?

miranda: PLEASE.

Another pause, and the symbols formed:

ariel: AN ARROW NEEDS A BEAU.

She read the cryptic message three times.

miranda: THANK YOU, CONFUCIUS. MEANING?

ariel: MEANING, SOME WOUNDS MUST OPEN TO HEAL.

Much clearer. She moved close to the screen, searching for the significance.

miranda: WHOSE WOUNDS ARE WE TALKING ABOUT?

ariel: MUST RUN. GOOD LUCK, MIRANDA. TA.

She logged out. Under a pile of papers inside her desk she found another snapshot, unframed, two young women in caps and gowns laughing in the sunshine. She'd been in better shape five years ago. Allie was thin and blonde. Each waved a diploma. Liz studied the photograph. The only thing she noticed was that the rolled parchments were aimed in exactly opposite directions.

▼ ▼ ▼

A police cruiser trailed Mike the last block to his apartment. He tried to walk a sober line. They blasted him with their spotlight as he reached the front door, and he realized he still had the moose under wraps. He exposed it for the cops, flapping his hand in what he hoped was a friendly wave. They killed the light and rolled on.

A yellow stickie decorated the cracked glass door of his building. His name was on the paper in Char's print-quality handwriting, with an arrow pointing down and sharply to the right. In the shrubs, he found a small paper bag, taped closed. He hefted it, juggling keys, wallet, dishtowel and antlers.

Inside the lobby, he tapped his mailbox with his finger for luck before exhuming the day's offerings. Magazine opportunities. Personal assurances from Ed McMahon. A postcard from Brazil, probably Uncle Ric, best saved for later. Three business letters, ominously thin.

He climbed the stairs. The elevator in the building was unpredictable at best, and the last thing he needed was a night in a hanging cage. As he walked, he counted the fifteen steps, hoping to divert his brain from the irrational lightheadedness that had almost led him to pass when the manager said he had nothing available at ground level. Afraid of heights. How come?

"I don't know," he told the stairs. It hadn't bothered him as a child. He couldn't pinpoint the emotional genesis. It was an acquired fear.

The one working fluorescent bulb on the second floor flickered erratically. He watched his hand move in strobe toward the keyhole. The bursts of light and darkness lent a marvelous feeling of significance to the gesture. Maybe this time something spectacular would happen when he opened the door.

▼ ▼ ▼

Liz hated to call anyone after 9 p.m., let alone close to midnight, but if she didn't do it right away it wouldn't happen. She hunched on the edge of her bed, studying the faded Holyoke logo on her shirt. They hadn't talked since the day after graduation, but it wasn't her fault. She gripped the phone and listened to the electronic hum. Only in response to the polite request for a name did she feel a pang of nervousness.

"Just . . . a friend."

The woman on the other end spoke with a soft drawl that revealed no annoyance. "I'll see if Miss Harper is at home, ma'am."

Liz wasn't sure she liked being called ma'am, even in a show of respect. While she waited for the maid, or whoever it was, to fetch Allie, she tried to picture herself living in the sort of place that not only accepted calls after eleven at night but apparently had someone on duty to take them.

A sound from the front yard caught her attention. Bud had insisted on a top-of-the-line alarm system for which the company had paid. Indicator lights on the bedroom panel showed nothing unusual.

The line rattled with the sound of someone picking up.

"Hello?"

She swallowed at the sound of Allie's voice. Through the window, she saw the yard suddenly illuminated. Someone had tripped the motion sensor.

"Hello?"

Her tongue was stuck. She peeked through the window, past the curtain. No sound outside her house. No sound inside her head.

"Hello? Is anyone there?"

The yard was lit in harsh brightness. She watched a small dog wander across the lawn, sniffing at the grass.

Wrong time. Wrong place. And forgiveness should be sought, not offered. She depressed the button and cut the call.

▼ ▼ ▼

The air in his apartment was stifling. Mike pushed the light switch up with his elbow, dumped mail, paper bag and newspaper on a rickety table, and drop-kicked the moose head onto the couch. Every piece of upholstered furniture in the room was draped, courtesy of Char, with brightly-colored bedsheets that did nothing to disguise the utter shabbiness of the place. On the couch sat an open suitcase, the only remaining evidence of last week's attempt to flee, abandoned for lack of a clear destination.

He pried open a window and propped it with a paint stirrer that lived on the sill. A dirty breeze pushed past him and nosed around the room, riffling the newspaper. He pushed the 'on' button for the portable fan, but remarkably the gremlins hadn't fixed it while he was gone. He flapped his arms to help the air circulate.

On the other side of what the manager persisted in calling the 'living space' was the kitchen, barely larger than the elevator. By the stove, Mike caught his hip on the drawer that wouldn't shut. It was jammed full of left-handed gizmos and gadgets Mom had buried him with during college, as if needing to atone for having produced such an ambitionless, wrong-armed son.

He held his breath, yanked open the refrigerator, and stuck his head in it to cool while he surveyed the battleground. Next to the 'throw out soon' pile was a chunk of cheese that looked salvageable. He was excising some of the bluer spots with a dull knife when the phone rang. The knife skittered off.

He watched the phone. When the caller gave up after four rings, he relaxed. No good could come of someone calling at . . . he looked at his wrist and saw only a fuzzy sleeve.

"Leave me alone, Carl."

He stomped into the living room, grabbed a fistful of darts from the table, and hurled them at the full-page ad for Pizzazzip on the dart board. The phone rang again. This time it wouldn't stop. On seven, he snatched at it.

"Hello. I can't come to the phone. Please leave a message and–"

"Shut up, Michael, you know you haven't got a machine."

"Char?"

"Daddy would buy one for you if I asked."

She was quick to volunteer someone else's help or money. Mike leaned on the counter. "Char, you can tell your father . . ."

"Yes?" Pure frost. Better than a portable fan.

"Tell him I'm fine."

"Why didn't you pick up before? Is someone there?"

"Of course not." What an idea. "I was . . . in the bathroom."

"I told you, hon, get a phone in there. It would be much more efficient."

"You're right, it would." Scientists were at work isolating the gene that made anyone care about efficient use of the toilet.

"Did you ask for the raise like I told you?"

"Sure did."

"And what was his answer?"

"Nothing definite."

"Well, it doesn't matter that much. You needed the practice mostly."

She made it sound as though the real performance didn't come until next Thursday. As he thought about it, Mike retrieved a foam ball from the floor and tossed it toward a hoop on the far wall. For the first time in recent memory, it went in. He pumped an arm into the air.

"Well?" Char said. "Is that all you have to say to me?"

Arm still raised in celebration, he froze. "Oh. Was there something else?"

"I left a package by your front door. Don't tell me those derelict neighbors of yours stole it."

"No, no, I got it." He stretched for the table, but the phone cord didn't reach. "Shit."

"What?"

"Nothing."

"Well? What did you think?"

"Uh, excellent." His fingers groped for the bag. "Terrific."

"Have you listened yet?"

"Listened? Well, no, I just got in from work." He lay on his back and used one foot to drag the table toward him.

"It's only a loan. I need to get them back next week."

"Okay." The table caught a floorboard and tipped over. He snatched at the bag as mail and newspaper cascaded around him. "Great, yeah, real thoughtful of you." He tore open the paper. Half a dozen audio cassettes spilled to the floor. *Finding the Right Job for You. Employment Despite Yourself.*

"Swell, Char. Perfect." He flipped them toward the couch.

"All you have to do is visualize. There's no need to fear success."

"Uh huh. I'll listen to them all."

"That's the idea, silly. If you'd get your headphones fixed, you could play them while you slept. They say it oozes into your brain. Much more sensible."

"Lots." The thought of sleep made him yawn. Impressive, really, how she managed to organize every aspect of his life from across town.

"Speaking of which, Michael, you ought to get to bed. Tomorrow's a big day. And we have a date bright and early."

"How could I forget?" Lucky she'd mentioned it.

"I'll pick you up in front of that place of yours. The usual time. Don't make me wait. You know I despise the way those vagrants stare at me."

"Right." He rubbed an eye and willed himself not to say, 'Maybe it's the BMW, did you ever think of that?'

He could almost hear her brain tick down the checklist. "Alarm set?"

"Absolutely." It would be. A dust ball skipped in the faint breeze.

"I wish you'd move. Get out of Southeast D.C., for a start."

"Right."

"You could afford a nicer place if you had a steady job."

"Can't argue there."

"I keep finding them for you. You keep losing them."

"Not on purpose."

"Twenty-six. Time to look beyond the pizza parlors."

"Well, thanks for the support." For an instant he entertained the idea that she'd sent Gray to find him.

"There's no need to snap. I'm doing my best for you."

The scary thing was, it was true. "I'm sorry." He watched an ant scout the wall. "A little tired, that's all. See you in the morning?"

"All right, then." Kissy noises from the phone. He held it away until they stopped. Her voice was tiny. "Love me?"

The question should be illegal.

"Don't be silly." He noticed his fingers were crossed. He pried them apart, mentally doing the same for his lips. "Of course I do." Who else would take the time to make so many decisions for him?

▼ ▼ ▼

Liz shoved the contents of her freezer around until she came across the last box of Girl Scout cookies. She rationed out three, then took a fourth and popped it in her mouth. Unwilling to face dreams yet, she had few options. She retreated to the study. The lily pads were back, and in a bizarre way they made her think of the island. Vacations were important. Was the new assignment so much more important? She tapped the space bar and went back to her Rolodex.

Someone had once suggested that the way to tell whether a tough choice was truly a toss-up was to flip a coin and, while it was spinning, figure out the side you were rooting for. Liz dug in the desk drawers but failed to come up with a coin. The closest she could manage was a paper token from a fast food restaurant game. Picture side, Virginia. Disclaimers, the island. She let it flutter toward the carpet.

Before it landed, she slid the ticket jacket from her travel documents. Time to do something. Time to confront the demons. She dialed the number for the airline, all multiples of three.

"Hello, this is, um, Laura Parker. I have a seat on Flight 162 on Saturday, July 2nd. My plans have changed slightly, and I was wondering: is there a possibility I could switch to the same flight on Tuesday, the fifth?"

Her game token lay on the floor. A grinning clown held a gold banner. Garish red letters on it spelled out, Instant Winner!

She hoped it was a good prize. A really good one.

▼ ▼ ▼

Mike wrapped the phone in the dishtowel and stuck it in the closet, in case Char felt the need to deliver an inspirational postscript. He rubbed his hands across his face. A siren whooped past beneath his window.

He moved the business envelopes to the bottom of the pile and opened each piece of junk mail, just in case. Lots of big offers, lots of small print. The Brazil postcard was indeed from Uncle Ric, operating at his usual level of eccentricity:

We've eaten some terrific food. I'd enjoy living down here, although really this iland goes about new growth abysmally. Pretty view, anyhow. Olé. P.S. You ought to come as soon as you can.	Mike Archer 447 4th SE #204 WA. DC USA 20002

Brazil. That was likely. He looked at the picture of Rio and frowned. Island? Brain fade for Ric. He hadn't even spelled it properly. And there was no clue as to the significance of 'we.' Ric had been a bachelor all his life. The only part Mike understood for sure was 'Olé,' Ric's signature on personal correspondence, his monogram in reverse. Mike's initials backward were ATM, a depressing thought for someone perpetually out of cash, but nowhere near as troubling as the anagram he'd discovered in Michael T. Archer: THE CHAR MIRACLE. He spun the postcard toward the kitchen counter but it hooked left, into the open suitcase on the couch. Olé.

The pile of mail dwindled to the three slim envelopes. He held them to the light but was unable to obtain any sort of preview. No point postponing. He tore the end off the first and withdrew a single sheet of stationery, which regretted to inform him, in response to his letter of June . . .

The others were close enough in tone and word choice that he could picture a wizened man in a dark room drafting rejection letters for all the businesses in town. Hey. Maybe the guy needed an assistant. He folded one of the letters into an airplane and sailed it across the room, out the window. As it disappeared, he realized his name was on it.

He spent a minute jiggling locks and chains on the front door, as if anyone might seriously want to break into the place. He turned off the light. In the course of navigating the apartment in the semi-dark, he tripped over a bulky pile. With all the rage he could muster, he gathered up the moose suit, snatched the head from the couch, strode to the window, and tossed it all toward the dumpster in the alley.

At last in bed, he lay on his back on top of the sheets, willing himself to feel the air cooling. He raised his hand toward the ceiling, reforming a clenched fist. His ribs were stiff. Alone in the stuffy room, he listened to the sounds of the sweaty June night.

Tomorrow. A big day. He wondered drowsily what she'd meant.

–3–

Mike struggled to keep his balance in the groggy pre-dawn light. The bump-bump-bump of roller skates over asphalt dealt shudders through his spine, turning his arms into windmills. With a noise between a whimper and a growl, he tried to steer a straightish line. Char skated backward, executing lazy figure eights around him on her flashy in-lines. Enough light had trickled into the sky for him to pick out some of the brighter colors in her Lycra costume. Her beautiful long legs swooped over the pavement.

"If you'd relax, you'd enjoy it more."

"That sounds familiar."

"Honey, it's good for you."

"So's a prostate exam."

Without warning, she veered onto the narrow pavement that led toward Memorial Bridge. Mike took an oblique angle to the path, bouncing over clumps of damp grass. Several turbulent moments passed before he hit the paved oasis that led to the bridge, already yards behind her. She didn't look back. He edged across the span, keeping his eyes on the Lincoln Memorial so as not to think about the drop to the water. At least there weren't any see-through, skate-catching metal grates.

On the Washington side, Char ignored the stenciled directions for traffic flow. Mike kept well to the side of the path and wished the Tidal Basin weren't so far off. The sun was gathering speed toward spotlight intensity. He could just make out Char's yellow headphones. Every so often she bobbed her head, with a dip of the shoulders, in time to private music.

As if she'd felt him watching, she turned around. He tossed a guilty wave, sensing the weight of the glove and the elbow pad, portrait of the artist as a four-star geek. She twirled and headed along the trail. In a few minutes she'd be around the bend, out of sight. His own progress was pathetic. Old ladies on foot, monster handbags and all, overtook him at will. He peeked at the wheels of his skates to see if they were dragging.

Char insisted that perspiration was a good thing. Sometimes he wondered whether she only wanted to make sure he'd do what she said. It hadn't been that way in the beginning. He looked behind, searching for his former self. Another moment of change that had slipped by unnoticed.

Her exercise mania was recent, an overreaction to quitting smoking. He'd been pleased about her decision, until she'd explained the logic.

"It's the statistics, hon. I finally got a look at the statistics."

"For lung cancer?"

"Dating services. Eighty percent of single guys prefer non-smokers."

He'd known before then the relationship was a bad idea. But that was one moment he'd recognized for what it was, the moment at which he saw she'd save him the agony of initiating a breakup. Not that he didn't have an eye out for a graceful way to exit.

He flapped his T-shirt away from his chest and settled into a pace just a notch above a shuffle. To travel through time, that would be nice. Which way was better? Back, to fix the past, or forward, to find out what would happen?

A woman ran by, alone on the lower path. She'd come from behind him. As she passed and pulled away with the rest of the world, he studied her stride. The tread was delicate, each footfall seeming to test the ground before settling. He let his gaze move up from her feet. She was tall, athletic, wearing loose black shorts and a tank top that revealed well-toned arms. A ponytail bobbed above her cotton shirt, which had lettering he couldn't pick out from a distance, the words shrinking as she ran out of his life.

Char, as usual, took the Tidal Basin clockwise. For the first time, he realized that, if he cut straight to the Roosevelt Memorial, he could wait until she passed on her way back, then pop out, cutting her lead substantially.

He came to the first section of giant blocks. Unconventional architecture. Jefferson, across the water in his marble columns, would not have approved. As

Mike read the carved messages, he was almost taken out by the captain of a three-wheeled baby stroller. He veered toward the edge of the path. A grassy slope, dotted with cherry trees, fell away from it. Beyond was a paved walkway that, without any railing, circled the Tidal Basin.

Over by Jefferson's dome, a neon dot became Char's leotard. He began to work up momentum, keeping well in the shadows of the Roosevelt. Beside the lower path, fifty feet away, a motorcyclist had ditched his bright red machine and stood facing away from Mike. Another motorcyclist. *Why howdy, jerks . . .*

The guy held one hand in the pocket of his windbreaker, as if he had a gun. A couple of speedwalkers hustled past him. Mike checked again. Char's leotard sped along the path in a hypnotic zig-zag.

A little way beyond the guy, Mike could see the white tank top and black shorts coming along the path. She must have turned just past the Roosevelt. Strange way to run the Basin. But she was even nicer from the front. Wraparound reflector shades covered a pleasantly thin face. The ponytail swung from side to side. Mike caught his breath. Perfect. And she'd come back after all. She was barely a hundred yards from the motorcyclist, closing quickly on her light feet.

Char was moving into the picture, too, skimming, gaining. Her mouth pursed into the grimace that, as a rule, preceded a lecture.

The biker pulled his hand from his pocket. Something metallic, shiny, tough to see in the glare from the water. Mike, on the upper path, was almost even with him. A pent-up desire for revenge collided with a tingling sense of chivalry. *I've got to let my feets run loose . . .* He pounded one gloved hand into the other and tipped his skates onto the grassy slope. It was steeper than he'd figured. He shot between two cherry trees, ducking beneath a low branch. From the corner of his eye, he saw Char skid to a stop.

The assailant raised his weapon. His victim was forty yards off, running toward trouble, oblivious. Mike locked his arms in front of him, clasping his hands into a battering ram. For once in his life, he'd figured it right. The angle was perfect. He slammed into the man, delivering a thwack between the shoulders as he flew past. The would-be assassin sprawled. His weapon sailed through the air, smashing on the pavement. In his moment of triumph, Mike saw photo film spill from it.

Things were getting worse. He'd reached the pedestrian path, careening beyond the possibility of braking, no rail to grab. Too-close water sparkled, a thousand devilish eyes. Dare you to jump. I dare you. Directly in front of him, a trio of old women blocked the path. He reached out to fend them off. Somehow the collision didn't happen, but he came away with a large handbag. He stared at it as a frail voice cried out behind him.

Now there was nothing between him and the white tank top but a man with a cat on a leash. The man walked on one side of the path, the cat the other. The leash hung between them like a lopsided grin. Mike neared mach speed. A change in direction would be fatal. He huddled into a crouch.

Nearer to the ground, things seemed to slow. The girl of his dreams reached the cat. As he closed on her, in the reflector shades he thought he saw mirrored images of himself. Her mouth formed the words, 'Hold on.'

She was going to save him.

He held out his arms, purse clutched in one fist. But she cradled the cat and jerked the leash taut with her other hand. The startled owner fell back on the grass. The barrier between them snapped to shin level.

Mike stood in horror. He had a strong impression of the faded instruction 'Just Do It' on soft cotton, beads of sweat on her forehead, and a tear-shaped pendant below a tanned throat. His ankles caught on the leash like a tailhook on a carrier. The world fell away from him, whirled, and slammed itself back, wet and cold.

He blinked water from his eyes. He stood in the Tidal Basin, immersed to his chest, torqued around to face the whole sorry scene: grassy bank, wraparound shades, and cat. Char stood on the upper path, hands on her hips. Where the giant policeman had come from was unclear.

"All right, zero. Let's see 'em." The cop was not a morning person, either.

Mike lifted his hands, still gripping the purse. Murky water sluiced into his face. He coughed. The cat clawed its way to the ground. The guy with the motorbike kneeled on the trail, gathering bits of camera. He stared at Mike, his mouth a slit, an axe bite in a tree trunk. On the path, the three shriveled ladies huddled together and shook their heads. They looked terribly Greek, and tragic.

▼ ▼ ▼

The voice at the other end of the line was indistinct.

"Your train leaves Union Station at three. Take it to Hartigan Gap."

"And when I get there?" Liz stood in her kitchen, wiping perspiration from her face.

"You'll be met."

"I'll be met. Great. Do I wear a flower in my buttonhole or something?"

That didn't produce a laugh, or anything close. She tightened her jaw and swept an unpopped kernel into the sink.

As she hung up, she caught herself thinking again about the skate guy, and his companion. Lycra was a privilege, not a right, but the woman was entitled. Liz poked a finger into her own middle.

She'd come down pretty hard on the guy. The scene had brought back such a load of bad memories. Maybe he really had lost control. If not, he was the most incompetent thief she'd ever seen. Too bad. He had a nice face.

▼ ▼ ▼

Mike hadn't spent time in jail before, and it wasn't shaping up to make the highlights reel of his life. The cop with the attitude took the cuffs off at the station, but only so Mike could help a raisin-faced booking officer live out some kind of vicarious finger-painting fantasy. The whole process felt unreal, as if it were someone else's hands at the ends of his arms.

There was no reason to panic, not yet. Char had watched it all, and she'd bail him out once she decided he'd suffered enough. Tons of other witnesses, too. Just an accident. Anyone could see that. Of course, it would have helped if the runner hadn't been so positive he'd done it on purpose. He was used to the world beating up on him, but today had a harder edge than usual.

Another cop led him down a sterile corridor. At the end was a holding tank filled with some of the largest and most impressively pungent bodies Mike had ever encountered.

"Say, looka what just crawled out the shitter."

The sliding door clanged behind him. A beefy guy in a rumpled shirt stood, belched in his direction and displayed an appalling lack of teeth. Mike turned away and found himself looking into several pairs of unfriendly eyes. Barefoot in shorts and T-shirt, which emphasized nothing so much as the physique of a bridge player, he tried to appear tough without actually flexing. They all stared at him and he concluded unhappily that he looked constipated. He squinted and worked up a sneer. It held for several seconds, until his lip started to spasm. He concentrated on imagining the color of the eyes behind the wraparound shades. As introductions went, it had been about as smooth as one could hope for.

▼ ▼ ▼

Liz sensed something wrong before she reached the office. She didn't believe in premonitions, but an undeniably bad feeling skittered in her as she pushed open the door with 'TekSekure' lettered across it. She stopped just inside. Joey never kept a neat desk; he was hacker first and secretary a distant second. But today was beyond any chaos even he could have created. File drawers stood open and wastebaskets upended. Papers covered the floor.

"Tell me you lost something, Joey. Tell me that's all this is."

A rustling sound came from under the desk and he emerged, still on his knees, holding a couple of disks and a looseleaf manual. Rust-colored hair hung in front of his eyes. He drew the locks aside as if they were a curtain. The silver stud in his left ear was a five-pointed star.

"Hiya, boss."

"Hell." She dropped her purse on his desk. "Was it like this when you got here?"

"Uh-huh." He pulled himself into a chair.

"Any idea what they wanted?"

"Dunno. Take a look. My stuff, they just tossed." He patted his monitor. "Nothing sideways on this set. I figure it must be one of yours."

Liz checked the electric eye.

"What happened to the alarm?"

"Bypassed, looks like."

"You call the cops?"

He shook his head, the movement dropping hair in front of his eyes.

"Good." Even though she couldn't trust a kid who didn't take his job seriously, there was no denying Joey was sharp. "What about Bud?"

"Nah, knew you'd want to. That's why he pays you the big bucks."

"That's it, all right." She grabbed her purse, waded through the paper, and peeked into her own office. The scene was much the same, except they'd gone to the trouble of removing the hard drive. Unbelievable.

A folder lay open on the desk, empty. She glanced at it. Hillton-Tanner. Much good that'd do anyone. The contents had been tossed against the base of the wall. So, whoever it was had seen it was nothing but a dummy file, stuffed with outdated material from an old TekSekure job.

She bit her lip. The H-T program must have had a trip wire that she'd overlooked during her first sweep. Careless. Very careless. She dialed Bud at home, moved papers from her chair, and sat. Twelve rings later, he picked up.

"Listen," she said. "We've got problems here."

He groaned. "Oh man. Sun's hardly up. I said I was sorry for calling late."

"You didn't. Anyway, it's not that. I'm at work." She described the scene.

He swore, and suddenly his voice was clear. "Joey okay?"

"Fine."

"What's gone?"

"I haven't figured that out, other than my hard drive, which isn't a big deal. Looks like they were interested in H-T; they flipped the dummy file. Someone may have frightened them away before they dug any deeper."

"Did you crosscheck?"

She stopped in the middle of organizing papers into a stack. "What's the point?" She didn't want to tell him the only disk was in her purse.

"Humor me."

She put down the phone and poked her head through to the outer office, where Joey was making his own ineffectual mounds of paper. She tried to sound casual. "What's the cross number for Hillton-Tanner?"

"It's your project."

"Thanks. So try calling it up on your screen."

"What's wrong with yours?"

She gestured toward the disassembled PC. "These brain trusts popped the skins and sucked out my hard drive."

Joey whistled and bent over his keyboard. "It's . . . two-two-seven."

Years before, when they were opening the Washington branch, she'd argued long and hard with Bud about where to store sensitive files. She thought she'd made a good case for a wall safe, but it was his company. In the end she gave up and let him go with the corny false-backed file cabinet.

She slid out the drawer until it caught, spun the combination lock and lifted out the dummy back. A dozen thin files, identified only by three-digit numbers, stood in the small compartment and didn't seem to have been touched. She rifled through them before picking up the phone.

"Everything looks fine."

"Even H-T?"

"Mm-hmm." She found it. "Even . . ."

"What? What?"

"Wait a sec." She pawed in the other files. "I don't like this."

"What?"

"It's all gone. All the H-T backup. Everything." She shook the folder, and a stiff piece of colored paper fell to the floor. It was a picture postcard of an island. Her island. She picked it up and read the typed message: *Having a wonderful time. Can't wait till you're here.*

In her purse, she found the H-T disk. "This isn't just a break-in, Bud." She shut the door and told him about the postcard.

He swore again. "What the hell's that about?"

"Search me. Are you sure we can trust Joey?"

"Hey, will you stop asking that? I told you, he's family."

"Your family. Not mine."

"What about it?"

"Excuse me for not finding that reassuring. Who else could it be?"

"Knock it off. He wouldn't do something like that. And if he did, he wouldn't stay around. You're not thinking clearly."

"I'm not thinking clearly?" She shoved the disk back into her purse. "What else would he do but hang around, knowing his uncle will stick up for him every time?"

"All right, all right. I'll be on a plane pronto. We're shutting down your operation until we sort this out. You'd better blow town."

She kicked the file drawer closed. "I'm leaving at three, remember?"

"Good. Have a drink to calm yourself."

"I don't drink, and I'm plenty calm."

"Sure you are, sure. Well, kill some time. Amuse yourself."

"I don't want to amuse myself. Can't I stay at the office?"

"No. We don't know what these guys are after. It may be you."

"That's ridiculous." But she squeezed the phone.

"Look, just find some place to lay low until three."

"I have to go home anyway, for my stuff."

"I guess so. Get things straightened up before you leave the office. I'll hunt you up over the weekend. Don't say anything more. We can't be positive the line's safe." The phone went dead.

It was the closest she'd ever heard him come to panic. TekInSekure, that was all they needed. It took three tries to get the receiver on the hook.

▼ ▼ ▼

"Archer!"

Mike spun to face the bars. Two hours of tensing, and every one of his muscles had cramped.

The guard scratched himself. "Rest of you girls, one giant step backward." A space cleared before the sliding door. It rumbled open, and he waved Mike out.

The interrogation room had no windows and smelled of despair. Apart from a metal table with a folding chair on either side, there was no furniture. Video equipment in a corner whirred softly. Mike noticed a small drain in the concrete floor, which was cold against his bare feet. He hoped Char had thought to dry the skates.

"Grab a seat, chump." The cop shoved him forward.

The door swung open and a small man came in, looking as if he'd been up all night, and maybe the night before.

"Swannie, kill the camera. Okay, here's the deal, Archer. I'm Detective Fry, and this is your lucky day. Your prints came back clean, which I hope to Christ is no surprise to you." He tossed a clipboard on the table and dropped himself into the other chair. "I got enough to bust you: petty theft, assault, destruction of property, half a dozen things I haven't thought of yet, but you know what? I'm letting you walk. It's Christmas in Ju-fuckin'-ly. I got a witness says you meant to grab the purse and another says no. First one calls back and now she could have got it wrong. I know just what it'll be, one monster pain in the ass in court, I can see that from here and I'm not wearing my glasses, it's all too fuckin' confusing, and you know what? I don't care. I just don't care. There's about five thousand and forty-six more important things for me to worry about today, and that's a fact."

Mike couldn't tell if he was supposed to comment.

Detective Fry mined some wax from his ear, studied it, and flicked it toward the drain. "So, here it is, chuckles, bottom line. You're out of here, but I want you thinking on this. I want you making restitution, which is the way a judge would put it, meaning pay that guy for his fuckin' camera, and I mean this week, or I'll come looking for you. That's number one, and two, I don't ever, ever want to see you in that chair while I'm on duty again, or I'm taking you down. You got it?" He stood and tossed a brown envelope on the table. "Sign for your junk and get the hell out of my life."

The door creaked shut behind him. His voice, bellowing orders, carried from the hall. Swannie looked on as Mike upended the brown envelope. His watch slid out. He shook the bag. Nothing more. He tried to remember. There had definitely been something. Change? That wasn't it. Wallet? Char had driven, so his wallet was back at the apartment. Back at the . . .

"Crud. Did I have a key ring when I came here?"

A glance at the clipboard. "One sports watch. Period. Which you got." The cop handed the board across. "Sign."

Mike scrawled his name. "Do you think I could have my free phone call?"

"You're not under arrest. You only get to call if you're under arrest."

"But I was. Before."

"So, you could have called, before."

"You didn't tell me."

"You didn't ask."

Mike took a deep breath. "Right. Could you bend the rules this once?"

"Bend this."

"Thirty seconds. It's a local call. And I'm having a really bad day. Really bad." The guy didn't loosen a bit. "It won't kill you."

"And?"

"And, if I don't make this call, she is going to kill me."

▼ ▼ ▼

"Senator D'Onofrio's office." The voice on the phone, a woman's, was less than welcoming.

Mike bent over the receiver. "Ms. Chamberlain, please. It's Mike Archer."

"Archer?" Her tone implied she was starting a trace.

Char's voice carried from the background. "Say I can't talk now."

"She can't–"

"No, no." He waved a hand at the phone. "Tell her this is important. It'll just take a minute." He caught the cop's eye and gulped. "Thirty seconds."

The guy had the decency to wander a few steps down the hall.

At the other end of the line was the sound of a hand rubbing on the mouthpiece. "Mr. Shapeable," he thought the woman said. He clenched his jaw, but at last Char picked up.

"What is it now, Michael?" And the Tidal Basin had seemed cold.

"Hi. I think I dropped my keys this morning."

"I know you did. I found them on the path, where you were trying to impress that woman."

"Where I what? God, you could have brought them to the police station."

"I had to get to work, Michael, some people do that. You're twenty-six, or so you claim. I assumed you could take care of yourself."

Forty seconds already. "So, where did you leave the keys?"

"I didn't leave them anywhere. They're in my purse."

"Great. Can you bring them by, please?"

"No, I can't. I'm busy."

"Fine. I'll come over."

"Are you wearing a tie?"

"They just let me out of the black hole. Of course I'm not wearing a tie."

"Oh?" She packed a lot of sarcasm into one word. "And how were you planning to dress for your job interview this morning?"

"Job? Interview? Shit." He stared at his watch for real. "It's nine already? Shit. Okay. Great. Thirty minutes. Okay, I'm going to run past on my way to the apartment. Can you meet me outside?"

"Honey, could you for once try to be a little organized? I've got better things to do than wait around for you all morning. The Senator needed this paper I'm working on yesterday."

"Oh, come on." She could have at least tried a credible excuse. "It's Fourth of July. Everyone in Washington's gone."

"He happens to be a hard worker; maybe you can't appreciate that. And he needs to take care of business before he leaves for the weekend."

"Fine, okay." Mike tried to jump start the brain. He'd agreed to the lousy interview to keep peace with Char and now he'd maneuvered himself into a full-scale meltdown. "Look, about those keys . . ."

"I'll drop them out the window. You can pick them up when you have an opening in your busy schedule. And don't forget this afternoon."

"No!" He fought to keep the scream down. "Don't do that."

Click.

He raced along the hall and down the front steps. Spineless. You are so spineless. He cursed the evolutionary path that left him in need of an exoskeleton. And cursed Char for providing it. Wretched symbiotic . . . The sidewalk was griddle-hot. He leapt for the shade and nearly collided with a man who was walking past, paging through a magazine.

"Back off, shithead."

"Sorry, I . . . Carl!" The day had turned into a mutant version of *This Is Your Life.*

"Archer, is that you?"

Mike glanced toward the police station. "It's not as bad as it looks. They didn't press charges."

"What the hell?"

"Gotta run, Carl. Late for an appointment." With a last look over his shoulder, he bolted down the street, clamping his hands over his ears. Just in case he still had a job, he didn't want to hear himself being fired.

▼ ▼ ▼

The Senate offices were ten quick blocks from the police station. Was Char's the second window, third floor? Or third window, second floor? He thrashed through the landscaping. In a stroke of needed luck, he found the keys behind the first bush he tried.

Barefoot, he gasped his way the mile home, taking the stairs three at a time, his T-shirt already off. She'd arranged a real interview this time, not slave work for her boss' nephew. It was an improvement. He panted as he reached the second floor. But no more family connections to launch job searches. None. Not after today.

On his doorstep lay a bouquet of wildflowers. He frowned as he scooped it up. She was so hard to figure.

Fifteen minutes to go, probably enough. Inside, he toweled away the sweat and grabbed his white dress shirt and the one suit, a belt already in the pants from whatever the last occasion had been. He found a bright tie with a hideous design Char claimed was stylish. He grabbed a comb from the bathroom, shoved it in a pocket and pawed through the closet for the box that held his good shoes. She'd picked those out, too.

Stupid interview. He didn't even want the job. But he'd promised to show up for it, and his word was the one thing he could keep when everything else washed away. At least he had that.

Dress shoes wouldn't work for the long sprint to the Metro. He wriggled into sneakers and hefted the box. Map. Another painful lesson learned. He grabbed a battered street map from a drawer in the kitchen. Just as he shut the door behind him, he remembered his wallet, and the portfolio with his resumé. He was in and out of the apartment in record time.

Ten seconds later, he went back for the address.

—4—

Sweat beaded along Mike's hairline as he stood on Constitution Ave. When he wiped at the moisture, he succeeded only in wetting his fingers. He waved his hand vigorously. People on the sidewalk stared.

He moved to a nearby bench. Inside the cardboard container, green felt bags swaddled the leather shoes. He peeled off the felt and kicked free of his sneakers. On second thought, the bench didn't look safe to sit on, not with a suit he wanted to keep clean. He hopped from one foot to the other as he peeled away his sweaty tube socks. The air on his bare skin felt good.

Dress socks. He pawed the bottom of the shoebox. Clutched the pockets of his suit. Checked under the bench. Nothing. The green wrappers. No. Yes. No choice. He sat on the very edge of the bench and slid a foot into one of the bags. It stuck on the sweat, but he yanked hard and worked it past the ankle. He repeated the process with the other bag and clapped the shoes on. When he stood, the trouser legs covered the makeshift socks, but he could feel them flopping against his legs. He bent, examining them from various angles. With luck, anyone who noticed would take it as a fashion statement. No time to search for alternatives. He shoved his sneakers into the box.

A revolving door whisked him inside the building. The security guard, who could have been Officer Swannie's twin, eyed him suspiciously. A fresh wave of uncertainty made Mike spend too long peering at the list of tenants.

Throat-clearing from the uniform. "Can I help you, sir?"

Mike looked over his shoulder.

"Oh. Torrey, Hart and Bellin. Third floor?"

"Fourth." The guard stared at the shoebox as if it might be ticking.

"Fourth." Mike gulped. "Thanks." He moved away as smoothly as he could without exposing his ankles. "Just taking these, um, shoes up."

He made it around the corner before he whacked a palm against his forehead. At the elevator, he gazed longingly toward the entrance to the stairwell, but the door had a sign promising to scream if he touched it.

The ride to the fourth floor seemed to last forever. He concentrated on visualizing the giant springs someone had assured him were at the bottom of every shaft. The ceiling was mirrored. He watched the reflection of himself staring miserably down, hanging by his toes. The sight made him ill, and he moved his gaze to the floor. Inside his trouser legs, the bags drooped toward his shoes. He clutched his box and portfolio tighter.

The law firm receptionist was professionally cheerful. "Mr. Archer, at last. Mr. Chamberlain is expecting you. Would you like some coffee?"

"Oh, no. Thanks." A cup would require a new level of coordination.

She inclined her head toward the box. "May I hold onto that for you?"

"No, it's okay." He sensed the need to elaborate. "Shoes." It sounded worse. "I guess you can have them after all. Say, would you mind if I took a couple of those rubber bands?"

She raised an eyebrow but motioned for him to help himself.

He worked his way to the window. A brittle, bald man in a well-pressed suit and a monocle sat reading a magazine. The varnished table before him held a half-filled coffee mug stamped 'TH&B.'

Mike, pretending to admire the Washington Monument, lifted one foot to a chair. With a quick look around, he slid an elastic band over his shoe, onto the ankle. The old man turned a page. Mike started on the other foot.

"Jake, good to see you." The voice, close behind, was a cannon. Mike jerked his hands from his ankle. The elastic snapped, stinging his fingers. The broken band flew into the coffee mug, where it floated on the surface like a sick grin. Monocle Man didn't notice. He folded his paper. Mike was working out how best to retrieve the elastic when he felt a grip on his shoulder.

"Michael."

He spun, stifling a shout of denial.

"Oh. Oh. Good morning, Mr. Chamberlain."

"Chuck. Please. You're virtually family." Char's father mangled Mike's fingers in a take-no-prisoners handshake, every bit the All-American linebacker. The guy could be subdivided. "Come on back to the cell."

"The cell?" Mike gasped, but Chamberlain ignored it.

"Jake, I'll be back in a minute. You okay for coffee?"

The old man nodded and raised the mug to his lips. Mike shut his eyes.

The 'cell' was a corner office the size of a handball court. It held a couch, a television and a jungle of plants. Some heavy work with a machete would doubtless uncover a wet bar. A marble-topped desk without a shred of paper occupied one end of the room. Eager to hide his feet, Mike made for the plush chairs grouped around it, but a vise clamped his arm and hauled him away.

"Oh, no," said Chamberlain. "That's not very friendly. Let's sit on the couch. You can tell me what you're hoping to get out of this."

Get out of this. That was it in a nutshell.

Chamberlain plopped down, looking as if the couch had been molded around him. "This isn't really the interview yet, so relax."

"Uh huh." Mike was trying to angle himself to block the view of his feet. He jammed his heels against the base of the couch, one ankle covering the other, a hand dangling by his side.

"You know," Chamberlain said, "I haven't heard what your father does."

"My father?" Mike contemplated the blank television, hoping to improve on the explanation that came to mind: He's in manufacturing. He makes mistakes. "Oh, he's . . ." he finally came up with, "an engineer." Close enough.

Chamberlain patted an armrest. "I was delighted when Charlotte told me you'd changed your mind about the law. Delighted, and surprised."

"Yeah, me too. I mean . . ." Mike gave what felt like a vacuous grin. "I just, I figured it wasn't right to be so set against something I'd never tried."

"Quite." Chamberlain stroked his lip. "Well, I hope your expectations aren't high. Work in a law firm isn't all you might think from the books and TV shows. We're not a front for the mob." He laughed.

Mike felt his face slip into another sick expression. "I wasn't expecting that." He studied the expensive-looking Rorschachs on the walls, hoping there wouldn't be a test. All the paintings looked like, well, pizzas.

"So, have you given much thought to schools?"

"I was in . . ." better upgrade, ". . . Georgetown last night."

"Fine school." Chamberlain thwacked Mike's knee. "Splendid. You let me know if you need a recommendation, and I'll set you up."

"Yes, sir. Thank you."

"Don't start sir-ing me, Michael, or I'll have to toss you out the door."

Corralling his attention back to the couch, Mike was horrified to see one of his own ankles resting on the other knee. He snapped his foot to the floor, too late. The most powerful lawyer on the planet stared at him.

"What is this, a joke? St. Paddy's was three months ago."

Mike remembered to smile. "I . . . I, it's a long story." Chamberlain wouldn't want to hear about jail. "On second thought, not long. My socks are with the moose suit."

He watched his unpotential father-in-law puzzle that one out.

"How unfortunate. Maybe we could . . . no, we need to get you to Kathy Laurence. You'll be seeing four lawyers, and things will ball up if we start running behind." He sighed, rose, and led the way to the door.

A tall woman looked up from behind a well-ordered desk.

"Mr. Chamberlain, your ten o'clock is here."

"Bring him back, would you, Jeanne? I'm taking Mr. Archer to Kathy, and she can join us when they're done. Oh, wait a second." He bent over the desk and mumbled something. The secretary made a note on a pad in front of her. Mike could imagine what it said: Guilty. And he hadn't even had the trial.

▼ ▼ ▼

Kathy Laurence, Mike figured, was what Char would have evolved into if she'd chosen law rather than politics. Laurence dominated the room, even seated. She pacified herself by fiddling with a knife-like letter opener, running a finger along the edge of the blade as she frowned at his resumé. He sat across the desk from her, bracing himself with the armrests.

A cuckoo clock on the wall broke the silence with lurching, grinding noises. Either it was fast or he was later than he'd thought. Below it hung fake pine cones. Mike sized them up, keeping an eye on the letter opener. He knew they'd make credible weapons if she turned hostile. He touched the scar high on his forehead. Twenty years, and Bob hadn't once apologized. Not that he ever apologized. Bob had ended up with the family self-confidence allotment. Bob wasn't afraid of heights. It had to be a recessive gene.

Chamberlain's desk had seemed to repel paper. Laurence's was a magnet. Stacks of manila files balanced against one another. A handful of telephone message slips were impaled on a spindle near a lump that might have been the phone, or a severed head. The one clear space on the desk was a small spot before her, over which she huddled like a poker player. Watching her red pen dissect his resumé, Mike began to fixate on what the surface of the desk looked like. Wood? Stone? There was no way to tell from above. Laurence abandoned the resumé and walked to the window. He slouched a little, angling for a better view of the underside. Not the politest thing, to peer under a woman's desk. But Laurence kept staring out the window. What the hell.

His neck was starting to ache by the time he'd bent far enough to see that it was made of glass. Papers were pressed against it, a collage. He had the sensation of being inside a copy machine. Some poor client was at the bottom of the pile. A label caught his eye. Westfield. Gray's name. He inched toward it.

". . . on earth are you doing?" Her legs were in front of him.

He clipped his head on the desk as he surfaced. "Ow. Sorry, I . . . tying my shoes." He rubbed his head, checking to make sure they weren't loafers.

"So. You want to be a legal assistant." She reclaimed her chair.

"Me?" He tugged the felt bags into place. "Oh. I mean, right."

She exhaled through her nose. "I should tell you it is highly unusual for me to interview paralegal candidates."

He wasn't sure what kind of response she was looking for. Maybe she wanted to test his courage. He searched for a suitable comeback.

"Oh, really?"

She pointed the letter opener toward him. "I suppose you've been told most legal assistants at Torrey Hart come from top paralegal schools."

He smiled. "Good for you."

"What?"

"Them."

She poked at the resumé with the opener's tip as if testing for signs of life. "You haven't been to paralegal school."

"No."

"University of Virginia, that's not Ivy League yet, is it?"

"No." He hoped she was trying to be funny. "Not that they told me."

"Have you at least taken pre-law courses?"

"No," he tried to match her humor, "I thought it would be more of a challenge–"

She held up a hand. "It looks as though at one time you thought you might be an actor."

"I did, actually." He straightened. At last, something he felt comfortable talking about. "You see, I've never really had a handle on what I'm good at. There must be something."

She dropped the opener and lunged across the desk, waving his resumé. "And just what is this?" The top entry wore an angry red circle.

It was Char's attempt to dress up Pizzazzip into something more. He had failed to convince her that 'leisure consultant for the maturationally impaired' wouldn't fool anyone and made him sound like a dork.

Laurence was waiting. Mike heard the rising tone of a siren as it raced down Constitution Avenue. Doppler effect, sound waves shoved closer.

"It was a job."

"But what is this?"

"Well, okay." If there was one lesson Dad had ever pushed, it was the importance of straight answers. Mike got to his feet. "Imagine antlers." He held his thumbs to his temples, fingers spread. He started to clunk around the office. "Imagine music." But it didn't feel right at floor level. He hopped onto the chair and shuffled in place. Might as well be hanged for a . . . moose.

He hummed the intro, keeping his thumbs pressed to his head.

". . . da dum da dum da silly goose, I've got to let my feets . . ." He shook one at her and she fell back in her chair.

The door opened, framing Chamberlain's secretary, Jeanne. Mike wasn't sure whether to stop or not. A vestige of artistic integrity goaded him on. Out of respect, however, he quit singing.

Jeanne turned to Laurence while Mike continued his silent dance. "You'd better come out. There's a man choking in the lobby. I think it's your ten o'clock with Chuck."

Mike flashed on an image of a floating rubber band. He slowed the dance but didn't quite stop as Laurence rose from her desk. Jeanne held something dark in one hand. She lobbed it toward him as he stumbled his way to the end. The missile bounced harmlessly off his chest, but instinct toppled him backward off the chair. Jeanne closed the door before he landed on the carpet.

The pair of dress socks, price tag still attached, rolled away from him. Laurence reached under the desk to pick them up. From the wall clock came a crunching sound. A yellow bird popped from its chalet and chanted at him.

Laurence looked at the bird and back at Mike. He sat on the floor, trying not to wince. Without a word, she picked up his resumé and extended it toward him, holding it between her thumb and forefinger as if it were a dirty diaper.

▼ ▼ ▼

Since she had time for it, Liz walked all the way home, slowly, so as not to let the humidity win. She was hot enough at the thought that someone had broken into her personal office to search for files. It was so invasive, so dirty. She needed a shower.

On the other hand, assuming it was a true break-in, there was no reason to take it out on Joey. Bud was right. If the kid wanted stuff in the office, he'd copy it and no one would ever know.

She rarely had the occasion to be in her neighborhood on a weekday morning. The number of people out and about was surprising. Maybe the invader who'd trashed the office was someone she knew. And he'd known where to look. Creepy. In three years at TekSekure, it was the first time she'd seen a target shoot back.

The mailman had just left her house as she turned the corner at the end of the block. He headed in the opposite direction, sweat stains visible on his short-sleeved shirt. Another person she didn't know. Another part of life that went on without help from her.

Five hours until the train. What a luxury. After the shower, packing wouldn't take long, and she'd have time to do . . . well, anything. Run a load of laundry. Sort bills. Drop a note to Vermont. Implode. How wonderful it was to live alone.

Her mailbox was empty. Not even a catalog. She found the keys in her purse and let herself in. The alarm warning went off, for once a comforting sound. As she keyed the sequence, a thought struck her, and her finger stayed on the last button. Why was the guy here, if not to bring mail?

She ran to her study. The computer was intact. The phone hadn't been bugged. Living room. Everything as it should be. That left the second floor to check. She crept toward the stairs. The house was quiet, which she didn't care for at all. Her breathing sounded loud. The bedroom held nothing to indicate anyone had been there since she'd left. Nothing except a postcard. It sat in the center of the bedspread, its edges parallel to the walls.

Bedroom. She looked more carefully and could see the drawer on the bedside table wasn't quite closed. He'd been in her bedroom. With a repellent sense of violation that made her want to scrub her insides, she picked up the postcard. Different picture, same island. On the back was no stamp, and a new message: *Missing you madly.* She flung the card to the floor.

▼ ▼ ▼

Slumped on a bench in Lafayette Park, Mike pondered his next move. He'd managed to retrieve the shoebox, so the day wouldn't go down as a total loss. On the other hand, he'd fled without the dress socks, and he'd left his portfolio somewhere. The limp, red-marked resumé went in with his sneakers.

A kid walked by, dribbling ice cream down his shirt. Mike had counted on a free lunch from Torrey, Hart & Bellin and, not to go out on a limb, it seemed unlikely there'd be any breaking of bread soon with Laurence and the gang. He'd have to kill time until his one o'clock meeting with Char.

A jet took off from National, flying low overhead. He wished he were on it. Heading somewhere Char had never heard of, if such a place existed. He didn't want to think about how she'd take the tidings, or the punishment she'd devise. Major silent treatment, probably, intended to make him convince himself he wasn't worthy of her. He pulled from his suit pocket the folding map of the District. Maybe it showed places for disappearing.

On the far end of the bench was a newspaper that didn't seem to have been used for anything quirkier than reading. He slid over and paged through, searching for the travel section, before he remembered it came out only on Sundays, even though midweek seemed the most likely time for people to think about getting out of town.

The paper opened to a spread of want ads, never a bonanza. Often he fell for the 'exciting opportunity to meet people' that ended up being a stint hustling timeshare units. Today's medley held nothing heart-stopping. The one title with any promise, *CHIEF,* turned out to be a misprint:

> CHIEF. Experienced cook needed for private business. Impeccable references. Ability to plan menu. Greek, Italian, French, Thai a plus. 555-7738 (3N).

He read it over twice, hoping for something more. Dead end for a guy whose culinary skills stopped at the peanut butter food group. He flipped to the personal ads, always a strange mix of optimism and despair. Running a personal was like buying lottery tickets. Only, with the lottery, the worst that could happen was you didn't win. Mike wasn't sure why he felt the compulsion to read other people's personals. To feel superior, maybe, or on the off chance it might trigger the event that would bring everything finally into focus. He ran a finger down the columns, hardly reading the words. Nothing. And more nothing. He turned the page and a personal jumped at him.

Most entries were intimate, cleverish, false self-descriptions. Others delivered messages to particular people. This took neither approach. It was addressed to no one and read:

> Get a job. Can't hide in europe forever. See the men you no on Friday. Bottoms up! USA North-east show me something. C.O.L.

Codes and riddles. The thought sparked a memory he couldn't connect it with anything. He turned back to the paper. *Can't hide in europe forever.* Who can't? *C.O.L.* or the unnamed reader? And why not capitalize 'Europe?' The ad was written in the imperative. Directions, most likely. *Get a job.* Maybe look for another clue in the employment classifieds? He scanned the pages, found nothing, and went back to the message.

C an't
h ide
i n
e urope
f orever.

Nearly choking on a piece of cracker, he raced through the job ads. No others came close.

CHIEF Experienced cook needed . . .

The dummy 555 prefix should have been a giveaway. Mike turned back to the personals. Fine. In the job ads, find *Chief. See the men you.* He got it: menu. A couple of pigeons edged toward his bench. He shook his arm at them and they scuttled away into a patch of sunlight.

He looked at the next obvious clue, the misspelled 'know.' *No on Friday.* Noon. Friday, today. He glanced at his watch. Past eleven. A phony number, *555*. Add the area code and you reached directory assistance, much good that would do without knowing who you were looking for. Unless . . .

He ran to the nearest pay phone, shoved in a coin, and dialed 555-7738. Maybe they'd rigged it to be a real number. As someone picked up, a truck roared by. He could hardly hear the sounds at the other end. "What?"

". . . call cannot be completed as dialed. Please check the number . . ."

Back at his bench, he tore out the personal and placed the ads side by side. Whatever happened at noon didn't involve calling. What was the number, then? An address? A . . . private business?

He pulled out his map of the District and put it on the bench next to the ads. No inspiration. *Bottoms up!* He turned the ads upside down. *555-7738* became BELL-555.

He gathered shoebox and clippings and ran across the park. Before he knew what he was doing, he'd hailed a taxicab. The driver swerved and drifted to the curb.

Mike leaned in at the window. "I need to go to 555 Bell."

"No such place."

"What?"

"Not in the District." The cabbie turned away and spat. "No such street."

"You sure?"

"I've only been driving a cab fifteen years, how could I be sure?"

"Oh. Okay. Forget it." Mike stared at the ad. *8ELL.* "No, hold it. What about 8th and L?"

"Sure. Northwest, northeast, southeast?"

3N. NƐ. Mike grinned as he hopped in.

"Northeast, of course."

On the way across town, he tackled the last bit of code. *USA Northeast show me something.* Another northeast. *USA Northeast.* New England? It didn't make sense. *Show me.* Someone's slogan. A state. Arkansas? Missouri. USA N.E. Missouri. MO. You say N.E.MO . . . you say 'Nemo.' A password.

When he laughed again, the cabbie shot him a look in the mirror. He shut up and began to work out why the name 'Nemo' seemed so familiar. Something other than submarines and mythology, he was pretty sure.

▼ ▼ ▼

At 8th and L Northeast, he paid and got out, and the cab sped away. Easy to see why. It wasn't a part of the city Mike spent much time in, or wanted to. Clumps of garbage bunched in the gutters. The buildings had an air of fatigue. No one was on the streets. His own neighborhood looked perky by comparison. It would have been better, he realized, to have stashed the sneakers somewhere. Too late now. He checked the ad again.

The four corners of the intersection were taken up by, respectively, a gas station, a drugstore, a vacant lot, and a six-story office building, most of the windows of which were boarded. 8ELL-555. Private business. Never one to overlook the obvious, he headed for the tall building.

The front door was missing. The lobby elevator bore a handwritten sign: 'Nope.' He took it as a good omen. The stairs were in good repair. Omen. Omen. Nemo omen. At five minutes to noon, he reached the fifth floor.

The hallway, lit by bare bulbs, offered a collection of dust and two rows of frosted glass doors that faced one another. Footprints, some new and some old, left confused tracks up and down the hall. As he moved along it, dust swirled around his ankles.

He paused in front of 555, wondering for the first time whether he'd stumbled into such a great adventure after all. Scuffling noises came from the other side of the door. Yes, this would be the right time to walk away. But . . . he couldn't do it. A jigsaw puzzle might turn boring three-quarters of the way through, yet he always forced himself to finish. He knocked.

"Whaddya want?" The voice was low.

Mike inhaled, sucked dust into his throat, and sneezed. "I've come about the job." In a strange way, it felt good to say it.

"What job?"

"Chief."

"Wrong place."

His shoulders drooped. After all that work. He started to turn away but stopped. *Impeccable references.* He hurried back to the door.

"It's . . . Nemo sent me."

"Nemo?"

"Yeah." He bit his lip and waited.

"That's it?"

"Yeah. I mean, no."

Another pause.

"You got something for me?"

Mike looked at the ad. *Greek, Italian, French, Thai a plus. G-I-F-T.*

"I have a gift."

"How good is it?"

He wrinkled his nose. How good? He peered at the scrap of newspaper. "It's . . . oh, it's A-plus."

The door swung open, revealing a tall, muscular woman in military camouflage and dark sunglasses. The name patch on her breast pocket had been removed, but there were insignia on the collar. Mike was trying to remember what oak leaves meant when she pulled him into the room. The door slammed behind him, and she gestured toward the scrap of paper in his hand.

"Nemo. Frigging codes. What's in the box? It wasn't supposed to be a real gift, you dope."

"It's nothing. Sneakers." He showed her.

"And the point of that?"

He shrugged. "Well, I . . . I could pretend to be delivering something, if anyone asked." It was the best his brain would do on short notice. But the lines around her mouth softened. He stuffed the ad into a pocket.

The window in the room was boarded, the light murky. He didn't know what he'd expected at the end of the puzzle. Not this. Trying to be discreet, he examined her more closely.

In her late forties, maybe, tanned and tough, and she wore the uniform as though she meant it. She chomped on mint-flavored chewing gum and her mouth tightened again as she pulled off her shades. There was something vaguely familiar about her face. A movie actress, maybe.

"Over there." She pointed toward a side door.

Belatedly he realized he hadn't thought through the down side of calling on Suite 555. The lady and the tiger. Two in one. He gulped.

The furnishings in the next room weren't much of an improvement, although with the window unboarded it was better lit. There was a fire escape outside. In a corner of the room, a child-sized statue was draped with a bedsheet, looking like a cut-rate Halloween ghost.

"Never mind that." Her voice was harsh. "I want you to see this."

A small folding table stood in the center, with a topographic map across it. Mike inspected the wavy blue lines. Beneath one corner of the map, a glossy black-and-white photograph was visible. He lifted the map and saw an aerial shot of a large house, with a lake and expansive grounds, surrounded by forest. She batted the map back down.

"We'll get to that in a minute. First there's blueprints." She unrolled a brittle set. At the bottom was a notation, an abbreviation, 'E.W.' East-West, presumably. She spread the sheets on the table. "I don't want to know your name. We'll use 'Worm.' You call me Colonel."

C.O.L. Mike put his shoebox on the table. She leaned closer, and he smelled recycled mint.

"They say you're good with computers."

"They do." It wasn't what he'd wanted his mouth to say.

She didn't press it. "How about maps?"

He shrugged. "So-so." The street directory, how would that be? In fact, now was the perfect moment to mention that it was all a mistake, a joke, he wasn't the person she wanted, just a guy who liked puzzles.

She glanced at the topo. "We'll see about that. Let's talk about TekSekure."

"Okay." TekSekure. Made as much sense as anything. "What about it?"

From the other room came a knock on glass, the knock of someone right on time for a noon appointment. The Colonel whirled.

"You bring someone?"

"I . . . no, I sure didn't."

"Wait here. Keep quiet." She pulled out an odd-looking device, like a flashlight with no lens, just two metal prongs. Mike felt his eyes widen as he took in the weapon in her hand. She had dirt under her fingernails. "Don't worry," she said. "Special issue stun gun." She slid around the corner.

Stun gun, excellent. He edged to the window. It opened on an alley. The fire escape was there, all right, but the ground looked far off. He could hear a conversation, urgent whispers. Nemo sent me, I've got a gift. To hell with it. End of investigation. Some adventures were too real to be fun. Any sally port in a storm.

The window opened with a squeak. He held his breath, tried not to look down, and scampered to the bottom of the ladder. Where it ended, he dropped the final endless distance to the pavement and managed not to sprain anything. When he stood, his knees buckled.

He didn't wait to see if people were sticking heads or guns out the fifth floor window. He didn't quit running until he left the northeast quadrant. And he didn't stop to think until then whether, during the escape, he might have lost something. Other than his mind.

▼ ▼ ▼

One appointment he was not likely to forget was his regular Friday rendezvous with Char. A few blocks off the Mall was a townhouse apartment maintained by Torrey, Hart & Bellin. It was intended for visiting lawyers from the firm's Los Angeles office, but so seldom was it used that Char had persuaded her father to give her the key, with the promise to have any of her fictitious friends out if the firm needed it. She considered it useful for taking a 'late lunch' on Friday afternoons.

In the beginning, Mike had found the clandestine nature of their meetings intensely arousing. The apartment, furnished but not decorated, had the humorless feel of a nice hotel room, and it was as if they had sneaked away for an affair. But after a few weeks the novelty wore off, and his lone thrill came from pretending an L.A. lawyer might walk in at any moment. It didn't help to find out that, for Char, the encounters were a matter of pure convenience, a way to keep herself from eating during the lunch hour.

Today the edge was back, because he could imagine how well it would go over if, say, Kathy Laurence were to drop by the place and find him there. Char had left the door unlocked for him, as usual. He took off his shoes and socks in the hall, so she wouldn't see the felt bags. It bothered him that he couldn't resist the pure animal urge to be with her. But there was no denying that their bodies fit together well, even if her main source of pleasure came from the burning of calories.

His mouth was dry. He went through into the bedroom.

"You have some nerve showing up, after your performance today." But he could tell that, under the sheet, she had her clothes off.

"I'm sorry about that, but–"

"Daddy's furious. He's had a horrible morning."

Mike sat on the edge of the bed. "I'm sorry about that, too."

"Stop saying you're sorry, you know you don't mean it."

"I'm . . . right." He stood and dropped his jacket on the armchair. At least she'd decided to talk.

"What am I to do with you?"

"I don't know, but the most incredible–"

"Stop interrupting."

"Right." He began to unbutton his shirt before he remembered he'd left the door unlocked. "Hey, could you hang on a–"

"I really don't see how you can come to the beach this weekend. Daddy would tear you apart."

He stopped at the door. "That wouldn't be fun."

"No. He has to be in a good mood. I want to borrow some money."

Mike stripped from his shirt while he waited for her to tell him the plan. She'd have one, and it would make sense. He stepped out of his pants and put them next to the fresh sheets she'd brought for making the bed with afterward.

"You'll never guess–"

"I suppose it would be best if you stayed in the city. We need to give him a chance to calm down."

"Okay." She'd said 'we.' That was good. She watched while he wriggled from his shorts.

"Since you'll be around anyway, you can have the oil changed in my car. The place I use is open Saturdays; you know the one. Yes, this should do it. I'll ride to the shore with Mummy. Daddy's got this horrible thing going on at work, so he'll take the helicopter. When I get back Tuesday night you and I can talk about how to patch things with him. Among other topics."

"If you say so." He slid in next to her, feeling the shock of her warmth. Not that he cared to wait in his apartment while mercenaries closed in. It wouldn't take them long to dust the map for prints. He pressed himself against her smooth, firm thigh. A bad sign, when you were in bed with one woman and caught yourself thinking about another. Especially when the other was the Colonel.

"I do say so. Are you paying attention? I don't like it when you get that tone. Come by the office this afternoon. I'll leave my car key with the man at the front desk. You know where I park?"

"I think . . . yes."

"Good. Remember, we close early today."

We close. Suddenly she was the entire federal government. He felt desire ebb from him. "You know, Char, I just . . ."

"Just what?"

He'd been about to remind her that it hadn't been long since the car's last servicing. Instead, he rubbed the tip of his nose along the side of her neck, the way she liked. "Char?"

"Mmmmm?"

"I just wanted to say thanks for the flowers."

"What flowers?" She pulled away. "What on earth are you talking about?"

▼ ▼ ▼

His telephone rang, muffled by the dishtowel and the closet door. Mike didn't let it interrupt the process of throwing clothes into his suitcase on the couch. The ringing kept up and at last he edged toward it. They wouldn't call ahead, would they? He lifted the receiver as if it might detonate.

"Hello?" He hadn't meant to sound like someone being strangled.

"Mikey?"

Never had he been so glad to hear mangled British.

"Gray!"

"Say, there's a welcome for a chum."

"Where are you?"

"At . . . well, where do you think? I just wondered if you'd changed your mind. About coming down."

"Yes! I mean, very nice of you. I think I might after all." He rummaged in a drawer and came up with a ragged length of twine.

"Terrif. You'll be catching the train, or motoring?"

Mike returned to the suitcase, stretching the phone cord to its limit. "Train, I guess. I don't have a . . . well, no, I'll drive." Char would understand. He wrapped the twine around the suitcase.

"Brilliant." Gray was silent a moment. "You know how to get, um, here?"

"Where's here?"

"Hartigan Gap. Not far off. Take 112 out of the city. Or is it 211?"

Bracing the phone with his shoulder, Mike eased the suitcase out the window and began to lower it to the alley. "I'll find it."

"Super." Gray sounded genuinely pleased. "Tell you what. I'll meet you at the Speckled Turnip. Lovely little eatery, right on Main Street. Nine o'clock tomorrow morning. We'll have a spot of brunch; I'll fill you in."

"Sounds fine." He checked his watch. Twenty hours. He could survive twenty hours.

"Oh, Mikey. Almost forgot. Can you get hold of a false beard?"

Mike stopped lowering. "Sorry, bad connection. I thought you asked if I could find a false beard."

“Right. Can you?”

“How should I know? I’ve never tried.”

“All right then, try.”

He made a face at the phone. “What for?”

“It would be . . . better. Look, this needn’t be a big production. Just strap on your tennies and run and fetch one.”

“My tennies?”

“Tennies. You know. Your sneaks.”

The twine zipped through Mike’s fingers.

“Yow!” He blew on his hands, visualizing a shoebox on a table in the Colonel’s office. Fingerprints? Who needed fingerprints? He’d left his resumé, with his name and address circled in red ink. He stared at the door and then the window. Some choice.

“. . . the important bit is, you have to be an archaeologist.”

“A what?”

“Archaeologist. You know. Archaeology. Wasn’t that your minor?”

“Anthropology, Gray.”

“Close enough. Mustache.”

“Mustache? A minute ago it was a beard.”

“No, no,” Gray said, more slowly. “Must dash. Gotta run. See you in the morning.”

Mike dropped the phone and hustled from the apartment, choosing the door. He’d had enough of windows to last a while. And there was no time to dawdle. He didn’t even stop to shed the felt bags. At the entrance to his building, he slowed and strolled outside, hoping he looked like a guy who might come back soon.

As he passed the alley, he ducked in. Too risky to lug the suitcase, which lay on the pavement beside the remains of Morty Moose. He untied the twine and stuffed it in his pocket. You never knew. He wrapped the costume around his luggage and dropped everything into the dumpster. For good measure, he threw the moose head on top and closed the lid.

He wiped his brow. So far, so good. No threat of spending the weekend in a suit without socks. And less than twenty hours to go.

He still didn’t have much of a plan, but at least he was packed.

–5–

The cab dropped Liz off right outside Union Station in plenty of time, but the cash machine by the ticket window had run out of money. She had to walk several blocks hauling her bulky suitcase before she found another, and that was perfect, just perfect, precisely what she wanted to be doing on a miserable summer afternoon. She yanked her money free and trudged back, threading her way through the oncoming foot traffic, forcing her mind to dwell on nothing in particular. There was no reason at all to get worked up about the new project. The answer was in a computer. The computer was in Virginia. And the postcard bastard could go stuff himself.

A few strands of hair had worked loose from the elastic, and she pushed them behind her ear. Without breaking stride, she reached into her purse for the hairbrush. Her fingers touched instead one of the business cards Bud had ordered for their more straightforward jobs. This was not a straightforward job, and the card shouldn't have been in the purse. With her hand still inside, she began to look for a litter basket.

She was a block from the station when she became aware of a skinny kid headed her way, wearing a Yankees cap. If it hadn't been for the logo, she might not have noticed. Here it was, practically the All-Star break, and the Sox ten games out. A curse on New York, and everything about it.

The kid stepped into her path. Now he'd offer to carry her bag, for a fee. At the last second he moved aside, giving her an odd glance. She turned to dispose of the business card. A jab in the kidney made her remember him.

"What the–?"

"Don't turn around, lady." He shoved whatever it was into her ribs.

"Stop it." She squirmed. "Get that out of my back."

"Gimme your purse. Don't turn around." She felt his panicky breath.

"You must be kidding."

"Gimme, or I waste you."

Suddenly there was no one else on the sidewalk. She scanned the street, but none of the drivers seemed to be looking. She hung her head. Not again.

"Now, lady."

"Shut up."

The memory of that mugging, five years distant, brought an edge to her voice. She turned to face him. "What the . . . huh?" Smaller than she expected.

He stepped away. "I told you, don't do that." He had a nervous look and waved something she was surprised to see really was a pistol. Too tiny to be real. He wasn't even as tall as she was. Beneath the cap, he wore one of those slash-and-burn haircuts that were so unaccountably popular. He shifted his weight from foot to foot.

"Lemme have that pocketbook." His voice slid toward a whine, the motion of his weapon more a tremble than a wave. "Come on, lady, move it."

"Would you stop calling me 'lady?' " Bud always touted those self-defense classes. But no one got mugged in broad daylight, half a block from Union Station. No one but a careless person. She tilted her chin toward the purse. "There's nothing in it."

"Yeah there is. He . . . gimme."

"Stop saying gimme."

"Fuck you."

She clenched her teeth. On a tropical island this would not be happening. He tugged at her bag. Safer to let him have it.

"All right, cool your jets." The strap was over the arm that held the suitcase. She set the bag on the pavement. Then she ran through the contents of the purse. Cash, of course. Cell phone. Driver's license, keys, credit cards, diagnostic disks. It flashed through her mind what a giant pain it was going to be to report, replace and recreate it all. From the corner of her eye, she saw the kid relax. His gun dropped to waist level. He gave a grunt of satisfaction as she disentangled herself.

She grabbed the suitcase and swung it at his groin. He gave a bigger grunt and tumbled backward. The pistol flew from his hand, skittered into the street and made an unsettling pop. She knelt on him, holding his collar with both hands, shouting toward the train station.

"Help! He's got a gun! He wants my purse! Help!"

But he yelled right back, even louder. "Help! She trying to kill me! Help!"

"Stop it! You don't get to call for help."

He looked past her shoulder. "Mister, you gotta do something, she crazy."

She turned, but there was no one behind her. She felt a shove in her stomach and fell away. The mugger rolled from under her and got to his feet as she landed hard on the pavement. She could see him searching for the gun, but it lay in the street, car wheels bumping across it. He cursed and began to lope down the sidewalk toward Union Station, clutching his privates.

She felt a surge of rage. Pretending there'd been someone behind her. What a cheater. Let him go, let him go, let him go. But she regained her feet, gathering her skirt and giving chase, tucking her purse under one arm, pursuing the memory of that other mugging, that betrayal.

He made it halfway down the block before he looked back. His eyes widened as he caught sight of her. His cap blew off, and he slowed. Vanity. He turned and resumed the sprint. She kicked into high gear, flying past the Postal Museum, twenty yards behind when he ducked around the corner.

She neared the intersection at full sprint. Holding her bag by the strap, she began to twirl it overhand like a bola. Thank you, Bud, for every one of these keys. The purse swung harder, ready to drop him. Toast. The kid was toast. She dipped a shoulder and took the turn as tight as she could.

▼ ▼ ▼

Mike walked, as always, with his eyes on the cracks in the pavement. The blow caught him in the chest and sent him sprawling. For nearly two hours he'd wandered the streets of Washington, trying to avoid the Colonel and her associates. Now they'd found him. He braced himself for the execution.

There was no blood, nor any sign of an entry wound. Maybe she'd used the stun gun. Stand up, dummy. Stand and run. In an instant, if they didn't shoot him, they'd bundle him into a panel van, blindfold and chloroform, the whole deal. He pulled himself to his knees, trying to guess the safest direction.

A woman lay close by, moving. Alive, at least. She rolled onto her side, and he saw her face. *The condemned man received a visit from the lovely . . .* He crawled toward her, grateful he couldn't speak, because the only thing he could think of was, 'Haven't we met?' She rose to her knees, wild-eyed. He held out a hand to her, but she waved it away and pointed at him.

"You . . . idiot!"

It was a bit much, even for Mike. He stood. "Excuse me?"

She stood too. "I've lost him."

"Lost who?" The sidewalk was deserted.

"That kid I was chasing. You must have seen him. He was just ahead of me when he ran around the corner."

Mike had an uncomfortable recollection of something along those lines. "Why were you chasing him?"

"Why was I . . . ? I wanted to marry him, what do you think?" She loosed a withering look. "He was trying to mug me."

"You were chasing him." Mike proceeded with care. "And you say he was mugging you."

"Is that a difficult concept?"

"In broad daylight."

She stared at him in an unpleasant, suspicious manner that made him realize she thought he was covering for the kid. As he searched for a plausible alibi, she shook her head and her dark ponytail swung back and forth. He had the vague sense that she felt sorry for him. Time to say something engaging. *Louie, I think this is the beginning of a beautiful friendship.* That wasn't it.

"Skip it. If I'd caught him I'd just have to fill out another of those damned police reports. Sorry about the pileup. Did I hurt you?"

"No, I'm fine." But the word 'police' clicked. He pretended to run a hand through his hair in order to shield his face.

"Hell. My suitcase." She ran back the way she'd come, moving with the same graceful step he'd seen that morning. Gone again.

A guy wearing a sandwich board and giant rabbit ears ambled toward him. Mike took a leaflet, out of sympathy. The flier was pink. DON'T WAIT

ANOTHER SECOND! HUSTLE YOUR BUNNIES! It was only an ad for used cars, but Mike took it as a cosmic sign. He crumpled the paper and ran after the woman.

He caught sight of her midway along the block, reaching down for a baseball cap. He drew closer. Funny, she didn't act like a Yankees fan, hadn't shouted obscenities or tried to pick a fight. And that was the difficulty with projecting a personality onto someone you'd never formally met. She didn't wear the hat, just stared at it as she walked toward a black suitcase that lay on its side near the curb. She jammed the cap into an outer pocket of the bag.

He was at max velocity for wingtips when she hefted the case and lurched toward him. He had to swerve to avoid another collision. She dropped the bag.

"You." When she said it, a small white scar appeared on her lower lip, slightly off center. Not an angry scar, a rather nice one. It made him want to touch it.

"I had to tell you, I wasn't trying to steal that purse." When she raised her eyebrows, he saw the need to elaborate and jerked a thumb over his shoulder. "This morning."

She glanced at her handbag, then peered at him.

"Have we . . . oh. The skater."

"Mike."

"Mike. Didn't recognize you in the suit. Nice tie."

"Yes, I . . . thanks. Listen, can I give you a ride somewhere?" He wasn't sure what he'd do if she accepted. He didn't actually have the car yet, just the key.

"I'm catching a train." She pointed behind him, toward Union Station.

"Train." He swallowed. "Well, I could carry your bag. To the platform."

She nearly smiled, he thought. "I'm okay, thanks."

"You're okay?"

"I'm okay. Really."

He sensed he'd fallen behind on points.

"Okay." He wished she would say 'you' again, so he could see the white scar. She gazed at the street. A pistol spun with the blows of passing traffic.

"Oh." He stepped back, half-raising his hands. "Is that yours?"

She gave him a sidelong glance.

"If you were a gentleman, you'd offer to get it for me."

"Um, all right."

"I'm kidding. It's not mine." Her eyes swept him, starting at the head. "You want a piece of advice, Mike?"

"Sure."

She pointed toward his feet. "Rethink the socks."

He stared at the green felt as she picked up her bag and headed off. Really, over the course of a day, it should be possible to do at least one thing right.

Where her suitcase had stood, a scrap of paper lay on the ground. He bent down to retrieve it.

TekSekure, Inc.
Liz Halloran
Vice President and Manager

Liz. Now he remembered: She'd given her name to the cop at the Tidal Basin. He looked up and waved as she disappeared into a group of pedestrians. A mustached man across the street was shadowing her. Mike shook his head. Enough with the rescue fantasies. Plenty to worry about on the home front.

He ran his thumb across the business card. No number or address. Weird. TekSekure. Colonel. Whoa. He pressed himself to the wall. But there was no one in uniform. He relaxed and slipped the card into his pocket. If he ever bumped into Liz again, she might want to know about the Colonel. A big 'if.'

▼ ▼ ▼

The run-in with Mugger Junior ended up costing Liz after all, as she reached the track in time to see the last car leave the platform. Consultation of a schedule confirmed the bad news: another hour until the next departure.

Taking the train hadn't even been her idea. But that was what the client wanted, and it was, in the final analysis, the client who was paying. Just as it would be the client who would now wait, since she had no way of reaching him to explain she'd missed her transportation.

She walked to a magazine stand and picked up a copy of *Sports Illustrated.* Damn the front-cover Yankees. She thought about Mike, wondering where he'd been headed. He was kind of cute, in a gangly way. She'd felt a gentleness in his touch when he tried to help her up, had seen genuine concern in his eyes. Potential, as Mother would say. Oh, well. Wherever he and his potential were going, it wasn't Hartigan Gap. Or anywhere else in the life of Liz Halloran.

The train, when she boarded, was full of perspiring commuters trying to get a jump on the long weekend. Midway along the car, she lifted her suitcase to an overhead rack and squeezed into a space between a woman with a lapful of knitting and a man in a brown suit who dozed with his face crushed against the window. As she dropped onto the seat, she realized it faced backward.

Across from her were a harried-looking man and two children just large enough to be unsafe. The father had made the tactical error of letting them sit next to each other. There was no way to change seats. Liz stretched her legs as far as she could. Late arrivals passed the length of the car, scanning. She peered through the window. On the platform, a face caught her attention, but he turned away before she could place him.

"My turn at the window."

"Go hurt yourself."

'You don't understand,' she wanted to tell them. Her parents had wanted another child. She'd heard about it often enough when she was five and would have liked a sister, maybe a brother if it came down to it, anything not to feel so alone and to blame for it all. Mother would tap her abdomen and fix Liz with a sharp look.

"You took it out of me, Elizabeth, you know that?"

'I'm sorry,' Liz had wanted to say then. 'I'd put it back if I knew what it was or where it went.' What she wanted to say now was, 'What a terrible thing to tell a child.'

The train found its rhythm. Liz closed her eyes, wondering if Mike of the green socks had been following her. Twice in one day. Kind of obvious. But an improvement over the postcard creep.

The conductor came through. With her eyes closed, she held up her ticket to be punched. The same man, twice in one day. It could be chance.

▼ ▼ ▼

The green felt protectors had absorbed their way into sweaty miseries. Unwilling to squish another step, Mike took refuge in a bus shelter. He placed the bag from the costume shop on the bench beside him and began to unlace his shoes. Someone entered the shelter, but Mike was past being embarrassed about the greenery. Without looking up, he stripped off the makeshift socks and remained bent over, inspecting his puckered toes, wiggling them in the air.

"I'll say this once." A gravelly voice. "I don't like you following me."

"What?" Mike eyed the man in the entrance.

"You been after me all day."

"Sorry, wrong person."

"I don't think so."

"Look." Mike stood. "Yowee." The touch of bare feet on hot pavement made him leap to the bench. "I'm telling you . . . oh. You." He crouched.

The guy had dark, deep-set eyes under brows that sloped down at the outsides, as if they'd snapped across the bridge of his nose. He was well dressed, not wearing a windbreaker, and not carrying a camera. Not any more. Mike scuttled along the bench.

The guy rolled his eyes. "Cool it, Archer, I only want to talk to you."

"How do you . . . oh." He'd been there for the whole sorry process of the arrest. The cops had taken his name, too. Rex, or Roger, something like that. Mike shrugged his shoulders. "Sorry about the camera."

Roger/Rex scoffed. "It was old. What I want to know is, why are you following me?"

"I'm not."

"Whaddya doing out this way, then? Live around here?"

"No." The beard story wasn't going to fly. "Just coincidence."

"Like it's a coincidence I saw you talking to Halloran by the station?"

"Halloran? Oh. Her. As a matter of fact, yes."

Rogex leaned against the shelter, blocking the only exit.

"What do you know about her?"

Mike felt the weight of the card in his pocket. "Hardly anything."

"You sure?"

"I never saw her before this morning, and I've been in jail most of the time since then. Or in . . . well, in business meetings."

Rogex squinted, as if trying out his new x-ray vision.

"Gave you something, didn't she?"

"No."

"She did. I saw you pick it up."

"Oh." Mike groped in his pocket. "She dropped this. I don't think she wanted me to have it."

"Lemme see."

Something in the urgency of the gesture made Mike hesitate, but he handed the card across. Rogex began a close examination, front and back. He held it to the light. He ran his fingers across the surface. He sniffed it.

Mike stared. "What . . . ?"

"Quiet." He picked at a corner with a fingernail in need of cutting. Rex, that was it. When the paper began to tear, he abandoned the effort and handed it back. "Okay. Sure she didn't give you something else?"

"Like what?"

"Anything."

"Nothing. No. No way."

"Maybe not." Rex frowned and tented his fingers. "Maybe not."

"What's going on, anyway?"

"Hunh. Can you keep this confidential, Archer?"

"I don't . . . sure. I guess."

The man withdrew a slim wallet.

"Special Agent Roger Donovan, Department of Justice." He flipped it open long enough to provide a glimpse of an official-looking card.

"What's . . . what are you investigating?" Mike had the sudden frightening thought that the Colonel worked for the government and had turned them loose on him. Donovan gave the shelter another visual sweep.

"This Halloran gal, she's into something bad. It's . . . deep."

"Deep?"

"Deep."

TekSekure. The Colonel wanted to talk about TekSekure. Mike swallowed.

"What is it?"

"Sorry, Archer. Classified."

"Okay." He nodded. Better keep quiet about the Colonel for now. "What do you want from me?"

"You really interested in helping?"

"Um, okay."

"There is a thing you can do."

"What's that?"

"Keep away from Halloran. We don't want to risk innocent targets."

Targets. Mike felt his shoulder blades tighten. "No problem there. No problem at all." He stole a look at his watch. Eighteen hours to safety. "As a matter of fact, I was just leaving town."

▼ ▼ ▼

Liz woke. Virginia farmland whipped past the train window, hurrying toward Washington. She listened to the cadence of the wheels. *I'm late, I'm late, for a very important* . . . No. That was someone else's crisis. There was nothing for her in the city. No dates to be late for.

The seats on either side of her were empty. Across the way, the Tots from Hell had gone, replaced by a thin man with thick glasses and a mustache that might well have been glued on. Liz smoothed her skirt over her knees and made the mistake of catching his eye. He leered at her. She turned away.

The car was mostly empty. She checked her watch. Thirty minutes to Hartigan Gap. On the other side of the aisle, a well-dressed man with graying hair studied the screen of his laptop and typed at a thoughtful pace.

The day after their college graduation, she'd been leaving the jewelry store where Allie worked part-time, just one last quick goodbye, supposedly. The guy on the bike had swooped out of nowhere, wrenching Liz's arm half off. But her reflexes were good and her leverage better. He let go and disappeared down a side street. When she looked in her purse she found the pearl necklace. It wasn't hers. The price tag was still on it.

Five years later, she still had to confirm that Mugger Junior hadn't planted anything. She snapped the flap closed and shut away the memory.

The goofball with the mustache kept ogling. She set her jaw and stared back, but he gaped on, doing something weird with his eyebrows. About time he got the hint. She raised her index finger, doubled it and jammed the knuckle into a nostril, rotating the finger for effect. He stood and bolted.

The intercom at the end of the car crackled. "Abbotsville, Abbotsville."

A burst of laughter came from across the aisle. The man in the suit closed his laptop and gathered up a briefcase. As he moved into the corridor, he winked and gave her a casual salute. She watched, faintly troubled, as he left through the narrow door. The train rocked and clacked. She slid across to the window and leaned her head against the cool glass.

▼ ▼ ▼

Mike collected Char's BMW safely. Unfortunately, the visor mirror revealed the main drawback to the beard; it failed to match the color of Mike's hair. Wearing it was like carrying a sign saying, 'I'm in disguise. Come get me.' He didn't dare approach his building, bearded or not, and parked the car in the next alley. To beat the garbage collector to his suitcase, he had to pay a juvenile graffiti artist five dollars to fetch it. The kid brought back Morty Moose as well and wanted to charge extra for that, but Mike held firm. Once he had the costume, however, he tossed it onto the back seat. You never knew. Fourteen hours to safety, and things were looking up.

▼ ▼ ▼

The heat was more tolerable in the country. Liz watched the train bend out of sight. From somewhere down the line came the sound of a crossing bell. No one else had disembarked at Hartigan Gap, not a soul. She breathed in the smell of freshly-cut grass. It was like stepping into a different world.

There was little more to the station than the platform and a clock that read 6:30. The ticket window was closed and didn't look likely to open soon. She passed through to the street side and could see that the railroad tracks ran along a valley, well below the town. Farther away, she spotted foothills, and the gap that presumably gave the place its name.

A solitary taxi waited on the street. She wondered what had become of her contact. The motor of the cab started. Liz shook her head at the driver, but he leaned over and rolled down the passenger window.

"Miz Halloran?"

She frowned. "Yes?"

He winked before popping open his door. "Been waiting a spell for you, Miss. Had to turn away a right crowd of business." He favored her with a bronchial laugh and heaved her suitcase into the trunk.

"I'm sorry. I was supposed to catch an earlier train."

"Oh, don't you worry about that." He held open the rear door. "Pulling your leg, miss. If you'll pardon the expression. Just the one bag?"

When she was settled he closed the door, slammed the trunk and hustled around the cab. There was no plastic divider between front and rear. Even taking into account that this wasn't the city, it made her uncomfortable.

"Have you there in two shakes, miss."

"I'm afraid I don't know where I'm going. There seems to have been a mixup. I think someone was supposed to meet me."

"Someone did, miss. Me someone. There's no mixup. Oh no no, they told me where to take you. Yes, they did. Have you up there in no time." He pointed toward the distant buildings. "Don't you worry about that little thing. Don't you worry about that a-tall." He chuckled and put the cab in gear.

They followed the meandering road. The river glittered with light from the late afternoon sun. The cabbie's window was open and the breeze blew on her face. It was all so pleasant that she began to worry.

Other than the lack of a divider, it seemed like a normal cab. Of course, the best traps worked that way. The trick was to lull the victim into exactly this sort of false security. Her hand gripped the edge of the seat. Across the fields, the sun reddened the foothills. The station was already out of sight.

She searched for the license on the back of the driver's seat. That was his picture, no question. Charlie Dodgson. She frowned. Charlie? Charlie? They don't put nicknames on licenses. Halloran, you are the queen of chumps. He didn't even have the meter on. Now he was staring in the mirror.

The first step in getting out of trouble was not to waste time worrying about how much of it you were in. She slid toward the door and reached for the handle. Her suitcase was in the trunk, but there'd be time to sort that out later. She readied herself to jump.

The cab stopped without warning, slamming her against the front seat.

"Sorry, miss." He hopped out and opened her door, grinning. "Here we are, Miz Halloran. You all right?"

She rubbed her shoulder. "Where are we?"

"Montclair Hotel. That wasn't so long a trip, now, was it? You step out, miss, I'll see to your bag."

She stood on the sidewalk, the adrenaline ebb leaving her legs weak. She put a steadying hand against the roof of the cab. Charlie slid the suitcase onto the pavement beside her.

"Like me to take that inside for you?"

"No." She reached for her purse. "It's fine. What do I owe you?"

"All taken care of, miss. Don't you be worrying about that." He pulled a card from his shirt pocket. "You decide you're ready to leave, give me a call."

Pleasant Cab Company. She stuffed the card into her purse.

"Do you . . . will someone else be meeting me?"

He climbed back in and pointed to the hotel. "In there. Leastways, that's where he's supposed to be. Not the most reliable one. You have a nice visit." He adjusted the seat and drove away. Dust whipped up behind the cab. It hung in the air, swirling, and settled once more to the ground.

▼ ▼ ▼

The Montclair wasn't much of a hotel. Uninviting bar to one side, uninviting restaurant to the other. Narrow stairs with patched carpet leading up. Under them a pay phone, out of order. One teenaged desk clerk camped on the house phone. On the wall behind her, three clocks showed the time in Richmond, Atlanta, and Washington, D.C. No hands on the last. The other two said 6:40.

Several chairs of too-red leather were ranged around a coffee table covered with a scattering of newspaper. All were occupied, two by the same overweight woman who used the second to prop her feet while she watched TV. She'd tethered a small child to the leg of the chair she sat in.

Liz surveyed the lobby again. In four years at TekSekure, she'd never run into such a screwed-up arrangement. The whole setup had begun to feel like a parody of a covert meeting. It had all the makings of a practical . . . Ariel. No wonder he'd been so off-handed about her trip. He'd planned it, the jerk. Bud was probably in on it. What a pair of comedians. The worst thing was that she'd fallen for it. What a professional. What a waste of space.

"Funny, Ariel. Very funny. Ha, ha."

The woman on the red chairs looked up. Her child worked free of the leash and crawled toward the dining room. Liz lifted her suitcase and turned to go when she heard a commotion from the restaurant.

"Darling!" A skinny young man in glasses burst through the doorway. He hurdled the child. "Darling. Frightfully sorry to be late."

She backed away, unable to place his features in the dim light, or his accent. "Who the . . . ?"

"Came as fast as I could." He covered a grin. "You know how it gets on the motorway."

He put a hand toward her. She grabbed his fingers and started to twist. He struggled, but she tightened her grip. He leaned forward, trying to kiss her. She ducked, and he ended up with his lips in her hair.

"Liz." His whisper was desperate. "For heaven's sake."

She froze. Ariel? But he was so young. She dropped his hand. He flexed his fingers and made as if to brush her clothes.

"Here you go, darling, let me take your case. So pipped you made it to the hotel on your own. Come through to the dining room, I've booked a table. We'll grab a bite before we head to the house."

A massive sense of disappointment filled her as he took the suitcase from her unresisting fingers. She followed him into the restaurant, feeling as though she'd just discovered that someone she admired was a criminal. He led the way to a booth in a dark corner. Mechanically, she checked for the closest exit. He parked her bag next to a fat black briefcase and had his face in an open menu before she could sit.

"What appeals, darling? Cup of soup? Salad? Something dead?"

She slid into the other side of the booth. The waitress arrived, plunked down glasses of water, and stood with a hand on her hip, not watching them.

The client ran a finger down the page. "Sandwich? Onion rings?"

"Nothing." Liz sighed. "Anything. Whatever you're having."

"Splendid. Matching tuna melts, Candace."

"Candy. It's Candy." She gave him a dirty look. "For your information, that's a real dumb accent."

When the waitress was out of earshot, Liz put her arms on the table. "For starters, you can stop calling me . . ." She gasped as she saw his face in the direct light. "But you were on the train. With a mustache."

"I know." He dabbed at his lip. "I tried to signal you, but you made everyone look. Where on earth did you learn that trick?" He doubled his index finger and examined it from various angles.

She picked up the nearest available weapon, a fork.

"I thought that mustache was fake. And where did you get off the train?"

"Abbotsville. Fifteen miles back. Had my car stashed, meant to beat you here. Stupid cows." His eyes lost focus. "Good thing I had Charlie waiting."

"But, Ariel." She put down the fork. "Why didn't you meet me at the station? Or just have me get off the train in Abbotsville?"

"Why do you keep saying that?"

"What?" Liz contemplated the butter knife.

"Aerial. Some sort of bird's-eye view? Or . . . oh, I see. Code name."

The piped-in music was awful, a syrupy version of a tune she couldn't identify. She pressed herself against the cushion. "Aren't you?"

"Hardly." He grinned. "It's Gray. Gray Westfield." He leaned closer and lowered his voice. "I'd, that is, I would shake hands, ordinarily, but it might look a bit odd. We're supposed to be engaged."

▼ ▼ ▼

Away from the alley, it became obvious that Morty Moose smelled terrible. Mike separated the carcass from the suitcase and threw it, along with the head, into the trunk. Had he been Gray, he would have worked out a plan for the night by now. With the Colonel in pursuit, he couldn't involve any friends in town, and that left him nowhere to stay. He pointed the car toward Virginia and waited for the rush hour traffic to ease.

Driving the BMW made him uncomfortable, as if he were wearing the wrong size pants. Even if it hadn't been lavender, it was too high-tech for him, loaded with every kitchen-sink option short of an autopilot. He didn't care for the bossy attitude it conveyed. Even the federal eagle on Char's key ring seemed to watch him with suspicion. The car came with a cellular phone. Of course, Char had removed it for the weekend, on the assumption that he'd have no one to call. He ran his fingers along the inside of the holder.

At the edge of the District, he stopped at a gas station and filled the tank, using the credit card she kept under the floor mat. He crossed the Potomac into Virginia and felt as though he'd made it into Switzerland.

"Them hills are alive with the sound of music," he sang to the cars around him, but no one sang back.

Somewhere between Washington and Hartigan Gap there had to be a place to sleep. The best way to find it, and the best way to shake off pursuit, would be to get lost, because if he didn't know where he was, no one else could. He drove a little past the Beltway and headed down a promising county road. A few random turns led him to just the sort of subdivision he'd been looking for. He pulled up in front of a house with two BMW's in the driveway already. With luck, they'd never notice the extra. Tomorrow, Saturday, everyone would sleep in, and the sun would wake him early. Perfect.

▼ ▼ ▼

"Let me get this straight." Liz forced down a mouthful of overdressed tuna. "You left the train early and drove here to make it look as though you were meeting me at the station?" Gray responded with a foolish grin.

The restaurant was permeated with an odor of staleness. She gave up on the sandwich. "What was the point of your taking the train in the first place?"

"I wasn't sure when you'd get here. You missed the right one."

"I was busy getting mugged."

"Oh, I know, I saw that."

"You saw? Thank you for the rescue." She poked the sandwich with a toothpick. "Hang on. If you have a car, why didn't you drive up to the city in the first place and bring me back?"

He fidgeted. "It seemed better this way."

"What's better about it? It couldn't be more convoluted if . . . and what were you doing in Washington?"

"That's not important. Just making sure you came down. Which was dashed difficult, you know."

She tossed her napkin on the table. "Who put you up to this? And what's that horrible accent supposed to be?"

He stopped smiling. "Everyone gives me a hard time about that. Even–"

"Yes, but I mean, why bother?"

"You wouldn't understand."

"I don't understand whether or not this is all a put-up of Ariel's."

"I told you, I don't know a thing about this Ariel person."

"You and I have never talked on the Net?"

"Some sort of computer deal, right? I'm no good with the frightful things. In fact, that's the problem. It's why I, we, had to hire you."

"Aha. There really is a job?"

"Absolutely. Dad's pulling his hair out. In a manner of speaking."

She laced her fingers on the table. "Suppose we start over, and you tell me straight what's going on."

He reached out and covered her hands.

"Stop it." She pulled back. He had mayonnaise on his cheek. From the speaker above her head, the same musical number repeated itself, and it was starting to grate.

"Really, I think it would be better if we discussed it at the house."

"Which is where?" Liz shot back.

"Up the road a jot." A crash of dishes came from the kitchen.

"And why do I have to be your girlfriend?"

"See here, I didn't want you to be my blasted fiancée. I've one already. I needed an excuse to get you in. If you've a better plan, let's hear it."

Liz draped a paper napkin over the remains of her sandwich.

"Best finish that," he said. "We'll be too late for dinner."

"Who else is in the house?"

"There's my father, me of course, and Mr. and Mrs. Liddell. They pretty much run the place. Don't let Mrs. L try any magic tricks on you. A few friends of Dad's coming down this weekend for the big party. He does it every year. Oh, and the person doing the digging. The excavation."

"Excavation?"

"You know. Civil War stuff. Cannons."

She closed her eyes. "Start at the beginning, Gray. Why did you hire us?"

"Because of the dratted computer."

"And what's happened with it?"

"If we knew that, we could take care of it ourselves."

"I understand it's some kind of riddle."

"Maybe. All we know is, she's done something to the thing. It won't tell us what we need to know."

Liz made a fist. " 'She' being who?"

"She? Dad's, um, partner."

"Partner in what?"

"Couldn't say. Consulting thing. Please. Best not to talk about this here."

"You chose it."

"My fault completely. Can we go?"

She moved from the booth. "You'll explain what's going on once we're in the car?"

"Absolutely." He slid a ten-dollar bill partway under his plate and stood.

She moved closer and embraced him, nuzzling his ear. "Sorry we got off to a bad start." She ran her hands down his back and over his ribs. He looked at her in surprise, a faint smile forming. She released him and headed for the door. One piece of good news. The lunatic wasn't armed.

–6–

By and large, things continued to sort themselves out on Saturday morning. Heading for what was, by all accounts, an elegant country house, Mike even had with him the suit and tie that would pass for emergency formal wear. It was a sunny day, he was out of the city, one hour from safety, and no one, least of all the Colonel and Nemo's pal, had a clue where to find him. The next exit pointed the way to Hartigan Gap. At the bottom of the ramp, he drove into a rain shower. It ended as suddenly as it had begun, disappearing into the blue sky. Afterward the car was clean, the temperature had dropped ten degrees, and Mike felt better still about the day ahead.

▾ ▾ ▾

By pleading train fatigue, Liz had forestalled an evening of inquisition at the hands of the man who thought he was about to become her father-in-law. This morning there was no way to avoid him. Gray lingered upstairs, and the Liddells were cleaning up after a terrific breakfast. Mr. Liddell came off a bit stiff, but Liz quite liked Mrs. Liddell. Mr. Westfield was okay, too, but she had to be careful around him. She followed him into the living room. He held a red apple and a paring knife.

"Elizabeth." He patted a place on one of the couches.

"I prefer Liz. Please." Mother was the only one who insisted on Elizabeth.

"Of course. You know, I'm just delighted Gray found someone who shares his interests."

She smiled, wondering, as she sat, what those interests were. A crib sheet would have helped. "Um, it worked out well for both of us."

"In what way?" He set about peeling the apple, making one long ribbon.

"I meant I was beginning to wonder if I'd ever find anyone myself."

"Oh, I can hardly credit that. A woman as charming as yourself?" He looked up from his apple. "But Gray's told me so little. I know next to nothing of your background."

"What would you like to know?" The guy was good, his interrogation a hundred percent sugar-coated.

"Your parents, for instance, where you went to school, what you do. That sort of thing."

"My mother is a judge in Vermont. My dad died eight years ago." He made noises of sympathy and she bowed her head. "Thank you. I went to Mount Holyoke and got my master's at Caltech."

Bud hadn't had time to create an identity for her. And it hadn't seemed necessary. The simplest thing, up to a point, was to tell the truth. Still, she hated having to play herself.

Westfield put an arm on the back of the couch. "What did you study?"

It wouldn't do to claim great knowledge of computer science. "Math. I teach it." Easy enough to fake, anyway.

"Math." He smiled. "So, what took you to Europe?"

She bit back a wiseass remark realizing the danger of the question. When had she supposedly met Gray? During the school year? Explain that, Ms. Math Teacher. The curtains billowed in the morning breeze as he waited for an answer.

She shifted. "I'm sorry, what was that?"

"I wondered why you happened to be in Europe."

"I won a trip. As a prize." Too damn complicated.

"How amazing that there was a mixup over your passports."

"Ye-es."

He laughed. "When the guests arrive, you'll have to give us the true account of the porcupine and the doughnuts. Gray is such a poor storyteller."

That would soon be the least of Gray's problems. The only solution was to corner him quick. They could get their story straight, or stories, and he could explain what he needed from the computer. Westfield held the single coil of apple peel from each end.

"Did you ever wonder about the true nature of the serpent in Paradise?"

She felt her back hit the corner of the sofa. Speak of the devil: Gray stuck his head through the doorway.

"Just off to town. Won't be long."

"I'll come with you," Liz said.

"Oh." He pushed his glasses up the bridge of his nose. "Not very exciting, I'm afraid. Groceries."

"That's all right. I'd like to see Hartigan Gap. Such a charming place." She tried to look enthusiastic.

Westfield discarded the peel. "You two run along. Matt and Marsha should be here any time. Liz, it's been a pleasure talking to you."

"And to you." She kept the plastic smile on her face as she hurried after Gray, imagining precisely how she'd place her fingers around his throat.

▼ ▼ ▼

Mike reached the Speckled Turnip after only six wrong turns. Leaving the highway had been a misplaced act of faith. The directional signs in the Virginia countryside seemed calculated to lead a person anywhere but the right way. And maps were no help. In the end, he arrived in Hartigan Gap by taking whichever road kept the sun out of his eyes.

A parking space was available just past the sign painted with the large turnip. Less than half an hour late. He climbed out and stretched, having concluded that kissing the ground would be an overreaction. Rolling his neck to get rid of the stiffness, he ambled down the sidewalk. At the entrance, he stopped and walked back to the BMW. While he was locking the car, he glanced across the street. Impossible. He looked away and back again. There she was. He pulled her card from his pocket, as if he needed to remind himself. Liz.

She walked into the post office without noticing him, not that he expected her to. Unless the Colonel had sent her to find him. What an idea. She was just a nice girl he couldn't stay out of the way of. As he reached the door of the Speckled Turnip, Gray came out. An odd and not pleasant odor followed.

"Ah, good. There you are." Gray adjusted his glasses. "Beginning to think you'd missed the place. Come on in. Hungry? They do a first-rate omelette. Low-fat mushroom something. Morelle Less, they call it."

Mike caught up to him at a small, rickety table. A piece of dried cheese had been shoved under one leg to stabilize it. "You actually eat here?"

"Yes." Gray lowered his voice. "But only when I'm dieting."

Mike's appetite died somewhere between orange quiche and asparagus pancakes. He dropped the menu. "Maybe I can wait until we get to the house."

"Suit yourself. Probably best. Say, I thought I told you to bring a beard."

"I did." He patted his pocket.

"The idea was for you to wear it."

"What, in here?"

"Certainly."

Mike leaned on the table. The wedge of cheese zipped across the floor.

"Would you mind telling me what's going on?"

Gray surveyed the room before answering. "You wouldn't happen to be a whiz on computers, would you?"

"I'm left-handed."

"Hadn't realized there was a connection."

"There is in my case. I can barely turn on a computer."

"Mmm. Afraid of that. Me neither. Pity."

"Does that mean I can ditch the beard?"

"No, no. That has nothing to do with it. I still need your help. With something else. And I merely thought . . . well, drop it."

Mike rubbed his temples. "Maybe we could start over."

"Why does everyone say that? It's exactly–"

"Just give it a shot. I'll jump off when it gets confusing."

"If you insist." Gray picked up a shaker and scattered salt on the table.

"Fascinating," said Mike. "Do you do tea leaves?"

"Shhh." He set about propping the beveled edge of the shaker on one of the grains. "It's to do with my father."

"I'm sorry. Is something wrong?"

"He's fine. But he lost something. It . . . it doesn't matter. That's not really what I need help with. There's this girl."

"Oh." Mike leaned back. There was always a girl.

"Don't be that way. This one is special. She's smart, and beautiful, and nice, and she rides horses. Horses."

"You don't ride horses."

"No, but she does. Isn't that grand? And she lives next door. Well, it would be next door if the woods weren't there. Only, she has this mother."

"Standard equipment." Mike clasped his hands behind his head.

"Oh, do shut up. The thing is, the mother distrusts me, you see. Thinks I'm lazy or something. That's where I need your help."

"Let me see if I understand this. You brought me down here as a . . . as a character reference?"

"Sort of. You could say that."

"And the beard lends, what, an air of credibility?"

"No, no, no. The mother's a problem because she thinks I'm dashed near as bad as they get. So I reasoned, with you around, I'd shine by comparison."

"Is that supposed to be flattering?" Mike bent the corners of his place mat.

"Well." Gray didn't make eye contact. "It was the natural connection. I got the idea from a TV show."

"Doesn't her father like you?"

"She hasn't one. There's a stepfather, very recent, but we haven't met."

"Shouldn't you give him a try," said Mike, "before you write him off?"

"No. Better not to test him. That way I'll be sure not to fail."

It made sense to Mike. "And the archaeology slant?"

"Oh, I told you, didn't I? There's some sort of dig not far from the house. This way it won't be suspicious when you show up."

"Show up for what? What do I tell the other archaeologists?"

"There aren't any. There was one, but she's gone, and I happen to know the new bloke won't be here until Tuesday. So you can be him for a few days."

Mike tried to get all four legs of his chair to touch the floor at once.

"It won't work. I met your father at school once. He'll know I'm not an archaeologist."

"No problem there. He's terrible with faces. There's a good chance he won't remember you. And he hasn't been following your career. He'll never know you haven't gone on to anything."

The scary thing about Gray's logic was that, while you were talking to him, there was no way to identify the step in the process that sent the train off the tracks. Mike finished folding the paper place mat and blew into it, forming a hollow cube. It was the only figure he remembered from a childhood origami fascination.

"Okay, archaeology. Was I supposed to bring a shovel?"

"You're missing the point. Look, I'd best give you directions to Briarwood. You can head over. I have to meet someone in a minute."

"The light of your life?"

"Er, no. You'll see soon enough. Whatever happens, go along with it."

Mike studied his friend's face, weighing the options. Now that he was on the scene, it was unclear that the sanctuary offered outweighed the mess he could be getting into. The very definition of friendship.

"And what do you need me to do with this flame of yours?"

"I'll give you details later, but basically act as though you're attracted to her. And don't call her a flame. It's deeper than that."

"What's deeper than a flame?"

"You know what I mean."

Mike felt a noose tug at his neck. "I'm not sure I'm the right guy."

"Why not?"

"I'm no good with women."

Gray looked relieved. "Is that all? No fear. You needn't do anything creative. Oh, stop with the look of gloom. I'm telling you, there's nothing to act so wet about. Do what I tell you. You'll see. It'll be bloody marvelous."

"You're guaranteed half right. Either marvelous or bloody." Mike crushed the paper cube. Forty-five minutes past safety.

▼ ▼ ▼

From the post office window, Liz watched Gray emerge with a taller man wearing a preposterous Karl Marx-type beard. They moved down the sidewalk, Gray doing most of the talking. The other man had his hands in his pockets and looked unhappy. They stopped beside a lavender BMW, the bearded one climbed in, and Gray continued to gesture expansively.

She returned to the telephone. "All I'm saying is, it doesn't feel right."

"What's not to feel right?" Bud's voice was faint, distracted.

"I've been here since last night, and I can't get near the computer. It's crazy." Liz watched an old woman buy stamps. "Of course, they're all treating me well, the mysterious fiancée brought home by prodigal Gray."

"What's the complaint?"

"I'm not complaining. It's all terribly charming and Victorian. I've got my own bedroom and everything. But it feels wrong. Too disorganized."

"Trust your instincts."

"What's that supposed to mean? The father's sweet on the surface, sharp underneath. But he doesn't have a clue why I'm here. And it's his computer. I'm beginning to wonder whether our boy Gray's trying to steal something."

"Uh huh."

"You're not paying attention."

"I am, I am, it's just we're trying to get the shop closed down. Come off it, Liz, you're an ace. It doesn't sound like a sophisticated system. Could take you maybe half an hour, and you've got all weekend. Relax."

"That was what I'd planned to be doing today, before you sent me here." Gray came in the door, grocery bag in hand. She raised her voice and stopped cupping the receiver. "Okay, Mother, talk to you soon." She hung up.

He frowned. "I say, no danger of your mum popping down, is there?"

"Oh. No, not likely." She smiled to encourage him. "Shall we go?"

On the way back to the car, he reached up to put his arm around her shoulder, but she brushed him off.

He cleared his throat. "See here, darl–"

"This is your last warning."

"Right. The thing is, it's going to look frightfully curious if we don't show at least a bit of affection."

"Why? People do it every day."

"Not engaged people. Not as a rule."

They drove down the main street to the edge of town. The Montclair Hotel appeared far less sinister in the morning light. Tacky, even. Gray half-turned his head.

"Did you get your errands run?"

"Let's cut the chitchat. I want to know what's going on at your house. This was supposed to be an encryption problem."

"It is. I guess. Oh, very well. It's all to do with a tiff my father's having with our neighbor, Mrs. What's-her-name-now, Owen. They're very keen on that genealogy stuff. It's become something of a rivalry, a race, each wanting to be the first to trace roots back to William the Conqueror, all that rot. Last year they got computers, so they could talk to people all over the world. My father's hopeless with the things. But she's a whiz. She was sort of tutoring him."

The road threaded its way through light-colored fields and dark woods.

"I don't see the problem." Liz couldn't remember ever needing so much time to get going once she was on site.

"They started bumping up against each other's families in their research. Silly things. Someone's ancestor ranked higher in the Civil War. Somebody else fought for the British in the Revolution. Then it got ugly. They found a common ancestor. Changed the dynamics. It became a flat-out race to get back in time. To be the first to link up with William the Conqueror. Dad was ahead. In fact, he'd latched onto some lead when she bollixed the computer."

"Are you saying you brought me down here to chase dead people?"

"Good Lord, no, there's more." They caught up to an overloaded station wagon, and Gray braked hard. "We need you to find something she's hidden."

"Call me a cynic, but I've found that it's difficult to find something without knowing what it is."

"Yes, well, it's a piece of paper. Valuable. I'd rather not say more just now. That's not critical to your work. She says the clue is on the computer."

He powered through a curve. To avoid leaning against him, Liz put a hand on the dash. "Yesterday you said this was about your father's partner."

"I panicked. That place was too public for conversation. Walls have ears, and whatnot. Dad and Mrs. Owen did once work together, that's true. It's how they met. Years ago, before we all lived here. I don't know the details. Dad's a bit close to the vest about it."

Liz ran through the screwball story. Phony, perhaps, but not obviously dangerous. "And the fiancée twist?"

"That's the simple part. I was afraid if she knew we had a professional in, she'd change the hiding place."

Liz watched more fields pass. "And why isn't your father the contact?"

"He doesn't know about you. The truth is, he thinks I'm something of a dolt. Can't find my shoes to tie them, that sort of bunk. I wanted to show him. He'll . . . oh, let's just say it would be useful if I could get on his good side."

▼ ▼ ▼

Mike regretted his decision not to write down Gray's directions. The street signs had gone from misleading to nonexistent, and the forest had grown so dense he couldn't tell where he was in relation to the town. He had about convinced himself to give up when he spotted 'Briarwood' lettered in gold paint on a wrought-iron fence that was nearly overgrown with ivy. He drove between stone pillars up a gravel drive lined with ancient oak trees. Fantastic. Exactly the sort of place the Colonel wouldn't think to look. His stomach growled. Another thing he regretted was his decision not to eat brunch.

The driveway ran roller coaster fashion for nearly a quarter mile before topping out short of a large white house with solid columns. A rectangular fish pond was on one side, a garage-type structure on the other. A line of low hedges blocked the view of the back yard. There was no evidence of other houses. He swooped down the final part of the drive to where the gravel ended in a circle around a burbling fountain. A late-model car sat by the garage building, where he almost expected to see a Model T. He parked next to it and adjusted his beard in the rearview mirror.

The solid slam of the BMW door echoed off the house. He waited. No sign of life on the castle grounds. The loudest noise was the splash of the fountain. At last, the front door opened. Gray emerged, poking his glasses into place, and marched across the crunchy gravel. He lifted a finger to his lips and addressed Mike in a voice that was too loud.

"Hello, there. You must be the new architect."

"What?" He hoped not. "Archaeologist."

"Right. Silly slip."

Mike opened the trunk. Gray peered over his shoulder. "I see you fetched the moose costume. Scads of use for that. And what a remarkable odor. Perhaps I should explain. It's July Fourth, not Halloween."

"Hysterical."

Gray pinched his nose as he surveyed the interior of the trunk. "Not to belabor the obvious, old man, but has it escaped your attention that you've a hydrant in there?"

"I'd noticed."

"Mmm. What I mean to say is, it's a fire hydrant."

"Yes."

"Training your dog, are you?"

"It's Char's."

"Dog?"

"Hydrant." Mike frowned. "Don't be dense. I told you about her Thursday night." But Gray continued to stare. "All right. It's plastic, see, with sand in the base to add weight. She uses it for parking in the city."

"Certainly. Who doesn't?"

He fought back a nasty response. "Say she's going to the movies. With this she can make sure beforehand she'll have a spot, then time things so she arrives right after the previews, which she hates."

Gray's brows rose above the frames of his glasses. "Is her time so valuable?"

"I suppose you could see it that way. For her, there's nothing worse than getting to a place too early."

"A formidable sort."

"You might say."

"Question. If I may."

"Yes?"

"Not to put too fine a point on it, how do you stand the blasted viper?"

Mike studied the house. "I don't do well on my own." It was the best he ever came up with when he asked himself the same question.

"But I thought you were going to grow out of this."

"Out of what?"

"This." Gray's sweeping gesture took in trunk, hydrant, moose costume, and Mike. "Hasn't it sunk in yet that it's all right for you to do okay on your own? You're not responsible for anyone else's mistakes. Especially not your father's. You have to live your own life."

Mike slammed the trunk. "I told you, don't start that again."

"Righty-o." Gray kicked at the gravel. "Still don't see the attraction."

"Okay. A good relationship has three aspects: physical, emotional, and intellectual." It felt strange to be quoting one of Char's loaner books. "We've got two out of three. And that ain't bad, as they claim in the song."

"I see. It's emotion that's missing."

"How did you know that?"

"Lucky guess. Come on, we oughtn't stand around all morning."

"No, really. Tell me."

"Well, an emotional connection would mean you love her, wouldn't it? And you don't. Obviously."

Obvious to whom? But Gray offered nothing more.

"Should I put the car in the garage?"

"It's not a garage, it's a carriage house. And you needn't bother. Not likely to rain. You'd best hurry off and act the archaeologist. I'll take your bag into the house, air it out, and sneak it to the cottage. That's where you're staying. Full tour later. Just ankle on over to the what's-it, the dig, would you?" He pointed beyond the fish pond. "Size it up, wander the grounds. The cottage is out back, near the boathouse, past the maze."

"Maze?" For the first time all morning, Mike sensed a focal point.

"You've plenty of time to work it out on your own. The door to the cottage is open. I've got to go shackle self to Lord of the Manor and chat up the guests. Best for you to lie low during the afternoon. Keep the beard on whenever you're outside. Meet me at seven-thirty in the gardener's shed."

"By the gardener's shed?"

"No, in. You'll see. It's near the garden. I'm sure you can manage." He hefted the suitcase and lurched toward the house.

Mike settled his beard and headed past the fish pond. Through a space in the lilac hedge that separated front yard from back, he glimpsed a vast lawn, a garden, and a sparkling lake.

The dig was near the edge of the woods, a hundred yards from the house, modest in size. It was shallow enough that no ladder was necessary to reach the bottom. Dirt lay piled on the grass. The archaeologists had begun where the lawn sloped down toward the woods that seemed to mark the northern boundary of the Westfield property.

For the benefit of anyone watching, Mike feigned profound interest in the mounds of dirt and small wooden stakes. Muttering "mm-hmm," and nodding, he walked the perimeter, taking occasional sightings of the sun for good measure. Closer to the house he found a gate in the shrubbery, latched but unlocked, through which he headed to the back lawn. The lake had a small boathouse. A formal garden occupied much of the grounds to his left, just short of the woods that marked the southern property line. Directly in front of him was a squarish mass of high boxwood that he took to be the maze.

He stood by the gate, soaking it in. He felt he had seen it all before, somewhere, from a different angle. He scratched his cheek under the beard. Maybe one of Gray's pictures at school.

Well, it wasn't important. His cottage was supposed to be near the boathouse. He hadn't ever stayed in a cottage of his own and rather liked the idea. It offered the right mixture of independence and protection.

The sun warmed his back. He sauntered across the wide lawn, whistling softly. His stomach growled. The hairs of the synthetic beard tickled his nose.

▼ ▼ ▼

The road swept through tall trees dense enough to provide shade from the noon sun. Liz ran at an easy pace along the left shoulder. She'd fled the house immediately upon returning with Gray. Still no chance to get to the computer, and she had little better idea what she was looking for. Besides, her cover was in danger of being blown. It was Gray's fault. The engagement scheme was flimsier than Bud's toupee, as had been made clear by her morning skirmish with the father of the goon.

Up ahead, the road forked. She consulted her watch, calculating distance as a function of pace. Far enough for a Saturday, anyway, a Saturday on which she was supposed to be working. She stopped, took her pulse and considered. The left fork led back to town. The right, unclear. Was it worth making a loop for the satisfaction of avoiding an out-and-back? In the end, she went with caution and retraced her route to Briarwood.

She felt the tear-shaped pendant slap against her collarbone and her mind went back to the first mugging. She'd returned to the jewelry store, desperate to unload the pearls before someone accused her of stealing. Back in the store, however, Allie was gone, and Liz had pointed at a pendant at random. While the clerk was off wrapping it, she'd dropped the pearls behind the counter. She couldn't imagine what could have prompted such an act. In five years, she hadn't seen Allie to ask why. But she wore the tear-shaped pendant every day to remind herself what happened when you trusted someone too much.

Beneath a stand of evergreens, a wash of pine needles covered the road. She swished through them, kicking the memory of the betrayal from her mind. Along the ribbon of pavement she kept her brain unplugged, letting the rhythm of her feet conjure memories of songs to which she didn't know the words.

Gray. The fool couldn't take a breath without complicating things. She turned at the driveway, past the wrought-iron gates that barely clung to their hinges. The drive rolled through the woods, and she picked up her pace. Stay smooth, finish strong. Lessons in life.

She gained the top of a small rise. Far ahead, a figure walked toward her, a man. One of the houseguests, no doubt. He disappeared from view, sinking like a setting sun, as she ran into the next dip of the road. When she reached the crest, he'd vanished.

Mike stayed flat on the ground, his face mashed into the dirt. A tree root pressed against his ribs. He could feel his heart thud as he drew the shallowest breaths possible. The footsteps neared and passed. He waited until they faded. Straining his ears, he pushed himself to his hands and knees. No human sound reached him. The beard had pulled away from his face in the course of the dive. He straightened it. All of Gray's cloak and dagger stuff, keep out of sight, wear a disguise. It was enough to set anyone on edge.

He crept toward the driveway, approaching at an indirect angle. He touched each tree he passed. His stomach growled louder. Seven-thirty was a long time off.

He was a few feet from the driveway when he heard a crunching noise behind him, the most fragile snap of twig, the delicate rustle that said he was being followed. He froze. She'd seen him jump into the trees, had circled around after going past. His fingernails dug into the bark of the tree.

Another rustling sound, nearer. He spun, hands raised in a caricature of a martial arts pose. A few yards away, a squirrel stood on its hind legs and blinked. Mike sagged. The animal dashed up the nearest tree.

He ran to the gates of Briarwood. Pine needles were caught in the false beard. He was picking them out when a car rounded the curve at high speed. He backed into the mouth of the driveway. The car, a silver convertible, whizzed past and skidded to a stop. The driver threw it into reverse, backing up in a weaving path that ended at the gates. A cloud of dust surrounded Mike, settling in his beard.

The driver climbed out, waving. "Boy, am I glad I found you."

"Me?"

He was maybe in his mid-forties, shorter than Mike and stout. A neat dresser, with a band-collar button-down shirt, and glasses that enlarged his eyes in a way that made Mike feel as though he were under a microscope. He wore a black leather fanny pack and had a Polaroid camera over one shoulder.

"Yeah, you. Of course you. Who else is there? I haven't seen a soul in ten miles. Say, I don't suppose you can tell me how to get to Abbotsville."

"Abbotsville? Afraid not. I don't live around here."

"Perfect." The man rubbed his hands. "Great. Randy Thomas. That's important. You need to remember that. You got it? Randy Thomas. Here's my card. No, that wouldn't look good. Maybe I should take yours. You got one?"

"Sorry."

"Okay, it doesn't matter." He made a hurry-up motion with one hand. "Go ahead and give me those directions."

"I just told you–"

"No, no. I don't care if they're wrong. Give 'em to me anyway."

"But why?"

"Why? Well, I'm supposed to be meeting Frances, and I'm late. Spent too much time tooling around the countryside. I need a good excuse. You ever meet Frances? Of course not. Trust me. She hates it when I'm late."

The man's story had a sad, familiar ring and Mike felt a sudden kinship. "I see. You're late. And you don't have an excuse."

"Oh, I have an excuse. But it's not very good. Not by her standards." The man passed a hand over his neatly-trimmed hair. "So I need you to give me bad directions. That way I can be lost."

"But you could just pretend you got bad directions."

"Sure, of course I could, but this way I can tell her the truth. I got lost, but it wasn't my fault." He waved the camera. "Here's how we'll do this. We'll take a picture of the two of us, right here, so she knows I'm not making it up. No, that won't work. No remote. You'd better take a picture of me."

Mike backed another step into the driveway. "What will that prove?"

"Prove? She's not a judge, for crying out loud. But it'll show I was talking to someone. Well, no, it won't. You're right. I'll take a picture of you."

"I'd still be suspicious if I were her. Do you often take pictures of people who give you directions?"

"Of course I don't. You just stand there. Hold it. Good." He snatched the square of film from the slot. "Great. Now. How about those directions?"

"Well, all right." Mike pointed. "Head that way. First right you come to, second left. Takes you straight to . . . where was it you wanted to go?"

"Abbotsville. Terrific." He grinned. "That'll work. Thanks." He looked at the developing photo. "Yeah, this'll be good. All I need is your name."

"My name?" Mike hesitated. Better to be safe. Chuck Chamberlain. How about that? Whoa. Death wish. No way was it a good idea to be Char's father. "It's Roger." He liked the sound of that. "Roger Donovan."

"Nice to meet you, Roger." Randy clambered into his car and started the engine. "Love the beard." The silver convertible made a tight U-turn as he dutifully followed the useless directions. Mike nodded. A man of principle. The car zipped down the road and out of sight, leaving him wondering whether he'd just had a peek at his own future. He hoped not.

▼ ▼ ▼

Liz marked the progress of the sun toward the horizon. It was nearly seven-thirty, and there'd been no movement toward the dining room. Perhaps they waited for sunset. Still an hour away. She gripped her tumbler of sparkling water and wondered how long Gray would insist on hovering around her.

They stood in the parlor, observing cocktail rituals and making extremely small talk with the rich married couple with unmarried names but identical initials, Matt and Marsha something and something else, who had carried on a running skirmish from the time they crossed the threshold. It was painful to be in the same room with them.

"Tell us." Marsha's gaze drifted to Liz. "How did you meet Gray?"

Liz tried to remember the thirty seconds' worth of detail he'd provided before they were interrupted. "It was . . . it was on a train."

Westfield, unobtrusive host and putative in-law-to-be, nodded from the corner. "Very romantic."

Marsha snorted. "The most romantic thing Matt ever thought to do on a train was pull the emergency brake. It was my birthday, and it dawned on him that he'd forgotten. He panicked."

Matt tossed back his drink. "You said you liked the feel of flying."

"I said you made me feel like crying."

During the silence, Liz watched bubbles in her seltzer die by the dozen. It was hard to feel sympathy for either of them, together for so many years and bludgeoning their marriage to death.

"Where was this train, Liz?" Westfield asked.

Behind his father, Gray mouthed a name at her. Something with an 'o' and an 'm' in it. She took a stab. "Nome."

"What was that?" said Westfield, as if she'd used profanity.

"Rome," said Gray. "She means Rome. It was between Naples and Rome. We called it Nome. There's no place like Nome." He swallowed a weak laugh.

Matt turned to Liz. "What sort of line are you in, anyway?"

"Counterintelligence." They goggled at her. "I'm kidding. It's advanced math. Chaos theory." At least she could bluff that.

Matt clapped Gray on the back, dislodging the eyeglasses. "I don't mind her being ugly, son, but did you have to pick a dumb one, too?"

"Was that supposed to be funny?" Marsha kicked her husband's ankle.

Liz forced what she hoped looked like a smile and turned aside. The crowd was growing, with two members of the house party arriving late. There was Westfield's college roommate, referred to as 'Senator' in reverential tones. And another no-show, a cousin of some sort.

While Matt and Marsha went at it, Liz moved away and bumped into little Doris, advertised as their offspring but as unlike them as it was possible to be. Her parents never stopped talking; Doris never started. She huddled in a chair in a corner, reading. Liz tried to think back ten years. Was that how fifteen-year-olds looked from the outside?

Westfield leaned against the mantel and spoke to her. "Cousin Jake is, in one respect, responsible for my being in this house. Our grandfather left the real estate to my father and the stocks to my uncle, Jake's father. It was 1929, before either of us was born. Who could have seen what was coming?"

Liz found an unoccupied section of sofa and sat.

"Luck of the draw," continued Westfield. "I have to say, Jake was pretty philosophical about it. He never blamed my father or me, just went out and made his own fortune. And quite a fortune at that." He slid his hand along the mantel. "But his sister Emma never forgave Dad for not evening things out. In time she blamed me as well. When she was twenty she disappeared."

"Disappeared." Marsha put a theatrical hand to her chest.

Westfield nodded. "She left before Jake made it big. For years I received postcards from all over the world, threatening to return and take the house."

"Postcards?" Liz sat up.

"Yes. They stopped without explanation. I haven't heard from Emma for, oh, twenty-five years."

"You see?" Matt nudged Gray. "Sometimes they vanish."

Gray poked at the ice cubes in his drink.

"Still," said Westfield, "Jake and I have kept close. I invite him out for the Fourth each summer. We love to shoot fireworks over the lake."

Reflex politeness made Liz look toward the back lawn, where she caught sight of a bearded figure.

"Hey. I mean, um, darling?" She touched Gray's sleeve. "Who's that man?"

"I didn't see a man."

"It's the person you were talking to in town."

Gray stared as if told he'd been eating live spiders. "Oh, that man. It must be the digging person. You know, the archaeologist. Harmless." He looked at his watch. "Be right back."

"Archaeologist?" said Matt. "Barton. What have you got going here?"

"Oh, nothing of mine." Westfield waved a deprecating hand. "Some pieces of rust they think may be from the Civil War. I've kept well out of it, believe me. Liddell's handling it."

"We knew an archaeologist." Marsha stretched. "Terribly dull fellow. Not quite as dull as Matt."

"The guy studied fossils. Big surprise, he liked talking to you."

Liz placed her tumbler on an end table. The noise sounded like a gavel. "I'm a little tired. Do I have time to rest before dinner?"

"Of course, of course."

She hurried from the room, but she heard Westfield say: "As it happens, I need to meet with someone myself. Pardon me."

In the foyer, Liz paused. It was a golden opportunity to start the search for Gray's missing 'valuable piece of paper.' There was no sign of Westfield, or of anyone else. She tiptoed across the living room to the library.

▼ ▼ ▼

The gardener's shed was dark and smelled of loam and fertilizer. Mike wiggled his fingers, pale caterpillars in the gloom. "Not to be a design critic, but has your father thought about windows for this place?"

"It's a shed, old man. People don't spend time in sheds. Not as a rule. What good would windows be?"

Fair point. Superfluous, really, in a building with two-inch knotholes. Mike pressed his face to the rough wall. Twenty yards off, he could see the edge of the formal garden that, with its straight gravel paths and neat rows of flowers, took up a chunk of the back lawn. It was dotted with statuary and had an odd, keyhole-shaped design in the center.

Farther away, the lilac hedge ran across his line of sight, stretching from the southern woods to the house. Mansion, really. The structure rested at the head of a lawn that swept up to meet its broad terraced steps, like the French chateaux on Uncle Ric's postcards. The terrace had trellises at regular intervals, on which climbing vines wrapped themselves. Above the trellises, the walls of the building glowed with the evening light.

In the darkness of the shed, Gray mumbled. "Mind the fireworks."

"The what?"

"Fireworks. For Dad's show on the Fourth. They're stored in here, but he's not very careful. The other day he found a box from last year that somehow didn't get shot off."

"I don't like it." Mike extended his hand but touched no boxes. "I don't like any of this."

"It's simple, old bean."

"Yeah, it is. Like Rube Goldberg. No plan of yours is simple."

"Now, that's unfair. This plan is perfectly simple, if you'd be quiet and let me tell you."

"All right. Tell me."

"Right. In five minutes, Allison will come along the path through the woods, proceeding straight into that garden."

Mike took his eye from the knothole.

"Allison being the object of your affections?"

"Who else would it be?"

"And you can predict her movements because your twin souls are one."

"No, because I called her and asked her to meet me at quarter to eight."

"Fair enough." Mike couldn't remember the last time he'd asked Char to meet him anywhere. Maybe there was something to Gray's relationship with Allison. "And the dread mother?"

"The D.M. famed in song and story, has a meeting with my father at that precise time. And here's the corker. She won't walk over, she'll drive. They're talking business, so he'll bring her into the library. Right over there, you see the French doors, on the left? That's the library. Where Allison's mother will be."

"I understand the layout." Mike pushed himself from the wall. "My role?"

"As advertised, quite simple. You jump out and attack Allison. I run through the hedge, by the side of the house. See that little gate? I'll come straightaway when I hear her scream. Then I beat you up. Well, not very much, just pretend to. You run into the woods. Her mother watches from the library and, what ho, embraces me as the savior. All objections to suitability evaporate. And a bonus: Dad realizes I'm not entirely hopeless."

"Stop, stop, stop. Let's look at that in slow motion. What do you mean, I 'attack' Allison?"

"Not actually." Gray laughed. "Not as such. Blast, I've dropped my specs. Can't pull this off without . . . ah, here we are. Look, you just sort of try to, I don't know, kiss her or something. On the cheek would be best."

"Yeah, sure. And when she thinks it's for real?"

"No, it's all worked out. I'm leaving now. There's a path that starts behind the shed and goes up through the woods. It crosses the one she'll be taking from Monte Rosa, her house. I'll just shoot up there, warn her about it, you know, not to worry and all that rot. Then I'll flank round to the front of the house and wind up by the hedge. Once I chase you off, you can zip into the woods and take the same trail back here."

"Did you have to wait until the last second to warn her?"

"I didn't want to give her enough time to decide it was a bad idea."

"Smart thinking. Supposing someone recognizes me as the attacker?"

"They won't. Enter the beard. Afterward, you take it off. Or I could have Liddell bring your moose costume, if you'd feel more comfortable."

"That won't be necessary." There was a certain symmetry in leaving Morty Moose packed up in Char's BMW, a neat compartmentalization of his current life.

"You can be gone by tomorrow, or whenever you want."

Mike touched the strands of the beard in his pocket.

"Forgive my asking, and this does show a little more thought than usual, but are you certain it'll work?"

"Can't lose, old top."

"So, why do I feel the chill of defeat?"

"Because you, my friend, are at heart a defeatist."

"That hurts." And it did. "Okay, I'll do it. Not for the sake of the plan. For the sake of, oh, I don't know, love. I might need you to do the same one day."

"That's the spirit. I tell you, Mikey, you shan't regret it. Allison's about the grandest thing that's ever happened to me. She's beautiful, and smart, and she rides horses. Horses! Mikey, she's absolutely–"

"Okay, okay. I get the picture. No music. No singing." He withdrew the beard. "I said I'll do it. Make sure you're there before the mother."

"Ha! That's a safer bet than picking last year's Derby winner. The woman has a bad leg. Uses a cane, the whole bit. You could outrun her on your knees."

Gray opened the door and slipped through the crack of twilight. Mike saw a stenciled sign on a crate: 'Explosives.' The shed went dark again.

Crashing sounds marked Gray's progress through the shrubbery. The noises stopped, and a whisper came through the back wall.

"Three minutes. Synchronize watches."

"Synchronize? To what?"

There was no reply. Mike peeked at the house and felt a tingle of doubt. It was a terrible plan, begging for trouble. Far better to duck out now. But he couldn't do that to a friend. The one good thing was, in five minutes it would be over. Barely twice the length of the Morty song. And not a motorcycle in sight. Piece of cake.

▼ ▼ ▼

The library was a mess. Liz found the computer under a pile of papers, but before she could turn it on she heard footsteps approach. The only way out of the room was through the French doors.

▼ ▼ ▼

Three minutes later, Mike started toward the door. His first step landed on a tilted surface. Metal clanged and balance deserted him. He reached out and clutched rough wood, which came away under his pull. He spun backward, landing on something spongy. Plastic pots bounced on the concrete floor as the room filled with dust. He launched himself toward the door, one hand shielding his mouth, the other held in front of him.

Outside, he twisted and turned to get away from whatever was choking him. A cloud of acrid powder trailed behind. It covered his clothes, clumped in his hair, dotted his beard. Lime. The slam of a car door carried from the other side of the lilac hedge. He looked up. Enter: one mother, on time.

And there was someone else. Standing in the center of the garden, gazing toward the house, was a china doll blonde. Her face in profile was a delicate pink in the waning light. Shoulder-length hair followed the curve of her ears above a sleeveless summer dress. Gray didn't deserve her.

At the hedge gate, no evidence of the would-be rescuer. The French doors of the library angled open, catching the afternoon sun. Hard to tell who was inside, just a matter of faith. Mike blinked away the dazzle, put his head down, and marched toward the garden. She whirled, a hand to her throat.

"Sorry. Sorry about that." He fiddled with the beard. "I'm Mike."

"Mike?" Her eyes narrowed.

"Er, yes." He brushed at the powder without effect. "Lime in the shed."

"You're not."

"What?"

"In the shed."

"Huh?" He sensed one of them was out of phase. "No, lime in the . . . I mean . . . never mind."

She averted her gaze.

He went for a running start. "I'm Mike."

"You said. I'm Allison." She gave him an odd glance and resumed staring at the house. Waiting for her mother to show, of course.

"I know who you are." She was not showing great enthusiasm for the performance. Maybe it was the powder. He scratched at his chin and dislodged the beard. "Any sign of Gray?"

She turned back with a pleased look. "You know Gray?"

Before he could pursue the implications of her question, a movement at the house caught his attention. The French door swung wider, and the reflected sunlight caught him full in the face. Through the brilliance, he could see someone emerge from the house. He drew himself upright.

"That's our cue, then. What do you think? Left cheek, or right?"

"Excuse me?"

The left, nearer, won by default and he went at it like a strafe bomber. Her skin smelled sweet. He drew back to survey the damage.

"Excuse me!"

He considered. "No. It's no good. That wouldn't fool anyone. Here. Give me your hand." He grabbed it as she started to pull away. "Maybe if I took your shoulder and just . . ." She was rigid. "Perfect. And a little . . . peck for good measure." More reconnaissance over her shoulder. A commotion by the library door, right on schedule.

Come on, Gray. Let's go.

She squeezed his fingers as he relaxed his grip.

"You know," he said, "I think that's . . . hey, cut it out!"

Still no movement by the hedge, but a new disturbance came from the woods. She turned toward it and screamed. "Hugo!"

Mike drew back. "Listen, we don't have to be quite so . . . hey!" She'd cut off the circulation to his fingers as she fumbled in her purse.

Hugo. Who the hell was Hugo? Her real boyfriend, maybe. Trust Gray not to list the full cast. The crashing from the woods grew louder. Hugo was large. He didn't bother with paths. Hugo . . . Mike tried desperately to free his hand.

"Listen . . ." Through the trees he glimpsed the stunt double for the Hound of the Baskervilles. He wrenched his hand loose, but her other arm came around with something in it. He barely had time to duck before she fired at his face. One eye went stinging blind. He stumbled up the lawn toward the lilac hedge. The dog thrashed through the last of the underbrush.

As he neared the shrubbery where Gray was supposed to be, an imposing woman with a cane blocked the opening. He gulped, veered left, and began to sprint along the back of the house, pressing a hand to his bad eye. A quick glance over his shoulder confirmed a piano-sized mastiff, gathering speed on an intercept course.

His fractured shadow bounced along the terrace steps. Another spot check: Cane Woman behind him, dog moving in at an angle. And worse: dead ahead, coming straight at him, was the person who'd stepped through the French doors, who'd run down the driveway that afternoon, who had none of the knee problems for which Allison's mother was famous, and whom, with a sinking heart, he recognized as Liz.

He gritted his teeth and broke left, clutching the beard. She moved to meet him. He cut back. She responded. With barely room to pass between her and the steps, he lunged forward, struggling to suppress an enormous sneeze. She took him down in a sliding tackle. He hit the grass and rolled hard before springing to his feet. The beard worked itself around to the side of his face.

A desperate look back showed Liz heading toward Allison, who stood in the middle of the garden like a piece of statuary. Cane Woman stared at her. The Steinway with fangs was gaining.

Impossible to make it to the gate on this side ahead of the dog. But a miracle: a gap appeared between the shrubs and the corner of the house. In three strides, he reached it and dove through. In that airborne and somewhat vulnerable attitude he suddenly recalled the relative positions of the house and the concrete fish pond.

His dive was shallow. He felt a stabbing pain in one knee before he came to the surface, shoving lily pads from his face, gasping. He could see with both eyes again. The water sloshed around him and spilled over the sides of the pool. He rose in the waist-deep water, streaks of fertilizer everywhere. Floating away from him like a drowned muskrat was the false beard.

Gray stood at the edge of the pool, drenched from the knees down. Hugo alternated growls with barking. Faint shouts drifted through the lilac hedge.

"Shut up, Hugo," said Gray. In response came a whimper. Mike turned. The dog sat wagging its tail. It had somehow shrunk to a tenth of its former size. Mr. Foolproof Plan knelt to where a goldfish wriggled on the flagstones. He nudged it into the pool and cleared his throat.

"On second thought, old man, perhaps this isn't the best–"

"Be quiet." Mike raked a sheet of water at him. Closing his eyes, he tested fingers and toes. The pungent smell of lime wafted around them. "Just . . . help me out of here."

When Gray extended an arm, Mike pulled him in. Hugo made a confused sound. "You know what the problem is with your plans? Bubbles. They're soap bubbles. When you touch one, this is what happens."

Gray leaned on the side of the pond.

"I appreciate that this might be a poor time to mention it." He smeared at his glasses. "But it would be best, I think, if you were to seek cover. I believe the police have been summoned."

–7–

Liz had taken down the powdered assailant before she realized it was Mike. He landed across her legs, and she felt a sharp pain in one knee. No time for him now. She scrambled to her feet and ran on toward the young woman in the garden. A small dog yipped past, headed the other direction. When the woman raised her arm, Liz saw the pepper spray. She skidded to a stop at the edge of the garden.

"Are you okay?"

"I'm fine." The voice was soft. "Has that lunatic gone?"

"I think so, he's . . . Allie?" She was struck, as she had been years before, by the flawlessness of the petite figure.

Allie took a step away. Her face hardened. "What are you doing here?"

Liz didn't know what to do with her hands. They felt like loaves of bread.

"I tried to call, a couple of nights ago."

"Oh." It was hard to read anything into the one word. "Why are you here at Briarwood now? What do you want from me?"

There it was, Allie in the power position. As if Liz should feel ashamed. For the first time in years, she couldn't come up with a cover story. "Why are you here?"

"I'm engaged to Gray Westfield."

"Funny, so am I."

Allie drew a quick breath. "I don't believe you."

No question, Gray had mentioned a real fiancée. But Allie? "I can explain." Liz wasn't sure that she could, or even that she wanted to. Her jaw tightened. She hadn't planned it, but maybe this was the retribution. "Anyway, it's not what you think."

"You're engaged to Gray, but it's not what I think."

"No. Yes. No." Come to think of it, how fitting to let Allie marry Gray. What a pair. "It's just a story."

"I don't believe that, either."

"Come up to the house and I'll explain."

Allie looked at Briarwood. "I can't do that."

"You can't. Why not?"

"My mother's here. Oh. She was, a minute ago. By the gate."

"Okay, your mother's here. Big deal."

"You don't understand. She's having a silly fight with Mr. Westfield. And she doesn't approve of Gray. I'm not supposed to be here on the grounds."

"She doesn't approve? Sounds pretty Romeo and Juliet."

"I'm serious."

"Okay. Is there someplace else we can talk?"

"There's a cottage near the boathouse. I don't think anyone's using it." On Allie's arm was the silver bracelet, Liz's graduation present to her. Strange. She couldn't have anticipated this meeting. There must be a reason for her to be wearing it.

"Fine." Liz made a fist around her teardrop pendant.

The cop who'd come to take her statement outside the jewelry store had said there'd been a series of these attacks, unusual in that the mugger always dropped the purse within a block and never seemed to take anything. And Liz had nodded, her face as expressionless as she could keep it. A hell of a scheme: embezzlement disguised as robbery. One thief inside, one outside. A clerk dropped the merchandise into the unsuspecting customer's purse and signalled her accomplice outside. He grabbed the purse, lifted the jewelry, and ditched everything else. When it was over, the grateful victim found nothing missing. The problem was, the one on the inside was Allison Harper. It had to be. Liz hadn't dealt with any other clerk that day.

Why she hadn't confronted Allie was another story. At first it was pure shock, but as time went on she convinced herself she didn't want to hear the excuses. Sometimes you had to cut your losses and move on.

Allie took a path that followed the curve of the shore, holding her head high, as if the only thing she had to worry about was whether someone was after her ridiculous boyfriend. The lake reflected the orange sky. From the front of the house came shouts and splashes. Feeling more prisoner than prosecutor, Liz kept her distance and followed.

▼ ▼ ▼

Mike lurked behind a tree on the northern property boundary. The lawn had to be clear before he moved. At last the voices by the front door faded. Cautiously, then with greater haste, he headed for the safety of his cottage.

▼ ▼ ▼

Allie tripped the light switch and Liz swept an appraising glance over the interior. Tastefully decorated. Luggage on the bed, suit in the closet, shaving kit on the counter by the sink. One occupant, male. No clear threat.

"You said they weren't using this."

"They weren't."

She inspected the room again. Interwoven with normal caution was the overwhelming need to match Allie's cool.

"Okay. I suppose we can stay a little, if we don't touch anything." She forced a smile. "I won't tell the three bears if you won't."

"To pick up where we left off, tell me what you're really doing out here."

"It's more 'down here.' I've been living in Washington the last few years. I know. I could have called." She couldn't get her mouth to shut up.

"We always had the best of intentions." Allie lay her perfect hand on the windowsill. During the awkward silence, Liz regrouped.

"The answer to your question is I'm working here."

"Working?"

It was so monstrously unfair that Allie should be the one to act hurt. Liz picked up the nearest object, a razor. Realizing what she'd done, she wiped away her fingerprints.

"I can't tell you more. Not without permission from my client. I'm sorry."

"So." Allie sat on the bed. "You're a lawyer?"

"Well, no, but it's the same concept."

"And Gray? The engagement?"

"It's nothing." She had to fight the urge to touch something, anything. "Look, I promise to let you know by tomorrow morning at the latest. And what about you? Why were you in the garden?"

"Gray's idea. Some plan for impressing my mother. I was supposed to meet him and he was going to explain."

"And you're really engaged?"

"We haven't told anyone, so I'm not sure it's official. But, yes."

"And how long have you known him?"

"You might say, 'congratulations.' It's considered polite."

Liz felt herself blush. "Congratulations." She avoided any particular comment about Gray. "When did he ask you to marry him?"

"Last week."

"After his father and your mother started their fight?"

"What a ridiculous thing to argue over. Yes, quite a while after."

Liz picked up a green felt bag, the kind used to protect shoes. "I thought this was wrong. I thought so." It was impossible to follow the convolutions of Gray's mind. "How much do you really know about him?"

"What do you mean, know about him? He's the boy next door."

"That may be, but I saw him talking this morning with the man who wears these as socks. The same man who attacked you. And that makes four times in two days I've run into the guy. Tell me it's a coincidence."

Wringing an apology from Allie wasn't first on her list of priorities, but it would be a nice thing to have. And now she could see how to do it without confronting her directly. Expose Gray as a fraud, and Allie would have to admit that Liz was right. To hell with fingerprints. She unlatched the suitcase.

"A quick background check never hurt any bride-to-be. What do you say we find out what those two are up to?"

Allie smoothed the corner of the comforter. "You never were good with people, were you?"

The earth's gravity seemed to have tripled. What kind of thing was that to say? First blood to Allie, but it was early in the contest.

▼ ▼ ▼

Mike crept down the lawn to the boxwood maze and made his way along its side. As he neared the cottage he straightened into a normal stride, head up, shoulders back. An honorable retreat. But twenty yards from home he saw two silhouettes against the window. He braked and backtracked before turning and running all the way up the slope to the hedge he'd just broken through. He passed through the gate and began to hurry toward the drive and the BMW. His only dry clothes were in the cottage, but at this point even the moose suit would do. The ground fell away and he sprawled face down in a pile of fresh earth. Archaeology Central. He extricated himself and heard a conversation come into focus as one of the people drew near.

". . . take a quick look." The beam from a flashlight swept past.

In the dusk, he searched for a hiding place. Anywhere, anywhere. A section of loose sod hung over the embankment. He maneuvered himself under. Footsteps thudded along the ground. Behind him, a smooth, hard surface pressed against his shoulders. He ran his fingers along it. Wood. A series of wide, unfinished planks leaned against the hill, hidden from view by the overhanging sod.

Through a crack in the dirt and grass, he watched the beam of light play over the dig. He pressed against the boards. They moved. When he explored with his fingers, one came away silently. He sensed a musty space behind them. The light came closer. He tumbled through, down a short flight of steps into stuffy darkness. With no time to reposition the planks, he huddled in the cave and willed the person away. The feet stopped.

"Mikey!" A whisper. "I say, old bean, are you down there?"

"Gray?"

Light shot through the opening. "What's all this, then?"

Mike rose, able to stand without hitting his head.

"I'm not sure. An underground storeroom. Come in with that light before the whole county gets here."

"Good Lord." Gray stuck his head past the sod. He fingered the planks and flicked the light around. "Who put this in?"

"Didn't you know about it?"

"I stopped by about three days ago, to see what they'd dug up. Nothing but dirt." Gray descended the steps. The light flashed on the walls. He, at least, had found time to change into dry clothes. He touched a wall. "It's brick. Some sort of little walled cavern."

"But what for?"

"I told you, I don't know a thing about it. Want the torch?"

Mike shook his head. "How did you know where to find me?"

Gray snapped off the flashlight. In the darkness, a green luminescence surrounded Mike's shoes. The light came on again.

"You made quite the apparition. I swept away the traces in the woods, but I had to warn you before they loosed more dogs. They think you ran down the drive."

"Why should they think that?"

"It's what I told them, once you managed to keep still."

"Then why look for me on the lawn?"

"I didn't tell them I was looking for you. You're not the only one with problems. Allison's missing. I rang her house, but no answer. The Dread Mother is encamped here, and not at all pleased."

"In other words, the plan worked perfectly."

"Yes, well, point taken. Rather opposite the effect I was after. Anyway, I'm concerned about what's become of Allison."

"Well, I can help there. She's in my cottage, not at my invitation. Now, do me a favor, go rescue your damn fiancée. And while you're at it, you might grab me some dry clothes."

"All right, no need to tear a fellow's head off. You know, thanks to you I too got wet. And no one believed I'd chased you into the fish pool."

"Which seems fair, since you didn't." Mike leaned against the wall and instantly recoiled from the cold brick. "Could you get a move on? Let's pretend this never happened. We'll start the whole thing over. And this time, we'll try it my way."

"Your way? How does that work?"

"It works great. Here's how it goes: when you ask me for help, I say no." He sat on the floor of the cavern. "I'm surprised I never thought of it before."

▼ ▼ ▼

Liz stood by the bed in the cottage, going through the contents of the suitcase. She lifted a pair of clean athletic socks. "Pretty straightforward. He packs like any guy who's off to the country for the weekend. No tools, no books. Not many clothes." A rectangle of paper fluttered to the floor. "Here's something." She held up one of her own business cards. "Where'd he get this?"

Allie went motionless. "I hear someone outside."

"Wonderful timing." There was no place to hide in the cottage. Liz slid the card into her pocket. "We'll have to tough it out."

The door opened. Gray. "Perfect. You're all right, then. Oh." He took a step back. "Liz."

"Yes, it's delightful to see you, darling." She stole a glance at Allie. "You didn't mention I was the second woman you're engaged to."

"Ah. You've met, then." He took off his glasses and put them back on.

"You might say that."

"All right." He closed the door. "No need for a snit. It's not as if we were really engaged, you and I."

Liz made an I-told-you-so gesture to Allie, who sat on the bed.

"Gray, what is this? How could you propose to both of us?"

He looked at Liz, but she shook her head. "Your secret's safe. For now."

"Oh, blast." He wiped his forehead. "See here, it's frightfully simple. Couldn't you trust me?"

"What a humorous idea," Liz said.

"Trust you?" Allie unclenched her fist. "Gray, that's what you said before. How can I trust you? There was a man with a beard. By the roses, while I waited for you. And Liz says you were with him this morning. He attacked me."

"Oh?"

"Mike," Liz prompted.

"Oh. Mike. I say, how on earth do you . . ."

"Listen, buster," Liz tapped him on the chest, "I don't know what you've got going here, but I'm thirty seconds from paying a visit to Allie's mother."

"No!" He moved to block the door. "I mean, that won't be necessary."

"You've got twenty-five seconds to tell us what's going on."

He stepped toward her. "There's really no need to–"

"Back off."

"Right-o." He began to pace.

"Please." Allie held a hand toward him. "Drop it."

"Drop it?"

"Be yourself . . . you know."

"Oh." He wilted. "That. Okay. All right." He took her hand. When he spoke again, the distorted British accent was gone, replaced by a southern drawl. "The fellow in the garden. He's a . . . a private investigator."

"A what?" Liz noticed Allie hadn't pulled her hand from his. "That guy couldn't find Lincoln on a penny."

"Ah." Gray raised an index finger. "That's what he wants you to think."

"Yeah? It worked. What's he doing here?"

"Investigating." He shot what was no doubt meant to be a significant look.

She ignored it. "Investigating what?"

Allie pulled her hand away, the first signal that it might not be two against one.

Gray removed his glasses again. "We've had . . . calls. Threats. All these people coming down for the weekend, you can't be too careful."

"Threats?" Liz laughed. "So, this guy's providing security. Which one are you trying to protect, Matt or Marsha?"

"That's rather harsh. There are others."

Allie twisted her bracelet. "Why did he try to kiss me?"

"Kiss you? He didn't, not really. I mean, why would he want to do that?"

"Very smooth, Galahad." Liz drew a tally mark in the air.

Allie knotted the bedcovers. "What are you saying?"

"Nothing, sweetheart. No. I'm sure you're right. Very improper. I'll have a word with him, right after I walk you home."

"Don't bother yourself." Liz snatched his flashlight. "I'll go. And we'll borrow this, if you don't mind."

Allie stood, smoothing her skirt. "I think that's the best idea."

"But Liz, see here." His fingers twitched like the legs of an overturned crab. "People will worry. Can I say you'll be back for dinner?"

"You can say I'm powdering my nose."

Outside the cottage, Allie turned to her. "You two are on very familiar terms. How long have you been here?"

"Yesterday."

"Staying in the house?"

Liz pointed. "That's my window. Above the library and over two."

"But that's across the hall from Gray."

"Does it matter?" So, Allie was jealous. They walked across the lawn in silence, Liz sweeping the light before them. Crickets entertained one another.

"I can't believe you'd come here to stop me from being with Gray."

"Excuse me? Be my guest. Not that I understand what you see in him."

"He's sweet."

"He's bizarre. What's with the accent?"

"It's just silly. He doesn't like the way his real voice sounds. He says people make fun of him when he goes places. This is an experiment. He thinks if he forces himself to talk that way long enough, it might purge the Southern."

"And that doesn't strike you as a little odd?"

"I think it's endearing." Allie wore a dangerously goofy expression.

"Blind." Liz shook her head. "I thought they said love is blind."

▼ ▼ ▼

Footsteps approached the dark cavern. Whoever it was didn't carry a flashlight. Mike retreated to the wall and hunched down, shivering.

"I've brought you clothes," Gray said in the darkness. "You still in here? Better change."

"Shine the light over."

"I can't. That's part of the . . . development. Take these." He came in and handed over a wad of clothes. "I think they'll fit."

"Aren't they mine?"

"They're mine. Should be close enough. Quit complaining. I told you, there's been a development."

"Development?" Mike felt through the bundle before stripping.

"Complication."

"It couldn't get more complicated." At least the pants fit.

"You're a detective. That's all you need to know. I'll explain later. Hurry."

"This should be entertaining."

"I'm doing the best I can, pal."

"Hey." Mike struggled into the shirt. "Your accent."

"Come on, then. I'll introduce you to Dad."

"As a detective." He felt for the shoes.

"For him you'll be my old college friend. Can you keep that straight?" Gray shoved his way through the opening.

"Slow down." Mike kicked his wet clothes into a corner and hurried up the steps. If only the guy would pick one story and stick with it. "What are you mad at me for? I did what you asked. Where the hell were you, Plan Man?"

Gray stopped in the entrance and his shoulders sagged.

"Allison's mother screwed up everything. I'm sorry. I made it through the woods fine, but then I saw her heading out back of the house, instead of through the front door the way she should have. Why do you think she did that? Anyway, in the rush, I never met up with Allison." He sounded miserable. "I thought it would work. I really did. I apologize." That was the thing about Gray. Once it was over, he didn't keep bullshitting you.

"Okay. It almost worked." Mike clapped Gray on the shoulder. "Come on, let's get this over with." When he went to button the shirt, he discovered it had a band-box collar, the kind the tourist had worn. A bad sign.

Gray took an indirect route toward the driveway. At the edge of the woods, he held up a hand. A police cruiser moved away down the driveway, directing high-powered beams into the trees on either side.

"Geez." Mike dove into the bushes. "The police really came?"

Gray joined him in the foliage. "Dr. Hatteras dialed 911 when the uproar started. He said something about loving a good show."

"What? I nearly walked up to the house earlier."

"Okay, don't panic. Now's your chance. Things will be better once you're inside. And no one got a good look at you. They'd never expect the attacker to stick around." The taillights of the police car disappeared over the rise. "They won't arrest you. I'll be your alibi. Just try not to look guilty."

Mike followed to the huge front door, practicing nonchalance.

▼ ▼ ▼

He hadn't been prepared for the inside of the house. The foyer alone could have held his apartment. Beneath an enormous chandelier, a staircase swept up to a landing and split like a wave on a rock. In a large room to his left, a well-dressed couple, part of the recent posse, stood guard over some hard-core drinks. They stopped talking as he and Gray entered. To his right, a living room the size of a soccer field ended at a fireplace that looked as though it used telephone poles for kindling.

While he gawked, an elderly man in formal wear coalesced beside him.

"Master Westfield."

"Liddell, this is Mr. Archer. He'll be staying for dinner. And the night."

"Sir." The butler inclined his head. "Shall I attend to his luggage?"

Gray looked startled. "No, that's all right. We'll deal with it later."

"Very good, sir. Perhaps the gentleman would care for a drink."

Mike felt the sense of having landed in a familiar dream, a performance in which he didn't know his lines, but everything went smoothly and would continue to do so without any effort by him. He looked at Gray, who pushed his glasses along the bridge of his nose.

"Bourbon, if you would, Liddell. And water, I think. Two." His accent had crept back toward something British.

"Certainly, sir." The butler faded away.

Gray nudged Mike. "Come into the parlor. Let me make the introductions. Ignore whatever they say."

They advanced on the well-dressed couple. Through another doorway, Mike glimpsed a cavernous ballroom. Gray made an odd little salute.

"Hi, folks. Old friend of mine, Mike Archer. Completely sane. Anyway." He faltered. "Matthew Hatteras. Marsha Harris. They're married. And doctors. And rich. Mike Archer. He's not."

"Hi." Mike wondered why anyone needed to vouch for his sanity. Neither guest moved. No one extended a hand. He hoped he wasn't expected to bow, or curtsy, or something.

At his side, Gray was suddenly pop-eyed.

"Um, yes. There you are. Say, why don't we find Dad?" He jostled Mike's elbow and hustled him from the room. "For your own good," he whispered.

"What is it?" Mike struggled to keep pace. "What? Do you think they recognized me?"

"No, no. That's not it." Gray pointed to Mike's waist, where a shirttail poked through the zipper of his pants.

▼ ▼ ▼

The butler appeared in the foyer, balancing a tray and two tumblers. Mike snatched one and accelerated toward the giant fireplace. In the middle of the room, he came to rest on an expensive-looking rug and took a vigorous swallow while he waited for Gray's direction.

"Is my father around, Liddell?"

As the bourbon hit Mike's throat, the room swung away and snapped back into place. The butler angled his head toward the rear of the room.

"In the library, sir. With a visitor."

"Come on." Gray swept past. "We usually dress for dinner on weekends, but you'll be all right. I'll loan you a shirt with a collar."

"You couldn't have thought of that before?"

"Shh." Gray knocked on a panel at the far end of the room.

"Come in." The voice was strained.

The door slid open to reveal a cluttered room that was reminiscent, in untidiness, of Mike's own apartment. Mr. Westfield, seated behind a mahogany desk, had aged much more than five years since Mike had last seen him. Across from him, filling an armchair as if it were a throne, was a solid woman dressed in black. She managed to appear even larger seated. Her cane lay on the floor. Mike stayed in the doorway, trying to look like a man who never wore beards.

"Gray," said Mr. Westfield. "Is Allison well?"

"Fine, Dad. Honest. Liz is walking her home."

"Liz?" Cane Woman gave Gray the death look.

"Yes. That is, yes. She's . . . she's . . ."

"My sister." Mike forced a weak grin. He didn't know why he'd felt the need to jump in. He wasn't sure whether he was protecting Liz or Gray.

"And you are?" The woman redirected her lasers.

He smoothed his damp hair. "Mike." It came out softer than he'd meant, a little slurred. She probably hadn't heard. "Mike."

She inspected him. "I don't suppose you saw a man about your height prowling outside? With a beard?"

"Beard? Hell, no." He concentrated on keeping his hand away from his jaw. "Definitely not. No way." Despite all his intentions, he rubbed his chin. He tossed back the rest of the drink.

She stared a moment longer. "Well. It appears Allison is not in danger at the moment. I shall be going. There is nothing for us to discuss, Barton."

"Helen, please."

"I told you before. You have the solution to your problems right here." She rapped her knuckles on the desk and stood.

"Is that a clue?" He rose. "You mean here in this room? The computer?"

Mike leapt aside as her cane swept a path to the door. She limped across the living room and into the foyer. Mr. Westfield slumped into his chair.

"Dad, you remember Mike Archer. From college."

"Mike? Of course." Mr. Westfield's face transformed itself into that of a southern gentleman. "How delightful to see you again." It wasn't clear whether he remembered or not, but he was nice about it.

"Hello." Mike ventured into the room.

"But your name isn't Halloran."

"Did I say sister? I meant half-sister." It still seemed a little incestuous.

"It's okay." Gray lowered his voice. "He's not her brother, Dad."

"Then why did he claim to be?"

"Yes," Gray said. "Why?"

Mike shrugged. "Trying to be helpful."

Mr. Westfield chewed that over.

"He was in the area, Dad. You don't mind if he stays tonight, do you?"

"Of course not. Any friend of yours is always welcome." The master of Briarwood turned a forlorn expression on Mike. "But if you wanted to be helpful . . . I don't suppose you'd know anything about computers?"

Gray had asked the same question in the Speckled Turnip. And yesterday someone else had been interested. The Colonel. Mike felt for the door behind him. It was too bad he didn't know anything about computers. Heck of a demand for qualified people.

▼ ▼ ▼

The cocktail hour and its social baggage had migrated to the living room. On the couch beside Mike sat Marsha, wearing a skirt with a hem she should have made peace with years before. He turned to face her, painfully aware he was in no position to criticize clothing. Gray's dress shirt gave up an inch to him at each wrist, and another half at the collar. Fastening it had been a challenge, and a mistake. Mike plucked at the top button, but it wouldn't come loose. He was going to pass out. It was only a question of when.

Marsha directed a surreptitious glance toward his waist. He rechecked the zipper. Still okay. He took a sip of bourbon, which at any rate no longer went down his throat wearing cleats. Still, he regretted not having put solid food into his stomach. The alcohol took a shortcut to his brain.

Mr. Westfield sat on the other couch, alone, morose. Matt Hatteras stood by the fireplace, having trapped Liddell in an animated discussion that seemed to have something to do with tea. Gray was gone, but the sound of books being reshelved carried clearly from the library. He hadn't bothered to explain what he was doing, and Mike couldn't guess. The edges of the room blurred.

Marsha stared in a way that suggested she'd asked a question. Mike smiled and mumbled, not even trying to form words.

"I beg your pardon?" She regarded him over the edge of her glass.

"That would be like you. So kind. So kind." He beamed at her, feeling warm inside. Big-time tunnel vision. With a puzzled look, she turned away.

His stomach gurgled. Dinner was tragically late. He tapped Marsha's shoulder and she stiffened. "Tell me something. Tell me something, Marsh. What is it you do, anyway?"

"My husband and I are psychiatrists."

"You are." He tried to focus on her face. "Oh, dear. I'm so terribly . . ." He touched her arm, but his fingertips felt nothing. She stood.

He considered stretching his legs on the couch, but something in the frown on Mr. Westfield's face made him stop. With great deliberation, he placed his tumbler on a side table. As Marsha reached her husband at the fireplace, Liddell broke free and headed for the kitchen. Somewhere behind Mike, a door slammed and brisk footsteps sounded in the marble foyer.

Mr. Westfield brightened. "Liz. Oh, Liz, come in." He stood. "How thoughtful of you to escort Miss Harper home. Gray!" He called over his shoulder. "Gray, Liz is back."

A crash of falling books. Mike was instantly sober. He sank into the spongy arms of the couch and hid behind his drink.

"Liz, this is Mike."

"We've met." She crossed the room without making eye contact, heading for a straight-backed chair. "Recently. He was taking a dog for a run." She settled herself and shot him a vicious glance.

"You must know Mike is an old friend of Gray's from college."

"Friend?" She snorted. "It's a friend now, is it?"

Mike was unable to scrape up a comeback, or indeed to coax any response from his mouth. Drinking bourbon was a bad idea. Time to do something sensible. Operate heavy machinery maybe.

"And Liz is Gray's fiancée," said Mr. Westfield.

"She's what?" Mike choked on his drink. This had to be rock bottom. "Sorry, I . . . did you say she was Gray's . . ."

"That's right. We're so pleased."

Now Liz looked uncomfortable. Mike tried to remember the discussion in the shed. Allison. Not Liz.

The couple by the fireplace migrated toward Liz on four well-heeled legs. She disappeared from sight, swallowed in chatter. Mike waited, half-expecting to see the pack move on, leaving nothing but bones. The angle of the ceiling had changed. Either the couch had risen, or he was slipping sideways. He straightened himself. Air. Now.

Liz freed herself from the parasites. "I'm going up to my room for a moment." No one made a move to stop her as she left.

"Excuse me," said Mr. Westfield. "I'll see what's keeping dinner."

From outside the window came the crunch of tires rolling to a stop on gravel. Mike peeked out the window into the darkness. Unmarked car. Police or Colonel. He placed his glass on the floor and tiptoed from the room.

▼ ▼ ▼

In the foyer, he felt he was being watched. A crosshairs-on-the-forehead sensation caused him to turn toward the central stairs. A third of the way up sat a girl in a pale cotton dress. She pressed herself to one side, as if trying to blend in with the carpeting or the woodwork. Unfortunately for her, they were burgundy and walnut, respectively.

"Found it!" Gray's voice carried from the library. "Here it is! I found it!"

Mike turned to see him spring from the library, both arms in the air. He vaulted a couch and ran the length of the living room. Matt and Marsha stared. In the foyer, he slid to a stop, wild-eyed, clutching a slip of paper.

"Have you seen my father?"

Mike pointed toward the kitchen.

"Terrific." He crashed through the swinging door. A little kid, eager to show his father what he'd found. Mike brought his attention back to the would-be chameleon on the stairs. She stared at him as if he'd been the one running through the house screaming. As he moved toward her, she stood.

"It's all right." He raised his hands. "I was only going to say hello."

She looked as if she might cry.

"I'm Mike. What's your name?"

She was older than he'd thought. Fifteen or sixteen, maybe. She had brown hair that hung straight to her shoulders, and she was barefoot. When he stepped on the first stair, she fled. At the landing, she chose the steps to the right and disappeared around the corner.

"Nice to meet you, too."

A heavy knocker sounded behind him. Statistically speaking, it seemed unlikely that the person outside was the Colonel. Or that she'd bother knocking. Liddell glided across the foyer and heaved open the door.

"Good evening, sir."

Not the Colonel, then. Liddell blocked any view of the caller, but Mike could hear the voice well enough.

"I'm the archaeologist who's taking over for Ms. Nishida at the dig here. Sorry I'm late."

"And what name shall I say, sir?"

"Donovan. Roger Donovan. I'll get my bag."

Mike's balance deserted him. He reached back for the wall and ripped a shirt sleeve near the armpit. 'Keep away from her,' the Special Agent had said in the bus shelter. Oh, sure. No problem there.

▼ ▼ ▼

The large table was set for six. Liz allowed Westfield to escort her toward one end since it seemed important to him. He indicated a chair.

"Would you be good enough to grace my right hand?"

"Of course." A casual dinner was more her style, but she wasn't going to make a fuss about dressing up. Westfield was nice enough. If he wanted to go formal, that was okay. No reason to visit the sins of the child upon the father.

Gray was, for some reason, making himself scarce. His hideous accent had crept back now that Allison was gone, but he'd contrived to be invisible for the last ten minutes. The last time she'd seen him, he'd looked as if someone had shrunk him by twenty-five percent. It was all very strange. Matt and Marsha had secured the two spots on the other side of the table and now wedged their miserable offspring between them.

"Fine. No, hold on. Where's Gray? Oh, and his friend. That makes seven." No one volunteered. Westfield turned his head at the moment the butler swept in. "Another place, Liddell, if you would."

"Very good, sir. Where shall I set it?"

Liz gave in to the petty fear that Mike would be seated beside her, but their host gestured to his left.

"Over here, I think. And you might hunt up Gray and his friend."

Marsha, who was beside the designated spot, gave an impatient toss of her head. "Honestly, Barton, we've hardly room enough as it is."

"That's right." Her husband waved from his corner, a good four feet away. "No room at all. Put him on that side."

Doris slid lower in her seat, looking horrified.

"Nonsense," said Westfield. "Plenty of space. Doris can sit next to Liz. Ah, but that would leave a married couple together. Let's put Matt next to Liz."

With a sullen expression, Matt moved to his new place. Marsha and Doris edged their chairs toward the foot of the table to make room for Mike. Liddell came back with the place setting and coughed quietly.

"Sir, there is the other guest."

Liz studied her napkin. Cousin Jake, or another of Gray's stooges.

Westfield rose. "How foolish. I've left him in the library." He hurried off. Liz caught the exchange of looks across the table. Served them right, the snots.

Matt turned on her. "You needn't grin. They're only going to put him on our side."

Sure enough, Liddell advanced with another chair, placing it between them. Liz set her jaw, trying to remember the last time she'd felt so out of sync with life. Gray led Mike, wisely beardless, into the room and pointed.

"You're on that side, next to Dad." He took a seat at the foot of the table. Mike was still wearing a shirt several sizes too small. He sat opposite her. Noting the ripped sleeves, Liz grimaced.

"Hi." He'd mistaken her expression for a smile.

She studied the tablecloth while Liddell set the place to her right. Whomever the mystery guest turned out to be, dinner would be excruciating.

Matt and Marsha conversed in stage whispers across the table.

"Hard to blame him. You'd be mad, too."

"And it's her fault."

"So I gather."

Liz flushed and was on the verge of denying blame for anything when Westfield reentered, stepping aside to introduce the large person behind him.

"Ladies and gentlemen, one of our archaeologists. Roger Donovan. Roger, come meet everyone."

Liz felt the blood drain from her face. Roger Donovan? Of all people, Roger Donovan? She twisted her napkin into a garotte. Roger met her gaze and winked. Across from her, Mike faced the table with eyes downcast, his face ashen. Not that he had anything to worry about.

"Roger, my friends." Westfield ripped through the introductions, ending with Liz. Roger bowed. Westfield indicated the empty chair. "Liz, of course, is engaged to Gray." She winced. As if there were an 'of course' about it.

Roger passed behind Mike and patted his shoulder. Mike went rigid.

"A pleasure." The voice held no trace of irony. "Congratulations to the happy couple. Honored to meet y'all." Good Lord, another overdone accent. "And thank you, sir, for inviting me to your table."

"Oh, delighted." Westfield smiled, taking in his guests. "We expected a couple more by this time anyway."

Roger grinned at Liz as he unfolded his napkin.

"Why are you here?" she whispered. "Did my mother send you?"

"You know, people," Westfield said, "Roger tells me they may be onto something significant."

"Really?" It was the first hint of interest Marsha had shown for hours. "And what are you . . . onto?" She made it sound obscene.

Roger lifted his water glass. "This property seems to have been the site of an encampment during the War of Secession. We know General Lee traveled past on his way to Appomattox."

"What have you found?" Matt seemed fascinated, more so than necessary.

"This and that. Usual camp things. Cookware. Bits of rifles. A couple of shovels." Liz felt his leg brush hers. She moved away with an irritated gesture Liddell interpreted as a signal for no wine.

"One other thing. There's a mausoleum by the dig. We found some remains inside, still in uniform. Or what's left of them. They'd been shot. We don't know whether they were casualties Lee hadn't time to bury, or deserters."

"Exciting!" Marsha draped her chest on the table. "Could you show us?"

"Sorry, we must preserve the integrity of the dig. It's too dangerous. The walls of that mausoleum could come down at any time. I'd advise everyone to stay well away until we have it stabilized." He glanced around the table.

Liz couldn't stand to look at him any more. Even Mike's face would be an improvement. She covered her eyes, knowing it wouldn't work long unless she faked a migraine.

"Who's this 'we'? " said Matt.

"My colleague and myself. She'll be here in the morning. Meanwhile, my advice is, stay clear."

Liz tried to imagine the poor sap Roger had duped into helping him this time. She opened her eyes to see Mike slide from his chair and hit the floor in a dead faint. With everyone else, she clustered around, trying to revive him. In the pandemonium, Liddell came in with dinner. Not until thirty minutes later when places were cleared did she find the postcard someone had slid under her plate. She dropped it into her lap before anyone else could notice. It was a shot of the island, and a scribbled message: *You'd be happier here.* An aerial shot. She felt as though someone had sucked all the air from the room.

▾ ▾ ▾

Mike's outlook on life had improved remarkably with the collar loosened and blood flowing to his head. Slumped on the couch, he stretched his legs. To hell with the coffee table. He wasn't sure how he'd made it through dinner, what with Donovan practically threatening to dismember anyone who came near the dig, and Liz, whom he could easily have watched through the whole meal, giving him the did-your-flying-saucer-run-out-of-gas look. The one good thing was that she didn't act as though she wanted anything to do with Gray. The other members of the party were on the terrace, admiring the night sky. Fresh air. Excellent idea.

Gray came into the living room and whistled. "Good thing we decided to shift your career."

"What if you'd introduced me to everyone as the archaeologist?"

"But I didn't." Gray took a seat. "See? It worked out fine."

"For you, maybe. Now they think I'm a detective."

"What's wrong with that? There was a detective Archer in a Bogart movie. Look what happened to him."

"He died."

"I thought he got the girl. It doesn't matter. Allison's the only one who thinks you're a detective."

"That's all?"

"Well. And Liz."

"Liz?" Mike propped himself up. "She knows that's baloney."

"You're wrong. She believes you to be a private investigator. A pathetic example, but a private eye."

"And the others? Those rich people. Even the little girl was staring." He could hear it again, the sound of one of Gray's waterfalls.

"Doris." Gray waved a hand. "Don't worry about her. Or her parents. They think you're my eccentric friend. I tell you, it'll work out."

"Just out of curiosity, how did you dream up this new story?"

"Well, you did attack Allison."

"Because you told me to."

"Yes, but the point is, I had to explain why you did. To Liz and Allison."

"And why did I?"

"A mistake. You were protecting her."

"From?"

Gray waved his hand again. "I left that vague."

"Quick thinking."

"I'm telling you, it's fine."

"It's not. There's something strange going on. And how did you end up engaged to Liz? I thought it was Allison."

"It was. It is." Gray sat on the edge of the coffee table and polished his glasses with a shirttail. "Trust me. It's part of the plan."

"What plan?"

"The plan to lull her mother into thinking I'm no danger."

Mike squeezed a sofa cushion. "So where does Liz fit in?" If only he hadn't fainted in front of her.

"Same as you, helping out. She's fixing the computer."

"You have to be engaged for her to fix the computer?"

"Something like that. She doesn't like me, if that's what concerns you."

Mike felt himself blush. "How do you even know her?"

"Friend of a friend." Gray paced. "There's nothing to worry about."

"And what about this Donovan guy?"

"Not a problem. I was expecting him. He's just a little early."

"Expecting him?" Just why Gray should be inviting the Department of Justice for the weekend was, at best, murky. "Might this have something to do with your shouting act before dinner?"

"What? Oh." Gray gazed out the window. "I suppose you might as well know. I imagined I'd found something."

"Something?"

"Ticket. You might have read about it. Lottery."

"The ten million dollar lottery ticket?"

Gray returned only a glum nod.

"That ticket?" The sleeves on the borrowed shirt were far too tight.

"Mmmm. The blighter expires on Monday. We've been looking for weeks."

"You lost it!"

"It was Dad who lost it, if you want to be technical."

"And you found it in the library?"

Gray swatted at a mosquito. "That turned out to be the wrong one. Right date, wrong ticket. Here." He dug a crumpled lottery ticket from his pocket. "Dad's into them by the truckload. We're about out of money, you see. Bad investments."

"How can you lose a ten million dollar piece of paper?"

"I told you, I didn't lose it."

"Yes, yes. How can anyone?"

Gray pressed his palms together. "It wasn't so much lost as taken."

"Okay, do I have to use all twenty questions, or will you simply tell me who took the damn thing?"

"Allison's mother. Probably."

"What? The future mother-in-law?"

"Probably, I said."

"Why would she do that?" Mike could tell his head had cleared, because an actual thought struck him. "You're still looking for it. How do you know she hasn't turned it in?"

"No one has. Didn't you see the paper? Unless it shows by Monday, the money disappears. Back to the state, or whatnot. Anyhow, when I say she took it, she's hidden it somewhere around here. She wouldn't actually steal anything. It's just, she's angry."

"About?"

"Not important. The point is, she gave Dad a clue."

"What clue?"

"He can't remember."

"This seems simple. He should ask again."

"He did. But now she won't tell. You were there before dinner. She said, 'You have the solution right here.' That was in the library. I figured it was a hint. So I looked between the books and, what ho, I found this ticket. Dad says it's not the right one. He bought several that same day. They're all over the house."

"That's a hint? 'You have the solution right here'?"

"No, I was guessing about that. She gave him the real clue a few weeks ago. The problem is, he didn't realize what it was when she said it. It was in the form of a riddle. Something to do with trains . . ."

Mike followed Gray's eyes. Liz had come into the room. He tried to look as though he weren't doing anything suspicious. Matt trailed her, munching a piece of cake, and dropped into an armchair.

"You talking riddles? I'm a pro. Try me."

Liz stood by a window, watching the darkness, or her reflection, or the room behind her. Mike and Gray looked at each other.

"Go on," said Matt. "Try me."

Mike tried to dredge up something. "Okay. A six-letter word where six different letters appear in alphabetical order."

"That's not a riddle." Liz didn't turn.

"Of course it is."

"Almost. Not quite. A riddle is, 'You hope I keep up when you mean you don't want me to. What am I?' "

"Sorry," Gray said. "What was that?"

"Rain." Mike had heard it before. " 'I hope this rain keeps up. That way it won't come down.' Rim shot."

"Yes." She looked surprised. "Yours isn't a riddle. More a puzzle."

"Well," said Gray, "being critical is easy when you don't know the answer."

She laughed. "Think so if you want."

Matt hunched in his chair, counting on his fingers.

"Okay." Mike took his feet from the table. "Do you have a better?"

"A better word puzzle? Sure. Use these in an eight-word sentence: defeat, deduct, defense and detail." She grinned. "You don't have to be a super sleuth to figure that out."

He felt as though she'd given him her phone number. She crossed the room and paused at the door.

"When you're done playing, I'd like to talk." Her steps echoed away.

Wow.

"Does she mean you?" Gray looked at him impressed. "Do you know each other from somewhere?"

"I'm beginning to think we must." He wasn't sure what he'd done right, but he prayed he wouldn't undo it.

"I give up." Matt whacked the arms of his chair. "What's the word?"

"The what? Oh. She said one of them. 'Almost.' "

He wanted to believe she'd done it on purpose.

▼ ▼ ▼

By the time Mr. Westfield left the room it was eleven, and the guests had started their yawning and stretching calisthenics.

Mike cornered Gray. "Am I still assigned the cottage?"

"Don't be a ninny. Donovan needs to stay there. We've got you in the house tonight. There's a room free since one of the guests won't be here until tomorrow. Take a right at the top of the stairs. It's the first door. Shall I have Liddell fetch your bag?"

"No, no. I can do that, at least."

He went out the front and around the side of the house. The moon lit the back lawn, and the crickets were in full voice. He passed a large oak tree and detoured around the maze. For the first time in a day and a half, he felt no concern. Or maybe it was a general numbness.

He knocked on the door of the cottage, just in case. Inside, he threw his clothes into the suitcase and snapped it shut. "Defeat the defense," he told the lock. "Deduct the detail."

As he passed the archaeological site on his way back, he remembered his wet clothes. The idea of groping among skeletons in a dark mausoleum was not appealing, but retrieval of clothes tonight meant avoidance of confrontation tomorrow. He slipped past the planks and felt his way down the steps. Arms outstretched, he moved to the wall, located the sodden clothing, and gathered it up. It reeked of fertilizer. Outside a shadow detached itself from the trees. Mike dropped suitcase and bundle.

"You kept me waiting half an hour." Donovan, all pretense at good humor gone, loomed large.

"I did?"

"Thought you understood at dinner. I was telling you to meet me here."

"You were? It took me time to break free. They were watching."

"You're a nuisance, Archer."

"I'm sorry."

"You're sorry." It didn't sound as though he believed it. "You know what happens to nuisances."

"Sure." Mike bent for his suitcase. In point of fact, he didn't.

"You were going to stay away from her. You said so."

"I didn't know she was coming here."

"Get off it."

"I didn't."

"And what's your excuse for complicating my life?"

"It's a long story." Mike picked up his wet clothes. "Gray invited me."

"That wasn't long."

"Oh."

Donovan began to circle him in a menacing fashion. "You heard about the lottery ticket."

"An hour ago. Why?"

"I'll let you in on something, Archer. We think Halloran's here to steal it."

"We do?"

"We do."

"Who's we?" Mike wasn't ready to be part of it.

"Your government."

"Really?" He wondered why the government would be interested in lottery tickets. On his next orbit, Donovan leaned closer. Bad breath.

"Her company, TekSekure, does this. They use computers as a cover."

"A cover? That doesn't seem likely." Mike rested his foot on a pile of dirt. "She isn't acting suspicious."

"Of course not. She doesn't have her instructions yet. They always wait until the victims accept her."

"But everyone thinks she's Gray's fiancée."

"Exactly." Donovan thwacked his fist into his palm. He kept circling. "She'll make her move tomorrow. Bet on it. Before time runs out."

"I don't understand." Boy, it would be easier if the guy would stand still. "Why should Gray pretend to be engaged to her?"

"Can I trust you, Archer?" Donovan lifted a clump of sod.

"Can you trust me?"

"That's what I asked."

"Well, sure."

"He's in on it. They're planning to do the old man out of his money."

"Come on."

"It's the truth." The dirt crumbled to the ground.

"And what happens to the ticket when they get it?"

"They've got a fence lined up in Washington. How will Westfield prove it was his to begin with?" In the face of such logic, Mike had to remain silent.

Donovan aimed a finger at his chest. "Your government's counting on you, Archer. You'll have to keep an eye open. Both eyes. She starts doing anything funny, you give me the signal."

"What signal?"

"You'll think of something." He backed away into darkness. "Remember. Don't let me down."

Mike waited, but no more came in the way of guidance. Clutching suitcase and wet clothes, he continued across the lawn. The full moon was clearer out here than in Washington, but smaller. In the city, joined with the artificial glow, it left hardly any darkness for the stars. Could you wish on a star if it wasn't the first one out, as long as it was the first you saw? He picked one. But a thing that bright had to be a planet. Probably bad luck to wish on planets.

▼ ▼ ▼

By the time he reached the house, he'd come back to reality. No reason to believe the news about Liz and Gray. Why should Donovan have a monopoly on the truth? Then again, Gray was acting oddly, even for him. And it would be good to figure out what Liz was up to. Or why a person's central nervous system shut down in her presence.

The lights were off in the foyer but, as he let himself in, he could see the moonlit steps of the main staircase. He left his damp clothes by the door. Liddell would know where to take them.

The big house was still. He made his way to the landing, where the stairs split. Which way had Gray said? Right. He turned and reached the top. The stairs ended in the middle of a long hallway, lined with doors. Moonlight came through a window at one end. It would be nice to sleep in a bed again.

The nearest door was closed but not locked. He pushed it open. Dark inside. He fumbled for the switch, but his hand brushed textured wallpaper. He gave up, shut the door, and felt his way across the room. The outline of a sleigh bed loomed before him. He dropped his suitcase, flopped onto the mattress, and landed hard across a pair of legs. Feet kicked at him. He rolled from the floor and into a crouch.

The kicker breathed hard. "Don't move. I've got a gun."

Liz. He caught her scent in the dark, a tangy, unperfumed, healthy-animal smell. The gun was a non-issue. He didn't want her to find out who'd broken into her room. Keeping his eyes on the shadow in the bed, he crawled away until he reached a wall. His ear struck a door handle.

In a single move he opened it, swung through, and slammed it shut. A key protruded. He turned it, panting in the semi-darkness. As his brain began to function again, it took note of small, curious details. Such as, bedroom doors never locked from the outside. And the hallway hadn't been tiled.

"I know you're in there."

He sagged against the wall, hand covering his face. The one good thing about the situation was he hadn't picked a closet. Pounding came on the door. Perhaps the bathroom had a window. The trellis, that was as good as a fire escape. And this was only the second floor.

He opened his eyes and was delighted to see not merely a window, but a door on the opposite wall. He strained his eyes. It was still there. Shared bathroom. With a muttered, "Thank you," to no one in particular, he pulled open the door and stepped into yet another darkened space.

After two faltering steps, he walked into heavy drapes. The noise from the far side of the bathroom grew louder. He dropped to his hands and knees and crabbed toward the far wall. A bedside light clicked on.

"What the hell are you doing here?" Matt peered at him from under a sheet. Mike stood and brushed his clothes.

Marsha sat up in the adjacent bed. "What the hell is he doing here?"

"That's what I asked."

"What did he say?"

"He just stares like a lunatic."

"Sorry," Mike said. "Sleepwalking. Terrible habit."

"But you're dressed."

"Yeah. I do that. Sorry."

With the lights on, it was easy to locate the exit. He reached the hallway and slammed the door behind him.

Gray stood in the hall, clad in a hideous pair of pajamas. "What do you think you're up to?"

Mike clenched and unclenched his hands. "You told me to take the right hand stairs."

"I told you take a right at the top of the stairs."

Sounds of commotion increased from behind the two bedroom doors.

Mike darted a glance toward Liz's bedroom. "It won't be long. She's going to figure out I went through."

"My room. Right there. Quick. Closet."

"Not the closet."

"Do it." Gray moved down the hall and started to pound on Liz's door. "Everything all right, darling?"

Mike shot into the bedroom. The closet was easy to find. Standing in the doorway, he had the brief, foolish hope that he could wake up and bring it to an end, but then he heard footsteps in the hall. He yanked the door shut.

He'd settled among the hanging clothes, and his breathing had come back to normal, before he realized what he'd done. Almost as good as a resumé. His suitcase was beside her bed.

–8–

Out in the middle of the lake, well away from Gray and his dangerous plans, Mike pulled hard on the oars. Despite his efforts to navigate a straight line, the rowboat was, under the disapproving eye of the morning sun, sweeping a wide arc across the calm water. A puddle had formed in the bottom of the boat, testament to the vigor of his rowing, if not the skill. His hands were warm from the friction of splintery wood.

The retreat to Gray's closet had been a bad tactical decision. In fact, each successive decision in the dark had been poor. There'd been no reason to run from Liz. Anyone could walk into the wrong bedroom by mistake. Better, far better, to apologize, wish her goodnight, and exit. A bird of prey swooped by, eyeing him as it passed. Hawk, maybe. He lifted the binoculars and tracked it through the sky. It flew across the sun. He turned away, rubbing his eyes.

He wasn't sure how Gray had managed to pacify the household. Indeed, much of the guy's behavior could stand explaining. Mike put his feet on the thwart and rested his arms on his knees. The boat drifted. Briarwood floated across his field of vision. The house offered a comforting sense of stability. Hard to believe anything suspicious was going on there.

But Donovan. Putting in time at the dig this morning, he'd said. What did the Department of Justice find so fascinating about Civil War artifacts, particularly in relation to lottery tickets? Mike stared at the house and grounds. From a distance, the topography was striking, as if he'd seen it before.

Codes in classifieds. Aerial photos and contour maps. The boat continued its slow rotation. Nemo.

Gray had been in the city Thursday night. On the way to meet someone. The Colonel. Gray could be Nemo's buddy. But that made Liz Nemo, and he didn't want to believe that. Just as he didn't want to believe that the Colonel had been on her way to Briarwood all along. Follow him? Hell, she could have given him a ride.

A movement on the lawn near the gardener's shed caught his attention. He fumbled for the oars and managed to slow the spinning rowboat. He raised the field glasses. Allison had just emerged from the woods, and Gray crossed the lawn toward her. So, she was in on it too.

The couple embraced and then held each other at arm's length. Allison reached into her purse and withdrew a container the size of a lipstick. She held it toward Gray's face. Not the pepper she'd used yesterday, too small. Gray opened his mouth, and she sprayed something in. A goofy smile spread over his face, and he took the canister. Now it was her turn for a shot. She put the breath spray away, and they pulled each other close and kissed. Hand in hand, they headed for the woods that divided the properties. Mike lowered the glasses, feeling nauseated. Definitely not the Colonel's kind of folks.

He looked at his watch. Another hour until his next meeting with Gray. There was nothing to worry about. Donovan was full of it. With a sigh, Mike took up the oars, pointed his back toward the boathouse, and began to row. Why would the Colonel have a map of Briarwood? She wouldn't, of course. Faulty memory. Imagination run wild. Wrong map. Wrong connection.

But there were other guests who hadn't shown yet. One of them could be Nemo. Where did Liz fit in? He pulled harder. No address on her business card. No number. Donovan was right. It was strange.

"Look out!" The voice was high-pitched, unfamiliar.

He looked over his shoulder and saw the bow slide under the dock. With a curse, he dropped the handles and ducked forward. Planks grazed his head. The pilings caught the blades of the oars, slamming the grips into his body. From somewhere near, yet far away, he heard the voice again: "Are you hurt?"

He snapped his head up, smacking the underside of the dock. He wanted to groan, but he didn't have the air.

Doris' face hung upside down over the edge of the dock, her brown hair trailing toward the water. "You okay?"

He sucked in enough wind to respond. "Fine. Thanks. Fine."

She reached out a hand and guided the boat free. He hunched over to avoid the end of the dock, hauled himself from the boat, and sat massaging his stomach.

"Thanks for the warning." The boat nudged his ankles.

"It's okay," she said. "You had your mind on someone else."

▼ ▼ ▼

Liz shut herself into Westfield's library and picked her way through the clutter. No more waiting for Gray. No more interruptions. Time to get on the computer. The house was quiet; Westfield and the odd couple had gone to town for the morning. She let her eyes and her mind adjust. The curtains let in a crack of light, and dust drifted across it.

The library seemed to be housing an experiment in entropy. Someone had started with the idea of a country squire's retreat, as evidenced by the stuffed moose head on the wall and the grand mahogany desk in the center. But the personality of the current owner had overcome all former stylishness. Sprawls of paper littered the desk, three chairs and much of the floor. The rest of the furnishings were eclectic: golf clubs, board games, half-built model rockets.

A pile of thick manila folders sat on the chair behind the desk. She moved them aside and settled before the monitor, where a keyboard rested on an old desk blotter. This would be the time for latex gloves, but, under the circumstances, fingerprints wouldn't be a problem. Westfield had bought her story about needing to check e-mail.

Her assumption was that whatever Allie's mother had put on the computer should be obvious to a person with any kind of background. She started with the 'docs' directory, working through it, finding nothing. A disk stuck out of the floppy drive, but when she pressed it in, it seemed to be blank. A de-install could confirm that.

She went back to the hard drive and ran down the list of applications. Nothing. So much for a quick fix. She settled back in her chair. Another slog. But at least it would be a slog ahead of the competition. If Mike or Roger could be dignified with such a title. They might be working together. She stared past the information on the monitor. Mike had certainly been tailing her since Friday. It was possible that Roger's appearance could be nothing more than coincidence. Mother wouldn't dare send him again. But he'd been there Friday, at the Tidal Basin.

It was a surprise to see him with such stable employment. Not that she'd kept up with him since that catastrophic blind date, when he'd talked straight through the evening, mostly about himself and his silly motorcycle. She didn't remember anything about archaeology. He seemed to think of himself as some sort of secret agent. She'd tuned most of it out. The one honest thing she'd told him that night was that she preferred to control her situations. He'd taken it as a hint she wanted to pay for dinner.

She dialed up the TekSekure server to check e-mail. While she waited for it to verify her password, she stacked loose papers on a corner of the blotter. A cryptic message from Bud, reporting everything okay with the office move, and another from Ariel, asking her to call when she could. She sent a zap to his mailbox, without text. It would dial his pager. She'd asked once for the pager number, but he claimed it was safer for her not to have it. That sort of protection wasn't very comforting.

She clicked the switch on the desk lamp and poked through the clutter of papers. Bills and receipts. At the bottom of the pile, a checkbook: Barton Westfield. She glanced at the entries. For the most part, it could have been her own account. Groceries, gas, credit cards. Then something stopped her eye. A five thousand dollar payment, referenced with 'E.O.' She flipped the pages. Another. And another. Every two months.

ariel: GOOD MORNING, MIRANDA.

She tapped at the keys with one hand.

miranda: HI, ARIEL. WHAT'S UP?

She flipped through more files. When she glanced at the screen again, he'd already sent his message.

ariel: NOT CAUSING TROUBLE, ARE WE?

She closed the checkbook.

miranda: OF COURSE NOT. WHAT MAKES YOU ASK?

ariel: I UNDERSTAND A CERTAIN OFFICE IN OUR FAVORITE CITY IS OUT OF BUSINESS.

She glanced at the label on a file while considering how to respond.

miranda: YOU SEEM WELL INFORMED.

ariel: MY SPIES ARE EVERYWHERE. SERIOUSLY, ARE YOU OKAY?

miranda: SWELL. I'VE SKIPPED TOWN.

She turned off the lamp.

ariel: EXCELLENT. COUNTRY AIR IS GOOD FOR THE SOUL.

She stared at the message and shivered. He seemed to know she wasn't on the island.

miranda: YOU'RE RIGHT. I'LL HAVE TO TRY IT SOMETIME.

She opened the file. The logo was distinctive, an H split by a T. But Ariel was writing again:

ariel: JUST WANTED TO MAKE SURE YOU WERE HEALTHY. GIVE A WHISTLE IF YOU NEED HELP.

She heard footsteps in the living room.

miranda: I WILL. MUST GO. TALK SOON.

Suddenly it didn't seem such a great idea to be caught reorganizing Westfield's files. The floppy disk would be safer in her purse, with her diagnostic disk. Oh, what the hell. She inserted the diagnostic and started a basic search program. She leaned a file against the monitor. The doorknob rattled. Quietly, she slipped once more through the French doors.

No one was under attack on the lawn today, which was good. Her mind was occupied trying to work out why Barton Westfield would have a stack of Hillton-Tanner financial files at home. It brought an edge to the assignment she hadn't counted on.

▼ ▼ ▼

Mike had only ever seen Doris sitting or running away. As they walked across the back lawn, she had to tilt her head up to meet his eye.

"Nice view from the lake?"

"The house, mostly." He glanced toward the woods where Allison and Gray had vanished. No sounds of dogs today. "Pretty impressive."

"Mom and Dad think so. They love to be invited down."

"How do they know the Westfields?"

She clasped her hands behind her back.

"They had season tickets next to each other for Orioles games. The Harpers, too. It was a long time ago, when Mrs. Westfield was alive, and Mr. Harper. Mom and Dad call it their former life. Before me."

Mike looked straight at her, feeling a lump in his throat. "Do you like baseball? I used to go to Orioles games all the time. With my brother. Dad gave us each one share of stock. Bird Holdings, isn't that a great name? He said they were worth two in the bush leagues. I tacked the certificate over my bed. The next year my parents divorced, my brother ran away from home, and Bird Holdings bought my share back. For the longest time I thought it was all related, but it wasn't. Life is lots of things. They're not necessarily connected." He kicked an acorn. "Why am I telling you this?"

"What was it like, when your parents broke up?"

He hadn't ever asked himself that one. "It was quieter, mostly. No more yelling. Except over the phone." He saw tears form in her eyes. "No, look, I wouldn't worry about it. That's just the way they are."

"Who are?" She rubbed an eye.

"You know." It killed him to see a nice kid like Doris have to go through that. They reached the big oak tree in the center of the lawn with a bench under it. "Come on, sit down. Do you have brothers or sisters?"

"Just me." She took the far end. "What about your brother? What's he doing now?"

In six months, Char had never thought to ask. "Following a star. Trust me, you're better off the only one." He stared across the lake, toward the hills. "Let's talk about something else."

"Such as?" She clutched her knees.

"I don't know. Anything. Anything but pizza. Or jail."

She laughed, a genuine laugh. "I think I can manage that. You're the only person I know who didn't ask in the first three minutes what I want to be when I grow up."

"Why should I ask that?"

"People do. I think I make them uncomfortable."

"No, you don't. Anyway. It's not the sort of thing I'd ask. Glass houses."

She traced a finger along the hem of her dress. "What did you want to be?"

"I'm not a generation ahead of you."

That made her blush. "I'm sorry."

"No, it's okay. I meant . . . well, never mind." He followed the patterns on the lake, textured clouds floating on water. "I think the problem is, I wasn't ever sure I would grow up, so I never bothered to plan anything out."

"You thought you were going to die?"

"Not exactly." He looked up through the leaves at a splash of sky. "I thought there was a chance I wouldn't figure out how to feel like an adult. Pathetic, really."

She rested her chin on her knees. "How did you find your . . . ?"

"My what?"

"Your, you know, girlfriend."

"Oh. Her. A mistake. I worked at the Library of Congress, shelving books, and she was researching something for her boss. I'd left a book on the table next to her. She thought I was reading it, and . . . that's how we met."

"And this is your first time visiting her? Down here, I mean."

"No, no, she lives in the city."

"She lives next door. I saw you kissing in the garden yesterday afternoon."

"Kissing? Ah." He held up a hand. "Allison. Not my girlfriend. And how did you know that was me?"

"It was obvious. When you . . . like someone, you can tell."

He smiled, then wondered whether anyone else had found it obvious.

"Are you all right?" she said.

"Of course."

"You hit the dock pretty hard. Maybe you forgot who your girlfriend is."

"I didn't forget. Allison isn't."

"I don't know, maybe we should go and ask her. I bet she'll remember."

"Go ahead." But when Doris walked away into the Hugo woods, some never before used big-brother instinct made him run after her.

▼ ▼ ▼

Hartigan Gap wasn't all that large, but it took Liz longer than she'd expected to find a quiet place with a phone. The Montclair, Gray's rendezvous, was out. The Speckled Turnip looked like a bad idea. The post office was too public, the Hartigan Tap not yet open. At last she discovered a coffee shop on a cross street that furnished the town with one of its three intersections. She even found a spot to park Gray's car.

The place was filled with a sufficient number of locals to reassure her the food wasn't poisonous, and the crowd would cover private conversations. Not so noisy, though, that you had to scream across the table. The shop had a fresh, bakery smell. The phone booth held a slim directory that took in several counties. She flipped through and found HARPER, H.A. She hoped Allie's mother didn't pick up.

"Hello?"

"Allie, it's Liz. I'm in town. The, um, Cinnamon Bear. Can you get away?"

"What's happened? Is it Gray?"

"No. Nothing horrible. We need to talk. Away from the houses."

"I can be there in ten minutes." There was something in her voice, as if Allie had been expecting the call.

▼ ▼ ▼

Mike found the path at the edge of the woods. A scent of pine carried on the breeze. No Hugo in sight. He caught up with Doris. Sunlight filtered through the trees in parallel shafts.

He laughed. "I just had an image of breadcrumbs."

"Good thing I don't like gingerbread," she said.

The path meandered a quarter mile and ended at a broad lawn. Another large house. Another wide driveway. Bad terrain for a frontal assault. Mike turned to go, but Doris was already crossing the grass.

"Come on. Are you afraid of what she'll say?"

"No, but this isn't such a good . . . rats."

They climbed together to the front door.

Doris pointed at the bell. "Go on."

"All right, all right." He pushed it. "Too bad, no one home. Let's go."

"Don't be silly. I hear them coming."

The door swung open. Behind it, Mrs. Harper leaned on her cane.

"Hi." He tried to muster a grin. "We were wondering, is Allison in? We wanted to speak to her. Didn't we, Doris? Have you met? This is Doris, a friend of mine. We just wanted to speak to Allison, didn't we?"

"Yes," said Doris. "We did. If that's all right."

"It's not all right. Not in the least. I know why you're here, but you won't find it on my property. You're out of bounds. It's in a safe place. Barton could find it if he put his mind to it. He doesn't need to send his son. Or his son's fiancée. Or her brother, for that matter. Doris, you should know better."

"Right," said Mike. "Of course. Sorry to bother you. Come along, Doris."

"Honestly, Mrs. Harper, we only wanted to talk–"

"I'm sure you realize I no longer use that name. At the moment, Allison is out. If you wish to speak to her later, you may telephone."

"Of course." Mike took Doris' arm. "We will. Thank you. Thank you very much." He led her across the lawn. "Wow. Near miss. Mad as a haddock."

"Hatter," said Doris.

"Maybe. I still think there's something fishy."

▼ ▼ ▼

Liz bought a muffin and juice and took them to a booth in the corner. The remains of the Sunday *Post* lay on the table. She paged through the sports section. Eventually, a conversation sifted through to her consciousness, a man and a woman in heated debate. She looked over her shoulder. The man waved a Polaroid.

"I told you, Frances. This is the guy. Roger Donovan."

Liz stiffened.

"I don't care if he's Roger Moore." Frances backhanded the photo to the edge of their table and glared. A busboy passed, knocking the photo to the floor, where it lay unnoticed. Another customer kicked it toward Liz.

"Honestly, Randy." Frances pulled a compact from her purse. "The fact you took a picture of a mental case proves zero."

Liz glanced at the photo. It was not Roger, but Mike. The beard had slid a quarter of the way around his face. Over his shoulder, the chipped gold 'B' on the front gate was visible.

"He gave me directions, hon." Randy held his hands as if in prayer. "No kidding. They were terrible."

"I'm supposed to believe that? Only an idiot would talk to this guy."

That was unfair to Mike, whatever his faults.

"Out of his mind," Frances said. "Take a look."

Randy pawed through the debris on their table with increasing agitation. He jumped from his seat.

"Gone. It's gone."

"Excuse me." Liz picked up the photo. He snatched it from her and scurried back to his seat.

"Look at this, hon, he's kind of pointing down the road."

"Give it a rest." Frances snapped her compact shut. "This wasn't taken within a hundred miles of here."

"Sure it was. It was real close. I'd show you, if I could remember how to get there."

Liz finished her muffin wondering what sort of trouble would ensue if Randy and Frances showed up at Briarwood. She was on the verge of offering directions when Allie glided past the window on a bicycle like something out of *The Wizard of Oz.* Liz refolded the paper, placing the sections in order.

Allie came through the doorway, looking great. She had on a sleeveless cotton mock turtleneck, and her cheeks were pink. She scanned the place and made her way to the back.

"What did you want to talk about?"

That was Allie, an arrow to the heart. Arrow. The word stirred a vague memory of archery. Liz leaned closer. "Do you recognize anyone here?"

Allie looked around. Randy and Frances were at the cash register. "Except for that pair, just about all of them."

"Is it safe to talk?"

"Safe to talk?" Allie sat. "About what? Overthrowing the government?"

"Let me put it this way. How much do you know about Mr. Westfield?"

"How much should I?"

"What does he do?"

"I'm not sure, anymore. He and Mom used to work together, but that was a while back. They did consulting."

"That's a catchall. What kind of consulting?"

"I don't know. Management something or other. I told you, it was a long time ago, at a company called Morveus Industries. What? What is it?"

Liz took her hand from her mouth. "Muffin down the wrong pipe."

Allie sat back. "This was what you needed to talk about?"

"Sort of." Liz touched her pendant. It was the perfect time to bring up the embezzlement, but the wrong place. She didn't want a public scene.

▼ ▼ ▼

A note lay on Mike's bed, in Gray's hieroglyphic scrawl: 'Marriage Noose.' He needed a good deal of study to work out that the actual message was, 'In Carriage House.'

In the gloom of the outbuilding there was a faint odor of motor oil and old wood. "Gray?"

"Up here, old sport." Some sort of loft.

"She took it. No question. Allison's mother is your thief."

Gray's face appeared at the lip. "How do you know?"

"She told me."

"She said, 'I'm a thief?' "

"Might as well. She said it's not on her property. In a safe place. Her exact words."

"That sounds like a clue. 'A safe place.' Come on up."

"No, you come down."

"Really, it's not that high. What are you afraid of? Falling?"

"Landing."

Gray laughed, but he climbed down.

"Okay." Mike leaned against a wall. "Suppose you're right. What's safe? Wait. Safe as . . . well, houses. 'Safe as houses.' "

"Some help. It's in the house."

As they went outside again, the sound of a car drew nearer.

"You know," Gray said, "there's an old . . . blast, the party's tonight."

"Swell."

"This Fourth of July thing Dad does."

"He must look forward to it. What's your point?"

"I mention it only because Allison's mother will attend."

"Tonight? I thought they were feuding."

"They're still friends. One has to observe certain niceties."

Mike looked toward the house. That was the sort of friendship that would keep a guy's blood pressure up. No thanks.

"You don't think she might try to get back the ticket?"

"Why not? It expires tomorrow. Maybe she figures time's up. She'll take it for keeps."

"Where was the last place your father had the ticket?"

"The library, he thinks."

"Which you've searched."

"Me personally only that once, but he's looked several times."

Someone else had expressed interest in the library, that very morning, at breakfast. He didn't have to strain to remember who. He'd been thinking about her all day.

▼ ▼ ▼

Mike paused with his hand on the library door. "Sure she's not here?"

"Absolutely. She took my car into town." Gray moved on exaggerated tiptoe, darting glances toward the foyer. "But what if she–?"

"You stay here. If she comes back, warn me."

"With what?"

"A warning, preferably. Use your imagination."

"It's snooping."

"It's your Dad's house. And he did want you to look for the ticket."

"I suppose. Be quick about it."

Mike stepped through into the library. The curtains were drawn, the lights off. One corner of the room had a greenish glow. In the darkness, his first impression was that someone had spent a fair amount of time ransacking the place. Unable to find a switch, he stumbled past unseen, shin-high barriers to the window and tugged on the drapes. Sunlight poured through clouds of swirling dust. No points for Liddell in the cleaning event.

Waving away the dust, he took his first good look at Mr. Westfield's inner sanctum. He shook his head. The idea of searching for a single piece of paper in this collection of debris wasn't worth considering. The moose on the wall favored him with a glassy stare. The sight made him feel strangely sorry for Mr. Westfield.

The desk was covered with manila file folders, some opened. One or both Westfields would have checked those. He bypassed them, stepping over bags of holiday wrap and odd-sized boxes stacked on the floor. Splotches of oriental carpet appeared beneath the clutter. He bent to inspect the rug, turned over a fringed edge, and was rewarded with a fresh stirring of dust.

There was a faint burning smell, which he tracked to the fireplace, and an ashen sheet of paper. Too big to be a lottery ticket. It crumbled in his fingers and fell through the grate. He looked for something to wipe his hands on and noticed, for the first time, a low hum. He followed it to a computer. Behind a file folder, the monitor zipped through a string of operations. The figures were incomprehensible, highly suspicious.

Several folders lay open to financial spreadsheets certain to panic an anthro minor. He flipped through the pages. All the same. Someone making pots of money. Hillton-Tanner, whoever that was. The computer whirred through its numbers and letters in what looked like high-speed code. He let his fingers hover above the keyboard, just to prove he could keep from touching it.

A thump came from the ceiling. He started, inadvertently pushing one of the buttons. The numbers began doing something different. He pushed the same button again. The display winked out. Nuts.

"Gray!"

A nose poked through the doorway, followed by spectacle frames.

"You'd better get out." Gray came all the way into the room. "My car's in the driveway."

"Okay. We've still got a few minutes."

"No, we don't. There's no one in it."

Mike bent over the computer. "Help me get this working again."

"Look, I really think this would be a good time to–"

"A good time to explain what you're doing in here?" said Liz.

▼ ▼ ▼

Liz took her purse from her shoulder. Look at them. The Tweedle twins. "This should be entertaining." She stalled for time. It was her own fault.

"I'm sorry." Mike indicated the room. "We were looking for something."

"I gathered." She craned her neck, trying to see what the screen showed. Stick to the game plan, damn it. Once the search program starts running, stay in the room.

"Didn't . . . didn't find it." Mike waved a hand aimlessly.

"Oh?" That was a break. Scare them off and get serious about the search.

"You wouldn't understand."

"I think I do." Still blocking their exit, she approached the desk. Gray backed away and Mike edged to the side. He stepped on a golf club, which rose up and whacked his leg. She stifled a laugh and looked at the blank screen.

"Pretty clever today, aren't we?" Let them think she was upset with them, not herself. Mike shrugged. She elbowed him aside. "Don't play stupid. I've been watching. Both of you." Should have been, anyway.

"Watching us what?" Gray said.

"You know perfectly well." She sat before the computer and tapped the F1 key, causing 'System Error' to flash in the upper left corner. She spun around, as if that meant something terrible. "Who touched this?"

Gray fled, but Mike, to his credit, stood his ground. "It was a mistake."

"You got that right."

"I said we're sorry."

"Have you any idea what you've done?"

"It can't be that bad. We only pushed one button." But she saw him sweat.

"You only destroyed two hours of work." Two minutes, more like, and the program would have saved everything, but he didn't need to know that.

"I'm sorry. You don't have to be rude." He pointed at the H-T files. "What about you? Finding everything you need?"

"What?" His counterattack was so quick, she'd never seen it coming.

"Call it a wild guess." He eyed the room. "I'd say someone spent a lot of time looking for something in here. Would you know anything about that?"

He lifted a folder, and she had to restrain herself from grabbing. The situation was flying out of control again. He thumbed through the spreadsheets.

"For someone who's supposed to be fixing a computer, you sure seem interested in papers. Like the one in the fireplace."

She advanced on him. "Get out of here."

"Mmmm, I should talk to Mr. Westfield. He might be interested in what else has been getting out of this room."

She felt her face flush. To be accused by . . . an amateur. "You're pathetic."

"But honest. And not known for pawing through people's stuff." He closed the H-T folder.

She stooped for the nearest weapon, the golf club. He hopped over a stack of debris and circled the desk. She came after him, making noises of anger and frustration, only partly an act.

"Okay." He made a gesture of surrender. "I'm going." At the door he paused. "Destruction of evidence. I believe that's a crime."

She launched the club like a javelin toward the wall. It connected with a moose antler and thunked to the floor. Mike looked unaccountably sad. He seemed about to say something but ducked out instead.

"And stay out!" She strode across the room and slammed the door behind him. Unbelievable. She leaned against it. Another slip-up like that, and she'd deserve to be fired.

▼ ▼ ▼

It took Mike a while to find Gray, who sat in the kitchen talking to Mrs. Liddell as if to establish an alibi.

The cook smoothed her apron as he walked in. "Luncheon, Mr. Archer?"

"No thanks." He liked being addressed as Mister. "A little early for me." He glanced at his watch to make sure the excuse was plausible.

She clucked. "You may as well check your stomach. Or your heart. Will Miss Halloran be joining us?"

"Miss . . ." He felt a touch of conversational whiplash. "I wouldn't know."

"You wouldn't, no, but you should. I'll be here if you need help." She headed for the pantry. He wished he could interpret the look she'd given him.

"Don't mind her," said Gray. "She's a bit . . . odd."

"By whose standards?"

Gray seemed to be searching Mike for signs of injury. "You got out okay?"

"Yeah, thanks for the help."

"Right. Well. Perhaps we should be going." He raised his voice. "Thanks for everything, Mrs. L."

Her answer was a whistled tune Mike didn't recognize. "What do you think Liz is up to in there?"

"Couldn't say. Same thing we were, I'd venture. Ticket."

"The difference is, we weren't looking through anyone's files. Or running some weird program on the computer. Or burning scraps of paper."

"Burning? Well . . . probably a school project."

"She's not in school."

"Work, then."

"Do you realize who she works for?"

From behind thick glasses, Gray slid him a furtive glance. "TekSekure."

"And you know what they do?"

Gray looked uncomfortable. "Find things."

"What? Where'd you get that?"

"It's not important. I'm telling you, there's no cause for worry."

"She had a bunch of open folders on that desk."

"Ah," said Gray. "Containing?"

"Well, I don't know. Too many numbers. Financial stuff for somebody called Hilltron, or something like that." Mike's head hurt. The nice long weekend would be over soon. Back to the sad reality of the job search.

"I just had a thought. Maybe we should check the mausoleum. That's a safe place, right? 'Safe as the grave,' isn't that the expression?"

"Quiet as the grave," said Mike.

"Close enough. I'll fetch a torch."

Mike watched him go, wondering about this sudden fascination with mausoleums. Gray sure wasn't interested in talking about Hilltron. And he hadn't wanted to know about the burnt paper in the fireplace.

▼ ▼ ▼

Mike ducked under the hanging sod and went down the steps.

"Hello? Anyone here?"

The beam from the flashlight picked up a small animal, immobile, which upon closer inspection he recognized as one of his own socks. Otherwise, the space was empty. Not merely tidy. Empty, as if swept clean. An old brick underground storeroom. Historical significance: zero.

"You can come in." He turned toward the opening. "Take a look at this."

Gray's face appeared. "What?"

"Well, I can't say I've spent a lot of time in crypts, but there seems to be something missing."

"Like what?"

"Bodies, Gray. Bodies. No caskets. No skeletons. No deserters shot by General Lee. Not here."

"Maybe they've been removed."

"It's not as if there were lots of room. This isn't a mausoleum. Now, why would Donovan lie?"

"Don't ask me."

"Do you know anything about the other archaeologist, Nishida?"

"Liddell handled all that."

Mike examined the space again. "If it weren't for that wall," he walked toward the bricks, "I'd swear this was . . ."

"Was what?"

He put his hand against the back wall. The bricks were soft fabric, stretched tight, that gave to the touch. He poked at them.

"Was what?" Gray repeated.

Mike found the edge and pulled the fabric aside. Behind the curtain, the room stretched into darkness. He aimed the light past. "Was a tunnel."

"Impossible." Gray's British accent was gone. "You've been re-reading your childhood books. This doesn't happen."

"See for yourself. The brick wall is painted on a curtain."

Gray drew closer. "This is sensational."

"And you didn't know about it?"

"Of course not."

"Hello?" Mike called into the tunnel. His voice echoed. He ran the light over the brick ceiling and walls. In pretty good shape, given their age. The floor was dirt, quite smooth. He directed the light along the wall. "Seems to make a straight shot for the house."

Gray pushed by. "Let's find out."

With an uneasy look at the ceiling, Mike followed, gripping the flashlight. After ten level yards, the floor sloped down into cool, stale air. He had enough clearance to walk upright, just. Trickles of water on the dirt floor made it muddy in spots. He turned the beam up to the ceiling once every few steps, until Gray finally called back.

"Knock it off, would you? Hard enough to see without your blasted Grand Opening routine."

Mike aimed the light toward the ground, just ahead of Gray's feet. The shadows of the two thin legs broke up the yellow oval. He began to whistle.

"Cork it," said Gray.

They squished along the tunnel, five feet apart, neither of them speaking. A sudden blow to the front of his head made Mike shout. He dropped the flashlight, and it went out. In the dark, he raised his hands in defense, but no further attack came.

"Ow. Ow ow ow."

"What?" Gray's voice echoed out of the blackness. "What is it?"

"I don't know." He listened hard, but there was no breathing save his own and Gray's. "Hit my head on something." He pressed his hairline.

The only sound was the dripping of water. He squatted and felt along the ground for the flash. When he had it working and trained it on the ceiling, the light picked out a small inverted pyramid resembling the bottom of a dreidel, which projected from the darker brick. He stood for a closer look. It seemed to be made of concrete. He rubbed his head again, as if seeing the cause somehow made the gesture necessary.

"There's something in the ground above this tunnel."

Gray retraced his steps and ran his fingers over the pyramid. "Wet, whatever it is." Concrete crumbled into his hand.

"Look out. The ceiling's caving in."

"It isn't. Whatever this is, it doesn't belong with the tunnel. Get a grip." Gray turned and resumed his exploration.

Mike didn't like it. A hundred yards along, or maybe it only felt that way, Gray stopped at a knee-high pile of dirt and stones. Just beyond was a reinforcement of new wood, where the walls showed signs of partial collapse. Someone had spent a good deal of energy digging through the obstruction. Gray tested the wooden support.

"Pretty solid. Like a mine shaft."

"Would you mind not disturbing that? It looks dangerous." Mike peered into the gloom. "We shouldn't both go, in case this gives way. One of us could still get back for help."

"Good idea." A thumbs-up gesture. "You stay."

"We could flip a coin." He tried to make it sound as though he wanted to spend more time in the tunnel. "I mean, I don't mind going on."

"I'm sure." The flashlight made Gray's grin macabre. "But if you think I'd miss out on this in my own yard, you've taken leave of your senses."

Mike handed over the light. "Good luck." He watched Gray's silhouette grow smaller. It gave him the sensation of falling backward through space. The light disappeared around a corner.

The air could be poisonous. It was worse than in the moose suit. He couldn't see the walls and didn't want to touch them. Waiting in the dark, he began to think about Gray and his denials. Maybe the tunnel hadn't been that much of a surprise to him. Maybe he knew where it led. Maybe he was going to get someone. Or something.

Suddenly, Mike wasn't at all keen on spending another second in the dark, near a wet, eroding wall. He felt his hands twitch. It was tougher not seeing them. He took a step backward, into mud.

Gray's voice caromed off the walls. "I'm at some steps. Leading up."

"Up?"

"Must go to the house. This last little bit's paved in brick. Hang on." The sound of shoes carried clearly.

Mike stood still, careful not to touch anything. If the tunnel led to the house, it made sense to curtain off the entrance to hide the fact that you'd uncovered a way to break in. But Gray didn't need a reason to break into his own house. The next report came in an unintelligible whisper. He edged into the blackness, holding his hands outstretched. The light became brighter, and the voice was clear again.

". . . a wall at the top of the steps." Gray rounded the corner and shined the beam into Mike's eyes. "I haven't figured out how to get through. But I can hear someone on the other side. Wait here."

"You wait. It's my turn."

"Nonsense. This won't take a second."

The light disappeared again, leaving Mike in endless darkness without a point of reference.

–9–

Bud's voice soared on the thermals of the cell connection. "Would you listen?" He sounded as if he were inside a barrel, which at the moment Liz wished he were. "It's one of those things, wheels within wheels, is all I can tell you."

"Why?" She watched lines of code scroll up the monitor. "I'm on top of this. I can handle it." She heard the tremble in her voice and hoped he didn't over the static.

"Did I say you couldn't?"

She withdrew the H-T disk from her purse. "But I'm through the first layer already. This is a cinch. It won't take long to wrap."

"Yeah, but the thing is, some of our friends have taken an interest."

"They're not my friends."

He made a noise that sounded like a chuckle. "They'll feel better if I'm in the area, that's all."

"There isn't room for another pair of hands." That was true. She tapped the disk against the monitor. "What does this mean? I'm done?"

"I'm not taking you off the job, of course not. All I said is I'm coming down. You'll hardly know I'm there. I'll stay with relatives."

That stopped her cold. "I didn't know you had relatives near here."

"Visit L.A. some time, I'll show you the albums."

She copied the H-T disk onto the blank from Westfield's computer, which had nothing of interest even in its deleted files.

"Why are you doing this? It's simple. All I need to figure out is–"

"Uh-uh-uh. The damn phones aren't secure."

"You bought scramblers, remember? To match your brains."

She hung up and stared at the monitor. Couldn't he act like a normal boss and spend his weekends watching TV, or drinking, or getting therapy? There was, of course, the outside chance that her irritation was driven by having lied to him. The code in the computer was simple. Probably. But there was still the question of what Westfield was doing with Hillton-Tanner files. And what he and Allie's mother had been up to at Morveus Industries. Morveus. That was a name she hadn't seen in a while. She watched the screen rip through several thousand combinations. And who the $5,000 payments were going to.

A scratching noise came from behind one of the walls. She made a face at it. Mice. The place was full of rodents. She didn't like it that the mousy little Doris kid had befriended Mike. He couldn't possibly understand the significance of the Hilton-Tanner files. And yet . . . he might be working for the government. Just the sort of incompetent they'd hire. A click from behind the bookcase, and a section of wall swung into the room. She dimmed the monitor. One more interruption.

Gray peered around the edge. "Oops. Thought you were gone. I mean, darling, how lovely to see you. Not still miffed, I hope."

She slipped both disks into her pocket. "Can it. There's no one here but us." She glanced at the bookcase. "Is that how you generally enter this room?"

He emerged, holding a flashlight. "Tell you the truth, I didn't know this was here. Isn't it marvelous?" He looked over his shoulder before swinging the door shut. "Drat. Should've figured out how to open it from this side first." He turned the beam off and back on again. "Well, I see you're back into the computer bit. Any luck?"

"As you may have gathered, Gray, I'm an old friend of Allie's."

"Oh?" He stood on tiptoe, scanning the books. "Don't seem to recall her mentioning you."

"We were at college. She wouldn't have had much reason to talk about me lately." *There was this friend I had. I stabbed her in the back.*

"Wait." His heels hit the floor. "Are you serious? That's wonderful."

"I don't see anything wonderful about it."

"No, but can't you understand, this makes things so much simpler. Or, on second thought, maybe not." He wavered. "Quite the reverse."

"Stop babbling. What I want you to know is, you've put me in a difficult position. I can't tell Allie the reason I'm here without your permission."

"You mean, you haven't yet?"

"Of course not. Not that there'd be much to tell, anyway."

He wrung the flashlight as if to squeeze a stronger beam from it. "You'd like to know what you're looking for, I suppose."

"It would help."

While she waited for him to think that through, she studied the titles, wondering which operated the latch on the hidden door. And where it led. Gray had needed a flashlight on the other side. Secrets. The house was full of them. She was good at secrets. But this didn't feel like a good thing.

"All right." He sat down. "It's some sort of instructions from Mrs. Owen."

"And who is she?"

"Allison's mother. What I told you about the genealogy is true. But there's more. She and Dad had a blowup earlier this year, and that's why she's so loopy. Something to do with this place they used to work. But that's not important."

Liz pressed her hands on the desk. Morveus fallout. Of all things to run into in Hartigan Gap. "Oh? And what is important?"

"If you can find the instructions, you'll help Allison tremendously."

Liz terminated the program. Here she'd thought Bud coming to supervise was the worst thing that could happen on this job.

▾ ▾ ▾

Mike eventually found Gray in his own room, staring out the window.

"See anything, Galileo?"

"No. Not especially."

Mike kept his voice steady. "Was it necessary to leave me in a dark tunnel?"

"Actually, it was."

"I had to feel my way the entire length of that damn shaft." He held out his dirty hands. "You took the nice clean stairs."

"Stairs that led to the library where I found your close friend Elizabeth."

"Oh."

" 'Oh,' indeed." Gray retreated to the bathroom. "You see why I didn't rush back with an invitation for you to follow." He returned with a towel. "Besides, once I closed the door, I couldn't figure out how to open the stinker. Sorry. Anyway, you managed to get out. All's well, and whatnot."

"What did she say?"

"Not much. Mostly she was doing things on the computer."

"What sort of things?"

"Computer things. Fixing the mess you made."

Mike tossed the towel aside. "It's not as if the ticket could be inside the machine. Why does she spend so much time working on it?"

Gray flopped onto the bed. "Some people are good at some things, others aren't. That's what she's good at. I can't see why you're worked up about it."

"I'm not worked up, I just don't trust her." Mike picked dirt from under his nails. "She has something going on we don't know about."

"Well, you're the detective."

"Hilarious."

"Don't take it out on me, matey."

"Please, not the Cockney again." He grabbed the window sill. "Okay, you're right. It's none of my business."

He stared down at the fish pond. Farther away, he could see the dig. The breeze played on his face. He looked at the mound of earth. Sighting along his finger, he traced the straight path from the pile of dirt to the corner of the house where the library was. He touched the bump on his head.

"They ran the tunnel under the fish pond. That doesn't make sense. It wouldn't take much force to punch through from above."

Gray came to the window. "What makes you . . . oh. Well, they probably didn't. The tunnel would have been there first."

"Then, when they built the pond, why didn't they realize there was . . ." Mike looked at his fingernails again. He'd seen dirty fingernails recently. Wrapped around a stun gun. "Of course. It's on the map."

"What map?"

"Of course."

"Stop saying 'of course' and tell me what you're talking about."

He grabbed Gray's sleeve. "I need to know where Donovan is."

"At the train station, I believe, meeting his associate. Or so he advertised."

"His associate. That means we're in big trouble." He wasn't sure where that 'we' had come from. An hour ago he'd persuaded himself Gray was in on it.

Gray pulled his sleeve free. "Why trouble?"

"Because," Mike decided to risk it, "I know who his associate is, and believe me, you don't want to meet her."

"You couldn't know that."

"I do. I ran into her, Friday. In the city."

"Whoa, slow down. What are you talking about?"

Mike gave the nickel version of his run-in with the Colonel. "She had a topographical map. It didn't mean a thing to me at the time. But when I was on the lake this morning, it all looked familiar. Those photographs and maps she had. The blueprint. It's your father's property. It's this house."

"Are you sure?"

"It was all there. Garden. Maze. Fishpond. Even the tunnel to the house."

"Lots of places fit that description," said Gray. "Several, at least. More than one. And how long did you spend looking at this map?"

"I'm telling you, she's planning an assault. The tunnel's her way in."

"No one would assault Briarwood. There's nothing for her here."

"Nothing but a lottery ticket."

"Oh." Gray deflated. "How would she know about that?"

"We didn't get that far. The real Nemo's associate showed up."

"The real . . . you mean, Donovan."

"Of course, Donovan. Okay, I didn't actually see him, but it had to be." Yes, it was a wild-ass guess. But the laws of probability said occasionally even a wild-ass guess would be right.

"I don't know." Gray fussed with his glasses. "Seems thin. Have you told anyone else?"

"Who could I have told?"

"Good. Let's keep it between us. No point getting everyone excited."

"And what do you suggest we do instead?"

Gray walked to his desk and back. "First off, we have no idea whether you've hit it, that this Colonel person is who's coming. Let's find out about that. If so, surprise is still on our side. She has no idea who you are, right? She won't expect to see you here?"

"Well, she . . . no, she won't expect that."

"Right. All we need is a plan."

"No." Mike raised his hands. "Please."

He didn't wait around to hear it. Gray's plans needed to incubate before they could hatch into complete and total madness.

▼ ▼ ▼

Westfield met Liz outside at noon, as she'd requested. They headed in the general direction of the boathouse. Under the bright sun, Liddell tended roses. A rusty wheelbarrow stood nearby. There was no sign of anyone else. Westfield clasped his hands behind his back as they neared the large oak that dominated the lawn.

"Gray seemed so serious. I hope there's no trouble between you two."

"There isn't anything between us. Nothing at all. It . . . there's been a deception." She took a deep breath. "And I'm part of it."

"Deception?" He led the way to the bench beneath the tree, beside a patch of daisies. Liz contemplated the flowers. Time for step one.

"The fact of the matter is, I'm not engaged to your son."

"You've broken the engagement?"

"No, no." It was worse, seeing that it bothered him. "I mean I'm not his fiancée. I never was. I hardly know him."

"I truly don't understand. Gray's been telling me for months about the wonderful girl he found in Europe. I've had letters since, oh, April."

The little schemer was thorough, you had to give him that. But no way would Allie benefit from Gray's machinations.

"That may be true, but it wasn't me. I've never been to Europe. And I can't tell you the story about the whatever, the porcupine and the doughnuts. I bet he never mentioned me by name."

Westfield pondered the leaves. "He didn't. Just that he'd fallen in love with a marvelous girl and wanted to arrange for me to meet her." He faced Liz. "You fit the description so well. I can't tell you how disappointed I am."

She felt a rush of fondness for the old man. “That’s sweet of you. But didn’t you find it odd that Gray wouldn’t tell you anything more?”

“No, I think he was afraid I’d run a background check on her, something ridiculous like that. And Gray does like surprises.”

“I’m sure he does. But you’ll have to talk to him about this girl. I’m only saying it isn’t me.”

“Then why come here pretending to be engaged?”

“That’s what I wanted to talk about. Gray seemed to think I needed an excuse to be in the house.” She ran her hand along the slats of the bench. Step two. “He hired me to take care of your computer problem. That’s what I do for a living. Computer forensics.” She pulled out the worn business card. Not very professional looking.

Westfield didn’t even glance at it. “You’ve been spying on me.”

“Not exactly.” Step three would have to be delayed. “That is, not at all. I haven’t gone into any of your files, your computer files. It’s pretty obvious what your neighbor has done. We call it a ‘cloak.’ I just need a little time to de-cloak it.”

“Why are you telling me this?”

An empty rowboat pulled at the line holding it to the dock. He bought the ‘cloak’ b.s., so maybe he didn’t know anything about computers. She might still have time to solve the problem before Bud’s arrival.

“There’s nothing sinister. Things were getting out of hand, and I don’t enjoy working for people who don’t realize I’m there.” While he digested that, she thought about some of her recent projects. “Not people I like, anyway. There’s enough deceit.” She gave him a meaningful glance, but he didn’t blink. “I finally told Gray if he didn’t let me talk to you, I’d leave.”

He seemed to realize at last that he was holding the business card.

“TekSekure. That’s who was recommended to me in the first place. I didn’t quite trust the source, so I never followed up.”

“We were recommended?”

“By Eric Owen.”

“That’s Allie’s stepfather, right?”

“Right. He and Helen haven’t been married long, and he didn’t want to upset her, but he’s sympathetic to my position. Or so he says.”

"Why would he take your side?"

"We go back a good long way. Professionally. And he met his wife through me. But, as I say, I couldn't quite trust his recommendation under the circumstances. Difficult to explain. I wonder how Gray found out."

"Let me guess. Owen worked at Morveus Industries, too."

Westfield's eyebrows drew together and for the first time he looked dangerous. "How do you know that name?"

Bad move. "Did he?"

"As a matter of fact, no. But my work there brought me into contact with him. You didn't answer my question. How did you know?"

"I told you. It's what I do."

"I see." He didn't sound convinced. "Well, I appreciate your telling me about Gray's efforts." He took her arm. "Shall we go to the library and see what you've found?"

She shrugged. "Not much, at this point, but I'd be happy to show you."

They started across the lawn. Not a soul was in sight. Even Liddell and the wheelbarrow were gone. Westfield gripped her arm in a way she found slightly threatening.

Two out of the three steps accomplished: no more engagement, and no more searching for lottery tickets without Westfield's knowledge. Still, she had the feeling she'd made shrewder decisions in her time.

▼ ▼ ▼

A sudden unpleasant thought caused Mike to run down the stairs. In the foyer, he nearly tripped over the butler.

"Liddell, great. Is there a gas station in town?"

"I fear it will be closed today, sir. Is there some way in which I might be of assistance?"

"I just remembered I need an oil change. For the car."

"Not a problem, sir. Mr. Westfield keeps a supply in the carriage house."

"Really?" Another piece of luck. "Thanks. I hope it's not inconvenient."

"What is that, sir?"

"Changing the oil for me."

"No, sir, I meant that you could change it yourself."

"Oh." There didn't seem to be a choice. "Well, if anyone wants me . . ."

"Dinner will be served at six-thirty. You will recall that gentlemen are encouraged to wear jacket and tie. I could arrange for a loan if you are in need. Cocktails will be available on the veranda an hour before."

"I'll be there. And I'm set for clothes." Another small victory.

"Your belongings have been moved to the Blue Room, sir. It was the only bedroom remaining. On the third floor, at the top of the stairs. I trust you will not find it too remote for your social obligations."

▼ ▼ ▼

Mike didn't feel comfortable with the BMW in the open, so he moved it into the carriage house. He felt a need for privacy, as if he were changing not oil but clothes. No need for a public display of mechanical ineptitude. He swung the big door shut. His parking effort had been less than perfect. A pair of bicycles stood dangerously close to the fender. He squeezed by, pushing them away from the paint job.

He had a momentary sense of embarking on a grand adventure, but it passed. Squatting by the passenger door, he shoved a plastic dish under the car like a bedpan. He slid across the floor after it, gripping the wrench. If all went well, he wouldn't have to spend a lot of time in the cramped space.

The plug was obvious, and he set to work loosening it. The pan was by his head. Smooth, smooth, smooth. He pushed air past his lips as he spun the last few turns. Dark oil shot out of the pan, surging across his hand. The wrench and the plug dropped into the plastic dish with a soft thunk-thunk. He stared at the hole, thinking unkind thoughts about automobiles. On his back, with his arm torqued around, he groped in the oily goo.

The carriage house door swung open and closed. He froze. From the sounds, there was only one person. He or she paced on the other side of the car. A click, the driver's door, and the chassis pressed against Mike's face. In momentary panic, he patted his pockets for the car keys. He could feel the oil on his fingers as he made contact with the cotton. Another click, the glove compartment. The metallic pop of the trunk release.

With every breath, his chest pushed against unyielding metal. He could feel his legs sticking out on the passenger side, like some sort of road kill. He tried to fold them under the car. Ruby slippers.

The chassis rose abruptly. The footsteps moved to the back of the car. He tried to recall the contents of the trunk: spare tire, jumper cables, fire hydrant, moose suit. Nothing to arouse suspicion. He'd forgotten to change the oil, not broken a law. He heard a slam, and a series of beeps. No one had any business in the BMW. With indignation and a vague sense of protecting Char's honor, he began to wriggle free when he heard Liz's voice.

"We need to talk."

He gripped the bottom of the car.

"No. I'm on my cell phone . . . As secure as it needs to be . . . Listen, will you? A close call, and some complications . . . Yes . . . Innocent bystanders and two bogeys with history at Morpheus . . . You heard me . . . No, but it's not your standard operation . . . I think you should stay away . . . Oh. How soon? . . . Great. Yeah, I'll try not to kill anyone before then . . . You know me, hardly a profile. Little Miss Nobody."

The rise and fall of her voice was nice, much nicer than her words.

"You've got problems? . . . Right . . . right . . . well, try the asynch volume card . . . Handshake conflicts, no kidding. Give me a minute."

Secret handshakes. That sounded suspiciously like the Colonel's crowd. Mike tried not to think about it. Morpheus. Sleep or drugs? Little Miss Nobody. A fragment of high school Latin surfaced. Nobody. Nemo.

His vision blurred. He realized he was holding his breath and had been for some time. No problem. Controlled, biathlon-style exhale. But his hand knocked the plastic dishpan, and the oil sloshed.

"I'm not sure . . . let's talk about it when you get here."

The carriage house door creaked open again, and closed, and he heard her cross the gravel drive. He slid from beneath the car and sat on the cool concrete floor. Normal breath crept back. His pants were covered in goop.

She hadn't quite shut the door, and daylight threw odd shadows across the shop area. In a daze, he retrieved a can of oil from the shelf. Liz was Nemo. Nemo was Liz. Oil glugged into the crankcase. And she was working with Donovan. Because they were after . . . the lottery ticket.

He slammed the hood closed and ran across the driveway. No sign of her. The front door to Briarwood stood open and he dashed through, delighted not to have to touch it.

▼ ▼ ▼

Liz strolled across the wide lawn. A moose costume in the trunk. Odd enough. The same for a fake fire hydrant. But both, that was weird. He must be planning something. She'd left the duplicate H-T disk on her dresser as a test. The original remained in her purse. If he really wanted it, he'd search the room. Last night's bedroom farce was too convenient to be an accident. Fine. This would give him a decent chance to steal the disk. Once he had it, he'd leave. Then she wouldn't be distracted, and she could concentrate on Westfield. Step three, a Morveus Industries confrontation, was in delay mode. In the library, he'd carried off the clueless routine, apparently satisfied with a few restored files, little more than sleight of hand. She hadn't learned anything new.

As she neared the oak tree on the back lawn, a movement caught her eye. Someone was hiding in its branches. She changed her direction to get a better angle and realized it was a girl. She stopped, because it was herself she saw, twenty years smaller and a thousand times more innocent, a little girl in a tree-filled park in Vermont. She sensed the moisture on her cheek. Time, time. She could never catch up to it. A rustling came from the oak.

"Who's there?" She raised her voice. "I can see you."

A face peeked through the leaves. Matt and Marsha's kid, Doris. Too old for climbing trees.

"What are you doing . . ." It was the very question she'd resented whenever grownups asked. Grownups. Long past that, surely. Another life. She thought of the Governor at Mother's robing ceremony, and his smoky breath. Deal with the present. If this nosey kid had been in the tree long, she could have overheard the conversation with Westfield.

"How's the view up there?"

"Okay." Doris scrunched her eyes. "You looking for your brother?"

"I don't have a brother."

"Get real. I was just with him."

"Believe me, I'm an only child."

"Then why'd he say you were his sister?"

"Who?"

Doris moved to another branch. "Mike."

"You've been talking to him." Liz felt her lip curl.

"So?"

"I'm not sure that's a good idea. And he's definitely not my brother."

"Is he your lover?"

"Certainly not." She felt her face grow warm. "That wasn't what I meant. I'm," she swallowed, "I'm engaged to Gray."

"You're lying."

"I'm not lying." Not about Mike, at any rate.

Doris twirled a plucked leaf between her fingers. "Then what do you care if I talk to him?"

"Look, I . . ."

"Don't think you have to be my friend. I know you don't like me."

"That's not true." Liz stopped herself before she could say, 'I hardly notice you're around.' She thrust her hands in her pockets. This girl was not a threat. "Do you like him?"

"Of course I do."

"Why?" The word hung in the air like an insult. "I mean, what do you like best?"

"He's nice to me. And funny."

"He is?" Good for him. "I don't suppose you know where he's gone?"

"That way." Doris pointed at the hedge maze. "Or was it over there?" She gestured toward the garage. "It doesn't much matter. Whichever way, he'd end up at the house. I mean, it has to be inside. That's the only logical answer."

"Wait." Liz lost sight of her in the leaves. "What has to be inside?"

"What everyone's looking for." The girl climbed higher. "It's made of paper. They wouldn't dare leave it outside."

"Yes. I suppose it could have been sealed in plastic."

The branches quivered. "And left outside? A ten million dollar lottery ticket? I'm sure."

"Oh." Liz swallowed her surprise. "Lottery ticket. How did you find out?"

"Mike told me. Mrs. Owen knows. She's full of hints."

"Oh. Mike did? And did he mention how he learned about it?"

"From Gray, duh. He's trying to find it for your future father-in-law."

"He who? Oh, I see. Gray hired Mike to find the lottery ticket?"

"Of course not." Doris moved out of sight. "They know each other from school. He's doing it as a friend."

"A friend. Right. This is where I came in." Liz rubbed her neck. All roads led to Mike's baloney. "I suppose I ought to help look."

"Don't worry about that. Mike will find it."

"Will he?"

"Sure." The only thing visible through the leaves was a grin. "He's smart."

"If you say so." Liz turned and walked across the lawn. Telling Gray about steps one and two ought to panic him pretty well. Smart. Mike, the master sleuth? The guy was a traveling train wreck. She headed for her room to see whether he'd managed to steal the disk.

▼ ▼ ▼

Mike crossed the foyer and reached the foot of the stairs. Gray was descending in a hurry.

"Oh, good. Good Lord. You look as if you've seen a something-or-other. And what's that muck? No, don't touch me. What is it?"

Mike held his hands away from himself. "We need to talk."

"We are. I saw your lips move."

"I meant in private."

Gray surveyed the room. "Oh, very well. Follow me. But stop with the Frankenstein imitation."

He ducked through a doorway beneath the main stairs. Mike lowered his arms and followed. He'd never noticed the door and had no idea where it led. Not another tunnel, he hoped.

It was a powder room with a mirror, in which he saw grease smudged across his face. He wiped at it and succeeded only in smearing it further.

"Okay." Gray closed the door. "Is this private enough? Or should I see that the toilet isn't bugged?" He made as if to look in the tank.

"That won't be necessary, thank you."

"Just stand still. Ordinarily I'd suggest a wash, but Mrs. L would have our heads if you touched her towels."

"I was changing the oil in the car."

"You don't say. I believe the idea is to put a bit of it into the engine."

"Very funny. Look, that's not important. I know who Nemo is."

"You said it was Donovan."

"He was the guy Nemo sent. Now I'm talking about the actual Nemo."

"Let me get this straight." Gray sat on the lid of the toilet. "Nemo is the brains behind the operation?"

"As far as I can tell."

"All right, who is he?"

"Not he. She. It's Liz."

Gray continued to stare, as if the translation hadn't caught up yet. "Liz? How can you say that?"

"I heard her."

"She told you she was Nemo?"

"Close enough. She was on her phone in the garage. I was . . . anyway, she didn't see me. I heard her talking to the Colonel."

"Sunglasses Colonel?"

"The same."

"You heard her talking. Saying what?"

"Not much I could understand." Mike put both hands together, figuring it was the best way to keep them out of trouble. "I think she's waiting for the Colonel to get here. She said she wouldn't do anything until then. But it seems to involve paratroopers."

"Sounds complicated." Gray turned on the tap and handed over a bar of soap. "So, who do we call? Police? FBI? Federal marshals?"

"Don't be ridiculous."

"I'm glad to hear you say that. Toss the soap in the wastebasket when you're done. I think you've got it wrong. Liz doesn't like Donovan."

"Well, naturally she'd act that way."

"But I was on my way to tell you, you were wrong about Donovan, too."

"Wrong?"

"Right. Didn't I tell you I'd work out a plan? I went down to the cottage, figuring with Donovan at the train station it would be a perfect time to do a spot of reconnaissance. Not to put too fine a point on it, he came back while I was there. Dashed bloody awkward, I can tell you. Then I remembered, what ho, it's my cottage. So I asked if he had a problem. He told me his colleague, this other archaeologist, had to take a later train. She'll be here this evening. Don't lean against that wall."

Mike's neat solution crumbled. "All of which sleuthing tells us what?"

"Nothing, perhaps. Not by itself. But," Gray raised an index finger, "there's more."

Mike sighed.

"Now," Gray continued, "don't get all snitty. Where do you suppose she's coming from, this colleague?"

"Washington?"

"No, you dope. It's Maryland. Eastern Maryland."

"So?"

"So, she's there with her family."

Footsteps sounded above their heads as someone descended the stairs.

"That doesn't mean anything." Mike thought back to the Colonel's deserted office. "She could have a family. Why shouldn't they be in Maryland?"

"You're not thinking." Gray wagged a finger in his face. "Was the person you met, the one with the maps, on her way to a weekend at the beach?"

Mike scowled. There was more, a detail that didn't fit. His capacity for rational thought seemed to have been affected by something. The beard, maybe.

"Admit it," said Gray, "you were wrong about Donovan."

"Not so fast. We don't know for sure where this colleague is coming from. You're taking Donovan's word for it."

"And what's wrong with his word?"

"Come on, he might have said anything. After all . . ."

"After all, what?"

That was the problem. Donovan could be a good guy posing as a bad guy, or the reverse. The mental course corrections were making Mike's head spin. "We need to talk to Donovan."

"We do?"

"It's the only way to find out what's going on. He's told me some things about himself. And Liz. Oh, you might as well know, if you can keep it a secret. You're in no danger. Nothing links you with Liz."

"Other than our supposed engagement?"

"Fair point. You can break it, but it's all the more reason to see Donovan."

"Let me see if I understand. This is the same Donovan you think is the Colonel's friend."

"So, I was wrong." He wasn't ashamed to admit it. You had to let go of theories that didn't work. Kind of like relationships. Huh. He'd never thought of it that way before.

"Donovan's with the Department of Justice. I didn't know whether to believe it, but now I do. They have Liz under surveillance." Mike lowered his voice. "It has something to do with the company she works for, TekSekure. And that's why I need to let Donovan know about this connection between her and the Colonel."

"Department of Justice?" Gray's eyes widened. He said something under his breath. Mike could have sworn it was, "Bad news."

▼ ▼ ▼

Liz heard someone call her name as she crossed the terrace behind the house. Mrs. Liddell's face appeared at a kitchen window; she lifted her hand and a yellow bird flew from it and perched on the trellis.

"Come in, dear, won't you? We have something to discuss."

A perfect, unexpected opportunity to get information about Gray. The kitchen fairly burst with the smell of freshly-baked chocolate cake.

"Have a seat, dear. Try some of this."

Liz wasn't hungry but didn't want to give offense. "Perhaps a tiny piece." Calories could be sacrificed for the sake of information. She'd go on a long run to make up for it.

The cook flashed an odd smile. "Try not to slump. It's bad for posture."

Liz sat straighter, knowing she should resent being made to feel like such a little girl. But there was something almost protective in the fussing that made it hard for her to stay annoyed.

Mrs. Liddell cut a slice of cake and put it on a plate, along with a fork. "Now." She carried it to the table. "What have you been wanting to ask?"

Liz picked up the fork, feeling that positions had been reversed while she wasn't looking. "Gray. Gray in Europe."

"Oh, no no. If you ask my advice, and I see you haven't, you're posing questions about the wrong young man altogether."

"I don't know what you're saying." Liz gripped the edge of the table, as if it might otherwise float away.

"You do." The cook's eyes sparkled. "You know exactly what I'm saying. It's my meaning that troubles you. And I always say what I mean."

Liz felt terribly small and unclever. Through the kitchen window, she watched a cloud drift over the lake. She shook her head to clear the cobwebs.

"Really, Mrs. Liddell. It's important I know . . ."

"It's important you listen. Not with your ears. With that." A bony finger shot out, and she felt a jab above her heart. "No need to be formal. Call me Mrs. L. Everyone does."

"All right. This is very good cake. And thank you for the advice. But all I'm trying to do is get an idea of what's going on."

Mrs. L smoothed her apron. "Look to the beam in your own eye, child. The beam in your own."

Liz flicked a hand in front of her face. "Poof. It's gone." She almost wished Bud would show. It would be nice to have one stable, predictable neurosis in this random madness. She snapped her fingers. "I hear you're good with magic tricks. Could you make my boss disappear?"

"Oh, no dear, no no no. I don't do the disappearances. That's another department. I'm only responsible for the appearances. Keeping up appearances, as it were."

"Oh, my." Liz put down her fork. "You know something, don't you?"

"Heavens yes, dear. Lots of things, and I'm here to help you learn them."

▼ ▼ ▼

Mr. Westfield held a vase of flowers. He stared as Mike and Gray came out of the bathroom. "Gentlemen. Have you been up to something?"

"Nothing, Dad. Mike picked up some grime changing the oil in his car. I showed him where to wash."

At the back of the house, the telephone rang.

"You haven't done a terribly good job of it, I'm afraid."

"We were just saying the same thing, weren't we? You should probably try again in your room."

"About that." Mike stared at his hands. "Are you sure it's all right for me to stay another night?"

Mr. Westfield put down his flowers. "Of course, of course. We had you in the Orchid Room, didn't we? Yes, we've moved you to the third floor, if you don't mind the extra flight."

"No problem." Mike gulped. "Thanks so much."

"Good, good. Ah, Liddell, there you are."

"Sir." The butler's gaze swept across Mike. "There is a telephone call."

"Is there? Who?"

A slight hesitation. Someone important, evidently. "A Mr. Chamberlain, sir. He identifies himself as an attorney."

Mike's knees were giving way. Bad. It could only be bad.

Mr. Westfield pursed his lips. "Chamberlain? I wonder what he wants."

"He gave the name of Charles Chamberlain, sir. Shall I take a message?"

"No, no, I'll pick it up in the library. Transfer it to my private line, would you?" He strode through the living room, and Liddell headed for the kitchen.

"Gray." Mike needed to sit. He didn't dare touch the furniture.

"Mmm?"

"The guy on the phone. You heard of him?"

Gray shook his head. "You know what I know."

"I'm sorry to say I know a bit more. It's Char's father."

"Really?" Gray brightened. "What do you suppose he's after?"

"I can't believe he tracked me . . . you don't think your father would say anything about me that's, well, damaging?"

"I shouldn't think this call's about you in the first place. I mean, you haven't done anything the fellow would be worried about, have you?"

"Not really. I blew an interview at his firm. Char wasn't happy, but I wouldn't think her father . . . oh." The Westfield file on Kathy Laurence's desk.

"What?"

"This relative of yours we've been waiting for. Cousin Jake. Is he by any chance our age?"

"Jake? Lord, no. Old as the hills."

Mike pressed a hand to his forehead and was rewarded with another oily sensation.

"Bald? Wears a monocle?"

"Yes, that's it. Are you acquainted?"

"We, um, met. In Chamberlain's office."

"Maybe that's why he's late getting here. He mentioned something to Dad about a wonderful surprise, and a change in his will. We've been hopeful."

"A change in the will? At his lawyer's?"

'There's a man choking at reception.' That was what the secretary had said. 'There's a man choking . . .' Mike smeared oil down his face.

"I need to tell you something."

Mr. Westfield reappeared, looking pale.

"Dad." Gray took a step toward him. "What's wrong?"

"Cousin Jake died in his lawyer's office on Friday morning. There was some confusion about the next of kin."

Mike lost his balance and had to support himself against the wall.

"What a shame," said Gray. "Had he changed the will?"

"Gray!" Some of the color came back to his father's face.

"Well, it's not like we're going to hurt his feelings now." Gray turned to Mike and said, in a stage whisper, "Bags of money."

"That wasn't the most pressing issue," said Mr. Westfield. "Such a shock. I didn't think to ask."

From outside came the sound of a car slowing on the gravel drive.

"You see," Gray said, "he wasn't calling about you."

Mike heard himself ask in a squeaky voice, "How did Jake die?"

"A heart attack in the lobby of the firm. They think he may have choked."

Mike put a hand to his throat. "How?" He was pretty sure elastic bands didn't pick up fingerprints. If they did, maybe coffee would remove them.

"The lawyer didn't say."

Loud chimes rang. The police. Mike searched for a hiding place.

Mr. Westfield reached for the front door, but Liddell hurried from the kitchen. "Allow me, sir."

On the threshold stood a large man in an expensive suit. A very expensive suit. His face was all too familiar. Char kept an eight-by-ten in her living room: herself with her boss, Senator D'Onofrio. He was bigger in person than Mike remembered. The part of the doorway that wasn't housing his shoulders was filled with his toothy smile as he extended a long arm toward Westfield.

"How you been, Bart?"

"Steve." Mr. Westfield shook his hand. "Come in, come in. You remember Gray, of course?"

"Certainly."

Gray stepped forward, mountain to Mohammed. "How are you, sir?" No messing around with British accents now.

"And this is a friend of Gray's. Mike–"

"Excuse me." Mike finished painting his face with oil. "Just came from the garage. Think I'll take a shower."

He ran up the stairs, reeling, trying not to brush against the wallpaper. Shower. What good would that be? There wasn't enough water in Virginia to wash away the mess he'd landed in.

▼ ▼ ▼

Voices drifted into the kitchen. Liz strained to hear the words, trying not to make her listening obvious. Westfield was doing most of the talking, but there was a new voice, a deep one. And Mike's. Him again. Mrs. L fanned a deck of playing cards.

"Do choose. Just one. You might learn something."

Feeling that she had no option, Liz drew from the middle. Joker.

"Heavens." Mrs. L winked. "How did he get in here?"

"Just my luck." Liz forced herself to stand. "You know, I might take your advice after all. There's someone I need to talk to."

She left the kitchen, feeling better for having made the decision.

▼ ▼ ▼

The water pressure on the third floor was almost non-existent. Mike stood in the shower and watched the stream of soapy motor oil, looking like weak cappuccino, spiral down the drain. His memory wouldn't leave the reception area at Torrey, Hart & Bellin, and a rubber band splashing into a mug. He touched his throat. Killer. Murderer. Detective Fry probably had a warrant.

There must have been some point at which he could have avoided the whole situation. Cousin Jake wouldn't have died if he hadn't choked. The elastic wouldn't have been in his coffee if Mike hadn't been wearing felt bags. He'd have remembered dress socks if he'd been on time for the interview. He'd have been on time if he hadn't been arrested. There'd have been no arrest if he'd stayed on the trail by the Tidal Basin. He wouldn't have left the path if Donovan hadn't tried to photograph Liz.

Donovan's fault. Much more comforting. Or Char's, for skating at dawn. Come to think of it, if the detective hadn't been lazy, Mike wouldn't even have been released from jail. He'd never have seen Jake. Detective Fry should throw himself in jail . . . maybe.

He stuck his face under the water and let the drops trickle on him, hardly enough in aggregate to be called a shower. More a Chinese water torture. Punishment before trial. He ran the soap under his nose and was rewarded with a perky freshness that made him think of a television ad. Halloran, that was an Irish name. Gray had to be right. Liz wasn't a friend of Nemo's. She was a good person. He owed her an apology for even thinking it.

Water, the universal something. Joint? Solvent. Water as dissolver. Maybe if a guy stood under a shower long enough it would dissolve him, wash him free of the taint of murder, wash him down the drain. He wouldn't have to explain to his friend that he'd done the family out of a fortune by killing off a distant relative at a job interview he didn't want in the first place.

His eyes opened. Or was there a chance for redemption? He twisted the knob, putting the sickly flow out of its misery. There was a chance. Right in the house, somewhere. All he had to do was find the lottery ticket. The water dripped from him. He stepped out, wrapped a towel around himself, and strode into the bedroom. The sense of purpose felt strange and heady. The Blue Room had a writing desk with stationery and a supply of pens. An apology, a fresh start. But he'd written no more than her name on the envelope when a knock sounded.

"Are you decent?"

He turned the envelope over and grabbed a bathrobe. Soft and thick, the sort swank hotels dared guests to steal.

"Come in."

Gray pushed the door open. The moment of confession: I'm sorry, I did you out of your inheritance. But Gray spoke first.

"That was rather abrupt. The man is a U.S. Senator."

"I am painfully aware of that."

"Bit rude to dash upstairs, though, don't you think? Left Dad with a spot of explaining."

"I'm sorry, but he's Char's boss. Char's boss, Gray. I didn't know what else to do. He could have recognized me."

"All right, so he can identify you."

"Yeah, that's great. Next week he can tell Char what a swell time he had in the country where her boyfriend was yukking it up instead of staying in the city having her car serviced, the way he said he would."

"Then maybe she'd break up with you and put you out of your misery."

"That's not how I want it to happen. She has to decide we're not right for each other. I don't want her to simply give up on me."

"Tell me honestly." Gray sat at the writing table. "What did you get in exchange when you gave up the brain?"

"The point is, I said I'd do it. And I didn't."

Gray flicked at the overturned envelope. "Maybe you should go back to the beard."

"I can't go around pulling it on or off, depending on which person I thought I'd run into next. Listen, there's something I have to tell you."

"Is it about the lottery ticket? Because that's all I want to hear about. Time runs out tomorrow."

"Look, you're just going to have to figure out where in the house you'd put something small and valuable."

"In the safe, ordinarily."

Mike stopped with one leg in his pants. "Say that again."

"The safe. Good heavens. A safe place."

"There's one in the house?"

"We don't use the silly thing. The lock doesn't work."

"Well, where is it?"

But Gray was already pounding down the stairs. Mike pulled on his pants and hustled to catch up. It was a dead heat across the living room. Gray pushed open the door to the library and stopped. Mike ran into him.

Behind the desk stood two people, motionless. Liz was recognizable, even from behind. Agent Donovan had his hands on her shoulders in a grasp that didn't look like any kind of arrest technique Mike had ever heard of. What was that all about?

For a moment, no one said anything. Then Donovan gave Liz a look that seemed quite meaningful and left.

She smoothed her blouse. "I thought I told you . . ."

Mike raised a finger to his lips. Gray dragged an armchair to the wall that held the moose head. He stood on the chair and tugged at the antlers. They swung to one side on hinges, exposing the safe.

"The combination hasn't worked in years." He stood on tiptoe to reach in. When his hand came out, it clutched a white envelope.

Liz stood behind the desk, looking like . . . someone waiting, maybe. Her face had been so close to Donovan's.

Mike guarded the entrance. "Anything else?"

Gray ran his hand inside the safe. "That's it."

He hopped down. The three of them converged as Gray tore open the envelope and withdrew two sheets of paper. Clearly, neither was a lottery ticket.

"Well?" said Mike.

Gray pushed his glasses along the bridge of his nose. "It says, 'Not nearly warm enough.' " He looked at the back. "That's it. Some help."

Mike took it from him. "And the other?"

"Oh, great. This is perfect." Gray slumped into a chair and dropped the paper to the carpet. "Just your thing. Some kind of puzzle."

—10—

The pace, Liz noticed, had picked up a notch or two. Something had happened to Mike. In his eyes was an intensity, a focus that she hadn't seen before. Perhaps she'd underestimated him. She wished she'd pushed Roger away sooner. Gray retrieved the second sheet of paper and tossed it onto the desk. She tried to read it upside down.

Mike snatched at the pages. "Not a good idea."

"What?" She made herself stare at the spot where the paper had been, rather than meet his gaze. "What are you two playing at?"

He wagged a finger at her. "I know who you are . . . Nemo."

"Wait a minute," said Gray. "I thought you decided she wasn't."

"Nemo, I said."

"Is that supposed to mean something?" She didn't know why he'd raised Ariel's old code name. She didn't care for his taking the upper hand. And she flat out hated not knowing what was going on.

"Knock it off," he said. "I know about the Colonel."

"That puts you ahead of me. I don't have the faintest idea what you're saying." She turned to Gray. "If that paper has anything to do with what I'm looking for, you'd better let me see it."

Mike's eyes became shifty. "What you're looking for?"

Her nails dug into her palms. She gestured toward Gray with her head. "Go on, tell him."

Gray kicked at the carpet. "It's . . . it's true. That is to say, we, or rather I, sort of hired her."

"Hired her? For what?" Mike held the paper but moved behind a chair.

"To get some information from the computer. It's not my fault. You told me you didn't know how to work the blasted machines."

"You could have mentioned this at the beginning."

Gray seemed to search for the right answer. "I thought it would be safer. Need-to-know basis. That sort of stuff."

"What's she looking for?"

Liz didn't care to hear him speak of her as if she weren't present.

"The same thing we are." Gray pointed. "A clue to the lottery ticket."

"And now we have one," she said. "Can we see what it says?"

Mike placed the paper on his side of the desk, oriented toward her. She studied the neat typing.

a song from the key of F

six by three right by two:

RRG

the very end(s)
in the very beginning

BSX2, on the nose

dig deep

She reached across and turned the paper over. Blank.

"B.S." Gray poked at the page. "That's the only part I understand."

Liz frowned. Mike circled the desk and looked over her shoulder. His breath on her neck was distracting. She pulled away before she had to figure out why.

"Six by three right by two." Gray held his hands a yard apart. "Coffinish dimensions. I suppose we've got to dig in a graveyard."

Mike repeated the clue aloud, as if that might clarify it. It irritated Liz to see him smile.

"What, you've figured it out?"

"Not yet. I just like puzzles. Still haven't solved the one you gave me."

Gray picked up a golf club and took a practice swing. "Pity, I don't read music. Do either of you?"

"What?" said Liz.

He swung again. "Key of F. Don't know what it signifies, musically."

"For goodness' sake, it's a code. It's not about real music."

He brightened. "There's a relief. Still, nice to know where to dig. Other than deep."

"No, no. Look." Mike jabbed at the paper. "That tells us where we finish. It's the starting place we need." He crossed to the window. "Somewhere out there, maybe, on the property. It reads like a treasure hunt."

"Fine." Liz was happy to let them go down that route. "You two better run along before it gets dark."

"Good idea." Gray headed for the door. "Wait. What about you?"

She waved a hand in a show of surrender. "I'm no good at treasure hunts. Never mind me. I'll stay here and work on this." She tapped the monitor.

"But there's no need to. We've found the clue."

"A clue. It didn't take computer skill to look in an open safe. I think there's more. I still haven't found whatever she's hidden in the computer."

"Suit yourself. Shall we go, Mikey?"

"Don't call me that."

"You know," Gray said, "you two are just made for each other."

Liz stared hard at the paper. "You want a copy of this?"

"That's okay." Without looking, Mike repeated it verbatim. He gave her a genuine smile. "I'll just run up and grab my shoes." He stepped past the model rockets.

Gray found a pen on the desk. "I'll have a copy, if you don't mind. We're not all as clever as Mike." He scribbled it down. "Cheers." He left.

Not all as clever as Mike. She felt cut adrift in a small boat.

▼ ▼ ▼

Liz blinked out of her trance. Someone was bound to drop by soon to steer the guests toward the inebriation ceremony, and she'd have to make complicated excuses to avoid it.

Gray had come dangerously close with his comment about music. She was glad they'd accepted her suggestion that the clue wasn't about that. They'd missed the natural relationship between music and numbers. So quick to rush off with their spades, they hadn't thought to sit down and work out the puzzle logically. Music and numbers. Numbers and music . . .

In the beginning, her feet had barely reached the pedals of Mr. Plecque's enormous Baldwin, but her hands were the problem, ten fingers that wanted to act as a group, to be doing the same task and not ten different things at once. As she'd grown into the piano and the months before recital had shortened to weeks, and days, Mr. Plecque had intoned over her shoulder as she wrestled with Beethoven, 'The sound, it could be so much better if we did not use our fists, no?'

Liz dragged her right hand across the keyboard, leaving a smattering of letters on the screen: PIOUYTFDSZ. It was the way she was beginning to feel.

She could probably explain each individual segment of the message, but what the hell did they mean mashed together? She hit keys at random. There was no sense forcing it. Music 232, freshman year, Professor Klotz: 'I suppose one could discover most anything one wanted, Miss Halloran, were one to analyze long enough.'

DIG DEEP. She leaned her forehead against the monitor, blurring the meaningless letters. For all the piano lessons, for all the music theory and all the math, she'd succeeded only in analyzing herself into a logical hole.

Her breath fogged a portion of the screen. She didn't want to acknowledge that he might solve the puzzle first.

▼ ▼ ▼

Gray lugged a couple of shovels from the shed. "Where should we–"

"Wait." Mike held up a hand. "Mark Hefy often goofs."

"Excuse me?"

"Mark Hefy often goofs."

"And who the devil is he?"

"I was hoping you would know."

"Of course I don't. Where did you hear of this person?"

"No, it's an anagram of 'A song from the key of F.' "

"It is, is it?" Gray held out a shovel.

"Look, it won't do us any good to start digging until we've narrowed the target area. It's a big lawn."

"Yes, and I don't see how your chum Mark what's-his-face will help find it. Besides, what makes you sure it's an anagram?" The trees that marked the property line rustled in the light wind.

"I didn't say I was sure. It's just an odd way to phrase it, don't you think? 'Song from the key of F.' Normally you'd talk about a song being 'in' a key."

"But you said it wasn't a musical clue."

"She said that, although I agree. And it's a good thing. I'm hopeless with music." The smell of fertilizer brought back unpleasant memories.

Gray swung his shovel. "Maybe we're supposed to find this key and then follow the directions."

Mike stared at the horizon. "You could have told me you'd hired her. She must think I'm the biggest jerk."

"If she does, would you care?"

Yes, thought Mike, but he didn't dare say it.

"In any case, I'm sorry. One has to diversify risk. I didn't think it was important you knew. I mean, was it?"

"Well, maybe I overreacted."

"Good." Gray clapped his hands. "I tell you what. Let's try things my way. First word to come into your head. Where's an F with a key?"

Mike closed his eyes. "Ferrari."

"Haven't got one, more's the pity."

"Fridge."

"Please."

He considered. "Frog feet on sky of ham."

"Would you knock it off with the bloody anagrams?"

Mike squinted toward the sun, downward bound, hours leaking away. "It's nearly five-thirty. Your dad wanted us at the house. Cocktails, or something."

"Shh." Gray mimed taking a key from his pocket, inserting it in a lock, and turning.

They shouted at each other. "Front door!"

Gray led the charge across the lawn. At the corner of the carriage house, he stopped abruptly and Mike caught up. He peeked over Gray's shoulder. Doris' parents elbowed each other on their way into the house.

"Let's make sure they're not spying on us. What's the next part?"

"It's 'six by three right by two.'" Mike wondered what Liz was doing with the computer.

"Directions."

"Apparently. Eighteen steps, turn right, and twelve more."

"Sounds easy."

"Unless it's six plus three, which would be nine, and then eight. Or nine then two. I hate math."

Matt and Marsha showed no sign of returning. Gray hurried forward, carrying his shovel. Mike watched him square his shoulders and march across the drive. The eighteenth step put him into the fountain. Undeterred, he made a ninety-degree course correction and executed twelve more paces. He stood now almost precisely where Char's car had been parked.

"I don't know. The ground doesn't look as if anything's buried there."

Gray swept away the gravel. "You're right. Let's try the other direction."

The results were similar: an undisturbed patch of driveway.

"Bother. We must be missing something. Maybe it's the 'song' part. Let's brainstorm. Can you think of a song with six in it?"

"A song with a six. There's *Now We Are Six.*"

"That's not a song."

"This is like a game show. Oh. 'Sixteen Candles.'"

Gray took a moment to mumble his way through the lyrics. "Doesn't mean a thing. Anyhow, that's not six. Give me another."

"You're pushing it. Wait, I've got it. 'Sing a Song of Sixpence.'"

Gray hummed the tune. "Right. Right. A bunch of birds, aren't there, four-and-twenty blackbirds?"

"So?"

"So, 'four' starts with an F. And twenty-four is six times four. I see, we're meant to take four times the number of paces."

"Nice brainstorm. Let me know when I need an umbrella. That would put you in the woods."

"Perfect. Where better to bury treasure?" Gray started to pace.

"This feels wrong. We got off track. What would the 'RRG' be?"

"The what?"

"The next part. 'RRG.' "

"Search me." Gray went back to his pacing. "Railroad grade? Real rock gravel?" He vanished into the trees amidst sounds of thrashing. Mike tried not to think of Hugo. Then he couldn't stop thinking of Liz.

Red Rose Garden. He hustled into the back yard. In the center of the garden was that odd, keyhole-shaped space. The flower key. THE KEY OF F. He faced the roses. A song from the flower key. *The Garden Song,* sung by a frog puppet. 'Inch by inch, row by row . . .' Inches. Inches instead of paces.

Eighteen inches was easy to approximate, and twelve to the right. He had to steady his hands. BSX2. ON THE NOSE. The answer eluded him. He scanned the lawn to make sure he wasn't being watched. Gray was probably searching every tree in the woods. Mike tore into the flower bed, dirt flying past his arms. DIG DEEP. He went down a foot and a half before conceding defeat in the hardpan. Defeat. Deduct.

X2. On a hunch, he tried doubling the measurements. Another three minutes, another hole. Gray came down the garden path. "Nothing doing in the woods, I'm afraid. But Donovan's back with that assistant he's been spouting on about. Much younger than you described your Colonel, so there's an end to that worry."

Mike stared glumly at the two holes. Either his mind wasn't as sharp in the country, or the Colonel's messages were easier to decode than this.

"I mean," Gray said, "one could describe her as serious looking, but I wouldn't go so far as to say military. You might watch what you do to Dad's roses. What makes you think . . . oh." He stepped into the key. "Jolly good. Found anything?"

Mike lifted a handful of dirt and let it trickle through his fingers.

"Pity. I've always rather liked this spot. A gnome used to stand here." Mike began an assault on another patch of dirt. "Dad called him Sidney. Wonder what's become of him."

"Wait a minute. What if 'BS' is shorthand for 'backwards?' " Mike stepped off the original distance, but in the opposite direction. "Times two." He repeated the exercise. Two feet down, the spade clinked against something. He bent to brush away the dirt. "Glass. It's a glass jar."

"Yes? Yes? Anything in it?"

"A piece of paper."

"The ticket?"

He pulled the jar from the soil. "A note. Hasn't been buried long." He unscrewed the cap and inverted the jar. The message was brief and Mike read it aloud. "A worthy effort, Barton. But a bit too literal. I was thinking more along Fulton County lines."

"Hell." He handed the note to Gray. "Wrong idea. And she knew it. She anticipated this."

"Where's Fulton County? Not around here."

"There's one in Georgia. Atlanta." Not that he could link Atlanta with A SONG FROM THE KEY OF F.

Guests would soon gather for drinks on the terrace. Mike began to fill in the holes. "Does Briarwood have a cellar? For wine, that kind of thing?"

"No." Gray stuffed the note into his pocket. "Perhaps we've taken the wrong end of the stick. You did say the important thing is the starting place."

Mike rolled the empty jar between his palms.

Gray shrugged. "We keep beginning with this silly song of F. Maybe we're meant to be at the other end."

" 'Dig deep.' "

"Right."

"Listen to me. 'Dig deep.' "

Gray looked peevish. "What's your point?"

" 'Dig,' " Mike said. " 'Deep.' "

"We agree on that."

"For crying out loud, Gray. It's the dig."

"I told you, it can't be. It wasn't exposed until recently."

"Not that end, the other. You start from the library, where Allison's mother left the note." Except, not today. Liz was in the library. A different route to the same end. He headed for the mouth of the tunnel.

▼ ▼ ▼

Liz made a face at the monitor. The ultimate clue to the ticket should be in the computer. Reasonable, therefore, to assume that the pre-clue gave the directions for getting into the computer. She studied the note again, and suddenly the first part was obvious. A SONG FROM THE KEY OF F. That had to be the F: drive. Not a deleted file, but something purloined, visible on the system. She executed a few keystrokes. Sure enough, the directory for the F: drive held an assortment of documents.

SIX BY THREE RIGHT BY TWO. That could be anything. Or could it? She scanned the file names, looking for 63, or 62, or both. Nothing. Six divided by three, and by two? That would be 2 and 3. She ran down the list of files again. Come on, come on. Show me a 2-3. Just one 2-3. One 2-3. Waltz time. A fragment of memory: balanced in stockings on Daddy's feet, age eight, arms up, twirling around the kitchen, wanting to dance as well as he could . . .

Hello. There was, in fact, a document last revised on 06-23, a short letter. No signature block, only brief text:

> BARTON, I HAVE TO ADMIT I DIDN'T THINK YOU'D GET THIS FAR. WELL DONE. ALTHOUGH I SUSPECT YOU'VE HAD A BIT OF HELP. DID I GIVE YOU A HINT? IS THAT CHEATING? WELL, NOT MUCH. THIS ISN'T THE END OF THE ROAD. LET'S SEE. WHERE CAN I POSSIBLY WANT YOU TO GO NEXT? OH MY. I SHOULD HAVE WARNED YOU. REMEMBER WHAT ALWAYS HAPPENED TO THAT NICE MR. PHELPS?

Shit. Liz stopped reading and hit 'Print Screen' as the letters dissolved on the monitor. A scraping sound came from the bookcase. The printer whirred and spat out the page. Useless. The text was illegible, mere fragments of letters. She crumpled the sheet. A new message appeared:

> VERY GOOD, BARTON. DON'T PANIC. NOTHING ESSENTIAL. I WANTED TO SEE WHETHER YOU STILL HAD STARS IN YOUR EYES.

Liz felt the hair on her neck rise. Advanced interactivity. The noise below the bookcase had stopped. She moved closer to the screen. The text blipped out, replaced by a new message. She didn't hesitate before printing.

> -DO SAVE THIS ONE, LOVE, OR MEMORIZE IT.
> SHUT THE DOOR AND COUNT AGAIN;
> STOP BEFORE THE BIG FAT H.
> BOXCARS ROLLING THROUGH THE TOWN;
> WHAT GOES UP WILL BRING YOU DOWN.
>
> THIS WILL HAVE TO BE YOUR LAST HINT. IT MIGHT BE IMPORTANT.
> OR NOTHING NEW. YOU'LL HAVE TO DO THE BEST YOU CAN.
> -SEE YOU WHEN I DO. FOR RICHER, OR FOR POORER.

While the paper fed through the machine, Liz tossed the other away, glad to be on the right track at last. There was enough clear space on the desk to fit the single sheet. She studied the half-poem, running her finger along each line. Again. And again. Her finger kept stopping on the non-rhyming 'H.'

"Lizzo!" The voice, behind her, was a thunderclap.

She jumped. "Don't do that to me, Bud." She draped a forearm across the paper. "What are you doing here?"

He closed the French doors. "I said I was coming down. Thought I'd drop by, see my friend Bart."

"What?" She covered her surprise by folding the paper and putting it in her pocket. "Well, nice of you to tell me that at the start."

"I didn't want you to get the wrong idea."

"That you were pulling me off Hillton-Tanner, you mean."

"Why would I do that?"

"I'm not sure. But when I saw these . . ." She searched the top of the desk. "They're gone. H-T financial files. Maybe you can explain what Westfield is doing with them."

"Nope. I can't."

"And you don't care."

"Of course I care." He patted the monitor. "Let's take this talk outside."

How unbelievably careless, not to have searched for bugs. She tried to remember whether she'd said anything important in the library. Damn. She followed Bud onto the terrace. Across the lake, the sun fired up streaky clouds. The heat of the day hadn't quite seeped into evening and yet she felt a trickle of sweat on her forehead.

"Forget H-T." Bud lowered himself into a rattan chair. "That game's over."

She stopped in the midst of tucking her hair back. "Since when?"

"Since Friday. The guy figured out we were after him. Good work."

She felt as if he'd slapped her. "I could have told them what the problem was if you'd let me stay."

"Forget it. Everyone's happy at H-T. The problem's gone. They didn't hire us to get their money back, just work out what was up."

She hated the chain on his wrist. She hated his California tan. Even the silence irritated her.

Flowering vines snaked their way up the trellis that shaded the terrace. She leaned against it. "I guess you were aware of Westfield's Morveus Industries connection."

He gave her a long look. "Yes."

"And Mrs. Owen, next door?"

"Of course, I . . . how do you know about her?"

Liz straightened. "I went to school with her daughter."

He rose and started pacing.

She hated that, too. "This smells wrong, Bud."

"It's nothing."

"You know what Morveus is. The place is a goddam . . ."

"I know, I know."

She grabbed his shirt. "A goddam CIA front."

"Was." He brushed her hand away. "It went out of business years ago."

"What's your point?"

"My point is, people retire. Circumstances change. Life goes on."

"Very philosophical." She snapped a flower off the vine. "You've got me poking at a situation I don't understand, I'm finding Casper the Spook all over the place, and, guess what, I don't like it."

"It's your job. You don't have to like it. Now, don't get all huffy, I didn't mean it that way. I'm telling you, the project we've been hired for, it has nothing to do with Morveus. Trust me."

"Take a number," said Liz.

"What's that supposed to mean?"

"It means I don't know that there's a person here I can trust. Everyone's either dishonest or crazy." Or Mike, whom she didn't know how to classify.

Liddell appeared at the end of the terrace. "Miss Halloran. Sir. Ah, good to see you, sir. Would you care for something?"

"Scotch."

"Miss?"

"Lemonade, if you have it."

He nodded and retreated.

Bud rolled his eyes. "I bet you even suspect the butler."

"Ha." It would be easy for Liddell to slip a postcard under a plate.

"Who, then?"

"Roger Donovan's here. The big mouth I told you about last winter. And another one who's been following me around. Mike Archer."

"Archer? Archer?" Bud searched the sky. "I wouldn't worry about him. The guy's a straight arrow. Straight arrow, get it?"

AN ARROW NEEDS A BEAU.

As she stormed across the terrace, Bud's voice rose. "What? What did I say? For crying out loud, it was a joke. I don't even know the guy. Come back."

Think clearly. If Ariel knew about Mike, he knew other things. Don't run away, find out. She put her head against the trellis. It was a mistake to let Bud see he'd found a way under her skin. She'd made too many mistakes lately. They were bound to catch up.

▼ ▼ ▼

One thing the Blue Room had going for it was a private bath. Mike stood at the sink, gouging his fingernails into a bar of soap. A solid hour of scraping, poking and digging, with nothing to show but dirty hands.

Maybe Liz had better luck with the computer. He wiped his hands on a towel. Not that she'd tell. 'Run along,' she'd said, as if they bored her. He opened the closet door. Next to his sport coat, Liddell had hung Morty. The moose head was on a shelf above. It produced an unsettling decapitation effect.

Liz would be interested in the jar. No she wouldn't. Still, he wanted to let her know he'd found it. Kind of annoying, solving a puzzle only to be told you'd got it wrong. SONG FROM THE KEY OF F. F you. Dinner first.

He poked through his suitcase. The wet clothes were dry again, and the other ones were oily. Strange, that Liddell knew where to look for Morty. Uncle Ric's postcard from Brazil lay on the bottom of the suitcase. 'We've eaten some terrific food . . .' Funny way to start a postcard, especially from a guy who found culinary excitement in ketchup and mustard on a hot dog. Mike looked at the picture again, and the text. With a shrug, he tossed the card onto the bed.

The bed was occupied. In the center of the spread sat a shoebox, lid on. It had been placed carefully, square to the sides. There was no ticking sound. No movement. No blood seeping from the corners.

Lighten up. Boxes did appear in houses from time to time. Another present from Liddell, no doubt. He lifted it. Heavier than a black widow spider. More unwieldy than a vial of nitro. Slowly, he removed the lid. Nothing but a pair of beat-up sneakers. Last seen in the Colonel's office, left there by a panicked interviewee.

He dropped the box and backed away. No, she wasn't expecting him at Briarwood. But she could have tracked him there. He grabbed his jacket and tie. Downstairs it would be safer. Much safer.

▼ ▼ ▼

The floor-length drapes had been gathered back, the windows opened to the warm evening. Seated on the ottoman in front of her dressing table, Liz caught the scent of honeysuckle from outside the window.

Cocktails on the veranda. What a delicious, civilized tradition. She had space at home for a veranda. A small veranda. Or a very small porch. She ran her fingers over the silken fabric of the ottoman. Briarwood was making her think stupid thoughts.

In the mirror, she saw she'd left the bedroom door ajar. She stared at the image, wondering if it might shut itself through the force of her will. And there was the bed, where he'd been. In the darkness. It had to be the disk he'd been after. Gone now, as she'd expected. There was nothing else he'd want.

She imagined the disapproving judicial voice: 'Two days after you meet the man, and you're in bed with him?' It's not what you think, Mother. He didn't expect me to be there.

Her gaze drifted to the dressing table and her limited choice in earrings. She'd never cared much about jewelry. Did he? She watched her shoulders lift in the mirror. The straps of the sundress pressed against her skin.

AN ARROW NEEDS A BEAU.

▼ ▼ ▼

Mike felt like a shooting gallery duck on the grand staircase, where the two sections met. Below him, black-tied strangers headed toward the ballroom. Band members, caterers. For hard-up folks, the Westfields were doing well. He descended a few cautious steps, trying to make as small a target as possible for the stun gun.

Footsteps behind him. Imagined. No, it was Liz. As she brushed past him, he could have sworn she'd blushed. Embarrassed about being caught with Donovan, probably. Mike was sorry he'd accused her of being Nemo. It was the product of a baseless jealousy he hadn't even known existed. She looked pretty in a blue and white summer dress.

Matt and Marsha stood in the living room. Mr. Westfield apologized; the senator had business in his room. Matt nodded in a way that suggested he didn't care. There was no sign of Gray, nor of Donovan or his newly-arrived assistant. Liz was swiftly pinned near the window by Marsha. Doris, in a party dress, was curled on a sofa by the fireplace, ignored by the adults.

Mike made his way over. "Hello there."

"Hi. You look good dressed up. Any luck with your search?"

"Yes and no. Thanks." He sat beside her. "Promise to keep a secret?"

Her eyes widened and she nodded. After a quick survey of the room, he told her about the clues.

"How excellent. Are you sure they're for the ticket?"

The thought hadn't even occurred to him. "I suppose there's one easy way to find out. Allison will be at the party tonight, with her mother. I could ask."

Doris grinned. "You did such a good job this morning."

Across the room, Liz said something that made Marsha break into shrill laughter.

"You like her, huh?" Doris scrunched herself tighter on the couch.

"Who?" He did a quick anti-Colonel sweep.

"You know."

"What?"

"I don't mind. I think she likes you, too."

"Who does? Really?" Over Doris' shoulder, he watched Liz talk, hoping to catch a glimpse of the little white scar. "What makes you think that?"

Doris smiled again. "I didn't used to think she was nice, but I could see the way she looked when I mentioned your name."

He checked on Liz again. "How did she look?"

"I can't describe it. But it's just, people should like each other. If they're going to be together. Right? Why be miserable? I mean, that woman with Roger Donovan. You can tell she doesn't like him, even though she pretends."

Mike failed to spot Donovan. Doris shook her head.

"They're not here. But you won't like her. She's not nice, like Liz."

Mike wasn't ready to talk about Liz. "Tell me about this woman with Donovan. Muscular? Middle-aged?"

Doris rolled her eyes. "She's buff. Fashion model pretty."

That didn't sound like the Colonel. But it was horribly familiar.

"What's the moose suit for?" Doris asked.

"What?"

"The moose suit. The trunk of your car was open. I was afraid someone might steal it. So I brought it up to your room. I hope that was okay."

"So it was you. Thanks. Just something I need to return. Sorry about the smell. Say, I don't suppose you happened to notice a box on my bed."

"What kind of box?"

Liddell approached with a tray of champagne flutes. Mike hijacked a pair and offered one to Doris. She squirmed.

"No. I mean, I can't. I'm not old enough, my parents think."

Holding wine in both hands made Mike reckless. "Who cares what your parents think?"

"Think about what?" Matt leaned over the arm of the couch.

Mike fought to keep the champagne in the glasses. He searched for an intelligent response in the bubbles. "About . . . whether I drink too much."

"Two glasses, one mouth," said Matt. "What's wrong with this picture? Dodo, time for dinner."

Doris rose. Mike waved a glass in salute and spilled a little wine. He took a sip to console himself, unloaded the second flute on another tray, and headed for the dining room. What a nasty thing to call your child.

Extra leaves in the massive table expanded it to medieval proportions. He was sizing up seating possibilities, sipping his champagne, when Donovan entered. The woman with him was hidden from view at first and then there stood Char. Mike took a bite out of his glass.

▼ ▼ ▼

Liddell served borscht, each bowl topped with a glob of sour cream. Liz breathed the thick beety smell, fighting off a childhood memory of crisp tablecloths and permanent stains. She shot a glance to her left, grateful for the empty place left by the senator.

There was an air of tension. She couldn't understand it. The only addition to last night's cast of characters was Charlotte, but her presence couldn't affect the mood so noticeably. She sat at the other end from Liz and seemed to be chatting amiably with Matt, Roger and, to a lesser degree, Gray. Her face generated vaguely unpleasant associations. Once or twice she sent Liz a look, as if expecting to be recognized.

Marsha blew into her bowl.

"That's cold soup," said Matt.

"So I can't blow on it?"

Doris' spoon clattered against the stoneware, and a red splash landed on the white tablecloth.

"I'm sorry." She picked up the spoon.

"Speaking of bizarre behavior, Bart." Matt directed a meaningful glance toward Mike. "I wonder if we could have the key for our bathroom."

"Bathroom?"

Mike lowered his gaze.

Liz heard her name pop from the conversation, Westfield speaking to Charlotte. "That's right, Liz and Gray are engaged. Oh. Not any . . ." He gestured to his right. "Mike, here, is an old friend of Gray's. From college."

Charlotte ignored Mike, who looked seasick. Too weird.

Liddell came through from the kitchen, swapping empty soup bowls for full plates of chilled poached salmon. Liz stared at her glass of ice water. After he completed the exchange, she checked under her plate.

"Not that fork, dolt." Marsha waved a utensil at her husband. "You don't use the little one for the main course."

"What, it's going to taste different if I use this?"

"Please," said Doris.

"Look at that." Charlotte directed her comment to Matt and used her own fork to point at Doris. "You're even passing bad manners to the next generation." Bitch.

Doris hastily set down the incorrect utensil.

"Do you suppose," Mike said to the chandelier, "when a butterfly sees a caterpillar, there's a flicker of self-recognition?"

Everyone turned to him, and Liz realized he'd wanted that to happen, not for his own sake but for Doris'. It was the most courageous thing she'd seen him do. He blushed deeply.

Charlotte broke eye contact first. "It's no excuse for bad manners."

Doris shrank into her chair, a movement that triggered for Liz another childhood memory.

"Knock it off," she said to Charlotte. "What did this one do to you?" And there it was, gloves off, this time with a woman she'd barely met. "You know," she looked to Doris, "I'm always getting that fork thing wrong. Can't set a table, either." Two needless lies, rewarded with a shy smile. Liz deliberately didn't check for Charlotte's reaction.

Marsha leaned toward Matt, mouth full. "Nice going, Captain Perfect."

"Please," said Doris. "Just be nice, can't you? Like they are." She pointed toward Mike and Liz.

Another silence. Liz felt her face go hot.

"Like they are?" Charlotte scraped back her chair. "Like they are . . . what?" Her lacquered nails caught the light.

Liz looked at those hands. Archaeologist, I think not.

"Hey, Doris, sit next to me, would you? I could use the company." She pulled the girl's plate over to the empty setting. As long as there was going to be a fight, it might as well be a good one. "So, Charlotte. Tell us about some of your favorite excavations."

▼ ▼ ▼

Mike stood gasping in the ballroom. Dinner in retrospect was a blur, sixty minutes of concentrated misery and mechanical actions. The food could have been ashes and it wouldn't have registered. He hadn't said a word, not a peep, throughout the meal, except the one time when Char had picked on Doris and he couldn't help it. Liz, across the table, had eyed him periodically with an expression he hadn't been able to translate, but she too had said little before launching an attack on Char. It was at that point that he'd lowered his head and waited for the ax to hit his neck.

And now he stood in the ballroom, next to the enormous punch bowl, watching the band ready itself. Precisely how he'd reached that spot without passing out or shattering something was a minor mystery. He drained another cup of punch and considered the merits of escaping through the French doors, sprinting across the lawn into the Virginia darkness.

Twin images of Gray hurried toward him. "I say, is something the matter? You looked ghastly at dinner."

Mike tried to bring the images into focus. "I'm a dead man."

"Because?"

"That woman Donovan brought down here." He laughed bitterly. "His so-called assistant."

"Rather attractive, I thought."

"Not the point." He inhaled another glass of punch. "It's Char."

"What, not your Char?"

"Excellent point." He studied the ceiling, but it insisted on sliding away. "Not any more she's not mine. Cheers." All that remained was the actual retribution, almost an anti-climax at this point.

"However did she find her way here?"

"As if I'd know? She's supposed to be with her parents at the beach this weekend. Maybe her boss sent for her. Unless . . ."

"Yes?"

"That's it." He clutched Gray's sleeve. "She hired Donovan to follow me. That Department of Justice stuff was an act. He's the private eye. When I saw him by the Tidal Basin on Friday, he wasn't watching Liz. It was me he wanted. Char must have told him we'd be there."

Gray freed his arm and smoothed his jacket. "What on earth are you babbling about?"

"I suppose it's not important. I've been expecting it. I just didn't think I was going to look like such an idiot."

"But why should she hire a person to follow you?"

"Control freak."

"And there was a danger of your being out of same?"

Mike gave him what was meant to be a withering look.

Gray shrugged. "I don't suppose she'll need her hydrant out here, anyway. Plenty of parking."

"Huh? Oh, no. The car."

"What of it?"

"I didn't have her permission to bring it out here."

"Steady on." Gray managed to float the ladle on the surface of the punch. "That seems rather much. I mean, you're an adult, aren't you?"

"No, no, with her it's all about trust, and openness. It's over. That's all there is to it. Over."

"Go easy on that punch. I didn't hear her say anything blistering during the meal. It can't be as bad as you think."

"No, that's just it. You didn't hear her say a word. Not to me. She's pretending we don't know each other. That wretched silent treatment. It can go on for days."

"Sounds like a plus."

"Thanks for the support."

Gray adjusted the cuffs of his shirt. "It's not the end of the world. All we need is a good plan to explain why you're here."

"Stop it. The last thing I need is another of your three-alarm plans."

"Still." Gray looked over his shoulder. "It could be worse."

"How?"

"I don't know. Just something to say. I mean, look at the bright side. Your Colonel isn't here. You were afraid Donovan was bringing her."

Mike gasped. "The Colonel."

"What of it?"

"I forgot. She is here. She brought my sneakers." He tugged at his tie and returned to the punch bowl.

"I'm afraid I should have told you," said Gray.

"Told me what?" He had the feeling it came out 'toll.'

"It's just that I was doing some thinking this afternoon. Allison's mother will be here. Suppose she were drunk. She might let slip about the ticket."

Mike was having trouble keeping his balance. The room had become fuzzy and warm. He stared at Gray, and the punch bowl, and Gray again.

"You didn't."

"Keep your voice down."

"What did you use?"

"Grain alcohol. Rather a lot, really."

Mike ran his tongue over his teeth without registering sensation. "What were you going to do, guard it?"

"Something like that. You got here too quickly. I did try to warn you. Wait, what are you doing?"

Mike pushed him aside. "What do you think? I'm having another quart of the stuff."

▼ ▼ ▼

He paced the terrace, gulping giant breaths of air. Silly to panic. What did Char have to be upset about? He had a logical explanation for everything that had happened. Everything. If she didn't like that, fine. Just clear the head a little, that's all, then go in and explain it to her rationally. Talk it out. End it like an adult. No, better stay outside another couple of minutes.

The band started up. Thoughts of dancing, and motion, made him vaguely ill. He sat down on the steps and stared at the lake. The moon hung in the sky, painting a stripe across the water. He listened to the frogs until he couldn't stand the racket.

The trellis looked inviting. Too bad it was so high. How wonderful to climb up, simply climb up and disappear. Unless, of course, the window he chose turned out to be Liz's bedroom. But that wouldn't be so awful.

The French doors stood open a few inches. He had to fight through thick curtains inside. Some dope must have closed the drapes. Or . . . Precisely as it was occurring to him that he'd gone in at the library end of the terrace, he heard noises inside. At the sound of Char's voice, he froze, tangled in drapes.

"What was that stuff you were doing at dinner?"

She was much too close. Whoever was with her must be farther off. Mike, caught up in the drapes, missed the answer.

"I still think this isn't the best idea. Your father would be furious."

The response was in a male voice, indistinct.

"No, but it won't be me who takes the blame. As you may recall, it was your great idea. I'm just a guest."

Mike strained to hear the man's voice. Gray? He found an edge of the curtain and peeked around.

Char stood in the middle of the room, talking to one of the walls. "And what about this Halloran woman? I don't trust her as far as I can toss her, especially now that I discover your supposed romantic involvement. You could have told me at the beginning. Besides, I've seen her before. She doesn't work on the Hill, does she?"

Mike wrapped the curtain tighter.

"No, no." She snorted. "I don't want to hear any more of your plans. I hate your plans."

Gray. Mike began to sway in the curtains. Please, no vomiting. He bit his cheek, too hard, and cried out.

"Did you hear something?" Char's voice approached.

He stopped breathing.

"Well, hurry up." Her voice rose. "I've seen all I needed to. Don't think I'm not grateful. It's opened my eyes. You know, I honestly believed I could make something of him. But I don't see why I should have to stay around here. It's not exactly the hot spot for Fourth of July parties."

This time he heard part of the answer. ". . . works."

"I'm sure it will be dreadful." Her voice grew louder again as she approached the French doors.

Mike took a step backward. With a shredding sound, the curtain tore from its anchor. He stumbled into the room and collapsed to the floor. His head popped free. Behind Char, a section of the wall stood open into the room. He looked up from the drapery and tried to flash an offhand smile.

"Hi, Char."

"Do I know you?" It didn't sound as though she were trying to be funny.

"Look." Mike stood and dusted off his clothes. "I'm sorry about all this, but I can explain."

"There's nothing to explain. You've mistaken me for someone else."

A grimy hand appeared at the edge of the wall, and the rest of Donovan followed, holding a flashlight. "You. I'm very disappointed, Archer."

Not Gray. Mike freed himself. "Would you tell her to knock it off?"

"Roger, do you know this person?"

Mike laughed uncertainly. "I told you, cut it out, Char."

"If the lady says she doesn't know you, buddy. She doesn't know you."

"But we were together the first time I saw you. By the Tidal Basin."

"Coincidence."

"That's ridiculous. Look, Char, I have your car keys."

"My car was stolen on Friday."

"Yeah, right . . . are you serious?" She must have worked that out at dinner.

"I'll take those," said Donovan.

"No way."

"Don't make me hurt you, fella."

"You must be joking." All the same, Mike leaned away.

"I'll count to three."

"That's impressive." It was the punch talking. Mike put the desk between himself and Donovan. Over the man's shoulder, the section of wall was still open, but he really didn't want to go back to the tunnel. He launched a desperate counteroffensive. "By the way, you're looking in the wrong place."

"What the hell are you talking about?"

"The little item everyone's so interested in."

"You haven't the faintest idea what's going on."

"Haven't I? Haven't I? Ask your friend Liz about that."

As Donovan turned toward Char, Mike bolted. He made it to the library door intact, and out into the living room. But his escape came with the sad sense that, in a day full of stupid moves, this had been the prize-winner.

▼ ▼ ▼

Liz stood near the wall, watching people mill in the ballroom. The band offered an inoffensive selection and had lured a few couples onto the parquet floor. She eyed the punch bowl and sniffed her drink again. Only the normal imprecise fruitiness, but there was a sharpness in the mixture she didn't trust. She dumped her drink into a potted plant, set down her empty glass and drummed her fingers on the edge of a table. Allie was somewhere in the house. Step four. No more avoiding it.

But as she headed for the door, Roger came through into the ballroom, craning his neck. Not what she needed, not now. As she turned away, however, he noticed her and crossed the room. The only person at this end she knew even remotely was Mike. He had his head tilted back and seemed to be silently reciting poetry, or memorizing lines. Still, for a damsel in distress . . . And he was a decent guy, except for stealing her disk.

A few strides brought her to him. "Let's dance."

"Oh, no." He waved her away. "I don't . . ."

"Come on, you can't be that bad." She took his hand and backed toward the floor.

"No, it's just that . . ." He let her pull him onto the parquet.

She staked out an open space and raised her right arm. "Here. You hold me like . . ."

"Yes, I know." He made a nervous, pointless gesture with his hands. But he moved closer and got the positioning right. She did her best to maneuver him around so she could find Roger. There he was, lurking beneath a large piece of art. The room pulsed and faded. Social buzz.

He wasn't such a bad dancer, hadn't crushed her feet. She glanced at his face, but he was staring behind her. The music had a tempo fast enough to let her get away with inspecting him under the guise of spinning out to arm's length. Actually, he looked pretty good in a suit. She checked the socks. Black today. She upgraded her assessment and swung back to him. Things would go more smoothly if she could like him. And after all, it wasn't that difficult.

The music stopped. He flashed a polite smile, and she felt him start to let go. Across the room, Roger stirred, edging around the perimeter.

"No. I mean, one more dance."

"I . . . okay."

'Feelings.' That was what the band decided it had to play next. She rolled her eyes but moved closer, resting her arms around his neck. The lights dimmed. Mike adopted a rice-paper hold, and she took it personally.

"I won't bite, you know." She slid toward him almost in spite, feeling unresisting hands glide across her ribs, around her back. A pressure against her stomach caused her to smile and raise her eyebrows. He was blushing.

"I'm sorry." He tried to step away, but she stopped him.

"It's okay." And suddenly she had a sense of, what? Of wanting to be held, and nothing more. She pressed herself to him. "It's okay." And she meant it.

He opened his mouth, but she raised an index finger and touched his lips. He kissed her fingertip and eased his body closer. His hands, on her back, began to stroke tentative circles.

She felt unaccountably drowsy. A voice in her head began to explain that this behavior was deliberate, needy. Be quiet. She rested her head against his shoulder and closed her eyes, letting her feet follow his lead, letting her mind drift. He smelled nice, clean but not overpowering.

"Mind if I cut in?" Roger's voice. "It would be best for everyone."

The gentle massage stopped. Mike's shoulders tightened. Notes reached her, but she'd lost the melody of the song, no more than a dull hum, far away. Roger, the five-diamond pain.

She whispered into Mike's neck. "Make him go away."

His throat vibrated. "Go away."

She held him tighter. No response from Roger. The hands began to move again. A thought tickled at the edge of consciousness. Something more important than this, something to do. Something to say. She shooed the thought away and let herself float in the warm, spinning darkness.

—11—

Slowly, Liz woke, ears first. Somewhere nearby was what sounded like a convention of small animals. Consciousness seeped through heavy lids as she teetered between regret for the world she was leaving and annoyance at the reality soon to come. It had been, it was, a beautiful dream, and she clung to it as it dissolved around her, wisps of greens and blues, filled with dancing and laughter and . . . gone.

She stretched out an arm and touched blades of short-cropped grass, and everything came back, fast-forwarded: a party, dancing, punch, a walk on a lawn . . . She opened one eye and stared up at the branches of an enormous oak tree. Its rustling leaves were lit in an odd, flat yellow that she eventually connected with the lights of Briarwood. The stars were out, the moon barely visible through the leaves. She squinted at her watch. Past midnight.

On her ribs she felt an unfamiliar pressure. Vague groping toward it led to the discovery of a warm, human hand. She ran her fingers lightly along the wrist, provoking no response. Turning her head with care, she opened her eyes and took in the slumbering features of, yes, Mike. He was asleep on his side. The arm not thrown over her was doubled beneath him, an open hand cradling his face. His mouth had relaxed into a smile.

She shut her eyes again and considered. Three hours to account for. They were both fully clothed, a good sign, but how had they ended up under the tree? What had they said? Or done? She'd read a study that had found a sober person, in the right social conditions, could persuade herself she was drunk. It seemed unlikely one could fabricate short-term memory loss as well.

Sounds of merriment carried from the house. Other dancers, other laughter. Mike groaned and rolled onto his back. The comforting smell of lilacs floated to her. With her cheek pressed flat on the grass and the cool earth, she inhaled. Five breaths, then get up.

A clang, very close by. She opened her eyes to the sight of a giant metal toadstool. By pulling her head back, she shrank it to a manageable size. She was propping herself on an elbow when the device shot a jet of water at her.

"Hey!"

She bolted past the streaming water, clutching her skirt, weaving her way among jets from the other sprinkler heads that were popping up everywhere. By the time she reached the terrace steps, breathless and lightheaded, the water had soaked her dress. Only then did she realize her feet were bare. But at least her head had cleared. She gazed across the darkened lawn and watched the water make silvery crescents in the lights from the house.

"Where have you been?" Allie stood by the French doors to the library holding a glass of wine.

Liz tipped her head toward the tree.

"Really? Doing what?"

"Ah, I'm not sure."

"Is there . . . is someone out there?"

"It's Mike."

"Is he hurt?"

"Huh. We can but hope." She caught the look of shock. "Of course he's not hurt. He passed out."

"Should we try to wake him?"

"No. I don't have to worry about him when he's unconscious. Come on, let's go." Her shoes could wait.

She crossed the terrace to the library, Allie following. Inside, one of the heavy curtains lay in a heap and she stepped over it. Through the open door she glimpsed the still form by the tree, in the center of half a dozen arcing sprays. Searching the room, she spotted a large umbrella in a pile of junk.

She timed her dash to minimize the effect of the sweeping showers. The wet grass felt cool and slippery under the soles of her feet. Beneath the tree, he'd curled on his side, still sleeping. Occasionally a hand pawed at the water.

Smiling, she opened the umbrella and propped it on the ground, to shield his head. Water from the sprinklers drummed on the garish pattern. She studied his sleeping face, feeling the droplets as they hit her calves like gently tapping fingertips. She reached toward his hand.

Allie called from the doorway, "Is he all right?"

Liz pulled her hand away. A little water wouldn't hurt anyone. Her sandals lay on their sides in the grass. She scooped them up. Gathering her skirt with the other hand, she darted in a barefoot zig-zag across the wide lawn, all the way to the terrace, without once looking back.

▼ ▼ ▼

He held her close as they danced in the darkness, but he could not feel her, or even his feet. She began to cry, and the drops fell on his face in a light pattering. He wanted so much to make her happy. He didn't know how.

▼ ▼ ▼

Allie picked up the curtain from the library floor and started to sing. "Someone left the date out in the rain . . ."

"It's not rain, and he's not my date."

"Really? You should give him a chance. I don't think he's so bad." Allie bundled the curtain into a chair. "Gray explained what happened yesterday in the garden. It was an accident."

"I'm not interested."

"Would you like some coffee?"

"I'm not drunk. I don't drink."

Allie shrugged. "I didn't say you were, or did. I just wondered whether you wanted some coffee."

If there was going to be a confrontation with Allie, it shouldn't be over Mike. "Thanks, yes, I'd love some."

Allie led the way to the kitchen, where she hunted through cabinets. As Liz watched, it occurred to her that she might pick up some useful information. Better not to confront her yet at all.

"Your mother seems to take a perverse delight in making Westfield suffer."

Allie shook her head. "No, I don't think she views it that way. It's more a game, a treasure hunt. She's a professional puzzle fanatic."

Liz tried not to look too interested. "Professional? What does she do?"

"Cryptography. But she's retired."

"And what's the unforgivable thing Westfield did?"

"It started with Mom's wedding, last year. For some reason, Bart objected."

"Don't tell me he was in love with her."

"He didn't want her to marry Eric. I don't know why. Perfectly nice man, even if he is hardly ever around."

Water from her dress dripped on Liz's foot. "And what Eric's history?"

"He runs his own company. An investment brokerage. He arranges the sale of closely-held businesses. High-tech, mostly."

"Sounds grim. I suppose it's strange, having a stepfather." She couldn't keep the image of Dad's funeral from her mind.

"It's okay, I guess." Allie lifted her thin shoulders. "As I said, he's never around. He was supposed to be here tonight, but some last-minute business problem came up. As usual."

"I don't see how Westfield's disapproval would matter to your mother."

"No, but there were other things. He . . . taunted her, would be the best way to put it. You wouldn't believe how competitive she is. It drove her crazy when he got ahead. Here, try this."

Liz took the coffee. Allie's mother should be the one to be punished. Westfield hadn't cheated. "Accepting for the moment that he demonstrated poor judgment, where does she get off stealing his lottery ticket?"

"She didn't steal it. She only hid it."

Now, there was a fine distinction. "Hid it. Do you know where?"

"Of course not, and I'm glad. Somewhere on the Briarwood property. I guess I'll go home now. I'm riding in the morning. I don't want to push my luck. There's a guy here I know from work, and I'd really like to avoid him."

"Anyone I met?"

"I don't think so. I didn't even realize he was coming. He seems to know the Westfields."

Liz sensed an opportunity to steer the conversation toward the jewelry store. "Where did you end up working?"

"Nowhere, now. I'm in between jobs."

"You said this guy is from work."

"I meant the last place. A little company called Hillton-Tanner. They develop educational software."

"Hillton-Tanner?" Coffee splashed the counter. "What did you do there?"

"Have you heard of it? What's the matter? I was in accounting."

"Accounting?" Of all people to surface in the H-T scam. "For how long?"

"A little over three years. You make it sound like front-page news. What else would I do with a degree in Finance?"

"Allie, we need to talk."

"Why?" Allie put her mug into the sink. "I thought we'd put it all behind us. You haven't changed a bit, have you?" She turned and left.

It wasn't fair that Allie should control their conversations. Liz thought of the anonymous note she'd sent the jewelry store, letting them know they had a dishonest employee. She hadn't mentioned names. Allie had nothing to resent.

▼ ▼ ▼

Liz was staring at the computer monitor when Joey found her.

"Hey, boss." He hadn't bothered to knock.

"What are you doing here?"

He sat on the other side of the desk. "Hanging with Uncle Bud. Trying to score a dance with Charlotte. Isn't everyone?"

"What are you doing in the library?"

"Looking for Colonel Mustard and the knife. I mean, come on, I could ask you the same thing."

"But you won't."

"We got the office closed. Now the big boss says blend into the scenery. I'm blending." He stood and prowled. When he reached the spot where the wall swung open, he stopped. Liz watched from the corner of one eye as he inspected the hinge and the latch release mechanism. He whistled.

"Cool. You been in here?"

"No." She didn't look up. Something about Charlotte . . .

"Why not?"

"Because I don't have time to go chasing down every rabbit hole in the place. Besides, there's no point. I want to find something that I shouldn't need to leave this room for. And I don't have a flashlight."

He tested the door, making it creak. "Aren't you at all curious?"

"As a matter of fact, I'm not. It's a character flaw." She smoothed the sheet of paper that held the clue. Charlotte was with Roger. An assistant. Where had he found her? Not in any archaeology class.

Joey swung the door. "Bullshit. You're curious, and you know it."

"Hey, when I need analysis, I'll let you know."

"Okay." He resumed his tour. "Nice moose." He swatted its snout, which gave off a small cloud of dust and swung back. A click came from the wall.

"Anything else you'd like to break while you're at it?"

"Geez, you're no fun."

"So I've heard." She didn't like the way the glass eye of the moose stared.

"Come on, lighten up." Joey snatched a piece of wadded paper from the floor and arced it past the moose head. She ignored him. He picked up the paper and shot from the other side. This time it lodged in the antlers.

"Okay." She slapped her palm on the desk. "You want to help, tell me this. What does 'big fat H' mean to you?"

"I don't know." He mimed another shot. " 'Headache.' Context?"

"It's some kind of clue. 'Shut the door and count again; stop before the big fat H.' I was thinking maybe 'shut the door' was a rebooting command. Or something to do with a disk drive."

"Yeah, make me laugh. You're so dense. Try a tougher one."

"What, you understand this?"

He picked up one of Westfield's model rockets and guided it through the air. "It's obvious."

"Well?" She struggled to be patient.

"Come on, guess."

"Joey."

"Okay. This door you're supposed to shut. It could be the one over there."

"It could?"

"But it isn't. Or the one behind the moose. Oh, all right. Ready? One, two, buckle my what?"

"Shoe."

"Three, four . . ."

". . . shut the door. Very entertaining. Oh. 'Shut the door and count again.' " She had to concentrate to come up with the nursery rhyme. "Five, six . . . um, nine, ten, a big fat hen. Hen."

"Ta-da!" He spread his arms. "I always thought it was a lame rhyme, myself. Look at the big picture. What kind of instructions is the kid getting? Put on shoe, go outside, collect sticks and close gate, then what? Poultry time."

"Fascinating. If we stop before the big fat H, we get . . ."

"Ten." He spread the fingers of his hands and looked at them from both sides. "You don't think it's a suspicious rhyme?"

"Terribly. Let me know when you publish. And the rest of the clue?"

He leaned across the desk to study the paper. "Unh-uh. Beats me. Boxcar. Six-pack of beer. Maybe it's a drink-and-drive warning."

"Good."

"Where'd you get this, anyway?"

She tapped the computer.

"Can I see?"

"It's gone now. This is what's left."

"Where'd you find it?"

"F: drive."

"Aha. As you have learned in our travels, grasshopper, F: is ordinarily a network drive."

She felt her cheeks flush.

"So." He patted the monitor. "Who's on this network?"

▼ ▼ ▼

The network seemed to have four users. She and Joey were searching for a form of identification when the library door burst open and Bud teetered against the frame. Faint music pulsed behind him. He jerked a thumb over one shoulder. "Liz, there's a guy out here with a glass slipper calling your name. Know anything about it?"

"Hilarious. Do you write your own material?"

"Come off it. Don't get all twisted. Ah, I see the flesh and blood has tracked you down. You should dance with the lad. Make his night." Bud bent in a mock-ceremonial bow. "You know my nephew, I believe?"

Joey turned red and disappeared behind the bookcase.

"You know, if you really wanted to help . . . What did you say?"

"About what?"

"Nephew."

"Merely teasing young Joseph, a great admirer of yours."

"Sit down." Her face felt cold. "Now. Stay there and don't move."

"What is it?" But he followed her instructions. "I love it when you boss me around."

"Shut up. Joey, get back in here." She sat before the computer, fingers trembling. Bud as Ariel? It couldn't be.

"Say, Lizzo, you mind telling me what's going on?" She ignored the taunt. "And will it take long? I gotta pee."

She logged in and called up Ariel. "Not long."

"Can I at least drink while I wait?"

"I don't care."

"Scotch and water, Joey. Light on the water."

"Oh, no you don't." She raised a hand and Joey froze. "Forget it. You won't get around it that way."

"What way?"

"Sending him from the room so he can dial in and pretend to be you."

"You feeling all right? Why would he do that?"

No answer from Ariel. Wasn't that a big surprise. He'd thrown her off track with that arrow stuff. How easy it had been.

"Liz, what is the problem here?"

"I suppose the name Ariel means nothing to you."

"Ariel?" There was the trace of a flinch, but his voice stayed steady enough. "Mermaid, right? In that kids' movie?"

She slapped the desk. "Don't patronize me."

"How can I when I don't know what the hell you're talking about? Do you know what she's talking about?"

Joey shrugged keeping his mouth shut.

"See?" said Bud.

"Damn you both. I bared my soul. How could you? How . . . ?" She was close to hyperventilating.

"Hey, you're upset."

"You're damned right I'm upset."

"About what?"

"About what? What do you think? About this. This!" She stabbed a finger toward the monitor. "Oh." Text filled the response window.

ariel: AT YOUR SERVICE, MAJESTY.

She glared at the two of them.

"Put your hands up. Both of you. Where I can see them. And keep them up." She tapped out the first thing that came to mind as a test.

miranda: WHAT AM I WEARING TODAY?

His answer came right back.

ariel: I'LL WAGER IT IS FETCHING. REGRETTABLY, I KNOW NOT.

She leaned back in the chair before typing.

miranda: TELL ME ABOUT YOUR NEPHEW.

ariel: YOU WOULDN'T BE INTERESTED. DAMAGED GOODS. HEART STOLEN.

She pushed the hair from her eyes.

miranda: NEVER MIND. SORRY TO BOTHER YOU.

ariel: NO BOTHER. SWEET DREAMS.

She stared at the keyboard and said in a flat, quiet voice, "Bud, I am really, really sorry."

"Can we put our hands down?"

"Oh God, of course."

He looked at his fingers as he lowered them. "What was that all about?"

"It's, no, I thought someone else was you. It's just that I've been under a lot of stress lately." She logged out. "Nothing you'd understand."

He pretended to shake blood back into his fingers. "You need a vacation." She gave him her darkest look. "And what was it you were going to tell me before we had our little diversion?"

"I don't remember."

"Sure you do. You were starting to say, if I really wanted to help . . ."

"Oh. That." She leaned her elbows on the desk. "Does the term 'boxcars' mean anything to you?"

"Boxcars? Double sixes on a pair of dice. Opposite of snake eyes. Why? Who wants to know?"

"Double sixes?" She found a pen and wrote, 10-6-6. That was the clue. 1066. William the Conqueror. "Joey, go find Gray Westfield. Please. Tell him we need to talk right now. On second thought, never mind." She snatched the paper. "I'll do it myself."

"Let's go, Joey," said Bud. "We've lost her." As she left the room, she heard him continue, "Snake eyes, boxcars. What's the diff? They're both losers."

▼ ▼ ▼

"Mike. Mike."

The voice came out of the dark, tinged with dampness. Mike opened his eyes and saw jumbled colors frighteningly close. He shut his eyes again.

"I say, feeling all right?" Gray aimed a horribly bright light at him.

"I was until you got here."

"Not to belabor the obvious, old man, but you're lying on some rather soggy turf, in what used to be a decent suit."

Mike shoved himself to his feet. A rush of sparkles enveloped his brain, and he toppled to the ground.

"Another thing. You've got an umbrella."

Mike lay on the ground, clutching his temples.

"Shall I show you how it functions?"

"Go away. You're giving me a headache."

"Self-inflicted, old bean. I did warn you. Would you like a hand up?"

Mike raised an arm and felt himself hauled to a sitting position. He opened his eyes. "How did I get here? Why is the grass wet? Where did the umbrella come from? Be specific. Speak slowly."

Gray waved the flashlight. "Afraid I won't be much help. The grass is wet because the sprinkler system activated itself, as is its nightly custom. We don't ordinarily camp out here. And the umbrella hails from the house. One of Dad's more unfortunate choices, fashion-wise."

Mike staggered to his feet. "These feel like rented legs. How much did you put in the punch? No, don't tell me."

"I agree. Probably best to forget all that."

"Speaking of forgetting, I have a scary memory gap. Tell me I didn't do anything asinine. No lampshades on the head, or anything?"

"Not that I noticed. You danced with Liz, but it seemed fairly orthodox."

"I did? How about that?" It would have been a nice moment to remember. At the terrace steps, he sank down. A tap on the shoulder jolted him awake.

"Hey." The voice was too loud. "Sure you don't want to go inside?"

He breathed gently. "Would it be too much to ask for some water?"

"Coming right up." Gray twirled the umbrella, spinning drops onto Mike. "But I'd have thought water was about the last thing you wanted more of."

"I get my laughs from the comic strips, thanks."

"Right-o."

"And, Gray? Just water. Nothing else."

While he waited, he tried to squeeze his skull back into shape. A breeze nudged his face. There was an annoyingly bright light above the lake, which he finally identified as the moon. He tried a few deep breaths, nothing fancy, relieved to discover that his lungs still functioned. Mostly.

Gray returned with the water.

"Thanks. Had you been looking for me long?"

"Truth to tell, I didn't realize you'd gone missing. Doris caught up with me a few minutes ago and told me you were out here."

Mike trickled water past his tonsils. "Why didn't she come herself?"

"She's supposed to be in bed. Anyway, I believe her parents insisted she stay away from you. After the incident last night, they're concerned." He examined his glasses. "They seem to suspect it was you who attacked Allison on the lawn."

"It was me."

"Ah. Well. There you have it."

Mike finished the water. With friends like this . . . "What time are we looking at here?"

"Working on two."

"I don't suppose Allison's mother told you where the ticket is."

"No. That is, no. She put in only the briefest of appearances. Never quite made it into the ballroom. Pity."

"I should have known. God, I should have known." Mike angled his face toward the sky. "Hey, why doesn't your dad just suck it up and apologize?"

"Oh, he did, long ago, but she said he was only doing it so she'd tell him the hiding place which is probably true. No help there I'm afraid. Come on, let's get you in. Whoa, not that way. Handful of guests clinging to the dance floor, best avoided. Let's enter through the library, shall we?"

"Good idea. You can open the bookcase and shove me down the tunnel. I bet I won't even feel the steps."

"Stop it. Self-pity isn't your finest look."

"Better a dark death than having to face Char."

"Stop worrying, would you? I don't think she's even in the house." Gray peered through the French doors. "If you'll hang in there a minute, I've worked out a foolproof plan to get you to your room."

Mike swallowed. "I was afraid you might."

▼ ▼ ▼

As it turned out, the library was occupied. Mr. Westfield faced a blank computer screen. Doris, curled in an armchair, read a book. She'd wrapped herself in the fallen curtain.

Gray prodded the rug with his toe. "Hullo, Dad. What's up?"

"Not right now."

Mike waited by the French doors, dripping. Doris smiled quickly at him and went back to her book.

"Oughtn't you turn the machine on?"

His father's shoulders tensed. "I don't want it to do anything. I'm trying to think."

"Mmm. Our talking isn't helping the effort, I suppose."

"Not a great deal."

"Excuse me." Mike ventured into the room. "Did you have an idea about the hiding place?"

Mr. Westfield took in the wet clothes and raised an eyebrow.

"It's all right, Dad. Mike knows about the ticket. In fact, he helped find a clue. Two, really." Gray put the flashlight on the desk and dug in a pocket. "I've been meaning to tell you. Here."

His father stared at the message from the safe. "When did you find this?"

"Earlier today. It was behind the moose. And this one," he handed the other across, "we retrieved from the garden. I say 'we,' but it was Mike who figured them out."

"That's wonderful news. I haven't made any progress in weeks and you found these in little over forty-eight hours." Mr. Westfield squinted at the messages. "What do they mean?"

"Ah, we haven't got that far. A bit stuck, truth to tell."

"She told me there was a clue on the computer. On the computer. I'm no good with the things, as she knows. I thought she might mean literally 'on.' Written in dust. But there's nothing. No dust, even. Hopeless idea."

"Pardon me." Mike felt himself grow more sober. "On, not in?" He shot Gray a dirty look. "I wish someone had mentioned that earlier. May I see?" He ran his hands along the sides of the monitor, peered at the back, tipped it to look beneath. He repeated the process with the computer itself. "Nuts. I was positive . . ." He lifted the keyboard. "Here we are." Taped to the underside was a plain envelope. He peeled away the tape. "For you, I believe."

Barton Westfield took the envelope as if it were crystal. "Would you look at that. Mike, you are a genius."

"Is it the ticket?" Gray hurried over.

His father's hands shook as he ripped open the envelope and snatched a square of paper from inside. His shoulders slumped, and he slapped the paper on the desk. Mike read over his shoulder, conscious of the wet wool smell from his own suit. The paper contained two words.

Mike read them aloud. "José Canusi."

"Canusi?" said Gray. "The baseball player?"

"Wrong name. Not even close."

"Maybe it's the guy with the next clue." Gray reached for the phone book.

"It won't be there," said Mike.

"How do you know? Oh. You're right. Then maybe it's one of your, what's-its, anagrams."

Mike closed his eyes. " 'O Jesus I can.' "

"Yes, well, perhaps not."

"You have good instincts." Mr. Westfield stood and patted Mike on the back. "Let me know if you come up with anything else. And get some dry clothes. You'll excuse me. I must see to my guests." He left.

Gray held the paper to the light. "It could be one of those invisible ink thingies. You know, hold it over a candle to get the writing to show."

"Try that." Mike removed his jacket. "Not to pry, but your family seems to be pretty well off already, even without lottery tickets or Cousin Jake."

"Would that it were so." Gray settled his glasses. "I gather we've run out of banknotes. That's the problem with inheritances. Dad never made much, and what little he saved went into bad investments. The ticket was all we had left."

"Then why throw an expensive party?"

"He'd sent the invitations before he lost the ticket and he didn't want to cancel. Always hoping for the best and keeping up appearances."

"He could have cashed in the ticket right away."

"I know, I know. The problem is, he didn't realize he had a winner until last month. Buys truckloads of the things and it takes him a while to catch up. When he finally did, he made a big deal about it, with this grand celebratory dinner and it was then he teed off Allison's mother. She took it that night and now here we are with the ratted thing expiring tomorrow." Gray consulted his watch. "Today."

"Okay, don't panic. We have time. You should be taking care of Allison."

"She's gone. I think Donovan said he'd give her a lift home."

"Why would . . ." Mike dropped his jacket. "Char. What happened to her?"

"In the cottage. Don't look so pale. The couch is a hide-a-bed. Speaking of same, do try to land in your own tonight."

"Wait. Wait. What about the plan to get me to my room?"

"Ah, the plan. Here it is: go up both flights of stairs and open the door with the handwritten notice that says, 'Mike's room.' I'm sure you can handle it."

In the silence that followed Gray's departure, Mike returned to the desk and studied the slip of paper. He rolled the flashlight back and forth, his lips moving as he repeated the name to himself.

A noise came from the armchair.

"Oh. Doris. Thought you were gone. Do your parents know you're here?"

"José Canusi?" she said.

"You heard."

She spoke again, more slowly. "O.J. canoe sea."

"Not quite, but close."

She paused between each syllable. "O. Say. Can. You. See?"

"O say can you . . ." He sat down. "Wow. You're the genius."

She pulled the curtain around her. "No, I'm not."

"Yes you are. You know who wrote the words to that?"

"Francis somebody. I stink at history."

"Francis Scott Key." He groaned. "The Key of F. The Key of flipping F. And guess when he wrote it." He smacked his forehead. "The War of 1812. 1812. Six by three right by two. We were so close." He ran through the rest of the puzzle in his head.

"Why is that important?"

Mike pulled Gray's also-ran lottery ticket from his pocket and showed it to her. "It means we've been digging in the wrong place."

▼ ▼ ▼

Liz gritted her teeth. After a lengthy search, she'd spotted Gray coming out of the library, of all places. Now he sulked on a sofa in the living room.

"I told you, they're racing to get back to William the Conqueror."

"Okay, then."

"What does this prove? That she wrote the message? Some breakthrough."

Liz looked away so as not to hit him. But it was true. 1066 told them nothing until they figured out the part about WHAT GOES UP WILL BRING YOU DOWN. 'I hope this rain keeps up.'

He gave her a tired smile. "Don't suppose you've heard of Joe Canusi?"

"It's a little late to be playing do-you-know."

"No, it's . . . never mind. Speaking of which, you don't happen to know this Roger Donovan blister?"

"Why?"

"Not a detective is he?"

"A detective? Why would he be a detective?"

"Nothing. It's just that Mike thinks he's following him." In response to her blank look, he tried again. "Donovan. Following Mike."

"I get it. Why would he be doing that?"

"Char hired him, Mike thinks."

"Char?"

"Charlotte," said Gray, on his way to the door. "Mike's girlfriend. You met at dinner." He disappeared.

Liz stomped all the way up to her room. Charlotte. She looked like a thousand other women, not as pretty as she thought she was but enough to turn heads. And damn good in Lycra. On skates. The sweatband-sunglasses combination had hidden her face but it should have been obvious. Liz locked the door against possible invasions and flopped onto the bed. Of course she'd known he had a girlfriend. Of course. And that wasn't a tear. It was sweat.

▼ ▼ ▼

Liz woke in the dark and lay on her back, thinking as hard as she could about anything but Mike. Stupid clues abounded on this job. Things that go up. That go up. Stocks. Baseballs. Blood pressure. Model rockets.

The house was quiet. She walked down the carpeted hall, carrying her damp shoes. The stairs groaned. She moved closer to the wall and hurried on.

In the library, she skirted dark objects to reach the desk. A flashlight lay by the computer. She turned it on and swept it from side to side, finally locating Westfield's three half-built rockets under a small table. She scooped them up and brought them to the desk. It was worth risking more light from the lamp. She cleared a space and, after pausing long enough to show a little respect for the man's modeling efforts, set about dismantling them.

Two minutes was enough to convince her the ticket wasn't hidden in any of them. She surveyed the wreckage before her. A setback to Westfield's space program, and to her search. She found the wastebasket and swept in the remains. As the pieces hit the bottom, she paused. Where had that first clue landed? She put the container on the desk and pawed through the trash, looking for the half-obliterated printout. No luck.

In the air was a faint odor of smoke. Wrong time of year for a fire. Mike had accused her of burning documents. There wasn't anything in the printout worth destroying. At the back of her mind wavered the recollection of having tossed the paper toward, but not quite in, the wastebasket. She sat at the desk and pantomimed ripping the sheet from the printer, wadding it, and pitching it away. The approximate spot where it should have landed was paperless.

She closed her eyes. Gray. Gray had fooled with the crumpled wad. She thought harder. Joey. Moose. The chair still sat against the far wall below the safe. She climbed up and groped in the antlers. Gotcha.

Back at the desk, she smoothed out the paper, pulled the light closer, and shook her head in disbelief. What had seemed nothing but meaningless dots was the classic circular burst of fireworks.

Fireworks. She studied the picture, hoping for a further clue, not that she deserved one. Bother. Bother bother bother. She should have paid attention when Westfield mentioned where he kept his pyrotechnics supply.

Computer forensicians don't lead treasure hunts. A monkey can connect the dots. Especially these dots. But, to have done so much of the work . . . a shame not to be in on it at the end. With a finger to each temple, she tried to imagine where a moderately sane person would store fireworks. Not in the house, surely. Even the garage was risky.

Time out. The shed. Cousin Jake wanted to launch them over the lake on the Fourth of July. Today.

She grabbed the flashlight and hurried through the French doors, down the terrace steps. The lawn was softly lit by the night sky. A breeze brushed wavelets across the lake to touch the shore with an unhurried lapping. She crept toward the outline of the shed, barely visible against the dark trees. Gripping the flashlight like a club, she pushed through, swinging herself past the edge of the door. The darkness smelled of fertilizer. She waited, holding her breath, until she was confident there was no one hiding. At last she turned on the light, blinking away the sudden brightness.

For the most part, the place held the sort of gardening paraphernalia she'd expected. Someone had had a run-in with a bag of lime and a few flower pots, and she could guess who, but otherwise things were neatly arranged. In the corner she saw impressive stacks of boxes marked 'Explosives.'

The quantity surprised her. He couldn't need all those rockets. It was a backyard display, for Pete's sake, not the royal fireworks. She checked her watch. 3:15. Several hours to dawn. Enough time to give it a whirl.

She played the light over the names on the boxes: Excelsior, Arrowhead, Liberty, Hastings, Colossus. She opened the carton on top of the nearest stack. Rows and rows of fireworks. She pulled out one and examined it. Nothing special. She shoved it back into place.

1066 and 'What goes up will bring you down.'

1066 fireworks.

She began to laugh. Rapid unpiling of the boxes in the next stack brought her to the one container labeled "Hastings Fireworks Company." It was already unsealed. Mrs. Owen's custom pyrotechnics.

There was nothing inside called 'King William,' or even 'Conqueror,' but after a moment of digging she knew which of the contents didn't belong. With a single exception, the several dozen rockets were green and gold. The misfit lay at the very bottom of the box, a huge item with broad red-and-white stripes running its length, culminating in a blue nose cone sprinkled with white stars. Frighteningly patriotic.

She hefted it, rattled it, tossed it. At last, holding the light close, she rotated the tube. Nothing unusual about the outer shell. She jammed the flashlight under one arm and twisted off the nose cone.

Bingo.

—12—

Monday morning was clear and sunny. Too sunny. Mike, having slept through the formal presentation of breakfast, sat alone in the kitchen. While he finished his tea, he tried to work out what to do. And whom he could trust. He wished it were Liz. Tea leaves formed indecipherable patterns at the bottom of the cup.

The door swung open and Gray walked in, altogether too cheerily. "Today's the day, old sport."

"Quiet, please."

"But you told me . . ."

"I know. I know."

Gray lifted plastic wrap from a pitcher of orange juice. "Hey. That's my shirt you're wearing."

"Liddell gave it to me. I'm out of clean ones."

"Oh, okay." He poured some juice. "Just saw Dad. He's rather low, but I didn't say a word. Do you really think we can solve the dashed thing? I have to tell you, I'll be relieved either way. At least it'll be over."

"Is that what you want? For it to be over?"

"Why not?"

"Don't you care if your father gets his property back?"

"Of course I care. What's the matter with you?"

"Nothing." Mike rested his forehead on one hand. "Long night. Anyhow, we're in the ballpark at last." He watched for a reaction. "That's a tiny joke." He explained the star-spangled breakthrough.

Gray dropped into a chair. "Bloody marvelous. Why didn't you tell me?"

"I figured the ticket wasn't going anywhere. Not before tonight."

"Meaning?"

"Fireworks, Gray. It's all about fireworks. RRG is 'rockets' red glare.' When Allison's mother told me it was in a safe place, she meant it three ways. The clue was in the safe. And the ticket wasn't safe in the long run, but on the other hand there was no danger of it being shot off before today."

"Stop. You're saying she hid the blasted item in the squire's fireworks? But he just had them delivered a few days ago. The ticket's been missing for ages."

"No, I didn't say she put it in one of your father's fireworks. There was nothing to stop her adding a box of her own. You told me yourself you found some left over from last year. Except they weren't. Allison's mother put them there when she hid the ticket." He patted Gray on the back. "Remember why your plan went wrong on Saturday? Instead of going in the house, she headed for the garden. I bet she wanted to check the ticket."

"Stuff the Sherlock Holmes act. Let's find out whether you're right."

It wasn't a question of being right. He knew he was right. The problem was, Mike wasn't quite sure what to do about it. He hadn't had much practice.

▼ ▼ ▼

Inside the shed, boxes of fireworks were stacked in piles. Gray began digging. "Move away from that door. You're blocking the light."

"I don't think you need to do that. She told us where to look."

"She did? When? Where?"

"The next clue is, 'the very end(s), in the very beginning.' "

Gray spent about five seconds in silent concentration. "I don't follow."

"The very end. The last line of F. Key's song, the national anthem. The line everyone cheers at the ballpark before the singer's done."

"I hate when you get smug. Oh, very well." Gray's head bobbed as he ran through the words. "It's . . . 'and the ho-o-me of the-e-e bra-a-a-ave.' So?"

"I should have figured it out when we found the glass jar. That was her final hint. She said, 'I was thinking more along Fulton County lines.' Fulton County Stadium. The old Atlanta baseball park."

"Baseball?"

"Baseball. The home of the Braves. A baseball fan would know that. And Allison's mother knows baseball. She used to go to games with your father. We need to find fireworks from the home of the Braves. Ordinarily, I'd say look for a box with 'Atlanta' on it. But there won't be one."

"The point of that being?"

"For starters, it wouldn't be enough of a challenge."

"It would for me." Gray picked up a flower pot and placed it on a shelf.

"But not for her. She loves layers. The clue is, 'the very end(s), in the very beginning.' You know where the Braves played before they moved to Atlanta?"

"You're going to tell me."

"Milwaukee. But hold it, we're not done. Before that, it was Boston."

"Blighters got around. And before that?"

"Well, nothing. That's it. That's where they started. The very beginning."

"Boston. Right. Boston." Gray scanned the boxes. "Not here. Hang on, these are made in Boston. Hastings Fireworks Company. I can't believe you figured this out. And it's open. Okay, what's next?"

Mike hadn't budged from the doorway. Even though he knew what was coming, he didn't want to face it. "An American flag. Or something that looks like one. 'BSX2.' The star-spangled banner. Broad stripes. Bright stars. B.S. B.S."

Gray whistled. He lifted a rocket from the box. "Fits the description. Oh, and look. Someone's taken it apart."

"Yes, she has. 'On the nose.' The nose cone. Check inside." He held his breath and moved closer.

Gray tipped the rocket upside down. "It's empty."

Mike let his breath go. "Is it?" Oh, Liz. He ran his fingers inside the rocket. "Something was taped here." He carried it to the door for a better look, his throat tight.

"I don't get it," said Gray.

"It's not hard to understand. Either we're reading the clues wrong, or someone's beaten us to it."

"Can't believe either one. Maybe there's another red-white-and-blue rocket." Gray shook the box.

" 'Dig deep.' That's all that's left of the instructions."

"I'm at the bottom of the dratted thing as it is. Who could have found it? How would anyone guess where to look?"

"Use your head. Who knew about the clues?"

"Allison's mother, obviously. The two of us. Dad. And Liz."

"We can rule out both parents. If her mother's taken it again, we've got zero chance. And we'd know if your father had it."

"But Liz? She didn't even have the garden clue."

"She didn't need it. You can solve it from the puzzle in the safe."

"Impossible. She'd have told me."

Mike could almost smile at Gray's confusion. The trickster tricked.

"Okay, if it wasn't Liz, tell me who it could be."

He hoped Gray would come up with an answer. A good puzzler he could accept. But he didn't want to find out she'd taken advantage of the Westfields. He didn't want to believe she'd stoop to theft.

Liz watched the shadow of the house retreat across the grass toward her seat on the terrace. She anticipated the feel of the sun on her face. Time marched on as always. This morning, for once, she was ahead of it.

The shade on the terrace was pleasant, not too cool for the sleeveless dress she'd chosen for her moment of triumph. She admired the lake and the distant hills, feeling that she'd conquered them, made them her own. Supposedly a person could like the beach or the mountains, but not both. This morning her island beckoned, but she could not deny the beauty of the dusky hills.

On the other side of the garden Mike and Gray emerged from the shed blinking in the sun like bears ending hibernation. She smiled to herself. A day late and ten million dollars short, boys. Amateurs.

She touched her hair a little self-consciously. It was arranged today in an unaccustomed style that had ended up more bun-with-wisps than she'd intended. Still, the change felt good, a step forward.

Gray said something about 'town' and headed for the driveway. Mike strode across the lawn with surprising purpose. She pretended not to see him and sauntered off at an angle, heading for the lake. Let him follow if he wanted. At the water's edge, she bent and gathered a handful of flat rocks. They were warm in her hand, smooth and solid. She cocked her head and began to skip them. The ripples spread, interlaced, disappeared. She heard him come to a stop behind her.

He cleared his throat. "You like baseball."

It was as if he were pretending last night had never happened. And then she understood he hadn't meant it as a question. Perhaps they'd talked baseball while they danced.

She loosed a rock that bounced off the water a dozen times. "Who do you suppose figured out that stones do this? What were they trying to accomplish?"

"Hit a fish, maybe. Where'd you learn to skip?"

"Where does anybody? My dad taught me. I think it's some kind of guy thing, this urge to push the world around, even on such an insignificant scale."

"You're lucky."

That was an odd way to put it. She threw another stone. "Do you have brothers and sisters?"

"A brother." The way he said it didn't invite follow-up.

After that the only sound was the plunking of stones on water. She reached for another handful and saw him reclining on the lawn. She thought about that. Perhaps disks weren't the only things he was interested in stealing. Even if he suspected her of having beaten him to the ticket, she could deny it. He'd been so sure in the library that he'd solve the puzzle. He might be a nice guy, but this was one conversation he wouldn't control. She threw the last of her rocks.

"Something you wanted to say to me?"

"Such as?"

"Such as, I'm missing a computer disk from my room. I thought you might know something about it."

"I don't. I don't know anything about computers."

She clapped her hands in mock applause. "And I suppose you've never heard of Hillton-Tanner."

"No, I have heard that somewhere." He seemed absorbed in watching the grass grow. "I . . . about last night."

The memory of his touch rushed back and stole her breath away.

"I hope I didn't . . . never mind. I was only wondering if you'd had any luck with the search." Mike's voice faltered. "You know, the ticket."

"Oh, that." As if the ticket mattered. Well, two could play. "Have you?"

"We thought we were on the right track, but it came up empty this morning. There was another clue. Maybe you saw it."

She watched a breeze track across the lake. "I did, although I'm surprised you figured it out. I thought you didn't know anything about computers."

"Fortunately, you don't have to know much to look under a keyboard."

"Under a . . ." Her cheeks went cold. "What did you find?"

"You mean you don't know?"

She refused to be sucked into his game.

"Nothing, really," he said, after a moment. "A name. José Canusi. You mean you found another clue?"

She searched the sky. "I suppose I can tell you. There was a message on one of the drives." She recited the rhyme for him. "And 'big fat H' is 'hen.' " As if she'd known it all along.

"Ten," he said, just like that. "And double sixes. William the Conqueror. What about the rest?"

He was quicker than she'd realized. "I'm not certain about the rest."

Thank God he hadn't been there when the messages flashed on the screen. She began to walk along the shore, toward the boathouse. Too dangerous to tell him anything more, or he'd put it all together and try to get the ticket from her. The sooner she talked to Westfield, the better.

"Planning to watch the fireworks?" He definitely wanted something.

"Why?"

"Gray says they're good. Rockets' red glare, bombs bursting in air."

"No, I don't think I'll stay for them. I'm flying down tomorrow to a lovely little Caribbean island."

He worked his way in front of her. "But you haven't finished here." He had a knack for making a person feel shifty.

"I pulled the clue off the computer. They didn't ask for more."

He took her arm lightly. "Could I persuade you to stay another night?"

She looked at his hand on her arm. The pressure swept her back to the dance floor. Time caught up and rushed past.

▼ ▼ ▼

Mike was vaguely aware that he still held her arm. Her tanned skin felt sun-warm. He sensed a trembling and wasn't sure which of them it was. With her back to the lake, the water danced blue and gold around her head. In the distance behind him, a door slammed.

She couldn't have missed the hint about the fireworks. And yet, she'd said nothing. There was no explanation except that she'd removed the ticket from the nose cone and now hoped to cover up her theft. Her gaze flicked away.

There was a sour taste in his mouth. "I think I should tell you . . ."

She brushed his hand from her arm. "Washington crossing the Delaware."

"Excuse me?"

"Friend of yours. Skater."

He looked over his shoulder. Char strode from the cottage, one arm raised toward him. Her first appearance in nearly twelve hours, and it didn't look as though her mood had changed radically.

"Michael." The voice traveled like a laser. "What are you doing?"

The silent treatment was infinitely better.

"You two must have lots to catch up on," said Liz.

He stretched a hand toward her. "Don't do this to me."

"Happy Independence Day." She backed away and headed for the garden.

He had roughly three and a half seconds to himself, not enough time to collect what remained of his thoughts. His feet stayed planted, but he started to lean toward the house.

"Stay where you are." Char's voice took a rare rise in pitch.

The monstrous unfairness of it all broke over him. She was the one staying in the cottage with a government spy. He, in contrast, was innocence personified. So, who gets accused?

"Come off it." He took a few steps in the direction of some nearby box shrubbery, more as an experiment than a plan.

She ended the march. "What was that?"

"You heard me. Why bother? You're not interested in anything I have to say." He chose the nearest exit, a gap in the boxwood.

"Hold it right there, buster." She hadn't caught up and he accelerated. "This isn't about what you have to say."

Another thing. She shouldn't get to pick when to talk and when not to. He'd made a peace offering last night and she'd rejected it. At least Liz would let a guy talk when he wanted to. Even if she was a thief.

He turned. "What's your problem?"

"My problem?" Char's voice came from the other side of the hedge. "I should think that's obvious. You tell me you'll stay in the city, and next thing I know you've taken my car to chase some bimbo all over creation."

"She's not a bimbo."

"I don't want to hear about her. Let's talk about you."

His hands twitched. It was as he'd feared, a patented sack-and-pillage tirade, with the bonus misery that she thought he'd come to Briarwood because of Liz. Really, it was too much.

"You didn't follow your itinerary, either." He faced the shrubbery in the general direction of her voice. "This doesn't look like the Maryland shore."

It didn't look much like anything. Boxwood surrounded him on three sides, eight feet high. He tried to flank the section ahead and found himself at a dead end. Brilliant.

"You know perfectly well that one of Daddy's clients died and we ended up having to cut the weekend short. I got back to the city and couldn't find you. What was I supposed to think? Just when I'm getting really worried, Roger calls and says you're here."

Good old Donovan. No sign of him all morning. Steering clear of the bloodshed, no doubt.

"I'm glad you mentioned that. What are you doing hanging around that guy, anyway?" Mike shoved his hands in his pockets and began a reflexive inventory as he backed away. Keys. Her keys.

"What am I doing with Roger?" Her voice grew louder and faded away, like a poorly-tuned radio. "What kind of question is that? I've told you a million times." The voice came back strong. "At least Roger's a true friend. I can imagine how long you would have carried on behind my back."

"I'm telling you." He lobbed his voice over the hedge. "There's been no carrying on." Too bad.

"Then what are you doing down here?"

"Gray's an old friend, you know that."

"I know no such thing." She seemed to be just the other side of the thick hedge. "Oh God, this is a maze." As if it were his fault.

He crouched. "So?"

"So stop fooling around and get us out."

"What makes you . . ." For the first time in memory, she was depending on him for something. Good. Let her see how it felt to be on her own. When he spoke again, he let the words fade. "What makes you think I know how?"

"That's too funny." Her footsteps moved away. "Not that I'd trust you to find your way out of a paper bag."

He crept in the opposite direction. She was still talking, but he couldn't make out the words, just the memory of the challenge. 'You don't have the nerve to leave.' He took a few random turns and came to another dead end.

The sun barely cleared the top of the hedge. East-southeast, that would be, the general direction of the house. Maybe what lay ahead wasn't certain, but he knew what he was abandoning. He touched her keys. The BMW would make the perfect getaway vehicle. Just one stop, for a call to Mr. Westfield, then don't look back until Washington. He'd even have the car overhauled before he dropped it at her apartment.

He forced his way straight through the boxwood. Branches clung to him, scratching his arms. On the other side he found another corridor, which he followed toward the sun. When the route ended, he broke through the wall again, using the same painful maneuver, and he was free, out of the maze. He looked back at his escape route. The hedge appeared to have had a cannonball shot out of it. No style points, but it had worked. Best of all, no sight or sound of Char. As inconspicuously as he could, he sprinted to the front of the house, giving the fish pond a wide berth. The car keys were in his hand. Matt and Marsha stood by the open door to the carriage house.

"What's the fool up to now?"

"I'm supposed to know?"

"Morning, folks." He jumped into the driver's seat. The car shuddered as he backed out, but there was no time to investigate. He struggled with the gear shift. Leaving behind a spray of gravel, he sped down the long driveway.

Char thought it obvious why she hung around with Donovan. Over the noise of the engine, he tried to concentrate. A small alarm at the back of his mind suggested he'd forgotten an important detail. Maybe two.

▼ ▼ ▼

From her half-hiding place behind the trunk of the old oak, Liz watched Mike burst from the boxwood and dash across the lawn. His solution to the maze was original, his speed impressive. He disappeared around the corner of the house, and, in a moment, she heard the sound of a car engine. She wondered, simply to have something to wonder about, where he was going. Not that she'd ever see him again.

Char appeared by the far side of the hedge, moving rapidly toward the house. She slowed as the sound of the engine faded. Her face was red and ugly. Liz smiled. But Char caught sight of her and marched toward the tree. Good. Nothing the harpy could do now. Liz yawned without bothering to cover it.

"I suppose you think it's funny," said Char.

"Should I?"

"He never used to be this way. He did what I told him. Then you pulled that stunt at the Tidal Basin."

"Stunt? I haven't done anything." Liz began to walk away.

"Of course you haven't, you've only ruined him." As if he were clay she hoped to turn into a bowl.

"That's crazy."

"Crazy? Crazy is the way he's acted since he met you. I mean, he's always been slow, but this is different." A bead of perspiration appeared on her temple.

"He may be quicker than you think. Anyway, there's nothing between us." She wished it hadn't come out so defensively.

Char emitted a harsh laugh. "Nothing on your side, maybe. That wouldn't stop him. He's like a big dumb dog."

"A what?" One thing he wasn't was a dog. How dense.

"I saw you dancing last night. He was all over you."

"That's not . . ." Liz felt herself flush. "What would you care? I don't understand why you're with him."

"It would ruin my career if people thought I couldn't find a boyfriend."

Liz took a moment to work that one out. "But you don't love him."

"Love him? Honey, have you spent time trying to find a straight single man in Washington? They're damned scarce. When you see one, you gotta grab him and hope he's shapeable."

Shapeable. She did see him as a clay bowl. But her demographic analysis was accurate. Not that Liz had ever reached that level of panic. Not yet. She made a grand gesture.

"Grab away. I'm not stopping you." It was a mess Liz didn't need to dive into. "Better hurry, though. Your big, shapeable dog seems to have driven off without his leash."

"He'll be back." Char pulled a handkerchief from her purse and touched it to her forehead. "You could save me time and tell me where he's gone."

"He didn't say." Liz looked for a way to indicate that the conversation was over without making it look like a retreat. There was little available as props. She stooped and picked a daisy, but the hint was too subtle.

Char returned the handkerchief to her purse. "You must have an idea."

"I don't." Tiresome woman. "From what I could see, he was doing his best to get away from you. That would leave a lot of possibilities, destination-wise."

Even that didn't send the woman packing. She gave Liz the fierce look that probably worked well on men. Liz resolved not to be the one who abandoned the field. She placed the stem of the flower in her teeth, kicked off her sandals, and climbed onto the lowest branch of the oak. As expected, Char declined to follow. Protecting her nails.

"Excuse me." Her voice chased Liz up the tree. "Just what do you think you're doing there?"

"Relaxing," Liz said through clenched teeth. To prove it, she removed the daisy from her mouth and stuck it in her hair. "It's simple. You ought to try it." She climbed higher. Too bad the tree didn't have helicopter seed pods.

Char snorted again. "You think you're so clever, but Roger told me about you. Easy to frighten if you're not in control. That's your weakness."

"What?" Liz slipped on a branch, scraping her palm.

Char stalked off. Liz touched the injured hand to her mouth. Roger had introduced Char as his associate. Trust him to blab about blind dates from his past. And Char was Mike's girlfriend, which meant a connection between Roger and Mike after all. That would start to explain why Mike had pretended to be Roger. But it didn't explain the beard.

Well, they could play all the games they wanted. You lose, guys. She reached into the pocket of her dress and touched the lottery ticket. It was the closest she'd ever been to that much money.

From high above came the sound of a jet. She looked at her watch. Less than twenty-four hours and she'd be heading at last to the elusive island. And no postcards since Bud's news about H-T. Only one loose end to tie up. When Allie returned from her horseback ride, they'd have it out.

The leaves around Liz fluttered in the breeze. It was a good climbing tree, plenty of places to stretch out. She pulled the daisy from her hair. Char did have a point. Where would he be off to in such a hurry? A lavender BMW. Obviously Char's. It didn't fit him at all. Liz twirled the flower between thumb and forefinger. No reason for him to want to drive the thing now.

Absently, she plucked one of the petals. Another. And another. She counted ahead, cheating. The daisy had an odd number of petals. Which meant . . . which meant nothing. Maybe they all did. It was fixed. Still, it felt good to be up in the tree. She leaned back against the trunk and laughed, letting the rest of the petals fall to the ground.

▼ ▼ ▼

"Come in."

The library gave off a tart, citrus odor. Westfield sat behind his desk, on the surface of which he had spread a large white napkin. A tangerine lay in the middle, peeled, impossibly, to the width of one section.

"Ah. Liz." He withdrew the wedge and motioned for her to come in. "May I offer you some?" Pretty cool for a man with ten million dollars at risk.

"No thanks." The desk seemed cleaner than last night. "I may have some news for you."

"Oh?" He stopped with the slice part way to his mouth.

"Yes. But I need to know something. Is it true that Mrs. Owen hid your ticket because you objected to her remarrying?"

He popped the slice in. "Somewhat simplistic, but essentially accurate."

"Why? Why would you care?"

"I know this sounds melodramatic, Liz, but the fact is, it isn't safe."

"For you?"

"For all of us. Let's not pretend. You're aware of our Morveus Industries background. Helen left a couple of years ago, shortly after I did. They're not high on reentry in our business. Once you're out, you must stay out. And Owen's still in the game. Don't mistake me, he's a remarkable man, but as long as he's working in that capacity, he's too dangerous to marry. Especially for an ex-player like Helen."

Liz turned up her lip at his slang. Evidently thinking it a reaction to his explanation, he held up a hand. "Ask your boss."

"Then you admit you know Bud."

"I've . . . I've known of him, for a while. We'd never met before last night. I'd like to stay retired."

"So explain why your butler knows him so well."

He freed another slice of tangerine. "All right. Yes, I've known Bud for some time. We need to keep a low profile, for a number of reasons."

"But all this cloak and dagger." Liz sat in an armchair. "What's the point? The last time we talked, you told me Owen sympathized with your position."

"He does." Westfield ran his hands across the desk, as if to smooth wrinkles in the wood grain. "We're friends, after all. And I don't object to him personally. It's the formal association that worries me."

Still no sign of the missing files on the clean desk. "And what about your association with Hillton-Tanner?"

"With whom?"

The tangerine rolled off the desk and thudded to the floor.

"The files on your desk. They were there yesterday afternoon."

"That name means nothing." He picked up the tangerine. "I'm sorry."

"Are you . . . you're serious."

She looked around the room without taking any of it in. Mike. He'd taken the H-T files. That was why he needed the BMW. Fine. Let him. That job was over. Concentrate on the present. Only one last thing prevented her from turning over the lottery ticket and walking out.

"This is an awkward question to ask a parent. Can you trust your son?"

"I suppose that would depend on what's involved."

"This is what's involved." She produced the ticket. "I found it in the nose cone of one of your fireworks." She recounted her search. As she finished, the telephone rang.

"No worry," he said. "Liddell will answer."

Liz put the ticket on the desk with her hand over it. "I'm not sure what Gray is up to. He hired us, and by all rights I ought to be giving this to him. But it seems to belong to you, even he admits that, so I'm going to turn it over and trust I'm doing the right thing." She slid the ticket across the desk.

"I never had a daughter. If I did, I'd want her to be you."

She fought down the lump in her throat. It was the sign she'd been looking for. He wiped his hands on the napkin and pulled the ticket close. He seemed to hold his breath. Since her discovery in the garden shed, she'd imagined many things he might say by way of congratulations.

"Liz, this is the wrong ticket."

She felt as though she'd shown up for the big party on the wrong day.

"This isn't the winner. Same date, January 4th. But the first number on the winning ticket is seven." He pointed. "This is three."

She closed her eyes, hoping the citrus smell would waft her to her island.

"In fact, this appears to be the one Gray showed me before dinner the other night. Are you sure you found it in a rocket?"

"Of course I'm sure. It's the only one I've seen." Gray. Gray wasn't smart enough to trick her onto a false trail.

Westfield rubbed his thumb over the paper. "I don't understand why anyone would want to put this in the fireworks."

"Excuse me, sir." Liddell entered. "The telephone. Mr. Archer."

"Mister who? Of course. Pardon me." He lifted the receiver. "Westfield. Yes, Mike . . . Why yes, she has, in fact. She's here at the moment . . . She did. No, the wrong one . . . She didn't seem to. Why? . . . Oh. One moment." He handed the phone across. "He wants to talk to you."

Liz took it, suspiciously. "Yes?" By now she expected a hidden camera.

"Hi." He said something else, but she found it hard to concentrate on the words. How strange to hear his voice on the phone, when they'd only ever talked in person. The telephone line was a tangible barrier, like seeing a person through a window, right there but not there.

"You owned up to finding the ticket." He sounded pleased. "That's really great. But it means I owe you an apology. And an explanation. Can you meet me in town in twenty minutes? I'm at the Hartigan Tap."

He hung up before she could think to ask why. He'd expected her to find the ticket. She picked it up from the desk to have something to focus on. And now he was telling her what to do and where to go. Not a good development.

▼ ▼ ▼

The Hartigan Tap served food, even on holidays. At just past one o'clock the place was jammed and it took Liz a few seconds to spot him. Mike sat at a dark wooden counter that ran the length of one wall, engaged in earnest discussion with the empty stool to his left. She edged closer. But there was no one else, just a soliloquy.

"Wonderful," he told the stool. "But I'm afraid she thinks I'm a space case, if not totally nuts. I have this way of making terrible first impressions. My second and third impressions aren't so hot, either . . . Well, easy for you to say, but it's all a matter of timing. I feel, I don't know, conspired against by fate and circumstance. More sinned against than . . . oh." He caught sight of her. "Thank goodness. Hello."

She managed a tense smile. "What are you doing?"

"Please, have a seat." He gestured toward the stool.

She eyed it, almost willing to believe there was an invisible someone there.

"Don't worry. People kept asking if the seat was taken. Eventually I figured I'd pretend someone was there, and people would leave me alone."

"Interesting approach. Have you tried it before?"

"No, I just thought it up."

She slid onto the stool and hung her purse from the back. "I suppose I should feel honored."

"Oh, these are for you." He gathered together a bouquet of wildflowers.

"For me?" The flowers were in her hand. Conversations around them blended into white noise. Everything went out of focus except for him.

He broke eye contact and slid a menu along the counter. "Please choose something. The waiter wasn't cheerful even before I came in."

After they'd ordered, she leaned on the counter. "Is this your idea of a private spot?"

"I never said we had to talk in private."

"Then why not come back to the house?"

He hunched his shoulders. "That's part of the problem. I borrowed Char's car."

"I noticed. So, return it."

"I would, only I was changing the oil yesterday and I . . . to make a short story shorter, the motor is now, I believe the technical term is, toast. I made it to a garage, but they can't fix it until tomorrow."

Divine retribution for having taken the H-T files. "You were hoping I'd give you a ride?"

"Something like that."

"It would have been a big help if you had mentioned that on the phone. I bicycled here."

"You didn't."

"Well, why shouldn't I?"

"Good point. I don't suppose it's a tandem? Okay, never mind. My fault."

With him not so much in control, she relaxed. "Was that it?"

"No, no. Of course not."

"Did you want to discuss Hillton-Tanner?"

"I told you, I don't have anything to do with that."

Someone jostled her from behind, and she had to move closer. She was intensely aware of the space between them.

"Then why were you in such a hurry to get away from the house?"

"I didn't mean to be. There's leaving, and there's leaving. But you saw her."

Liz hadn't intended to make 'her' the topic of conversation. She balanced her knife between the tines of a fork. "It didn't seem as though you'd done anything you needed to be worried about."

"That's not really the issue with her."

"But she was upset." The knife reflected the image of her fingers twitching on the counter. She stilled them.

"Yes. To tell you the truth, I think I'm a letdown."

"How so?"

A party nearby erupted into laughter.

"Promise," Mike said.

"Promise what?"

"She says I've got lots of it."

"Maybe you do."

"I'm wasting it, she thinks."

Interesting, that neither of them had uttered Char's name. Liz hooked her feet on the crossbar. "Pardon the observation, but I'd say the only thing you're wasting is the time you spend with that woman. Who died and left her in charge of your life?"

He paled. "Who died?"

"You know what I mean. She's a headache on legs."

"Oh." He freed her knife from the fork and laid it gently down.

"Look." She fixed her place setting. "If there's one thing I've learned, it's that we don't need anyone inside our skulls but ourselves."

"That's the problem. I'm not even sure I'm in there. Do you feel certain about things? I don't. I don't even understand my life, most days." He looked toward the kitchen. "I'm beginning to believe I've got a kind of paralysis."

"Meaning what?"

"We get one shot at the world. I don't want to screw up my life by doing the wrong thing, so I end up afraid to commit to anything."

"Oh, but you have to try. You can't be afraid of success."

"Exactly. Success at what?"

She looked him in the eye. A nice eye. "Do you think there's supposed to be some kind of revelation or something? Is that what you're waiting for?" Lucky thing she couldn't see herself in the mirror.

"No. Yes. I don't know. I'm not sure whether to believe in fate or not. The night before we met, I was watching the stars and I stepped in a dog pile. I was wearing a moose costume at the time."

"You what? Why?"

"I just was. You probably saw it in the trunk of the car." He blushed. "I couldn't scrape the stuff off, so I pitched the whole boot in the trash. With a bare foot, I had to keep my eyes on the ground, looking for broken glass. And I came across a length of cotton string. A sign, I thought. So I followed it along the sidewalk, as if it were a high wire, not checking to see where it went, ready to go anywhere. You'll think this sounds dumb, but it was my yellow brick road, an umbilical to adventure. Then it veered into a dark alley, midway along the block, and I had to abandon it. It wasn't my fate."

Something in the way he said it made her rest her elbows on the counter. A curious attitude toward life, taking things as they came.

"Over the last few days," Mike said, "I've started to wonder whether my fate isn't something different, very different."

Their legs touched. She didn't press closer, but she didn't pull away, either. Let it happen. See how it turns out. A waiter stumbled, dropping a tray to the floor. Splatters of guacamole flew through the air, landing on the wall. Mike reached up to clean the food off with his napkin.

"You know, this is something of a relief to me. I can sit here and say with absolute certainty that I'm not responsible for that."

"Are you usually?"

"Things tend to come unglued when I'm around." He put down the napkin. "This is a nice change."

She waited, but there was nothing more. "You are stuck."

"That's what I was saying."

The small part of her that had hoped the conversation would head in another direction went back to sleep. She dug in her wallet.

"I may have something that could help you. It's advice my dad gave me, a long time ago." She pulled out a faded square of red construction paper and handed it across.

He peered at it, front and back. "Nothing's written here."

"That's right. Sometimes there aren't any answers. You have to take the leap even when you don't know where you'll land." She stuffed the square of paper back in her wallet. "Now, how about that explanation? Or did you just want to talk about Char and life?"

"No. Definitely not."

She felt a rush of elation, and that scared her. It wasn't as if Char were a woman to be jealous of. Mike drummed his fingers on the counter.

"I told you on the phone, I owe you an apology. I put the dummy ticket there last night. You see, I wasn't sure what you were up to. Once you brought it to Mr. Westfield, thinking it was genuine, I knew you were okay."

"You were testing me?"

"Sort of. I didn't plan it that way."

A boisterous group in the corner began singing the national anthem. Testing. He had the nerve to do that, after he'd stolen the H-T files.

"I'm not sure I like that. In fact, I know I don't. How could you be sure I wouldn't know it was the wrong one?"

"If you knew, there wouldn't be any reason for you to try to pass it off."

My God, he'd worked the whole thing out. Five moves ahead in the chess match, at least. The smell of deep-fried food was beginning to make her ill. She ran her palms along the counter.

"So, what are you saying? You found the real ticket?"

"In the rocket." He looked uncomfortable. "Last night. Ten minutes before you got there."

From the kitchen came the sound of glass shattering. He smiled and gestured toward it. "I didn't do that, either."

"Screw the damned glass. How could you know when I was in the shed?" A hideous thought struck her. "Were you watching me? How? It's impossible. You couldn't have known which box to look in. You didn't have the clue."

"But I did. There are parallel clues. You don't need all of them."

She tried desperately to regroup, anything to salvage some pride. But there was nothing. He'd won at every turn. "Okay, where's the real ticket now?"

"I hid it again, right away. It's in the . . . oh, no."

She turned to see. In the doorway of the Tap stood Gray, panting. His hair had been cut quite short. On only one side.

▼ ▼ ▼

Mike made sure the bartender wasn't going for a weapon.

"The problem with chasing after life is sometimes the string you need to follow is behind you." He nodded toward Gray. "Case in point. Excuse me a moment."

Liz shrugged, a bit of a disappointment. He preferred her smile.

"Did you see them?" At the door Gray was wide-eyed.

"See who? You look as if you escaped from brain surgery pre-op."

"Damn. I must have been too far back. Left my blasted specs at the . . . you know. Not many places open today, with the holiday and whatnot. I figured they must have ducked in here."

An oppressive silence descended on the room as patrons stared.

"There had better be a serious head blow to explain this behavior." Mike gave Gray a gentle shove through the doorway and followed, waving to let everyone know he had it in hand. They stood in the street.

"I know how this looks," said Gray.

"Do you? I wish I had a mirror."

"What? Oh." He ran a hand through what was left of his hair.

A bicycle leaned against a blue mailbox. Mike touched the handlebar. "Have you got a story that won't get you committed?"

"It's perfectly simple. I was sitting in the barbershop when through the window I spied Allison's mother."

"Uh huh. Which caused you to leave in the middle of a haircut."

"Yes, as it happens. I popped out in time to see her round the corner. Loosed the smock and followed at top speed, but lost her."

Mike looked up the street, almost expecting to see the barber's cloth. "I'm surprised you found a shop open on the Fourth."

"Earl has a special on major holidays. A half-off deal."

"What, left side only?"

"Yes, yes. We haven't time for your wit. We need to find her."

"Bad news, pal. You sacrificed your trim for nothing." The table in the window was filled with gawkers. "Come on, let's get away from here. We don't need Allison's mother any more."

"Well, of course, I know that."

"No, that's not what I–"

"You don't understand. It wasn't her I was interested in. It was the person she was talking to."

"And that was?"

Gray lowered his voice. "Donovan."

"Really? What would she want with him?"

"Aha. Well might you ask. He can't be after Allison. She hates the blister. He practically drove her from the last place."

"My question was what would the woman want with him, not what wouldn't she."

"How should I know? You're the detective."

"I am not. You made that up."

"So I did. Still, you were always the bright one. I just do the organizing."

They headed for a nearby park, a rectangle of green surrounded by a five-foot hedge, with a bandstand and a statue of a soldier on a horse. It was neatly maintained and, best of all, empty.

"Okay, since I'm in charge of thinking, here's what I think." Mike headed for the bandstand. "The only way we can find out what they're up to is if we actually spy on them, right? But they're not here now, and I'm in the middle of something kind of important, so could we just drop it?"

"But I'm afraid the Donovan item will ruin everything."

"What everything?"

"Everything everything. Allison."

Mike sat on the steps of the bandstand. Donovan was good at ruining things, witness how he'd brought Char to Briarwood. On second thought, it might be worth finding him just to say thank you. No, that was the wrong way to look at it. Gray needed help. A little help. That wouldn't kill anybody.

"All right, I'll give you two minutes, then I have to get back."

"Terrific. They can't be far off. I came straightaway."

"Well, there's a hotel a block from here. Did you try it?"

"Disgusting." Gray shuddered. "The Montclair? No one stays there."

"I didn't mean it that way, chowderhead. They could be in the lobby." Mike followed the path that cut across the park toward the hotel. It didn't look like a yellow brick road. But it could be the leap Liz meant.

▼ ▼ ▼

The lobby of the hotel was filled with a comfortable darkness and little else. Three plush chairs were grouped around a television set, which was off.

Gray gave a half-salute to the clerk as they approached the front desk. She regarded him coldly.

"Y'all need something?"

"Not really. Pay us no mind."

The dining room was closed. Through the doorway to the bar, Mike saw the back of a lone elderly figure hunched on a stool. A basket on the counter held books of matches with the hotel's name stamped onto them. Just above the basket was a 'No Smoking' sign.

"Okay." Mike grabbed a matchbook. "We came up empty. It was worth checking. Excuse me," he said to the clerk. "You didn't happen to see a couple of people come in, did you? A middle-aged woman with a younger man?"

She rolled her eyes. "Why would I see anyone like that in here?"

"I've just had a thought." Gray retreated to the front window.

Mike tossed his matchbook in the air and caught it. "Bound to happen."

"Shut up and listen. What if Donovan's not really with the government? He doesn't have a very plausible story. What if he works for Allison's mother? Could be a plant."

"Plant?"

"Sure." Gray snapped his fingers. "Sure, she can't access our place all the time. Once she hid the ticket, she'd need someone to keep an eye on things. Maybe she paid this Nishida archaeologist to take off for the weekend in order to sub in Donovan. If we came close, he'd know how to snatch the ticket."

"No, you don't understand. I–"

"Look, there she is." Gray dropped to his hands and knees and peeked over the window sill. "Get down, will you?"

Mike kneeled, although there didn't seem much danger of being spotted by anyone. The window was grimy. He had to rub a circle on the glass before he could see through. Across the street, a tall woman moved briskly along the sidewalk. He wouldn't have recognized her as Allison's mother. She wore a loose pants outfit and had on sunglasses beneath a floppy hat, a more casual look than she'd had whenever Mike had seen her before. A child's red wagon trailed behind her, containing a two-foot statue.

Gray squinted. "What's she hauling?"

"It looks like a garden gnome." Mike rubbed at the glass again. "It is."

"Garden gnome?" Gray pressed his nose to the window. "What would she want with that?"

"Believe me, I'd tell you if I knew."

"Hold it." He squeezed Mike's arm. "Dad used to have a garden gnome. I told you. Sidney."

"Your point?"

"What if she hid the ticket on Sidney, and since Dad didn't find it she's reclaimed it?"

Mike pulled the shirt free. "I told you, the ticket was in the fireworks. That gnome hasn't been in the garden all weekend."

"Okay, so why drag it around in a wagon?"

"There, I admit, you have me."

Gray scrambled to his feet. "You'd better go after her."

"I'd better?"

"Of course. I can't risk her catching me following her. Anyway, I've got to fetch my specs. Tell you what: I'll meet you."

Mike's knees had begun to throb. "You don't know where I'll be."

"Oh. You haven't one of those homing gizmos, I suppose?"

"Gee, I guess Q forgot to give me one for this mission."

"Good point. Okay, I'd best stay here. You call when you find out where she's headed." He pointed to the matchbook. "The number's right on there."

"This is nuts, Gray. How do you know I'll end up at a phone?"

"Quick. She's getting away."

"Let her."

"What, are you afraid?"

Mike stood. No reason to give in to another of Gray's ill-considered plans, and every reason not to. Liz was waiting at the Tap and would soon start to wonder. On the other hand . . . there had been something odd in the woman's appearance. And she was, after all, hauling a gnome. He shoved the matches into his pants pocket.

"Here's what I'll do. You have five more minutes of my time. I'll follow her that long. In five minutes, I'm turning, no matter what." Gray opened his mouth, but Mike spread his fingers. "Five."

"Oh, blast, very well. You'd best be off."

Outside, Mike glimpsed the wagon rounding the corner. He crossed the street and hurried along the sidewalk. At the end of the block, he crouched and peered around a brick building. She was making good time. He had to pick up the pace to keep her comfortably in sight. And still something in her appearance troubled him, something more than the gnome, which rocked with a gentle drunken motion that made him expect it to tip over. It faced backward, as if keeping a lookout. He didn't care for its expression.

Allison's mother pulled up beside a parked van. With nowhere to hide, Mike had to brazen it out. He lengthened his stride and turned his head toward the row of closed storefronts. The air held a slight odor of mint, generating negative associations he couldn't immediately place.

As he drew even with the van, a movement was reflected in the plate glass. Before he could face it, something dropped over his head, something dark and soft. He'd barely identified it as cloth when he felt a sharp blow. His legs gave way beneath him. No time to be scared, just a tingling regret as he fell forward into a world that went briefly white, and then black again.

–13–

Wishing she'd thought to do so when he'd left, Liz looked at her watch. Knowing how much time had passed would have helped in arriving at the right level of irritation.

He'd gone to help a friend. There was probably a good explanation for the fact that he'd been away for, well, twenty minutes at least. Something bad could have happened. For all she knew, he was lying in the street bleeding, while ill-tempered, inconsiderate Liz worked up a petty rage over being left alone at a lunch counter, precisely the kind of stunt that awful Char would pull.

She watched thirty more seconds sweep past. Reality time, Liz. The guy didn't have a clue. He'd probably forgotten where she was. It had to be some kind of hormonal defect in her that attracted the hopeless ones. She abandoned the remains of lunch and left a generous tip. At the last moment, she gathered up the flowers. Outside, the street was all but deserted; odd for a small town at noon on a national holiday. At least no one had taken the bicycle.

They could have planned the whole thing. Perhaps Gray had stood in the entrance for ages, waiting for Mike to tell her about the ticket, then giving him an excuse to leave. Her stomach churned. A straight setup, nothing but a dose of humiliation.

She eyed the bike, contemplating the exertion of the mostly uphill way back to Briarwood on a warm afternoon. Not that there was anything to hurry back for. She could picture it: in she'd come and there they'd be, laughing at her. She clutched her flowers and walked the bicycle along the sidewalk, past the stores, watching her reflection jump from window to window.

A few houses stood on the outskirts of town, and then nothing. No cars passed. The road cut across a small field and entered dense woods a quarter mile farther on. She followed it, thinking of Mike but not wanting to. As she walked beneath the fragrant canopy of evergreens, she caught sight of a low fence off to the side, lengths of rusty iron and granite posts. An overgrown path led to it from the road. It had a familiar, sad look.

She leaned the bicycle against a nearby tree. For once without a place to be or a deadline to meet, she walked through the brush, still holding her flowers. The air was heavy with balsam. Brambles on either side grabbed at her shorts and scratched her legs. She hugged her arms to her chest.

The path ended at a gap between two of the fence posts. She walked into a square enclosure, perhaps twenty feet on each side, covered with pine needles. In the center, eight slabs had settled at dejected angles. She ran her hand along the nearest; smooth, partially covered with moss. It had a date, 1745. Everything else was gone. The next, much the same. The third bore the beginning of a name, *HAL* and faded away. She scraped off the moss but found nothing more.

She slid down, her back against one of the posts and her hands pressed to the ground. Her throat tightened. The pine needles felt brittle and sharp against her palms. She raised teary eyes toward the sheltering evergreens. Through the branches, she could see specks of a blue sky that seemed very far away. In the tiny cemetery, she hung her head and wept.

▼ ▼ ▼

He was running up a staircase made of stone, an endless spiral, a north tower in a medieval castle. Boots slapped on the steps below. Something in the design favored the uphill combatant. He ran on. Higher was better. Swords. Right-handed swordsmen had an advantage on a spiral staircase. Bastards.

To hell with swords. They were shooting. Sparks flew around his head. Fireworks. He burst through a doorway and onto a roof. It was night outside, dark. He did not want the roof. More stairs, more stairs. A low railing circled the top of the tower. No weapon. Nowhere to go.

The Colonel appeared in the doorway, panting. She brandished her stun gun. "We told you about coming. We told you."

He backed away until the railing caught him behind his knees. Beyond, he sensed a bottomless void. Leap, and don't worry about landing.

Liz left the flowers by the grave and pedaled slowly back into town. At the intersection with Main Street she stopped, even though there was no traffic, and rested a foot on the ground. Her shadow stretched toward Briarwood. At the unexpected pressure on her arm, she jumped.

"Take it easy." Bud's unwelcome voice was the last thing she needed. "I've been looking all over for you. How do you get lost in a town this size?"

She shook free of his grasp. "I don't know. Why not try it?"

"Whoa, settle down."

"What do you want?" She sat on the bike seat.

"World peace and a royal flush. What's eating you?"

"I need a little space today." She pedaled across the street.

He jogged to catch up, huffing. "No problem. Can we talk a minute first?"

"I suppose." She coasted.

"Give me a break, Liz, get off the bike." He grabbed for it and missed. "There's a bench in that park there, in the shade."

She preceded him past the war statue and dropped the bike to the grass.

"Sheesh." He steadied himself on the bench. "I hear you found the glass slipper. You're the best. I always said it." He pulled an inhaler from his pocket.

"Glass slipper?" She glanced at her sneaker. A lace had come loose. "Oh. The ticket. You're well informed."

"Goes with the territory."

"Swell. So you wanted to compliment me?"

"Of course I did. But you're right. There's something else. A bit delicate."

"Well." She bent to retie her shoe. "You're just the man for it."

"The fact is, I ran into Westfield Junior. I gather you beat him and his friend to the hiding place. He sounded real irritated."

"Did he?" There was a plaque at the base of the statue. 'This park dedicated by the Daughters of the Confederacy.' Damsels of the Lost Cause. Either Gray was a terrific actor or it hadn't been a setup after all.

Bud grunted. "Yes, he did. Real irritated."

"And?"

"To put it mildly, it made me curious." He cleared his throat. "Here we have Liz with the magic ticket. The guy who hired her doesn't know where it is. Leaving me to wonder, maybe, just maybe, she neglected to turn it over."

"What are you saying?" Liz looked at him.

"Nothing. I'm not saying anything. I'm asking."

"Asking whether I stole the ticket?"

He wiped his forehead. " 'Stole' is a harsh word."

"So is 'fuckhead.' Did it occur to you I might have given it to Westfield?" Unbelievable for Bud to come up with this kind of slander.

His eyes narrowed. "Did you?"

"No, I didn't."

"Then fork it over. No more fooling around."

"I don't have it to fork."

"Where is it?"

"Search me. And I don't mean that literally. Your friend Archer found it. He substituted a phony for gullible old me to find. It's the one I gave Westfield this morning, and boy did I feel stupid."

He digested her news. "If that's true, why doesn't young Westfield know?"

"It is true."

Bud's brow furrowed. "I don't believe it."

"Not my problem." She watched a car stop in front of the Tap. Maybe Mike deserved another chance. Maybe pigs are rocket-powered.

"This is for real." Bud reached out but checked himself when he saw her expression. "I need that ticket."

"For the reputation of the company? I'm telling you, I don't have it."

"Doesn't have anything to do with the company. It's personal. I told Helen I'd get it."

No way did Liz want to hear about Bud's love life. "Helen?"

"Helen. Helen Owen. My sister. The one who hid the ticket in the first place. The one who left the clues in the computer. The one who never figured our client would hire me to find the damn thing."

▼ ▼ ▼

Mike regained consciousness with the sense of having belly-flopped onto concrete. He lay on his stomach, breathing hard and staring into blackness. Rough cloth pressed against his face, and he felt something wet. Saliva? Blood?

He tried to roll over and couldn't. His arms were torqued behind him at an awkward angle. When he made any effort to move one, the other tugged across his back, and rope bit into his wrists. He tried his legs, but his feet were held together as well. He worked on not hyperventilating and figuring out why anyone would want to tie him down. And whether they were nearby.

Several minutes of tense thinking produced only the conclusion that the situation would improve if he could establish where he was. He shook the hood from his head. He was lying face down on a cot, perhaps a foot or two off the floor. A pillow, pungent with mildew, supported his chin. Floorboards above him creaked, and muffled noises followed.

The room had a cool and different quality of dark, filled with the smell of earth and cat urine. At first he thought it might be the tunnel, but there was carpet, a flight of wooden steps and unfinished walls. The steady throbbing in his neck brought his thoughts back to the van, and to Allison's mother. It might be the basement of Monte Rosa.

He had the sensation of being watched. By not staring directly at it he could pick out a shape in the corner, possibly someone hunched on a stool. He shut his eyes and rested his chin on the pillow, trying not to inhale its foulness. Then he peeked. Concentrating now, he could tell that it was a man, motionless, a short man with a hat, a silly, pointed . . . oh. He opened his eyes wider and stared at the garden gnome. It stared back.

"So," Mike said bitterly, "don't just stand there, give me a hand."

"I don't think so." Under the metallic rasp, the voice was clearly female. "Anything worth doing is worth doing on your own."

He tried to sit up on the cot and felt stabbing pain in his shoulders.

"You see the value of learning to tie knots properly."

No obvious response came to mind. Okay, the gnome was rigged for two-way audio. It couldn't see in the dark. He struggled against the ropes.

"I wouldn't bother. Inherited your father's stubbornness, I see."

Deep weirdness. But wait a minute. If there was one thing Dad had never been, it was stubborn. The realization that the kidnapping was a mistake made it better, somehow. "I'm afraid you grabbed the wrong guy."

"Not likely."

He focused on her voice. It didn't sound like Allison's mother, even taking into account the tinniness, but it was something familiar. He heard the rattle of a door handle, and a shaft of light appeared at the top of the stairs. The clunk of footsteps descending, and a pair of legs came into view. Jeans, not a dress. And the tread was heavy, a man's tread.

"Don't try anything cute." Another familiar voice. Unfortunately, he could place that one right away. The owner of the legs ducked under the low ceiling as he reached the bottom of the steps. He stood in the cellar, backlit from above. At least it explained the high-tech garden gnome. It was just the sort of toy those government guys loved.

▼ ▼ ▼

Bud drove her toward Monte Rosa. The trunk of his rented Mercedes wouldn't close with the bike in it, so he'd rigged a bungee cord. Occasionally Liz looked back and saw the trunk flapping up and down, as if chewing.

"Who is this Archer guy, anyway?" said Bud.

"A thorn in my side, since you ask."

"And how'd he beat you to it?"

"I haven't figured that out." It galled her, having to admit it. "He claimed not to need the computer, but that's a lie. No formal training, though."

"And what's he done with the real ticket?"

"He didn't tell me." She watched shadows of tree branches flicker on the gleaming hood. "He was about to, when Gray broke in on us."

"In the middle of what, Mata Hari?"

"Up yours." She stared out the window. "Lunch, if you must know."

Bud made traveling a competitive sport. Liz slouched in the passenger seat, feeling that her life was unraveling, and that it was all somehow Mike's fault. Not that he was worth thinking about. She put her feet on the dash.

"Tell me how Gray knew to call TekSekure in the first place," Liz said.

"You tell me. Is that bad luck, or what?"

She thought about it. "But you said Helen didn't expect Westfield to hire you. She must have known you were old friends."

"An overstatement. That was why she thought he wouldn't call. It would have put me in an awkward spot."

"But, when Gray called, it must have occurred to you she might be involved in this project."

"I knew Helen was down here, and it's a small place, but it never crossed my mind to investigate any connection. You can't expect me to figure she was the one who hid the ticket. We're not so close she tells me everything."

Liz leaned against the window. "It's a waste of time to see her."

"No, it's not. We've got to clear the air about how TekSekure fits in."

"We've got to clear the air? This is your mess." Helping Bud with family relationships. Things couldn't get worse.

They passed the entrance to Briarwood and he waved toward it. "Joey's still fooling around in there. When we get to Monte Rosa, call over and tell him to knock it off. We need to get back to Washington."

"Explain 'fooling around,'" said Liz.

"Looking for something."

"The ticket?" She sat straighter. "You've got him searching my stuff."

"There was a chance you'd stolen the ticket, Liz. I had every right."

"The hell you did. You have some nerve, you jerk."

"I did what I had to."

She dug her fingers into the shoulder belt. "How is it you never told me you were related to Allie?"

"For crying out loud, I wasn't hiding it. There's a lot you and I haven't discussed about my relatives. I bet I never told you about my crazy aunt."

"Don't be a smartass. I bet your aunt never worked at Hillton-Tanner."

The car swerved. "What?"

"Now you're going to tell me you didn't know Allie worked at H-T."

"What makes you think she did?"

"She told me."

"No kidding." He whistled. "That complicates things."

"You don't say."

"Yeah. If it's public enough that you know about it, there's no way I couldn't. Helen's going to think I spend my life snooping on her family."

"Would you listen to yourself? Embezzlement's a crime, in case you've forgotten. You should be slightly worried your niece is involved." Again.

"Slow down there. Seems to me it wasn't many days ago you accused my nephew of trashing your office. Use your head. If you're a friend of Allison's, you know she isn't capable of something like what happened at H-T."

"We don't always know people as well as we think."

"You can't be serious." He glanced across. "You are serious. Come on. H-T must have a hundred fifty employees. There's nothing to connect Allison with the disappearing cash."

"She used to work in the accounting department."

"Used to." He tapped the gearshift. "So she's gone."

"That has nothing to do with it."

"Did she tell you when she left?"

"Couple of months ago, it sounded like."

"All right, then." He tooted the horn.

"Proving nothing. The bug artist runs on auto-pilot, I told you that. It would be easy enough to set a timer if you wanted." She looked at her watch. Half past two. More than an hour since Mike had walked out of . . . the Tap.

"I wasn't through, okay? Do you have the exact date Allison started?"

"Why?"

"Sometimes you can be awfully dense for such a smart girl."

"Oh, you've been taking tact lessons." She moved away from him.

He turned the car into the driveway of Monte Rosa. "With me, what you see is what you get."

"What I see is a myopic, sexist jerk."

"A jerk who pays your salary, sunshine."

"Not for long." The house had a lily pond out front. Maybe Bud would fall in. Just like . . .

He killed the engine. "You're too loyal. You wouldn't dare quit."

Too loyal? "Oh, wouldn't I?" So, excessive loyalty was the tragic flaw. She threw open the door. "Watch me."

▼ ▼ ▼

"Man, you can't stay out of trouble." Donovan untied the knots at Mike's ankles. "Stretch your legs. No heroics."

Mike did as he was told, feeling the blood rush into abandoned patches of skin. Escaping shouldn't be a problem. All he had to do was free his wrists, take half a dozen karate lessons, and manage to catch Donovan unaware.

"Where am I?" It was a start.

"Here." Donovan reached around the gnome as if he were scratching it behind the ear. Mike heard a faint click, like a light switch turning off.

The cellar offered little in the way of walking space. Not much to work with either: stacks of boxes along the walls, a coiled garden hose, a couple of broken chairs, and the cot. High in one wall was a square ventilation screen. Big enough to hide behind, maybe. The opposite wall had a door, closed. He paused in front of it, wondering whether he could get through and whether he wanted to. From above came the sound of water rushing through pipes.

"Archer, you're making my life difficult. Whatcha got going? Tell me."

"Nothing. I've got nothing going. I don't know what's happening."

"What's happening is you're screwing up a very delicate surveillance operation. I've got Nishida right where I want her. She trusts me, okay, thinks I'm helping. Then you come barging in and you're gonna trash everything. I gotta get you out of town. Don't have much time. She'll be down any minute."

Mike worked his jaw back and forth, feeling as if he'd stumbled into a foreign language class. "Nishida?" That was the other archaeologist.

"Japanese for 'Westfield.' " Donovan fitted a key to the door and swung it open. Mike could see nothing but darkness. He tried to concentrate. Nishida. Mrs. Harper as Nishida. Mrs. Harper as archaeologist. It was like being unable to fit the last piece of a jigsaw puzzle into the only space left.

▼ ▼ ▼

It was all very well to make a dramatic exit, Liz discovered, but the effect was rather spoiled without a handy curtain to disappear behind. Having slammed the car door in Bud's face, a satisfying feeling as far as it went, she found herself standing in the driveway of Monte Rosa with no place to go.

Bud got out of the car and stretched. "We going in, or do you want to kick all the gravel off the driveway first?"

She hadn't even noticed her toe gouging the ground. Liz followed to the front steps and watched as he let himself in. Bud and Allie, related.

"Helen?" He shouted again from the hall.

Empty coat rack. Umbrella stand with cane. Mirror on the wall by the door. Expensive-looking art throughout. Like Briarwood, the house was cut from Gone-With-the-Wind cloth, except the staircase here wrapped around two sides of the foyer, unlike Westfield's split monstrosity. There was no reason to stay. Charlie the cabbie could whisk her to the train, which was what stood between her and the end of the damn job. Bud peered toward the head of the stairs, as if expecting some sort of royal procession.

"Helen?" He rested a foot on the first step. "Maybe she's having a nap. Make yourself at home." He took the steps two at a time, and it was only then Liz realized he was worried.

She pushed open the door to the adjoining room. At Briarwood it would have been the parlor, but here it was a study. Light-colored furniture, simple in taste. No papers, only a computer on the desk. Pictures of Allie, several, and an older man. In a short bookcase was a collection of genealogy materials. So much more went on in Hartigan Gap than she understood. It might be better to get away, before any more foolishness occurred.

The sun pushed shadows toward the front of the property. Aside from the indignity of having to march through the woods simply to pack the pieces of her life into a suitcase that Bud had Joey rifling, there was the problem of Mike. If he hadn't returned to Briarwood already, he would soon. She could envision the scene, with him producing the lottery ticket, Westfield beaming and bells pealing, fatted calf and all that. She just didn't want to see it.

There must be a better excuse for sticking around. It wasn't confronting Allie, because that was a pure dead end. At least Allie's mother had no H-T files around. After checking for security cameras, Liz approached the computer. The desk was uncluttered. She ran her palms across the surface. The older man in the picture. Laptop. Train. Allie's stepfather, hiding all weekend.

Noise from above signaled Bud's movements, a room-to-room search. Time was growing short for stabs at the computer. She powered it up and drummed her nails on the desk. A quick look. Thirty seconds, tops.

A door slammed somewhere in the house. She whipped through various directories, scanning for something, anything. But there was no evidence of encryption, nothing suspicious. Wait, an F: drive. Methodically, she turned it inside out. Genealogy stuff. She'd seen the same files in Briarwood. There must be more; it couldn't be so straightforward. Footsteps in the hallway.

Westfield and Mrs. Owen shared a network. The logical explanation was that the celebrated feud was a sham. The footsteps stopped behind her. She heard a growl.

"Don't worry, Bud." She repositioned the mouse. "I'm getting out."

"Take your time, dear."

She spun in her seat. Leaning against the door frame, a small dog beside her, was Allie's mother. Bud's sister. It didn't seem fair that the person who stole the lottery ticket could claim the moral high ground.

▼ ▼ ▼

Donovan flipped on a light on the other side of the door and Mike saw that the next room was a garage. There was a van, and a red motorcycle.

"Come on. We need to get you back to the city."

Mike edged toward the door. "Why would anyone want to capture me?"

"Easy enough. She thought you were Gray Westfield."

"That seems extreme. The guy's only in love with her daughter."

Donovan gave him a hard look. "Simple. She figured he'd follow from the barbershop. Before you go, has Gray asked you to do anything unusual?"

Mike stopped in the doorway. "Define 'unusual.'"

"Oh, helping him with something odd."

Ten million dollars. Not so odd. Indeed, it was even. Mike had never been much good at finessing, but he went with one now. "Not really. Stuff around the house, mostly." Maybe Donovan knew about the attack on Allison.

"But you made a pointed comment last night. Something about looking in the wrong place."

It was the ticket. As Mike pressed against the frame, he felt the matchbook in his back pocket. So much for finesse. "Did I? Shooting my mouth off again. Someone told me there was a scavenger hunt, and I was only saying that because . . . because I was upset Char wanted to spend time with you."

"Well, what do you expect, when her boyfriend . . ."

But Mike stopped listening. The woman in the sunglasses, the voice from the gnome. It could have been Char. If she and Donovan had something going, this could be a ploy to get Mike on a train and out of the way. Carefully, he pulled the matchbook from his pocket.

"You know, you're wasting your time with Westfield."

"What?"

"Gray. He doesn't have a clue." He groped for the hole in the metal plate where the door latched.

"No shit. But it isn't information she's after."

Mike coughed to cover the sound of tearing cardboard.

"Time to go. Train leaves in fifteen minutes," said Donovan.

Mike took a deep breath. "I don't think so."

"What? You have to go. We don't have much time."

"No." He thought of Liz and felt braver. "I have things to take care of before I go. But I appreciate your help."

"If that's the way you want it. Don't say I didn't try." Donovan lifted a rake and thumped on the ceiling. "Come on then, back to your crib."

The door at the top of the stairs opened. Mike stuffed the cardboard into the strike plate and returned to the cellar, fingers interlaced behind him in an impromptu prayer. Another pair of legs appeared on the stairs, and he had his first close look at the Colonel in three days. She still had on the clothes she'd worn for dragging the gnome.

Yes, the voice had been familiar, but it was not Char. And not Allison's mother. No cane, that should have been a giveaway. She'd marched along the streets of Hartigan Gap, towing the gnome, without any sign of a limp. What a dummy he'd been not to spot it.

"You were right," said Donovan. "We're safe. He hasn't learned a thing."

For the second time that day, someone clubbed Mike over the head. His knees buckled. Hasn't learned a thing. No kidding.

—14—

Liz felt as if the room had shrunk around her. In the doorway, Allie's mother leaned on her cane and held the dog by its leash.

"I suppose there's an entertaining explanation here."

"No." Liz gave up her effort to hide. She turned back to the desk and logged out. "I'm here with Bud. He's looking for you." She pointed toward the ceiling.

"I should have known." She bellowed up the stairs. "Nigel! Get your useless self down here!"

Nigel. That was a secret Liz hadn't needed to discover. "Look, you two probably have a lot to–"

"Nonsense. This concerns you as well. Let's go through to the living room. Come, Hugo." She stooped to pick up her shopping bag. The dog trotted ahead, nails clicking on the wood floor.

The living room was as large as that of Briarwood, but the furniture looked more comfortable, the beiges and blues more relaxing. There were no servants in sight. A grandfather clock stood against one wall, ticking softly.

Allie's mother put down her bag. "Sit there."

Liz took the armchair, feeling as if she'd missed curfew, wondering what the punishment would be. Something mild. Helen acted the disciplinarian, but up close she wasn't that threatening. On an end table lay a collection of three-dimensional wooden puzzles. Liz began prodding at one, trying to take it apart. She'd never been any good at them.

Bud appeared at the far end of the room. "Hey, sis. Where you been?"

"We'll cut the pleasantries, Nigel."

"Aw, geez, don't do that to me." At the sight of Liz, he winced. "It's all because–"

"Please." She held up a hand. "I've learned enough about you today." The puzzle rattled. It probably had a marble inside.

"Take a seat, Buddy." Helen pointed to another chair and followed her own advice. "Let's straighten out a few things. Do you have the ticket?"

"We're working on that."

"I don't want a progress report. Either you have it or not."

"Not." Liz didn't look up from the puzzle. The trick, obviously, was to figure out the first move.

"Is that true?"

"Um, yeah." Bud shifted in his chair.

"But you said she had it."

"I said I thought she had it."

"And what makes you think she hasn't?"

Liz felt a need to inject herself into the conversation. "I told him."

Helen slapped Hugo's snout from her shopping bag. The dog gave a yelp and curled up by her chair. "You'll pardon me for not finding that wholly reassuring, from someone I've caught digging in my computer files."

"You what?" said Bud.

Liz kept her attention on the puzzle. "Academic curiosity. Besides, if I'd found the ticket earlier, I wouldn't be hunting in the computer."

Helen aimed the tip of her cane at Liz. "You might, to throw us off track."

"Ridiculous. It's nearly three. The thing needs to get to the lottery office."

"You could be setting up an alibi." Bud straightened. "Meanwhile your accomplice cashes it in."

"Accomplice? Was your skull vacuumed today? All you have to do is check tomorrow's paper to see who turns it in. I can't believe I'm having this conversation. I told you, I don't know anything about where the real ticket is."

"The real ticket?" Helen leaned forward, hands crossed on top of her cane.

"Oh, for pity's sake." Liz recapped her discovery of the switch.

Helen picked up her shopping bag. "I'm wasting my time. The person I need to talk to is Mr. Archer."

"Take a number," Liz said, under her breath.

Bud lay sideways in his chair. "The guy's long gone by now."

"Why do you say that?" She couldn't believe she wanted to defend Mike.

"Don't be naive. Ten million dollars, and he tells you he's hidden it? What's he waiting for?"

"If he planned to steal it, he'd have cashed it in. He wouldn't hide it, not this close to the deadline." She looked at them. "Would he?"

"Don't ask me, Lizzo. He's your boyfriend."

"He isn't." Somewhere on the planet there had to be someone who believed that.

"Be quiet, Nigel. If the man says he hid the ticket, I'm willing to take him at his word. That means we must find it, or him, as soon as we can. I knew I should have retrieved it the other day."

Liz returned to the puzzle. "You were going to give it back?"

"Of course. I'd made my point. I even picked up a peace offering." She reached into the bag and withdrew a package of sparklers.

"And now it's too late." Bud stood.

"It isn't, you ninny." She shook her head. "I've been trying to tell you. We have until tomorrow to turn in the ticket."

"Because the lottery office is closed today?"

"It isn't." Liz stopped fidgeting. "The paper said it would be open."

"I know. But you're not thinking. They give you a certain amount of time to claim the prize." Helen smiled.

Bud paced. "Six months. January 4 to July 4."

"No," said Liz. "It's not 'six months.' That's not what the paper said. It's 'half a year.' "

"Same difference."

"It isn't," Helen told him. "Count the days from January 4 to today."

While he took time to do the math in his head, Liz felt her stomach tighten. Anyone could read the paper. Even Mike.

"It's 181," said Bud.

Helen nodded. "Half a year is 182 and a half days. We have another day."

The puzzle fell apart in Liz's lap. She looked down at the pieces of wood, instant chaos. The rattling hadn't been a marble. It was a heart of white porcelain, with a hairline crack down the middle. And she realized she'd been wrong earlier. He'd laughed at her, but not because he'd beaten her to the ticket. He didn't plan to give it back.

In the Tap, when she'd finally acknowledged he wasn't returning, she'd thought she couldn't feel worse. She dropped the remains of the puzzle on the end table and rushed from the room. She needed a private place to scream. Not in front of Bud.

▼ ▼ ▼

Mike's face was back in the pillow when he came around. The Colonel and Donovan talked nearby.

"You sure he knows nothing?"

"Not a clue."

"How does he explain the fact that he and I were spending quality time together last Friday, before you managed to drag your sorry ass over there?"

In another heartbeat Mike realized that he'd been right the first time. Donovan was Nemo's protégé. He tried to relax as he thought through the implications. For starters, he'd made a total ass of himself by accusing Liz.

Donovan cleared his throat. "He followed me."

Mike stopped breathing. Donovan's statement had been delivered emphatically, as if gleaned from an interrogation.

"Followed you?" The Colonel snorted. "Is that what he said? Best job of following I ever heard of. He got there five fucking minutes before you did, you sack of shit."

Mike began to appreciate that he was in a load of trouble. Playing dumb wouldn't work, since he'd rattled off the code so cheerily on Friday. Surely this pair wasn't sick enough to resort to violence. He hoped he wouldn't embarrass himself by wetting his pants.

"Wake up," said the Colonel. He felt a jab in the ribs. "You've slept enough this afternoon. Wake up. Let's get this straight, Archer. How'd you know where to find me?"

He raised his head and swallowed. It should have been so easy to tell her he had read it in the paper. These people seemed to think they were dealing with some kind of unbreakable code. Instead, he listened to a voice, his voice, say in a sneering tone, "How do you think, Colonel?"

"What?"

Donovan rose to his feet. Mike continued his pathetic bluff. "Who knew you were in that building?"

"No one knew. No one." She stared. "Wait. Nemo?"

Mike smiled.

"Nemo." Donovan's voice was derisive. "I don't believe it."

"Shut up, Crab. Let me think." She pulled out a stick of gum.

It didn't seem fair that Donovan got to be 'Crab' where Mike was only 'Worm.' But a flicker of hope rose in Mike's heart. Neither of them had met Nemo. There was a chance.

The Colonel folded the gum into her mouth. "You been letting everyone think you're a buddy of Gray's."

"Is there a rule I can't be both? Use your head."

"You're so young."

Mike made himself laugh. "Loose thinking." He hoped it sounded better to her than it did to him.

"I suppose it's possible," she said at last. "And you'd have no way of knowing what I had in mind when I asked for help."

At this point the divide-and-conquer theory advised attacking the weaker, Donovan. But it wouldn't be easy. Or plausible, come to think of it, since Nemo-Mike was supposed to have supplied Donovan in the first place.

"Sorry this guy didn't work out. At least he was sharp enough to decode the puzzle."

That got her thinking. "If you're Nemo, why show up at the rendezvous?"

"That should be obvious. I wanted to see how secure your operation was." He paused, not so much for effect as from lack of inspiration. "Not very, it seems." He shut up, afraid he was spoiling it.

She ran a finger along her nose. It was as much of a concession as he could hope for.

"Look," he said, "it's your show to run. Your show. But I'd be grateful if you'd let me out of here. Or at least untie my hands."

It was going to work, amazingly enough. But she shook her head.

"Damn sight too convenient. You may be Nemo. I can't prove you're not. I also can't afford to let you go. We gave you a chance to get out on the train." She looked at her watch. "In a couple of hours it won't matter. The deed's nearly done. Hell, it's practically in my pocket. I think we'll hold onto you a while yet."

Mike didn't care for the sound of that phrase, the deed being done. Donovan sneered. But there seemed to be a hint of respect in his eyes.

▼ ▼ ▼

Liz hated to be tricked almost as much as she hated to be wrong. In a way it was the same thing viewed from different angles. But trickery required the active participation of another person. That meant someone else to blame. Being wrong you did all by yourself. She yanked the front door of Monte Rosa behind her. Enough. Time to pack the suitcase and get out of town. Let someone else take the abuse.

He'd sat in the tavern on his stupid stool, feeding her a line of Grade A baloney about how difficult it was to get a handle on life, and she'd actually believed him, had felt sorry, was even beginning, maybe, to like him. And all the while he'd laughed up his sleeve, wanting to let her know who'd be cashing in the lottery winner while she went back to the same old no-prospect job, taking pointless orders from a reptile.

She reached the Mercedes and hauled out the bicycle. But when she put it on the ground, she could see the rear tire had no air. Closer inspection revealed a gouge chewed through by the latch mechanism. With a wordless cry of rage, she threw the bike to the ground. Conspiracy. She slammed the trunk closed. Full-fledged, no-holds-barred, grassy knoll conspiracy. She leaned on the car, panting, fighting the bitter taste in her mouth. Even swallowing was a challenge. She kicked the bike.

▼ ▼ ▼

"Here's what we're doing, Crab. Try to keep up. Before we move, we need to account for George Washington. I should lay low a while yet, but you check out the weeds and the pink hills. Obviously, they don't suspect. Take the van. The chopper draws too much attention. I'll look around town and check the train station." She crumpled her gum wrapper. "Meet me back here at 1600 hours. You've got the cell number if there's an emergency. Don't let there be." For the first time, she took off her glasses. "Make sure you pack up our ears."

She stomped up the stairs, leaving Mike wondering what the hell was going on, and where she'd managed to stash a helicopter. Something about her appearance troubled him, but he couldn't corner it.

"Hey," he said to Donovan, "how did you get my sneakers to Briarwood?"

"Char brought them. I told her a friend of mine had a package for me. The Colonel gave them to her in Washington."

Mike was so annoyed that he didn't think before saying, "You can quit looking for the ticket. Mrs. Harper has it back."

"Owen."

What a dope. Her name wasn't Owen. That was Uncle Ric's name.

Donovan patted the top of Mike's head. "Thanks for the tip, pal. Make yourself comfortable." He unlocked the door to the garage and went through, failing to see the matchbook cover in the strike plate. The door creaked as it swung shut. To cover the silence that would be there instead of a click, Mike bounced on the bed. While he was at it, he tried to put strain on the rope and was reassured to feel it give a little. He heard the sound of the van's engine. A minute later, a door slammed above him. He forced himself to lie still.

George Washington could be Gray Westfield, same initials, which meant they did plan to kidnap Gray. Mr. Westfield had no cash for the ransom. He did have the lottery ticket, technically, if that was what the Colonel wanted. But there had to be a simpler way to get it, a way that didn't involve dressing up as Allison's mother.

Nemo hadn't met the Colonel, but he'd sent her Donovan. That suggested he was dumb, dumb enough to pick Crab as a sidekick. But someone who had no trouble supplying muscle secretly, and who used code names. An organized crime boss. Someone in government.

Nishida. Westfield. Something pinged away in Mike's brain. What would Liz do under the circumstances? Know better than to get herself into the mess. And not think much of a guy who ran out during a lunch date. Date. Right.

He couldn't remember whether he'd told her where the real ticket was. Not knowing would be less dangerous for her. He smiled at the thought of protecting Liz, even indirectly. But the Colonel was right. In a few hours it wouldn't matter.

He yanked his hand free of the rope and stepped to the door leading to the garage. No movement from the gnome, no sound. With a deep breath, he pulled the handle. The door swung open, and he slipped through into the darkness behind it. The light switch eluded him. After precious seconds of groping, he gave up and fumbled for the matches, striking one with a shaky hand. In the glow, he found a button. Behind him the garage door began to rumble upward.

It was now, he told himself, nothing more than a matter of walking out, and yet he hesitated. Sunlight filled the garage, illuminating the motorcycle that stood against one wall. He edged closer. A shell helmet, biker-gang style, sat balanced on the seat. A leather jacket hung from one of the handlebars. The key was in the ignition. Not once in his life had he ridden a motorcycle. He ran his hand along the seat. Pity. It would have made for a stylish escape.

He thought to check the time. Little more than an hour and a half since he'd been at the hotel. Ninety minutes past when Gray should have begun to worry, and Liz to wonder. He tried on the helmet. It fit. What the hell. He'd ridden a bicycle before. It couldn't be all that difficult.

▼ ▼ ▼

Liz took a deep breath. Tantrum over. Time to see about more productive use of brainwaves. She tried to identify which among the long list of irritants bothered her least. There was surely a problem for which she could devise a solution, something that would bring a sense of accomplishment, a salvaging of a shred of, oh, dignity. Professional pride. Self-respect.

She hauled herself onto the trunk of the Mercedes, propped her elbows on her knees, and rested chin in hands. Forget the lottery ticket. Think about Westfield and Morveus. Think about, for that matter, Westfield and H-T.

Bart Westfield and Helen Harper Owen had worked at Morveus. More recently, Helen's daughter had worked at Hillton-Tanner. Westfield had H-T files on his desk. Bud had dismissed the suggestion that Allie had any involvement in the H-T embezzlement. He must know something.

A car shot up the driveway. Perfect. The timing of the angel couldn't be better. Liz hopped to the ground. In fact, it wasn't a car, but a white panel van. It skidded to a stop not ten feet from her, and out jumped . . . Roger. He left the engine running. She didn't know whether to laugh or to scream.

"You?" She struggled for a more civil tone. "What are you doing here?"

He frowned. "Have you seen Gray?"

"Yes." The unexpectedness of the question surprised the response from her. "A couple of hours ago." Nice. Very professional.

"Where?"

"In town. At the Hartigan Tap." Odd that he should be so interested in Gray. It was the first time all weekend he'd shown curiosity about anyone other than her. Correction: other than her and Char.

"No, I know about that. I mean, since then."

She shook her head. "That's the last time."

"Shit." He kicked at one of the tires. "What about Archer?"

"What about him?"

"Do you know where he is?"

"I don't know, and I don't care. He can fall into a bottomless pit for all it matters to me."

"I don't believe it." Roger's expression hardened. "I saw you last night."

"Doing what?"

"Dancing. I watched the way you danced."

"What way?" Hell, everyone seemed to have caught the act. They should have charged admission. "I danced with him, Roger, so I wouldn't have to talk to you. Honestly, do they install this super-dense filter on all men, or just the ones I meet?"

"There's no need for that."

"You're right. I'm sorry." She couldn't find anything appropriate to do with her hands. "It's just that I'm a little irritated at the moment."

"By Archer?"

"No. Well, yes." Perhaps Roger wasn't so dense.

He looked toward the pond. "I could take care of him for you."

"You could?" His words were more threatening than he usually managed.

"Nothing permanent. Unless you want. Just make his life more difficult is all. I have friends who will mess with him for me."

"You make it sound as though they do it on a regular basis."

"They do. It's not hard. Just takes a phone call. You aren't the only one he annoys. There's a demand for this sort of service. You'd be amazed."

She tried to imagine the market he served. People Mike annoyed. Could be a decent-sized club. "Thanks anyway, but I told you, it doesn't matter to me what happens to him."

"Yeah, me neither, any more. I got what I wanted."

"Did you?" She couldn't stop herself from asking. "What was that?"

"Char, of course." He laughed. "It took a while, but once I convinced her what a total write-off he was, she was glad to cut her losses."

Liz waited for the punchline but he appeared to be sincere. How about that? A break for Mike. Not that he deserved it.

"Still." Roger contemplated the gravel. "I need to see Gray."

"Sorry, I can't help you. Have you checked Briarwood?"

"Just came from there. I guess I'll have to keep looking. Want to come?"

"Gee, wonderful as that opportunity sounds, I have other things to do."

"Sure." He grinned with malice. "You gotta get to your island."

She felt as if a balloon had inflated inside her and she had to fight to contain it. "How do you know about that?"

"Oh. You mentioned it. Last night. You'd been drinking."

"I don't drink."

"Well. You did mention it."

"Did I?" She forced a shrug. "Maybe I did. Anyway, you're right. I'd better move if I want to make my train."

He extended an arm toward the van. "I'll give you a lift."

"That's okay. I need to pack."

"Suit yourself." He climbed in.

She turned and headed for the trees, searching for the path to Briarwood. Behind her, the van roared away. With Roger gone, a swirl of images filled her head, bumping into one another. Postcards, H-T files, and half-recollected phrases: *I know why you're there. You're easy to frighten.*

Things had been a touch blurry the night before. But she was certain of one thing. She'd never mentioned the island. Not to Roger.

▼ ▼ ▼

The unsettling principle about motorcycles, Mike soon discovered, was that maximum stability could be achieved only at maximum velocity. While speed was desirable in the context of putting distance between himself and his kidnappers, it was not a notion with which he was especially comfortable. Nor was he excited about the prospect of cornering on a two-wheeled death machine. He'd therefore shot out of town on the first road that presented itself, exulting in the magnificence of the escape but not quite daring to peel his fingers from the handlebars. Not until he saw the train station in the distance did he realize he was heading toward a rendezvous with the Colonel.

He slowed to a gentle stop, got off, and pushed the machine around until it was pointing back toward Hartigan Gap. The smell of gas reminded him of the BMW and made him feel slightly ill. He threw a leg over the seat.

As he throttled up to hang-on-and-pray velocity, he tried to take his mind off the vibrating steel cataclysm between his knees, growing warmer by the minute. By any rational measure, the first order of business was to warn Gray of his imminent abduction. Forgiveness from Liz was important, and sooner rather than later. On the other hand, a few minutes delay wouldn't get him much deeper into the compost. Plus he hadn't worked out the tangible demonstration of his apology. Something more dramatic than flowers, that was certain. Though a return to Briarwood was mandatory, to rescue the ticket for Mr. Westfield, Donovan might have thought of the same thing. The Colonel had wanted him to check out 'weeds and pink hills.' Briarwood and Monte Rosa, presumably, as supported by the fact that the van hadn't sped past along the road to the station.

Fields whipped by on either side. Vibrations sprinted up Mike's spine in waves, making his fingers tingle. The cycle had a low screen, the helmet no visor. Wind pummeled his chest and face, bringing tears to his eyes. He squinted through the moisture, keeping his back rigid and his mouth clamped shut against the arrival of flying insects.

Gray's exact whereabouts were a mystery. He'd been at the hotel less than two hours ago and might still be. On the same principle he used to guide his searches for keys, Mike headed for the last place he'd seen the missing object. In this case, the missing person.

He was a block away from the Montclair, nearly even with the horse statue park, when a figure charged out of a store front and ran into the street ahead of him. Mike swerved before he recognized the crazed pedestrian as Gray, which triggered the fleeting thought that it would be nice if apartment keys could run out when they were lost. He had the impression of a second person following Gray, and then his thoughts centered on the motorcycle.

Involuntary easing of the throttle meant his speed had decreased to the point he was able to avoid both Gray and a complete wipeout. The resulting unsteadiness, however, took him in a wobbly, unrelenting line toward an inconveniently located cluster of bushes at the edge of the park. The front wheel slammed into the curb and he went airborne.

The flight through the warm afternoon had an element of familiarity, the first sense of comfort he'd had the entire weekend, other than talking with Liz in the Tap. All the same, he was glad to be wearing a helmet.

He executed a full rotation in the air, skimmed the bushes and, upright, hit the ground more or less running. The jarring impact buckled his knees. Three sinking strides brought him to the base of the statue, and as his head hit the granite he became truly grateful for Donovan's helmet.

He bounced off and staggered to a halt, panting, trying with all his might not to fall to the ground. A victory waited inside the disaster; he could sense it. Behind him, the motorcycle wavered between silence and explosion. He was congratulating himself on having maintained his balance through the ordeal when he felt himself tackled from behind. His face met the ground and a great weight landed on his back. A frantic, whispered voice in his ear was accompanied by the strong scent of hair tonic.

"Stay down, you silly blighter. He's chasing me, and he's got a gun."

Mike rolled from under the weight and sat up. Adrenaline coursed through him. "What the hell are you doing?"

"Trying to save you, blast it." Gray's glasses dangled from one ear.

"Hey. You finished your haircut." It seemed terribly important.

"So?" Gray was still prone.

"So, how was that supposed to save me? I disappear for hours and all you think of is your personal grooming."

"That's not important now." Gray fumbled with his glasses. "Stay down. We're in great danger."

"The Colonel?"

"No, you imbecile. Him." Gray pointed to the edge of the park.

On the grass was a man dressed in casual clothes. The good news was he wasn't Donovan. The bad news was he held a hand in the pocket of his windbreaker in a way Mike didn't care for. It reminded him of something else he'd seen recently.

Gray's breathing quieted. "He was in the barbershop. That's a gun."

"I don't believe it." Mike tugged off the helmet and rubbed his hand down his face. The blow from the statue must have been harder than he'd thought. "He looks like my Uncle Ric. Harmless."

The man laughed. "Hey, Mike. It took you long enough to show up."

"Whoa." The ground pitched under him. "It is Ric."

"I'm not quite following." Gray raised himself to his knees and looked from one to the other. "Why should your uncle want to shoot you?"

▼ ▼ ▼

Bud shouted at her from the front steps of Monte Rosa. At the edge of the path, Liz turned and saw him standing by Helen. They both gestured at her to come back.

"Can you get the ticket from Archer?" Bud yelled through cupped hands.

She spun on her heel and strode away toward Briarwood. Let them find a way out of their own mess.

▼ ▼ ▼

"Of course it's not a gun." Ric pulled the hand from his jacket pocket. He held a ring of keys.

"Blimey," said Gray. "Thought I'd have a bloody heart attack."

"I don't understand." Mike dropped the helmet. "You were in Brazil."

"Brazil? Are you nuts?" Ric laughed. "That's a joke. Brazil. Nuts. Oh, come off it, lighten up." He ducked out of sight around the hedge, and the motorcycle grew silent. "That's better." He straightened, only his head and shoulders visible above the foliage. "Yes, I was in Brazil. The operative word being 'was.' Past tense."

"Do you really know this bloke?" said Gray.

Mike waved him aside. "Okay, fine, why are you here?"

"Wait a minute. You got the postcard. Otherwise you wouldn't have known about Brazil."

"Sure. Thanks for thinking of me."

"Didn't you read what it said?"

"Very amusing," said Mike. "What's your point?"

"No, I mean what it really said." Ric came around the bushes again. "The message. The code."

"Code?" Mike had a sinking feeling.

"'Island.'" Ric threw up his hands. "I said 'island.' Brazil's not an island, an obscure fact I assumed you knew. I thought you'd get the hint. I even misspelled it. Maybe I should have made it more obvious." He pulled out a notepad and scribbled on it. "Something like this, if I remember right."

We've	Here	Growth
Eaten	Although	Abysmally
Some	Really	Pretty
Terrific	This	
Food	Iland	View
I'd	Goes	Anyhow
Enjoy	About	
Living	New	
Down		

--Olé

P.S. You ought to come as soon as you can

Mike returned the page. "When you put it like that."

"Are you telling me it was dumb luck you got here?" Ric said.

"Not exactly, but . . ."

Gray raised a hand as if in class. "Why did you want him to come?"

"What's it to you?"

"Sorry." Mike made motions of introduction. "Uncle Ric, Gray Westfield. Gray, my Uncle Ric."

"Yes, I know." Ric chuckled. "The troublemaker."

"What do you mean by that? Say, you're awfully familiar."

"I have that sort of face."

"No, hang on a bit. I've got it. You were on the train, Friday."

"Was I? Well, so I was. And you were wearing a preposterous mustache."

Gray reddened. "And you–"

"Stop. Stop." Mike waved his arms. "We're straying from the point. Why was I supposed to come here?"

"Several reasons. The most important of which was, I thought Bart might need help finding his property, the lottery ticket. You've always been good at puzzles, and I knew you were a friend of the family. I didn't think he'd hire professionals."

"By 'Bart,' you mean Barton Westfield."

"I do."

"You know him?"

Ric gave a half smile. "Of course."

"Okay." Best to take it in stride. "Returning to the main theme, what are you doing?"

"Keeping an eye on people." The other half of the smile caught up. "A little of this, a little of that."

"Which people?" Mike feared he might be one of them. "Did Mom send you to check on me?"

"No, no. People people." He made a temporizing gesture. "Not you." The distinction wasn't reassuring.

"Speaking of watching." Gray brushed the dirt from his clothes. "You let Allison's mother get away. It shouldn't have been a challenge."

Ric froze. "What was that?"

"I nearly forgot." Mike clutched Gray's arm. "You have to hide."

"Hide? From what?"

"They want to kidnap you."

"Are you daft?" He struggled loose. "Who does?"

"Take this helmet. Use it for protection."

Gray fought off Mike's attempt to put the thing on him. "Protection from what? Get a grip. What are you talking about?"

"I spent the last few hours with Donovan and you know who." Mike mimed sunglasses. "They want to kidnap you."

Gray stared at him, then at Ric.

Ric scratched an ear. "'You know who?'"

"Yes. It's another long story."

Gray passed the helmet back. "You're making this up so I won't get mad about your disappearance."

"I'm not."

"Then you're hallucinating."

Mike threw the helmet to the ground. But he began to wonder.

"I don't think your motorcycle is going anywhere in the near future." Ric put an arm around Mike's shoulders. "Can I offer you guys a ride?"

"I've got my car," said Gray.

"Car!" Mike smacked his forehead as a chain of associations collided. "Oh, no. I've got to get back to . . . damn." He pictured the empty counter at The Tap. So much for priorities.

Gray stuck out a hand. "Nice to meet you, Mr. . . ."

"Owen. Eric Owen. Call me Ric. And, really, the pleasure was all mine."

A perfectly conventional response. Mike couldn't imagine why Gray had suddenly lost all color in his face.

–15–

Roger's words echoed in her mind as Liz threw her suitcase onto the bed. She'd told no one of the island. No one. Surely. Who else was aware of her plans?

Bud. Bud. That was who knew about the island. Not some stranger she'd spilled the beans to in a moment of weakness, but a man who absolutely, positively knew. Who could have told Roger. And that would explain the taunting postcards, Roger to the core. How dense not to have figured it out. She paused in the act of slamming a blouse into the suitcase. Why assume Roger had acted on his own? Bud could have helped. Maybe Bud had left the postcards himself.

No. She dropped the blouse. No way. Bud couldn't leave any cards. He hadn't been on the right coast when she'd found the first two. Or so he said. He could have forwarded his calls and come to Washington days ago. That would explain the ease of the TekSekure break-in. And the forced entry to her house, ripping through the company's own security system. The thought of Bud with not only a key, but the access code, was not nice. She went to the window and looked out at the afternoon sun sparkling on the lake.

But he had no reason to plant sinister postcards. What threat did she pose? Perhaps he wanted to keep her from discovering something, such as Allie's involvement in the H-T embezzlement. Once he'd shut down that project, though, he didn't gain anything with the postcards.

Nothing made sense. Even Roger's story about looking for Gray sounded phony. He wanted something at Monte Rosa. Bud. That's who he'd been on his way to see. She'd messed up the plan by appearing at Monte Rosa herself. Okay. She slammed the suitcase and fastened it before digging the cell phone from her purse.

It took a while for Charlie to pick up. "Pleasant Cab."

"This is Liz Halloran. I'm at Briarwood, the Westfield place, and I'm ready to go. Can you take me to the station?"

"The station, Miss?" His voice crackled on the poor connection. "I could do that, of course I could. Only thing is, there's no train either direction for a few hours now. Holiday schedule today."

She flipped his card into the wastebasket. "All right, so when's the next train to Washington?"

"That'd be eight-fifteen, Miss, next train to Washington."

She looked at her watch. "Could you pick me up at, say, seven-thirty?"

"Seven-three-oh, Miss. You got yourself a cab."

"Thanks." She hung up and closed the suitcase with a sense of having achieved the smallest victory. She glanced around the room one last time. Near the bed, she could almost see the shadow of Mike's suitcase. The other guests might return soon. She had no wish to face them. There was nothing left to say. Perhaps the grounds had a quiet nook where she could be alone with her self-pity and her luggage. Come to think of it, she knew just the spot.

▼ ▼ ▼

The Tap was deserted. The sour-looking waitress denied any recollection of Liz. Mike ran his hand over the counter. Some desperate part of his brain persisted in believing if he stayed in the restaurant long enough she'd reappear.

"Maybe she's in the women's room."

"Maybe." The waitress crossed her arms. "Wait out here if you want. You try going in, I'll call the cops."

"Hello." Gray waved a hand in front of Mike's face. "Hello? On the next orbit, could I have a word?"

"Sorry. What is it?"

"You made a bloomer. Fine. Cut your losses. She's probably back at the house. You can apologize there, or whatever you have in mind."

The place had been wiped clean of evidence they'd ever sat together. Gone. Not a speck of guacamole. Mike leaned his head on the counter. "I'm not sure what I have in mind. I can't think straight. Liz is gone. Ric never told us why he chased you from the barbershop. We haven't figured out what Donovan's doing with the Colonel, or why she's dressed like Allison's mother."

"What kind of ridiculous story is that?"

"It's not a story."

"Aha." Gray pointed at Mike's chest. "You admit it's ridiculous. In any event, you raise excellent questions. Few, I think, to be answered in this establishment. Shall we adjourn?"

Mike shrugged. "You're the one who'll be kidnapped."

"Oh, do stop it with that. You can't scare me."

They took Gray's car and sped toward Briarwood. Mike rested his elbow on the window frame. The breeze bent the hair on his forearm, miniature trees in a hurricane. "So, what's the program now?"

Gray turned to make eye contact. "What happened to your program?"

"If you see it, let me know. I think it must be traveling in disguise."

The car swerved. "Disguise?"

"It was a joke. Watch the road."

"No, no. Disguise. Colonel. Allison's mother."

"Come on, Gray, buy a verb."

"It's obvious, isn't it? Why do you disguise yourself?"

"Because you tell me to."

"No, I mean, what's the purpose of a disguise?"

"Not to look like yourself, I suppose."

"Usually," said Gray. "But if you deliberately make yourself look a lot like someone else?"

"You confuse people. And let me tell you, you're succeeding."

"Pay attention. I'll assume, for the sake of argument, it really was the Colonel dressed as Allison's mum."

"Very generous, after the abuse you've been giving me."

"You still don't follow." Gray hunched forward. "Come on, Mikey. Use your imagination. She'll impersonate Allison's mother. After the abduction."

"The abduction of you?"

"Of the mother, dolt. No one wants to kidnap me, I told you. What value am I? They need her to tell where the ticket is."

"But it isn't where she hid it any more. I figured–"

"Yes, but they don't know that. Good Lord, can't you see what this is? It's the perfect chance for me to shine as hero. It's wonderful. If I play it right, I can save Allison's mum. Then she won't dare come between us." He switched on the radio. "Blimey, I hope we're not too late."

"'Blimey?' Are you out of your mind?"

"You're sore," said Gray, "because you didn't think of it first."

"I'm proud, because I didn't think of it at all."

The song ended and an ad came on. A horribly familiar ad. *Why, howdy kids . . .* Mike snapped off the sound and wedged himself into his seat. He had the depressing sense of having reached a high water mark and fallen back.

▼ ▼ ▼

Liz laced her fingers together on the window sill. Perhaps coming to the cottage hadn't been such a good idea. Roger wouldn't show for a while, but someone else might. Someone like Char. Maybe the woman had seen the error of her ways and dumped Mike for Roger. How convenient for all concerned. Char had a shapeable man and Mike had a get-out-of-jail-free card. Everyone's life should work out so neatly.

On the lake, a fish jumped. Somewhere in the distance, an engine roared to life. Car. Mike returning. No, not a car. Lawnmower, or chain saw.

An idea came to her. A wonderful, awful, grinchy idea. What if Char learned something bad about Roger, something that would make Mike a saint in comparison? She would head back to Square One in an instant: Mike and his new-found riches. He'd have a hell of a time prying her away. Serve him right.

Liz turned from the window, scrutinizing the interior of the cottage. Her gaze came to rest on the bed. That would do. From her suitcase she withdrew one of her bras, an old one. After some artistic consideration, she dangled the bra at the foot of the bed. The covers were stretched tight, a little too neat. She rumpled them and bounced on the mattress for effect. The springs creaked, a revolting cheap-motel sound. She indulged herself in another bounce. Lipstick would be nice, for a message on the bathroom mirror. *Love you, sweetie.* But she didn't carry any and had to go with a note printed on a scrap of paper: 'Darling: running errands. Back soon. Keep things warm.' She placed it with studied indifference on one of the pillows. The plan would succeed provided Char came first to the cottage. If Roger beat her back, well, Liz would be out one old bra. Worth the gamble.

No sign of life at Briarwood. She hauled her suitcase across the wide lawn to the woods. In the stillness of the afternoon, she thought she heard the faint sound of a woman's shouts, but when she stopped to listen, there was nothing.

She stashed the suitcase behind a tree, not far off the trail. A curious feeling of emptiness settled within her. She pulled the square of construction paper from her purse and examined both sides. A last glance at the cottage, and she set off along the path to Allie's house.

▼ ▼ ▼

Gray parked in front of Monte Rosa. Mike inspected the two cars in the driveway. A bicycle lay abandoned behind one. It made him think of Liz.

Gray, Mister Action Hero, ran to the front door. Mike extricated himself from the passenger seat and followed at a more cautious pace, not ready to be trapped in another strange house. He stopped at the foot of the steps and was scoping out the path to Briarwood when Liz emerged from the trees. He wished he'd spent time on the exact wording of the apology.

She stopped short. "You left me."

"Um, yes." He swallowed. "I'm glad you . . ."

"You left me." She seemed on the verge of tears. "You left me alone."

She was mad because she'd had to pay for their lunch. He fished out his wallet while looking over his shoulder, not wanting a public scene. The front door opened. Gray made choking sounds.

"Why, hello again." Uncle Ric's voice came as a complete shock. "You two made good time." He walked down the steps.

Mike froze, hand on his wallet. "How did you get here?"

"Surface streets, how else? This is my home. Didn't I mention it? Helen and I married earlier this year. Minuscule wedding, or we'd have invited you."

"You." Liz ignored Mike and stared at Ric. "From the train."

He smiled. "Nicely done." He held up a finger and examined it.

Gray spun to face Mike. "Your uncle. Allison's stepfather." He pointed back and forth in the air. "Same person."

Mike sensed he'd fallen a lap behind. From the house he heard growls.

"Hugo." A deep female voice. "Stay."

"Uncle?" Liz looked at Ric and seemed to stagger. "Nephew?" Back to Mike, with a hand at her throat.

"Hell," said Ric. "This wasn't the way I wanted it to come out, Miranda."

Miranda? Ric knew Liz as Miranda? That didn't sound good. It was Mike's turn to do the tennis match thing. This time, Liz really did stagger. Afraid she might faint, Mike took a step toward her. But she caught herself.

"You." The white scar was not in evidence when she said it. Her eyes blazed and she turned to Ric. "You, too. A set-up? With Mike? Of all the . . ."

In the doorway appeared a short, tubby man. One of the guests at the Briarwood party. Mike was too busy decoding Ric's and Liz's expressions to put a name to the face.

"Problems?" said the man.

"Shut up, Bud." Liz shook a finger at him. "This is all your fault. You staged that break-in."

Mike looked for a graceful way to exit. Any way at all.

Bud smoothed his hair. "You're crazy, you know that?"

Inside the house, the growling escalated to full-fledged barks, and Hugo appeared in the doorway, straining against a leash. At the other end was yet another woman who looked like Allison's mother.

"Liz." She stepped onto the porch. "Hugo doesn't care for your brother."

"My brother?" Liz advanced on Mike. "Who else thinks we're related?"

"Oh, God." He pressed a hand to his face, trying to wipe everything away. "I just wanted to apologize . . ."

He opened his eyes to see her bringing her arm around. For an instant he thought she was reaching out to hug him and he relaxed. Then he saw the fist. His nose absorbed most of the shock, and a blinding light filled his brain. Noises around him wavered and grew hazy. The driveway lifted itself up to catch him. Through the haze he heard gasps. Someone with atrocious breath began to lick his ear. He became dimly aware of Gray's voice, farther off in the fog.

"Miranda? Some kind of warning thing? I say, are you all right?"

Mike's body had taken a lot of abuse over the past few days. Having Liz punch him was the first thing that really hurt.

▼ ▼ ▼

The bleeding had pretty much stopped by the time he stumbled from the woods on the Briarwood side. His nose felt about the size of a watermelon. He held Ric's handkerchief against it. Matt and Marsha, strolling in the garden, stared as he lurched to a halt.

"What's the fool doing now?" said Marsha.

Matt pulled out glasses and set them on his nose. "Bleeding."

Mike resumed flight. He would have preferred to go straight to his room, but the likelihood of making it up two flights without staining the carpet seemed remote. He chose the boathouse, which at least offered cleansing water and privacy. As he passed the boxwood maze he heard rustling. Even Char should have found her way out in three hours. But it was Doris who stepped from the entrance. A piece of luck.

"Are you okay?" She glanced toward the garden. "Did Char do that?"

"Thang you." He pressed his nose. "No. It wad Liz."

"You must have said something awful."

"Are you kidding?" He released the handkerchief. "I was in the middle of apologizing. Actually, I'd rather not relive it just now, if that's all right."

"You could wash up in the cottage. It's empty now."

He wondered why she'd phrased it that way. "Anyone around the house?"

She took a deep breath. "My parents are out in the garden, fighting. Mr. Westfield's been tearing the library apart. Liz went to Monte Rosa, but I guess you know that. Let's see. The so-called archaeologists were poking in their dig. No sign of the senator since breakfast, or Gray. Who's left? Oh, Mr. Liddell's getting fireworks ready. Mrs. L must be busy with dinner."

Mike gazed at her with respect. "Quite a report. Have you been tracking movements all day?"

"Not really. I spent some time finding my way around the maze. Those were big holes you left. I did my best to pull them back together."

"Really?" What a great kid. "Thanks. It was an emergency."

"I saw. I've been keeping an eye on you. From over there, mostly." She pointed to the oak tree. "And there." An upstairs window. "You can see lots."

"I couldn't ask for a nicer guardian angel."

"Gosh, I never thought of myself as an angel. You'd better wash. They'll think you've killed someone."

▼ ▼ ▼

The inside of the cottage was a mess, clothes and underclothes everywhere. Someone had gone the best of three falls on the bed. It wasn't tough to guess who Donovan was hosting in the cottage. Mike sighed. Concrete proof that it was over at last.

"Any idea of the time?"

Doris took her eyes from the chaos of the bed. "Close to four."

An hour to go for the ticket. He splashed water on his face. While he dried himself, Doris rummaged in the medicine cabinet.

"Here, try a cotton ball."

"Thanks." He dropped onto the couch. "And for paying attention last night. It was . . . helpful."

"I didn't do anything. Did you find the ticket?"

He examined the red-stained E.L.O. on the corner of Ric's handkerchief. "I did, thanks to you, but my plan was to hide it until I could sort through what's going on."

"Which is what?"

"I'm not sure. It didn't turn out to be much of a plan. Did you see Donovan with a tall woman today, kind of mean-looking?"

"Other than Charlotte?"

He laughed. "Other than her."

"I don't think so. Who is she?"

"I'm not totally sure of that either. Some type of commando. She's extremely interested in the house, I don't know why. This afternoon she dressed up as Mrs., you know, the next door neighbor." He hadn't adjusted to Allison's mother as his aunt. "I think she's trying to get at the ticket."

"Then why not call the police?"

"I wouldn't know what to tell them. They wouldn't believe me. And what would they do, post guards?" He folded the handkerchief. "The ticket expires today. I should give it to Mr. Westfield so he can take it to the lottery people."

The door handle turned. Doris covered her mouth. Even before it swung open, Mike knew it would be Char.

Her clothes were covered in dirt, and she held her hands in front of her in a way that suggested only the nails were still intact. She looked terrible, almost human. As she came through the doorway, her brow furrowed.

"What are you doing here, Michael? What are you doing with this girl?"

"Nothing." He looked to Doris for confirmation. She remained silent.

"And I suppose that's nothing, too." Char pointed to a bra near the end of the bed. "Honestly, Michael, is there a woman within ten miles you can keep your hands off? This one hasn't reached puberty."

"That's not fair."

"We're way past fair, cowboy." She laughed without mirth. "Let me guess. You had no idea that someone hit me on the head and tied me up in a cave."

"Really? The same thing happened to me. Except not a cave, a basement."

"Spare me, Michael. We don't need more of your stories. I'm perfectly aware that you did this to me, God knows why. I shouted for help. You must have heard." She picked up a piece of paper that lay near the pillows. "'Running errands?' Checking on me, I suppose. I tell you, if it hadn't been for Roger, I can't think what I'd have done. You're in a pile of trouble. Daddy will sue you for everything you're worth, all ten dollars of it."

Doris clenched her fists. "I saw–"

"Shut up, twerp."

"Hold on, there." Mike didn't understand the note, or the attack on Char, or what Donovan had to do with it, but for once he knew he was blameless. "Look here, under the circumstances–"

"I want my keys back. What've you done with the car?"

"It's in the garage."

"Keys."

She hadn't asked which garage. He pulled the ring from his pocket, removed the key to his apartment, and handed the rest across. He did it with dignity. No groveling, no shouting. He tossed his apartment key in the air and marveled at its lightness.

A perfunctory knock. Donovan entered the cottage and looked at the three of them. "What the hell is this? How did you . . ."

Mike's legs gave way. He sat on the bed.

"That's what I planned to find out," said Char.

Donovan pointed at Doris and jerked a thumb over his shoulder. "Out."

She looked to Mike for guidance. He smiled weakly. "Better go ahead."

When she'd gone, Donovan closed the door. "All right, Archer, I'm done with the games. I want that ticket, now. If I were you, I'd hand it over. I have a call in to some associates who'll be more persuasive, if that's what it takes."

"What good will that do?" Mike sat on his hands, determined to play out the bluff. "I told you, Mrs. Owen has it back."

"Yeah, you told me, and it turns out to be complete bullshit. I checked."

"Well, of course she'd deny that. Anyway, what right do you have to it?"

Donovan looked smug. "The right of the U.S. Government to impound fruits of illegal enterprises."

That didn't sound good. "Illegal enterprises? What illegal enterprises?"

"Treasonable activity."

"Hold it," said Mike. "You're the one who kidnapped me."

"Honestly, Michael." Char examined herself in the mirror above the sink.

"You're delusional." Donovan was very much the man in charge. "We've had Westfield and his co-conspirators under surveillance for weeks."

"You have?" The window was open, maybe leaving enough room to squeeze through if he could shove past Donovan. "What co-conspirators?"

"They're being rounded up. It's not your concern. Your best chance is to put as much distance between yourself and them as you can. Cooperate, and things might go better."

"He's right," said Char. "You're in trouble. You'd better cooperate."

"Wait a minute." Mike stared at Donovan, feeling the anger build. "Are you seriously suggesting Liz is mixed up in this?"

Char crossed her arms. "You're better off forgetting about her."

Donovan took a step closer. God, the guy was big. "We're not sure how involved she is. But it's a fact you'll be charged as an accessory if you don't hand over that ticket right now."

"How many ways are there to say I don't have it?" Mike didn't want to believe that about Liz. He couldn't. The story was too far-fetched.

"Where is it, then?"

A firm knock sounded on the door. Char and Donovan exchanged glances. Another knock.

"Popular place," said Mike. "I'll get it."

"Shut up." Donovan turned and opened the door. "Oh." Beyond him, Mike could see a broad shoulder. The Senator stepped through the door.

"Roger, I wanted to see you." He stopped. "Ah. I thought you were alone. I . . . Charlotte?"

"Senator." She'd never looked so pale, so vampirish. "I had no idea you were visiting Briarwood." She glared at Donovan. "You told me–"

"I thought," said her boss, "you were in Maryland." He lifted the brassiere from the bed. "These aren't your clothes I find in my son's cottage, are they?"

In the corner, Char was a trapped animal, hyperventilating. She glowered at Donovan. "Why didn't you tell me?"

Mike squeezed past the gathering at the door. "Excuse me, folks. I don't mean to crash the reunion. Gotta run. Goodbye," he said to Char. "And I mean that in a permanent way." Incredibly, no one made a move to stop him. He closed the door and ran like hell for the house.

▼ ▼ ▼

Uncle Ric had commandeered one of the rattan chairs on the terrace of Briarwood. A slim briefcase stood beside him.

"Ah, there you are." He gestured. "Have a seat. Take time to enjoy the sunset. How's the face?"

"Roughly holding shape. Why are you here?"

"I should apologize. It was me Liz was mad at."

"About what? How does she know you?" Mike checked the cottage door. No sign of activity.

"She doesn't." Ric's face twisted in an odd way. "It's complicated. I'll explain later, I hope. The important thing is, she tells me you found the ticket. Sit down. Is it true?"

Mike eyed his uncle. "Why?"

"If it is, we can wrap up this whole misunderstanding."

"Meaning?"

"Meaning, my wife is in the library with Bart Westfield, waiting for you, and I believe I can orchestrate a resolution."

Mike glanced at the briefcase, wondering what it held. "You want me to fetch the ticket and give it to Westfield." The handle had a laminated name tag. ERIC L. OWEN.

"Not exactly." Ric tipped his head back and forth. "You give it to Helen, and she'll pass it to Westfield. That's the way it needs to work, politically."

"I see." Mike stood and dried his palms on his pants. "And when will this take place?" OWEN.

"As soon as you produce the ticket."

"Ticket. Okay." He took three steps across the terrace.

NƎMO.

His chin dropped to his chest. "Not okay. Not at all. Nice try, though."

"What?" said Ric.

"Nice try. You know, it almost worked."

"Almost worked? I'm afraid I don't understand."

"I bet you don't. I bet." The scary thing was how innocent the guy looked. It dawned on Mike that revealing knowledge of Nemo might be a bad idea. "Good cop, bad cop, isn't that what they call it? Donovan threatens me, then you come along talking all sweet. I must still be groggy."

"Mike, you're not being rational. What are you worried about?"

"Stay away. It's not a question of being worried. I'm not worried. Why should I be? Tell me how this looks. Three days ago, I run into a colonel with blueprints and maps of this place. This afternoon I see her in town, dressed very much like a woman I now find out is your 'wife' of whom I had the barest glimpse at 'your' house before I got socked. You have her inside now, haven't you, and you want me to hand over a valuable lottery ticket. No thanks. I don't think so."

"Time out, time out." Ric made a T with his hands. "You know about the Colonel?"

"I'm sure that's a surprise."

"It is. But not for the reason you think. Let me get this straight. Donovan's threatened you?"

Mike gestured toward the cottage. "He's there now, sharing the delusion with Senator D'Onofrio that they're related."

"They are."

"Get out. They don't have the same name. What is it, an alias?"

"Donovan is his real name now. Roger never came to terms with his heritage, and he changed his name years ago. It's the nineties. People do it all the time."

"But . . ." Mike took a step away, thinking hard. "Mr. Westfield acted as though he'd never met Donovan. Wouldn't he recognize the son of his college roommate?"

"Maybe. Roger's always been a bit of an embarrassment to the senator. I don't suppose Bart's seen a picture since the kid was ten."

Mike felt his guard going down. He spent a moment reliving the image of Char caught sleeping with the boss' son. She'd probably enjoy looking for a new job. She had all those tapes to help her.

"Okay, very entertaining. What about the Colonel?"

Ric picked up his briefcase. "Come into the library. You don't have to do anything about the ticket until you're positive I'm not trying to sneak one by you. Just let me do the talking."

▼ ▼ ▼

Mr. Westfield stood behind his desk, examining a smashed model rocket. Across from him, her cane resting by her chair, was the woman who'd assured Mike the ticket was in a 'safe' place and who was definitely not the Colonel. She had a grim expression, but the resemblance ended there.

"I don't understand," said Mike.

"Don't worry." Ric motioned him toward a chair. "I'm not certain anyone here is prepared to say what's going on. And that includes me. But I can promise you this, Bart: everything that had you worried has been taken care of. Do you understand? It's taken care of. Go ahead and say to Helen what you want." He stood behind the woman and rested his hands on her shoulders. She did her impersonation of Whistler's Mother.

"Your name is Owen, too." Mike had assumed Nemo was a man.

Mr. Westfield cleared his throat. "I have made two fundamental mistakes, Helen. The first was advising you not to marry Eric. Obviously, the pair of you have things under control."

She lobbed a frosty stare at him. "The other?"

"The connection I told you I'd made to Thomas of Bath. I was, well, mistaken. It seems we don't have a common ancestor. Which I suppose means I won't need this." He lifted the blotter and withdrew a photocopied sheet. The writing looked old. Very old.

Helen took the paper with a skeptical look. As she studied it her features relaxed. She looked up and spoke in a whisper. "You realize what this means?"

"It takes you back into the twelfth century. A generation from William the Conqueror, maybe two." He winked. "But I might catch you yet."

"I wouldn't count on that. All in all, very gracious of you, Barton. And I gather from this gentleman's presence," she nodded toward Mike, "that you didn't need to surrender. I therefore accept the apology in the spirit offered."

"That's it?" said Mike. "That's what the big fight was about?"

"Excellent." Ric rubbed his hands. "Mike, if you'll do the honors, you can give the ticket to any one of us. I guarantee it will end up in Bart's hands."

"Why wouldn't it?" said Mr. Westfield.

"I'll explain later. What do you say, Mike?" He tapped the side of his briefcase. "We're ready to take it to the lottery office."

Mike looked at each of them, ending with Helen. "Then, you're not . . ." For once, he couldn't think of an explanation. "It's not here. I'll have to get it."

He rushed from the library and across the living room, taking the stairs two at a time all the way to the third floor. At the end of the hall, the door to the bathroom stood open. He went to the toilet, lifted the cover from the tank, and peered inside. The plastic zipper bag was taped to the porcelain where he'd left it. The paper envelope into which he'd placed the winning lottery ticket, however, was gone.

–16–

Allie appeared in the doorway of the greenhouse. "There you are. I've been looking everywhere."

Liz ran her fingers over a mound of potting soil. "Why?"

"I was worried, of course. Mom said you'd just disappeared." She stepped inside and closed the door. "I mean, what kind of question is that?"

The kind of question someone would ask when her knuckles hurt and she wished they didn't. "You spent a long time riding."

"Sorry, no one mentioned a time limit."

"Let me ask you a question." Hothouse heaviness surrounded them. No more chasing after life. Here was Allie, and here was the moment. And Liz couldn't do it. After five years of waiting, she couldn't do it.

"Yes?" said Allie.

Liz stared. "Have you ever punched someone in the face for no reason?"

"I've never punched anyone for any reason."

"It's not like I make a habit of it." Liz wiped the soil from her hands. "Too bad you were riding for so long. I needed a voice of reason."

"To say what?"

She poked at a red flower. "To keep me from hitting Mike." She realized how stupid that sounded. "I thought he was in on it. But now it turns out your stepfather acted on his own."

"Are you okay? It sounds as if you were the one who got hit."

"Oh, I got hit all right." AN ARROW NEEDS A BEAU. It was perhaps the one thing more important than making sense of the past. Ariel. Eric.

"Oh, my God. Mr. Westfield's checkbook. Your stepfather's initials are E.O." Ariel, a blackmailer. Impossible. "Tell me why you left Hillton-Tanner."

Allie's expression revealed nothing. "Why are you so interested?"

"Just tell me."

"Combination of things. I couldn't stand working with Roger."

"With Roger." It clicked. "Roger Donovan."

A large plant in the corner wiggled. Liz rushed to it, determined to expose him, but behind was only a bird, Mrs. L's canary. Roger Donovan was the easiest connection to make, absolutely the easiest, and she'd missed it. She tried to keep her voice calm.

"So, Roger works at Hillton-Tanner."

"Not any more." Allie edged toward the window. "He used to."

"He never told me that."

"Why would he? Do you know each other?"

"Socially. My mother fixed us up once on a date, a disaster. I'm certain he didn't mention anything about H-T."

"When was that?"

"Earlier this year."

"Well, no wonder. He'd probably just left."

Liz forced herself to count months. "How long had he been there?"

The canary hopped from behind the plant, probably hoping for food.

"Mmm, about a year, I guess. He had six months' seniority on me. That was one of the worst things. He always needed to be in control."

A familiar feeling, and what Roger must have told Char. *The thing with Liz, you gotta keep her off balance. Out of control.* She ticked backward through the calendar. The first embezzlement had been four months after Roger's arrival. But two months before Allie started.

"Did I ever mess up," Liz said. "I owe someone an apology. Where's your . . ." she choked it down, "your uncle Bud?"

"Heading to Washington with Joey."

"Perfect." Liz stabbed a trowel into the dirt. "He must have known you and I went to school together. Why didn't he mention it?"

"I asked him not to."

"You?"

"Sure. I knew you'd be upset if you found out I helped you get your job."

Liz sat down carefully. "Try that again."

"Didn't he tell you?"

"No. But you'd better."

Allie put her hand on the glass. "I saw your Master's thesis."

"And how did you see it?"

"I've been . . . keeping track of you. Anyway, I sent it to Uncle Bud."

Liz felt the ground fall away. "You knew I'd never ask him for a job if I found out he was a relative."

"You always had to do things on your own," said Allie.

The greenhouse air was unbearably humid. The canary took flight. Liz watched it circle near the ceiling.

"I don't believe it." Her stomach hurt. It was like having a huge trig test you'd studied for turn out to be calculus. "You found me my job. After . . ."

"After what?"

"When you worked at the jewelry store." She advanced on Allie. "I never understood why you would do that."

"Do what, for God's sake?"

"Put that necklace in my purse. The day I came to say goodbye."

"Necklace? I didn't put a necklace in your purse."

The bird crashed against the greenhouse window and began to panic.

"You must have. There's no other way it could have ended up there. And a guy on a bike swooped by and grabbed my bag and knocked me down and there was the necklace and," Liz sniffled, "I mean, how could you do that to me? I thought we were friends."

Allie looked flash-frozen. "You haven't talked to me in five years. Because you thought I used you to steal jewelry from the store."

The bird cried out. Liz wanted to make it stop, but she didn't know how.

"Look at me," said Allie. "Look at me, now. They caught the clerk who committed those thefts. He confessed. He went to jail. I had nothing to do with it."

"I . . . I . . ." With some people, you could tell by looking at the face.

"You never asked." Allie brushed the back of her hand down Liz's arm. "You never even gave me a chance."

"Oh, God." Liz felt her voice shrivel. "I'm sorry. I am so, so sorry."

But Allie said nothing. She simply unlatched the greenhouse window and let the canary free.

▼ ▼ ▼

Mike headed down the stairs more slowly, more philosophically, than he had gone up. The discovery that a toilet is not a sacred throne might shatter any man's faith.

Helen aimed her cane at him. "I knew it was too good to be true."

"Don't you have it?" said Ric. Mr. Westfield edged forward in his chair.

Mike turned weary eyes toward his uncle. "Someone appears to have helped himself."

"Who else knew where it was?"

"Nobody. I didn't tell a soul. I never got a chance."

"Helen," said Mr. Westfield, "you haven't gone and hidden it again."

"Of course I haven't, you ninny."

"Settle down." Ric patted the chair beside him. "Let's take it step by step."

"I found the ticket in the fireworks last night." Mike picked up one of the crumpled model rockets. "At first I thought it was in one of these. When I found the ticket I brought it back to my room and put it in an envelope. I sealed it in a plastic bag. I taped it to the inside of the toilet tank. And now the envelope's gone. The last time I checked was this morning, before I confirmed Liz had taken the other one."

"Toilet tank?" Helen seemed almost amused. Mr. Westfield didn't.

"Presumably," said Ric, "Liz wouldn't have shown Bart the wrong ticket if she'd known where the right one was."

"Then I'd say," Helen thumped her cane on the floor, "it's a matter of figuring out who had the opportunity to take it."

"Anyone in the house could have been in that room," said Mr. Westfield. "Are you sure no one saw you hide it?"

"Sure, I'm . . ." *I've been keeping an eye on you.* Not Doris. No way.

Ric paced. "Has anyone left the house since this morning?"

"Who are you?" Helen laughed. "Columbo?"

"It's a reasonable question," said Mr. Westfield. "There've been the usual comings and goings." He turned to Helen. "Your brother's gone back to Washington with his nephew. That kid was around the house all afternoon."

Ric stopped pacing. "Doing what?"

"Claimed to have lost an earring last night."

"And naturally you gave him the run of the house."

Mr. Westfield closed his eyes.

"You guys must be joking." Helen settled into her chair. "I think we can assume neither Bud nor Joey took the ticket."

"Why?" said Mr. Westfield. "Because they're related to you?"

She hefted the cane. "Don't start that again."

"Okay, people. Okay." Ric held up a hand. "Let's suppose it wasn't them. We can eliminate the four of us. Allison's been riding since dawn. Gray would have come forward, surely. Who does that leave? Your guests?"

"Wait a minute." Mike felt the attention shift to him. He swallowed. "The number one suspect has to be this woman you're protecting. The Colonel."

"Woman?" The new Mrs. Owen gave her husband a dangerous look.

"Colonel?" said Mr. Westfield.

A faint thought swam through Mike's brain in search of articulation. He had the feeling there was something he needed to tell everyone.

▼ ▼ ▼

The greenhouse was more bearable with the window open. Allie touched Liz's shoulder. "This can't be the first time you've been wrong."

Liz passed her hands over her face.

"Please," said Allie. "I just want to go back to the way it used to be. Back to being friends."

"We can't go back. Time doesn't work that way. I don't work that way."

Allie dead-headed a flower. "Maybe you should. Or are you waiting for your punishment?"

"No, no, I've got the punishment. That job you found me, I just lost it. I called Bud a crook."

"You do that rather easily."

"I guess I do. I was supposed to start vacation tomorrow. If I go now, I won't have an office when I get back."

"Eric could help. Uncle Bud listens to him."

That was true. Bud listened to Ariel. Everyone listened to Ariel. All she had to do was bring herself to face the man. She bowed her head.

"Do you know where I can find him?"

"Eric? He went to Briarwood with Mom."

Briarwood. Where Mike had gone. Another apology. Liz's head throbbed. "Back to Briarwood. I'm beginning to feel like a pinball. Come on, Allie, let's see if we can light the bonus."

▼ ▼ ▼

"It's work," said Ric. "Leave it at that." But Helen's look made it clear she wouldn't. "Oh, hell. The Colonel is an old contact." He turned to Mike. "Government stuff. Nothing to interest you. She's what we call a free agent, paramilitary. We've had our eye on her because she's been acting a little odd."

"A little odd?" Mike threw all the disbelief he could into one look. "She's planning an invasion."

"Yes, I know. She's been here posing as an archaeologist."

Gray's father leapt to his feet. "You let a free agent loose on my property?"

"She's no threat, Bart. I've kept an eye on her personally. You've seen her. She calls herself Nishida." Ric used a matter-of-fact tone, as if the whole thing should have been obvious. Mike didn't care for it.

"Yeah, Nishida. As you may know, it's Japanese for Westfield." Nishida. Westfield. In his mind, another thought swam after the first. "Hey, you've been keeping an eye on her? Then you are Nemo."

"Yes, but . . . how do you know about Nemo?"

"Wrong puzzle." Mike walked to the window. "I solved the puzzle that wasn't meant for me, and missed the one that was. You sent me that postcard. And you sent Donovan to the Colonel."

"You have been busy," said Ric. "Yes, unfortunately, I was a little too cute. Roger worked for me four or five years ago. The senator wanted to make something of him and persuaded me to take him on."

"Stop." Mr. Westfield flopped back in his chair. "Roger is Steve's son?"

Ric nodded. "He washed out. When we let him go, he said things he shouldn't have. So I've kept tabs on him. When the Colonel came to me wanting help, I steered her to Roger. How much trouble could they get into?"

Mr. Westfield's face hardened. Suddenly he was no longer the southern gentleman. "It sounds as if you played with fire."

The thoughts met up in Mike's brain. That map in the Colonel's office. 'EW' didn't mean East-West.

"You're right, Bart." Ric gave Westfield a strange look. "When I heard Roger had surfaced this weekend, I broke cover myself."

"What about this colonel?" Helen stopped twiddling her cane.

"She doesn't have the ticket." Ric shook his head. "Not her style. It's not what she's interested in."

"That's right. She came for the family reunion." Mike studied the moose head on the wall. Things had been so simple four days ago. "I really should have seen it in the eyes." He saw those same eyes now, in Mr. Westfield. "Your Cousin Jake's sister. Emma. She's the Colonel."

▼ ▼ ▼

The drive in Allie's car passed in silence. Liz wondered what she'd do if Bud wouldn't give her back the job. They pulled up in front of Briarwood. The carriage house door opened and Gray emerged, looking furtive.

He blinked in the sunlight. "Allison. What are you doing here?"

"We could ask the same thing," said Liz climbing out of the car.

"I live here. And I'm looking for the ticket. Surely that's obvious."

"Spare us. We know Mike took it." She began to advance on the house.

"He did? What makes you think that?"

"Nothing much. Only that he told me."

"He did?"

"Would you stop saying, 'He did?' "

"Dash it, now." Gray flushed. "Mike went with me to follow someone, then he vanished for several hours. He reappeared, claiming to have been kidnapped by Roger Donovan. Oh, I see your point."

"Roger Donovan?" She didn't believe there'd been a kidnapping. But she was relieved, in a way, to confirm the Mike-Roger connection. She'd been half afraid Mike's accomplice would turn out to be Char.

Gray kicked at the gravel. "Forget Donovan. I mean to say, when was it Mike told you he had the ticket?"

"Around lunchtime."

"But I'm sure he doesn't have it. He would have told me."

"No, he wouldn't."

Allie frowned. "You mean he was going to give it to Gray's father?"

"No, he was going to keep it for himself."

"Steady on," said Gray. "If that were true, why come back?"

"To throw suspicion off himself, of course. Which he's done."

"Gray," said Allie. "Why'd you think the ticket was in the carriage house?"

"Well, I didn't." He covered his mouth. "Oh. I mean . . ."

Liz slipped past him and threw open the door. The place was mostly empty, an ordinary garage. She was turning to go when she saw a manila file sticking out from beneath a tarp.

"Let me guess." She closed her eyes and touched a finger to her forehead. "I see . . . a stack of Hillton-Tanner files."

She heard twin gasps and opened her eyes.

Allie stared at Gray. "What are you doing with those?"

"There's no 'those.' Just one." Gray put his arm around her. "I moved the rest from the library. But I just found this one, and someone was coming, so I came here to hide it."

Liz rested her hands on her hips trying to ignore how Allie seemed to fit into his embrace. "Why were you doing that?"

"Allison has nothing to do with this problem. She's innocent."

"I know." Liz lifted the file.

"Whatever made you think I had anything to do with it in the first place?" Allie wore the unhappy expression Liz had wanted to see earlier, but not now.

"Anonymous phone tip."

It was all too pat for Liz. "How did you happen across the files?"

"In a briefcase in the Left Luggage room at the Abbotsville train station on Friday. Per instructions. Where I returned the case today. Also per."

So, the files would be back at H-T by Tuesday, and if anyone missed them before then, Gray would make a convenient patsy. Liz was genuinely impressed.

"Who gave you the claim check? Roger?"

"Lord, no. The man slipped it to me on the train."

"The man?"

He nodded. "The man who turned out to be Allison's stepfather. Eric."

▼ ▼ ▼

Mike still occupied the center of attention, a position he hated.

"Emma?" Mr. Westfield's jaw worked, but no other word came out.

Mike turned to his uncle. "You knew the whole time."

"I knew she was in Washington. Not that she wanted anything out here."

"Say that again?" Mr. Westfield's voice was gruff.

"I'm sorry, Barton. I didn't know how to tell you. She's not entirely balanced. I thought it best to keep a low profile and simply watch, as long as she wasn't an overt threat."

"You what? And how long have you been God?"

Mike thought back to his first encounter with the Colonel. Photos. Maps. And something else. "It's as if she thinks there's something valuable in the house. She's been digging in the tunnel that leads to the study."

"Tunnel?" Mr. Westfield dropped into his chair.

"Yes. She hung a fake brick curtain at the entrance. Why would she do that?" Mike held up a hand. "Rhetorical question."

No one spoke as they waited for him to explain. It would have been fun, if only he'd had an explanation. The tough thing was to make it all fit with a kidnap plot. He turned from the window. "When did Nishida turn up?"

"Last weekend," said Mr. Westfield.

"Emma always resented not having Briarwood. True?"

"Yes."

"Maybe she's not after anything inside the house. She said something to me about the deed being in her pocket. The deed. Maybe what she wants is the house itself."

"And how would she propose to acquire it?" asked Helen.

Mike searched the desk for pencil and paper. "Here's what she has." As he listed each item, he said it aloud. "A map. A photograph. Blueprints. An empty tunnel. A van with some equipment. And Donovan." He pointed toward Ric with the pencil. "Thanks to you. A scheme to kidnap someone, possibly Gray. Oh, and an electronic garden gnome."

"A what?" All three spoke at once.

"A garden gnome with a two-way radio. Are you missing one?"

"Not exactly," said Ric. "The plans for that device were stolen from a company called Morveus Industries some time ago."

"Yeah, well, Emma has the prototype."

Helen twisted the top of her cane. "We know how she came across that."

"What would she want with it?" Mike looked at his list. "I mean, put it in the garden and you can listen to birds. Not exactly cutting-edge military use."

"Good heavens," said Mr. Westfield. "I wonder if Emma knows about her brother."

Mike drew a dollar sign. "Maybe she had her plan in motion already."

"Plan?" Helen turned those intense eyes on him. "What plan?"

"I haven't worked that out." He drew a square around the dollar sign.

She made a tsk-ing sound. "Let me know when you do. I need to use the facilities."

"Hey," said Mike, after she'd gone. "Do you think Emma planned to kidnap Gray and ransom him for the lottery ticket?"

Ric coughed politely. "The same ticket you hid?"

"That's right. We got off track from trying to figure out who took it."

Mr. Westfield looked at the grandfather clock.

"In thirty minutes it won't matter who has it. If they don't turn it in, it won't be worth the paper it's printed on."

Both men looked at Mike. Only fair, since he'd lost the ticket. But he wished they wouldn't. He wished he weren't in the same room. Or on the same planet. "Here's an idea. Why don't I check the bathroom one more time?"

He raced up the steps to the third floor, trying not to think about the height. There was an awful lot of pressure on him. It was going to take something fairly spectacular to make it all work out.

–17–

Eric Owen gave you Hillton-Tanner files?" Liz had hoped the surprises were over. "Why?"

"He didn't tell me that." Gray closed the carriage house door. "The person on the phone said to be on the train and suggested I look through the files, otherwise there might be a problem for Allison."

"A problem for me? How?" Allison raised her head from his shoulder.

"He didn't explain, and I couldn't tell."

Liz examined the H-T file. "You did your review in the study, figuring the paper would be lost in the clutter."

Gray looked glum. "When you started spending time in there, I realized I had to move them."

"You lifted the H-T disk from my bedroom."

"Sorry, don't know what you're on about there."

"Roger, then." She put the file on the hood of the car. "It must have been Roger, trying to cover his tracks."

"Could be. Anyway, you're wrong about Mike. Solid as they come. He wouldn't try to steal the ticket even if he had it. In fact, you've given me an idea. I'm going to look in the shed again. Liddell's set up the launching apparatus. Pity to have the ticket go up in a shower of fireworks."

"Forget about the ticket," said Liz. "I don't understand why Ariel would give you the H-T records. You, of all people."

"Search me. This anonymous caller asked if I knew anything about counting, which of course I did, then he told me how to get the files."

"Counting? Counting? You dope, he asked about accounting."

Gray went pale. "Accounting?" He ran toward the back lawn. Allie followed a few steps and stopped by the hedge. Liz caught her at the gate and watched him disappear into the garden shed. Someone, two someones, had a rowboat on the lake. The oars appeared to have drifted away. The boaters used their hands to paddle toward shore.

"You know something?" Allie squinted toward the hills. "I'm about as confused as I ever hope to be."

As they passed through the gate into the backyard, Liz pondered the ground. "Let's assume the best about Ariel. Eric. If he heard about the H-T problems, he might have thought there was a danger you'd be implicated. He arranged access to the files and slid them to Gray. At the same time, he had Bud pull me off the case and send me here where he could keep an eye on me."

Allie twirled her car keys. "If you're right, what's Roger doing here?"

"I certainly want an answer to that before we leave."

A launcher sat outside the shed. Liddell hadn't yet brought the fireworks out. A crash came from inside the structure.

"Much too late to find the ticket," said Liz.

Allie pointed across the lawn. "It's Roger."

A trio emerged from the cottage and moved toward the house. Roger, and Char, looking disheveled, and . . . Liz started.

"That's the senator?"

"Looks that way. He must have decided to get some air."

"But he was the governor who swore my mother in as a judge. He was fatter then."

Roger's voice carried across the lawn. "Dad, you don't understand."

The three disappeared around the side of the house. A new sound came from the direction of the road. A high-pitched whine, coming nearer.

▼ ▼ ▼

In the middle of the ballroom stood someone wearing a moose costume that sagged around the ankles. As Liz and Allie entered the room, the moose fled toward the parlor.

"Not another party," said Liz. The engine noises grew louder. Motorcycles. A bunch. She tailed Allie into the foyer. Mrs. L came out from the kitchen.

"What on earth is that racket?" The aroma of roasted peppers wafted behind her. "Oh, Liz, dear. Allison. You've come for the fireworks."

"We were looking for my stepfather. Have you seen him?"

"I believe they're all in the library. This is for you, Liz." From her apron pocket she pulled a white envelope.

"Who sent it?" It was sealed and slightly damp. Her name was on the front. She could tell that there wasn't much inside.

"I couldn't properly say." Mrs. L looked past them, out the window, and frowned. "I really couldn't say." She dipped her head and made for the stairs.

Liz studied the unfamiliar writing. She was about to break the seal when Matt and Marsha staggered in, their sleeves soaked. Marsha draped herself on Liz. "There you are. You've missed all the excitement."

"Just a pair of oars. No call to go fainting." Matt made a show of peering into the distance. "I don't suppose anyone's seen Liddell with the drinks. We could use a Saint Bernard."

"A saint won't help you," said his wife. "You need a priest."

Liz pointed with the envelope. "I think he's outside with the fireworks."

"Speaking of fireworks." Marsha took firmer hold of Liz's shoulder. "I wanted to talk to you about the engagement party."

Liz looked at Allie and smiled. "Sorry. The engagement's definitely off."

"What?" Matt followed. "You had the sense to cancel?"

Liz glanced toward the closed door to the library. "You might want to catch Liddell now."

A commotion arose in the foyer, and a small group entered the living room. Roger and Char were easy to spot, looking unhappy. The senator didn't seem pleased either. The fourth person stayed behind in the shadows. Liz could see only that it was a tall woman. The others stopped, as if waiting. All of them held their hands stiffly, close to their sides.

"What's your mother doing back there?" said Liz.

"That's not my mother."

The swinging door from the kitchen burst open, and in ran the moose, waving a piece of paper and prancing.

"It's Archer," said Roger. "I told you he had the ticket."

Char gasped. "Michael?"

The moose vaulted a couch and sprinted across the room, clutching its prize. It fumbled with the library door. The antlers had just disappeared into the next room when the door frame emitted a puff of smoke. The woman in the shadows moved into the living room. She crouched with her arms extended. What she carried was now clear. It couldn't be legal for civilian use, a stun gun that fired electric bolts.

▼ ▼ ▼

Mike dutifully examined the inside of the toilet tank. Hearing footsteps in the hall, he hefted the tank lid, let it drop into place with a grinding clank, and stepped to the sink. The tap water ran over his motionless hands. He peered at his reflection and another bathroom, everything the same but backward. Maybe things worked properly in that room. Maybe that toilet tank had a lottery ticket in it. He turned off the water and dried his hands. No time left for fantasies. In the hall, he ran into Mrs. Liddell, wearing an apron with fresh food stains on it.

"Young man," she said, planting her fists on her hips. "Could I trouble you to step inside for a moment?"

He gulped. "Did I break something?"

"Not that I am aware of. We need to speak."

"Oh. Sure."

When they were in the Blue Room, she headed for the window. As she passed the bed, she brushed her hand across the quilt to smooth a wrinkle that was, to Mike, invisible. He stood in the doorway while she fussed with a square of blue silk draped over a small table. On it stood a flower in a vase. With a snap of her wrist, she flicked the silk from under the vase.

"Very good," he said. "Actually, I need to . . ."

She raised a finger to her lips, made a fist with her other hand, and stuffed the silk into it. From the bottom of the fist, she pulled out a red, white and blue square.

"Nice." He tried to give an encouraging smile.

"Things," she shrouded her fist with the silk, "are happening. Downstairs."

He straightened. "Are they?"

"They are. You, on the other hand, remain upstairs." She whipped off the silk, revealing a small yellow bird. He couldn't think of anything to say.

She stroked the bird. "This one's not tame. Quite wild, in fact. For, oh, ages she wouldn't come near. I'd put out a bit of seed for her, ordinary food. But that wasn't what made her dare to come near. I cared for her, that was it, and she learned to trust me. People can be like that."

"I see." He didn't. "Anyone in particular you had in mind?"

The woman indicated the floor with her eyes. "I told you. Things are happening downstairs." Still holding the bird, she moved to the window and opened it. From outside came the sound of unmuffled engines, bringing to mind Donovan's abandoned motorcycle. The bird chirped and wriggled.

"I've done what I can." Mrs. Liddell faced him. "You couldn't stop her from flying away, of course, unless you kept her in a cage. But if you're gentle, she might remember and come back. Would you like to pet this little one?"

Mike crossed the room with the sense that he was being offered more than a lesson in ornithology. He reached out, and the bird bit his finger. "Hey!"

It flew out the window. He examined the welt on his knuckle.

"It takes practice, dear. Practice and patience. You can't expect miracles."

"No." He sucked the side of his finger. "Speaking of which, you wouldn't by any chance have seen a sealed envelope lying around here this morning, would you?"

"You mean the one in the loo?"

He froze. "Yes. Yes, that's exactly what I mean."

"I have been known, on occasion, to clean the bathrooms in this house."

He hardly dared breathe. "Terrific. What did you do with the envelope?"

"I delivered it, of course."

"Delivered it. To who? Whom?"

She continued to look at him in the way grade school teachers often had. "To the addressee, naturally."

"Addressee?" He fell against the wall. "It wasn't addressed to anyone." But then he had a picture of himself at a writing desk, and a more recent picture of himself grabbing the first envelope that came to hand.

Mrs. Liddell fiddled with the end of her apron string. "Eyesight has not abandoned me, young man. The envelope was clearly addressed to 'Liz.' Hmmph." She closed the window. "Of whom else have we been speaking for the past several minutes?"

▼ ▼ ▼

"Allie." Liz eyed the taser. "Keep very, very still."

The crazy woman waved her weapon. The maximum range for a device like that was twenty feet if you bought it in a spy shop, but God only knew how far the military could make it go.

"Everyone through that door." The gunwoman pointed toward the place where the wooden frame smoldered.

Liz came into the library just ahead of the gun. Char promptly huddled in a corner and buried her face in her dirty hands. She looked as if she'd been buried alive. Westfield and Allie's mother and stepfather stared out through the open French doors into the afternoon sunlight. Beyond them, near the hedge maze, the moose dashed across the last piece of open ground. As the room filled, the three turned to face the newcomers.

Westfield gasped. "Emma. Good Lord, he was right."

"Can it, Bart."

The moose disappeared into the maze.

"Don't worry." Roger leered at the woman. "I told you those guys would come in handy." He pointed toward half a dozen bearded men in leather and chains who lumbered with boisterous shouts across the lawn. One by one, they disappeared into the maze. Roger's friends. The ones who messed with Mike.

Emma pushed through the crowd and took up a firing position on the terrace. Sounds of a struggle came from inside the boxwood, and the moose suddenly appeared above the foliage, rising high in the air before falling back into the maze. There was an eerie silence, followed by a collective shout, and it reappeared. Cheers reached the house. "Moose. Moose. Moose."

Matt lifted a drink from the table. "Twenty bucks says they get him higher on the next throw."

"Stop it." Liz clenched her fists. "This is insane."

Emma retreated to the room. The front doorbell rang. Liz turned to Ariel/Eric. "Can't you do something?"

He shrugged and gestured toward the weapon.

"Emma." Westfield hadn't stopped staring. "What are you doing?"

"Hang on, Mikey!" Gray's shout came from somewhere near the garden.

The doorbell rang again.

A whizzing shriek ripped the air, and the evening sky filled with color. In the glow, Liz spotted Gray, crouched by the launching device. Three more rockets arced through the sky, aimed more or less at the hedge. Emma pointed her weapon through the French doors toward Gray.

"No!" Liz lunged as the taser sent a bolt of electricity into the shed.

Allie dragged Liz back. "Don't be stupid."

"Are you kidding? That's your fiancée she's shooting at."

"Gray can take care of himself."

Helen stifled a snort. "That'll be a first."

"Fiancée?" Westfield steadied himself against the wall. From across the lawn came a white roar. The shed was on fire. Gray, silhouetted against the flames, sprinted for the woods.

▼ ▼ ▼

From the safety of the dining room window, Mike watched the growing chaos outside. He would have felt pleased about being entirely blameless had it not been for the tiny detail that, by failing to turn over his find, he'd brought it all about. Now Liz had the ticket, which would ordinarily have been good, but the explosions and the fire were definitely bad. He still had a few things to iron out. And there wasn't time for it. The banjo clock on the wall said five. Zero hour. Expired lottery tickets and deadly rubber bands. Destruction of a family fortune twice in one weekend. It had to be some kind of record.

▼ ▼ ▼

A gentle cough came from the door to the library. Liz turned to see Liddell. "Sir, a gentleman at the front door wishes a word with Mr. Donovan."

Emma turned to Roger, who shrugged. "Don't look at me."

Westfield pushed himself from the wall. "Thank you, Liddell. Could you deal with it?"

"Oh, my." Marsha giggled hysterically. "This should be interesting."

Liz turned back to the lawn. The moose had just freed itself from a hole in the wall of the maze. Limping, it headed for the side of the house. The unseen bikers continued to thrash in the hedge.

The gunwoman took aim. There was a click, and nothing. Liz held her breath. He was going to make it.

"Don't worry." Roger pushed through the crowd. "I'll get him." He dashed from the terrace toward the stumbling animal.

"Roger!" said the senator, who took three running steps before Emma had the gun working again. She felled him on the grass. Liz took a sharp breath. It was the closest thing she'd ever seen to an assassination.

"I'll be leaving, then," said Helen, but she stopped when Emma aimed at her. "Not yet, I guess."

▼ ▼ ▼

Somewhere in the house, a door crashed open. Mike heard running steps.

Gray came through from the kitchen. "There you are. How did you do that so quickly?"

"I had nothing to do with it."

"Sod that. Can't you see what's happening?"

"How could I?"

"Not the bloody fireworks, dolt. It's your colonel. She's in the house."

▼ ▼ ▼

The smell of phosphorous filled the air, and flames licked the garden shed. There was going to be a major explosion soon. Liz took cover behind a chair. Out on the lawn, near the oak tree, Roger tackled the moose. The two went down with a thud and rolled over. Another handful of fireworks launched themselves simultaneously, tracing random paths over the lawn. In the multi-colored light, Roger tugged at the antlers. At last, the furry head tore away, revealing the dark, straight hair inside. Marsha fainted. Matt dropped his tumbler. Inside the headless moose suit, Doris' eyes were triumphant.

▼ ▼ ▼

"I know all about the Colonel," Mike said. "She's your cousin Emma."

"Please, don't start with the bloody theories again." Gray put his ear to the wall. "I'm trying to figure out what's going on in there."

"It's not a theory. Uncle Ric told me. You want a real theory? I finally figured out what it is with you and the accent." Fireworks set themselves off in batches. "You can't figure out who you are. For all the complicated plans, for all your organizational skill, you don't have a clue. You're no better off than I am. It's another way of doing the same thing, waiting for life to happen to you. That's my theory."

A lull came in the pyrotechnics display.

"Interesting," said Gray. "Assuming you're right, how would you suggest I get out of it?"

"Be yourself. Just be yourself."

Gray looked as if the concept were not only novel, but insane. "So," he said. "Emma Westfield is the Colonel. Why?"

"Why what? Why is she here? Because her father inherited the stocks in 1929. Because, more than anything else, she wants this house." Mike moved to the window. "That's why she has the garden gnome."

"Okay, I'll pretend you didn't say that."

"No, it's all right." Mike turned to follow the flight of a rocket. "The gnome in the wagon. It's some goofy surveillance device. The plans were stolen from the government, and Emma got her hands on them."

Gray continued to wear a blank look.

"What's more, she was going to plant it here and tip off the feds. You and your father would have been hauled off to jail. He would have had to sell Briarwood to fund his defense. Or, if you both got convicted and the house was seized, she'd buy it at the sale."

Gray looked askance. "Preposterous."

"I'm telling you, she's not interested in the money so much as making sure your father has to give up the house. With her it's revenge, nothing but revenge. I bet she'd have destroyed the ticket even if she'd managed to put her hands on it." He peered through the window. There was something almost admirable about a person who could walk away from ten million dollars.

"What do you mean, would have? Do you have it?"

"No, fortunately. Mrs. Liddell gave it to Liz. Don't ask. The important thing is, it's safe."

▼ ▼ ▼

Roger yanked the paper from Doris' hand and ran toward the house.

"I've got it!" He waved something, far too big to be a lottery ticket.

Lottery ticket. Liz became conscious of the envelope she held. The one with her name that suddenly seemed to weigh twenty pounds. She ran her fingers over it, squeezing the small rectangle inside. Me. He gave it to me.

There had to be a way to get rid of it before Emma noticed. She tried to imagine what Mike would do under the circumstances. Hoping not to draw attention, she slit the envelope with her finger.

Emma rose as Roger neared. "Let me see it."

A rocket zipped by. Roger crouched to run the last few steps. As he reached the terrace, he made a triumphant display of his spoils. Emma snatched it away and scanned it.

"You imbecile." She crumpled the paper and threw it to the floor. "It's a train schedule."

"Hey, what the heck is going on here?" In the doorway to the library stood a stout man wearing a leather waist wallet on his stomach. "This crummy butler says no one's home, but I know he's bullshitting me. We could see the fireworks from the road."

▼ ▼ ▼

"The ticket is not safe," said Gray. "Liz is in the library right now, with the Colonel and everyone else."

Mike rushed to put his ear against the wall. The fireworks made it difficult to hear anything.

"The library of course. You realize she's going to escape through the tunnel she's spent the last two weeks clearing." Mike pressed his hands against the wall. "If only we had a way of blocking it up." Staring at Gray, he touched the bump on his forehead. "Quick," he pointed toward the carriage house. "Get a hammer and the biggest nails you can find. I'm going in there."

"I wouldn't advise that. She's not too friendly. She shot at me."

"Someone's got to stop her."

"Fair enough. I shouldn't think walking into the library is the answer."

"The answer?" There wasn't any construction paper handy. Mike cupped his hands as if holding a firefly. He opened them and showed Gray his empty palms. "Sometimes," he said, "there are no answers."

▼ ▼ ▼

It took Liz a moment to recognize the tourist from the Cinnamon Bear. The guy with the picture of Mike.

"Who the hell are you?" Emma hid her taser.

"Randy Thomas, if it's any of your business. Where's Donovan?"

Emma gave Roger a look.

"I've never seen this guy in my life," he said.

Liz ran her finger along the crease of the envelope. Other than Ariel, who briefly met her eye, everyone was busy looking at the new arrival.

"Not you." Thomas shook his head. "I mean Roger Donovan. The guy with the beard."

"I'm Roger Donovan, and I've never had a beard."

"Don't mess with me, kid. I've got a picture of the guy I'm talking about." As Thomas dug in his waist wallet, a beep came from it. He withdrew a mini cell phone. "Yeah, this is Randy. Gimme a break, will you, Frances, I just got here. No, I can't find the guy . . . I am not making him up." He covered the phone. "She doesn't believe me."

The door opened again, and Mike walked through.

Emma raised her weapon. "How did you get out?"

"That's him!" Thomas pointed with the antenna. "That's the guy."

"Michael," said Char, as Roger moved toward him.

"Is there a problem here?" Mike ignored them both.

Thomas snapped the phone shut. "Thank God you showed. I've been looking everywhere. You gotta come out to the car so Frances can see you."

"I'm not going anywhere," said Mike. "I finally realized what I didn't want to be when I grow up. Or who."

Roger grabbed Mike's wrist. Emma aimed the taser.

"Oh, put that thing away," Thomas said. "I should warn you, I've got a concealed weapons permit." He reached for his wallet.

Before Liz could decide whether the tourist was bluffing, Emma zapped him. His body convulsed, and his cell phone bounced on the carpet. From the receiver came a shrill, tinny voice. As he crashed against the desk, his photograph of Mike fluttered to the ground. Char, of all people, began to cry. In the commotion, Liz slipped the envelope into her purse, upside down, and tried to shake out the ticket. Another round of fireworks exploded. And another. The stun gun pointed at her head.

"I'll take that," said Emma.

Liz stared at the weapon. From the corner of her eye, she could see Mike standing motionless. No help from Ariel, either. With a leaden arm, she handed over her prize.

Emma glanced inside the envelope. "Plus contents, if you don't mind."

Liz reached into her purse and produced the ticket.

"Much better." Emma placed it on the desk and admired it.

Mike caught Liz's eye. His eyebrows inched up, a question. She shook her head minutely. Emma pulled a lighter from her pocket, flicked it once, and touched it to the paper. She held the ticket in the air while it burned. Westfield gasped. Helen shook her head sadly.

"Wait!" Roger lunged for the burning ticket. "You can't . . ."

He slumped to the floor. Even though she'd watched it happen, Liz couldn't believe Mike had clipped the guy behind the ear so precisely. Nor could she understand why he'd done it.

As the paper became ash, Emma looked at Mike. He flexed his fingers, as though he'd hurt his hand but didn't want to acknowledge it.

"I told you earlier," he said. "Your show to run."

"Yeah." She crushed the ashes with the butt of the stun gun. The envelope dropped to the floor. "So, you really are Nemo."

Nemo. Liz tried to navigate through the mental smoke clouds. How many people called themselves Nemo? Ariel stifled a cough, and Mike sent him a dirty look. Then he smiled at Emma.

"Don't worry. I won't hold your sense of prudence against you."

"Why would you do this, Emma?" Westfield lifted a bit of ash.

"Work it out. Okay, Nemo," she said to Mike, "fair enough. You can leave through the front door. The rest of you, on the lawn. Not you, sunshine." She grabbed Char by the arm. "Anyone follows us, she gets it."

Roger and Thomas lay motionless on the floor, breathing. Liz moved onto the grass with the rest, past the still form of the senator, toward where Doris lay. She kept a wary eye on the burning shed. The explosions had tapered off somewhat, but you never knew. She turned around in time to see Emma close the French doors. The glitter of bursting fireworks reflected on the glass. She couldn't tell what Mike was doing inside with Emma and Char. Liz had the feeling she'd never see him again. She wanted to talk to him one more time, to ask whether he'd set the whole thing up.

▼ ▼ ▼

Gray waited outside the library, clutching a hammer.

Mike closed the door and whispered hurried instructions. "Gray. This time we try my plan. Wait for the sound of the bookshelf closing. Then get in there and nail it shut."

"How do I know where to nail?"

"Figure it out. Do your best."

"And where are you going?"

"Fishing. No time to explain." Mike climbed the staircase in bounding strides, filled with an unfamiliar sense of purpose. It would take her time to get the bookcase open. Fifteen steps into the tunnel, say, then several yards . . .

On the second floor, he hurried down the hall. But the window facing north wasn't big enough. He stuck his head into Gray's room. Wrong angle.

It would have to be another flight, and the roof. He clenched his teeth and clambered up the stairs. Leap. Leap. The dormer window in the Blue Room was fairly large. He pried it open and squeezed through. Balancing on the gutter, he straightened, not daring to look down.

Here at the front of the house, things seemed relatively calm. Only a few of the fireworks soared high enough to explode above the roof. A silver convertible idled outside the carriage house. The driveway seemed a long way off. Char would resist, probably, so that would slow the Colonel a little. A very little. He set his jaw and scrambled to the peak. The back lawn spread below him. He swayed. The sun hovered above the foothills. An empty rowboat drifted on the lake.

From the burning shed by the garden, fireworks erupted in irregular bunches. Multi-colored light flashed on Matt and Marsha as they knelt by a still figure on the grass. He saw the moose costume and recognized the face. What a grand, futile gesture. He felt a lump in his throat.

Most of the people on the lawn had clustered near the oak tree. Ric and Allison tended to another body on the ground. Several bikers, having thrashed their way from the hedge, trundled toward the side of the house.

Liz stood alone, near the spot where she'd once tackled him. As he watched her, she looked up. He raised his hand, more a salute than a wave. He could sense his momentum ebbing, but waiting would only make it worse. He ran along the ridge as fast as he could, imagining as his target the tormentors of Morty Moose. Bastards. A rocket burst not twenty feet away, showering him in red, white and blue.

"No!" In the din, her voice was faint. He lost himself in the sense of release as he leapt into space. It was like jumping into another world. His form was perfect: legs together, arms raised. The wind rushed by and roared its approval. There were no other sounds, no sounds at all. The figures on the lawn were statues. Even the fireworks had stopped.

No miscalculations this time, no mistakes. He knew where he would land. Sparkles from exploding rockets glittered below him, captured in a small rectangle of water. His feet pointed like twin daggers toward the crumbling fish pond above the Colonel's escape tunnel. The reflection of color and light rushed to embrace him.

–18–

He lay in darkness, listening to a rhythmic beeping that came from somewhere close by. A soft cocoon spun itself around him, clean and marvelously cool, except for his legs, which felt warm. He risked opening an eye. Whiteness. Nothing but whiteness. He closed it again. Repeating the process with the other eye produced the same result.

To the extent he'd spent much time wondering what death was like, not once had it occurred to him that it might resemble a hospital.

▼ ▼ ▼

Allie insisted on driving Liz to Dulles. "We need to talk," she'd said, but now they were in the car she didn't seem so eager.

Liz gazed without interest at traffic going the other direction, toward Washington, people headed for work, people like Bud and Joey and Matt and Marsha, and even Eric. But not Liz Halloran, not this morning. The broken white line whipped toward them like so many darts.

"Send me a postcard?" Allie took her eyes from traffic.

"I'm kind of off postcards for a while. But I'll drop you a note. Where should I address it?"

"That depends." Allie grinned. "How long will you be gone?"

"A good while, I hope."

"In that case, send it to the Chevy Chase address. Gray says there's no reason we can't move in after Jake's funeral."

"Your mother's all right with that?"

"Yes. Isn't it wonderful?"

"Of course it is." Liz fumbled in her purse for the crumpled Polaroid photo. There he was, dopey beard askew, looking lost.

"What's that?" Allie spared another glance.

"A memory. A possibility." She put away the picture.

A black convertible overtook them on the left. The day before, she would have seen something ominous. Today she noticed only the way Allie's golden hair made a sharp contrast with the dark paint. It was dangerous to jump to conclusions. Westfield's payments to Eric Owen, for instance. Investments, not blackmail. She hunted in her bag without looking for anything, needing something to do.

"I'm sorry I thought you were mixed up in . . . everything."

"Forget about it." Allie changed lanes. "We're starting over. No harm done. Speaking of which, do you plan to call Mike before you leave?"

"No." Liz slid her finger along the dashboard.

"Why not? He could use some cheering up. And you were wrong about him. Don't you think he deserves a chance?"

"Allie, he jumped off the roof. Does that strike you as particularly stable?"

"No. But then, I wouldn't think you needed a whole lot more stability in your life."

Liz stared out the window. "There isn't time. There just isn't time."

"Make time." Allie smiled. "No one makes it for you."

Traffic slowed as they neared the airport.

"One thing bothers me." Allie hit the brakes. "I can understand Roger burglarizing your office once he realized you were on to him, but why leave the postcards?"

"Probably something he saw on television. He wanted to scare me, and he couldn't resist letting us know how clever he was." Liz began to search for signs to the international terminal before deciding Allie could handle it. "He was right, in a way. I wasn't very smart."

"Because you let it bother you?"

"Because, in the end, there were only a few ways anyone could have picked up that information. But instead of securing my line, I went ahead blabbing to

Bud and Ariel. Eric. At dinner Saturday night, Roger's postcard told me he knew why I was there. I should have figured it out from that."

"If he knew you were heading for Briarwood, there was no reason to stage a mugging."

"It wasn't staged. They were really after this." Liz tapped her purse. "At the Tidal Basin, he tried to take a picture to show to the kid he hired. Then Mike came along."

She removed the H-T disk and held it up. "Roger guessed I was carrying this when he didn't find it at the office. He'd already removed the renegade file to wipe out his footprints, so this was the only thing left that showed where the money had gone."

"He shouldn't have cared, if it went into a numbered account."

"That's the weird thing. It shouldn't have mattered to him at all. I guess it became personal."

"He's definitely going to transfer the money back?" said Allie.

They swung onto the departure ramp, and the sun hit Liz in the face. She flipped down the visor.

"He will if he doesn't want his father turning him in for, among other things, impersonating a federal official. Or a human being."

Allie stopped the car. "Well, this is it."

"I'll call when I get back. Take care." Liz pulled her suitcase from the car, then reached back in and gave Allie's shoulder a squeeze.

As she passed through the automatic doors, Allie called after her, "I still think you should give him a chance," but Liz was far enough away to be able to pretend she hadn't heard.

▼ ▼ ▼

Something about the whiteness was eerily familiar. Mike opened both eyes. Patterned whiteness, warp and woof. Cotton sheet. A cotton sheet covered him. Not a hospital. A morgue. Awfully soft mattress for a slab, though.

▼ ▼ ▼

Liz waited in a short line and gave her folder to the agent. He glanced at her passport and stamped the ticket.

"Your flight's had a brief delay. A minor mechanical problem." He pointed toward the monitor, and she found the flight number. The 'brief delay' was estimated at three hours. She looked back to the unloading zone, but Allie was gone. The agent flashed his teeth. "Sorry for the inconvenience. Here's your boarding pass. I'm afraid we're out of windows and aisles."

She shoved the folder into her purse, and her fingers brushed two other pieces of paper. She pulled them out. The first one, she'd planned to mail from the airport. She held it next to the torn envelope with her name printed across the front. With the lightest touch, she traced the letters he'd written.

▼ ▼ ▼

Mike reclined against the propped pillows and surveyed the hospital room. Outside the sheet, the white motif continued. The walls were white. The visitors' chairs were white. The curtain forming the makeshift fourth wall was white. The television set braced near the ceiling was white, except for the screen, and that was snowy. The open door revealed a white corridor. On the table beside him, the spray of wildflowers made a wonderful contrast.

A nurse had brought them half an hour earlier. "No card. Secret admirer, it looks like." She sounded jealous.

A steady wheeze came from the other side of the curtain. Moving with care, so as not to cause his ribs undue alarm, he brought his arms up and placed his hands behind his head, adjusting his skull toward a window he couldn't see. Sunlight splashed across the wall of the room, illuminating the dividing curtain. He listened to the brisk click of heels on a tiled corridor. Above his head, conveniently out of reach, were two large buttons. One was green, the other red. He wondered what they might do.

The floor warden bustled in, thin and muscular. Mike did not miss her during the prolonged periods when she was gone.

She set a plastic cup on the bedside table, along with a glass of water. "Ibuprofen for pain. I will be back to adjust the bed. You have a visitor." A visitor of whom she did not approve. "Do not excite yourself." She left.

The white-faced wall clock flirted with noon. Mike held the pills and waited to see who would come through the doorway. Light footsteps drew near.

Around the door peeked Gray's spectacles, followed by the rest of him.

"How y'all doing?" It was his normal voice.

"We're great, all of us. Thanks for asking."

"Aw, hell. Meant to bring you something. Sorry about that. Next time."

Mike shrugged carefully. "I was hoping there wouldn't be a next time. With any luck, I'll be out tomorrow. They just want me for observation." He held up a cautionary finger. "The walls have . . . eyes."

"Suit yourself. What in the name of sweet Mary set you to jumping off the roof? I wish I'd seen it."

The tableau on the lawn rushed back. "Is Doris all right?"

"A few bruises. One good thing about it, scared the bejesus out of her parents to see her in your costume. I think they went thirty minutes without insulting each other."

Mike let his head drop back to the pillow. "It's a start."

"I thought you might have wanted to know about someone else."

"Liz?"

"Char."

"Oh. Is she okay?"

"Intact, if that's what you mean. Not highly pleased. You destroyed her car. Someone stole her hydrant. She's lost her job. Her pal Roger is in it deep. And a chunk of fish pond concrete gave her a bloody lip. She also broke a nail."

"I'm sorry about that. I would have thought it was a small price to pay for being rescued."

"Might have been." Gray sat in a white chair. "The problem is, she wasn't technically a hostage by the time you crashed the tunnel. After all, what good would it have done Emma to drag her along? Char was on her own, pretty much. She didn't like it, though. Second time that day she was cooped up in the tunnel. Of course, it didn't collapse on her the first time."

"How did she get down there earlier?"

"Someone bopped her on the head and left her tied up. She swore it was you until I convinced her you were in town with me when it happened."

"Donovan."

Gray applauded. "See, you're not in such bad shape after all. He told her it was you. Some bizarre plan to make himself look good by rescuing her, I guess."

Mike gazed levelly at his friend. "I'm glad I don't know anyone dumb enough to try a stunt like that."

The nurse returned. "Your medicine, Mr. Archer. Now."

"Sorry." He hoisted the pills and she left.

Gray settled in the chair. "Who sent the flowers?"

"No card."

"I see. Secret admirer."

"So they say." Mike pushed at the pillows with his elbow. "Ironic, isn't it, that if Emma had inherited Jake's money, she could have bought property just like Briarwood, without going through this phenomenal trouble."

"Didn't you know? Oh, no, you wouldn't. Jake did change his will last week. He wrote her in. It was on the way out of his lawyer's office that he keeled over. The choking thing had nothing to do with it, Dad says."

"On the way out?" The medication seemed to have taken effect, because Mike felt a whole lot better. "That means I didn't . . . I'm sorry you didn't get the money."

"Oh, well. You win some, you lose some. Tough to complain."

Pretty philosophical for a guy whose family had lost an inheritance and a lottery fortune.

"You haven't heard the kicker," said Gray. "Remember that business I was talking to you about last week?"

Mike winced. "The pizza place?"

"Well, yes, if you have to call it that. The point is, I've found a partner. Matter of fact, I was on my way to pitch the idea to him when I ran into you that night. You were so damned negative about it, I didn't get to tell you the rest. He thought it over all weekend and said yes this morning. I came over here to give you one more chance to join us. It's a no-lose proposition. The guy's already in the business. It was Dad who arranged for me to meet him, through the senator. They're related in some fashion."

"What?" Mike felt dizzy again. "Your partner is related to the senator? Are you saying . . ."

"He's outside. Let me get him." Gray stepped to the door. "Hey, pal."

Mike fought to hold onto consciousness. A figure walked in, and Gray swept an arm in introduction.

"Meet my new partner. Mike Archer, Carl Handley."

"Carl." Mike was too weak to continue.

"What do you say?" Gray edged closer. "Will you join us?"

The room smelled of antiseptic. Carl stood beside the bed, blurring. Maybe the idea behind all the whiteness was to embarrass germs from the place. With a sense of relief, Mike let it slip away.

▼ ▼ ▼

A muffled voice, dehumanized with amplification, hummed in the hall. *Lock the batteries in for free.* That wasn't it. *Dr. Hatteras to O.R. Three.*

He opened his eyes to the vision of Liz. She stared at his leg with a look of concern. Beneath drowsy lids, he studied her, admiring her face, stupidly pleased that she didn't know he was watching. She had her hair pulled back in a ponytail. Sunglasses dangled around her neck, secured by a bright blue strap. She looked great. With a rush of disappointment, he realized it wasn't happening. None of it. Just a dream.

His legs made a tent of the white sheet. He wiggled his toes, happy to see movement at the tip. Liz was oblivious. He wiggled again and felt shooting pain in his right leg. "Ouch."

She smoothed a wrinkle in the sheet. "You're awake."

"The way you're eyeing me, it's a wonder I'm alive." Since it was a dream, he could be bold.

"Don't be silly. It doesn't look that serious."

"Really?" He pouted. "They won't tell me. I thought they were afraid."

"Busy, more like. Broken ankle, bruised ribs . . . I think most doctors can deliver that kind of news."

He smiled. "Say what you want. Things will change when I'm awake."

"You are awake."

"That's what you're supposed to say."

"You're impossible." She tweaked a toe, sending a wave up his left leg. A good wave.

"Okay, okay. Did I ask to be pinched?"

"You didn't believe me."

"No cause to pinch my toe."

From the other side of the curtain came a raspy voice. "For God's sake, shut up you two. You're making me sick."

Liz stifled a laugh. She tipped her head toward the curtain and raised her eyebrows. Mike shrugged.

"Honey," continued the voice, "would you by any chance be Liz?"

"Yes, I am. Why?"

"Take your whiny husband home, willya? The guy's drivin' me nuts. All he does is call out for you in his sleep."

Mike's ears pounded.

"Oh." She touched her lower lip, just beside the white scar. "But he's not my husband."

"Jesus, do the world a favor and marry him then, for crying out loud." The voice degenerated into spasmodic coughing.

Mike's face grew warm. He felt exposed, just a thin sheet over a hospital gown. Trying to look relaxed, he laced his fingers across his stomach.

Liz inspected the room. "Nice flowers."

"I was thinking the same."

"Someone must like you quite a bit."

"Must they?" His gaze had drifted to the static on the television set, but this brought it back.

"Yes." She looked right at him. "Yes, I think so."

He cleared his throat. "I guess . . . you're on your way to the airport."

"The flight's had a big delay." She searched for something in her purse. "You . . . you missed the excitement yesterday."

"Actually, I had about as much as I could take."

She laughed. "The funny thing is, I'm sure Emma Westfield never thought of herself as a bad person. It must have seemed unfair that you could jump through the tunnel to stop her."

Mike did not want to replay that particular moment. He adjusted his pillow. "Will Gray's father press charges?"

"I don't think so. He's well disposed at the moment. Although–"

"You two talkin' all day, or is there a chance of a guy getting some sleep?"

Liz raised a finger to her lips. "I'll be right back."

While she was gone, Mike devoted some thought to how hurt he'd have to pretend to be to get her to stay all morning. When she returned with a wheelchair, he gave her a skeptical glance. "What will the doctors say?"

"They'll say it's good for you. Let's go."

He maneuvered himself toward the chair, conscious of how thin the gown was. She was thoughtful enough to hand him a white bathrobe that had been hanging, camouflaged, on the wall. They rolled into the hallway. Outside his door, the name ARCHER was typed on a slip of paper in a plastic frame. Below it, WHISKERSON. Liz's fingertips grazed his shoulder. He put his hands in his lap and concentrated on anagrams of his roommate's name.

▼ ▼ ▼

Liz blinked away the sunshine as she pushed the wheelchair into the garden. Other visitors propelled other patients into similar health. She chose the nearest stretch of asphalt. Flowers had been arranged in tidy beds along the paths.

Mike's exposed toes wriggled in the breeze. He twisted his head over his shoulder. "You didn't raid the gardens for that bouquet, did you?"

"That's my secret." She put a hand on his shoulder and let it rest there.

He started to touch her fingers but drew back. "Did you leave a bouquet at my apartment on Friday?"

"I wish I could say yes, but I believe it was Roger."

"Donovan? There's a frightening thought."

She covered a laugh. "I didn't mean he had a special interest in you. He wanted to make Char mad."

"Char? I don't see how she fits in."

Well, there it was. He'd asked straight out, and he deserved a straight answer. She stopped wheeling the chair.

"Don't shoot the messenger, but Roger's had a crush on Char for ages. He's gone out of his way to make her break up with you."

"All he had to do was ask. But I thought you two were . . . you know."

"Were what?" She wrestled with the news that he didn't care about Char.

"When I saw you in the library the other day. You seemed . . . intimate."

"Intimate? What an appalling idea. My mother fixed us up on a date once. When you saw us, he was trying to steal a computer disk."

"He and Char deserve each other," said Mike. "Tell me more. Why is Mr. Westfield well disposed?"

"Because she didn't cost him the ticket." It was almost criminal, stringing him along like this. Almost. If he hadn't done the same thing to her, she'd have felt bad.

"But I saw you give it to her."

"I gave her a ticket. It happened not to be the right one."

"What do you mean? I took that ticket from the shed."

"No, I took that ticket from the shed. Where you'd put it."

"Where I'd . . ." He searched in the sky. "You've lost me."

No, she thought, quite the opposite. He looked sweet, with his bathrobe and his bare toes. It had taken her so long to see.

He traced the air with his finger. "I found the right ticket late Sunday night and left the wrong one in the fireworks."

"And I still had the wrong ticket. Then Mrs. L slid me the envelope with the winner. Her magic tricks gave me the idea. While Gray launched fireworks at the bikers, I did the same thing you'd done earlier and switched the tickets. Emma never checked the numbers, and she had no reason to expect me to have an extra. I did try to let you know, before you jumped from the roof."

"That's why you waved. So, you ended up with the real ticket."

"Yup. I turned it in and put the money in a numbered account."

"You did?"

"Of course not." She grinned. "Get a sense of humor. I gave the ticket to Westfield, and he redeemed it this morning."

"But it's too late. The deadline was yesterday."

"Funny, that's not the position the lottery people took. And it's a little late for them to ask for their money back."

He looked at her in a way that made her uncomfortable. A little too . . . admiring. She reached for the wheelchair handles and began to push. They gained the shade of a huge tree, its branches spread to the sky.

"If I weren't in this chair, I'd be hugging you now."

She felt a surge of pleasure, too intense. She ducked under a branch. "Something to work toward."

She angled him into shadow, set the brakes, and sat against the tree trunk. He kept on admiring. The dirt at her feet was suddenly fascinating. With a twig, she drew interlocking circles. There'd been another tree, a big oak tree, not long ago, in the dark. She wanted to lock away the memory of this warm sun, the drifting shadows of clouds, the suddenly bearable songs of birds. From the corner of her eye, she watched him fiddle with the hand brake.

He cleared his throat. "There's something I've been meaning to ask. That riddle of yours. 'Defeat.' You know."

"Oh. That." She tried to smile. "It's nothing."

"Tell me."

"Don't you want to guess?"

"Stop tormenting me."

She paused slightly longer than was dramatically necessary. "Defeat of deduct . . . go over defense . . . before detail."

"What?"

She repeated it.

He began to laugh but quickly clutched his ribs. "Ow. Is it okay with you if I use that?"

"Be my guest."

"Well." He cleared his throat again. "Mr. Westfield must be pleased. To have the ticket. All that money."

She gave up on the line drawings and turned to an invisible thread on her skirt. "Mmm. But not the way you think."

"Oh? Mount Helen insisted on half?"

"Not quite. In fact, she didn't make any claim on it. She was happy to have the ancestral clue." A dandelion grew by the tree, its yellow petals faded to gray feathers. Liz plucked it. "I guess she planned all along to give him the ticket today."

"Huh. Remind me not to count on her next time I'm in front of a firing squad." He looked toward an old man shoving a walker across the lawn. "What do you mean, he wasn't pleased the way I thought?"

She blew the seeds into the air between them.

"He's not going to keep all the money."

"He's giving it to Gray?"

She smiled. "Some. About a quarter, I think. On condition he invest it in that business he's starting."

"He'll need it."

A trim figure in a white uniform strode toward them and resolved itself into a glowering warden. As she zeroed in, Mike reached for the wheels. Liz coughed softly. "You haven't heard about the rest of the payoff."

"I hope he's putting it to good use."

"Most of it." Rehearsing had been easy enough, but now the words wouldn't come. "A hefty chunk . . ." She pointed at Mike, paused, and stabbed her thumb toward her chest.

"What?" He mimicked the gesture. "You? Me?"

Slicing between them like a starched missile, the nurse gripped the chair, pulled the brakes, and spun him around.

"This patient is not to be ambulated by non-hospital personnel." She bumped him across the lawn. Liz scrambled to her feet. She heard mumbles about charts and access. They were halfway to the doors before Liz caught up.

"Look, it's not that big a deal . . ."

The nurse shot her a look meant to injure and stepped up the pace. As Mike, near-recumbent, shot past, Liz dropped the stamped envelope onto his lap. A claw snatched at it, but she saw him stow it in the pocket of his bathrobe, and the nurse had the decency not to dive after it.

▼ ▼ ▼

Back in the sterile room, pinned between sheets with nothing but head and arms and leg cast exposed, Mike studied the thin envelope. His name wandered across the front. There was a stamp, but no postmark. He held it to the light and shook it.

Through the dividing curtain, he heard the restless creak of bedsprings and a snore from Mr. Whiskerson. Sunlight coated the bare white wall under the white TV. From the hallway drifted sounds of doctors being paged. There was no sign of Liz.

Mike ripped the end off of the envelope and withdrew a sheet of pale stationery filled with more of the same graceless handwriting. The name 'Westfield' was etched across the top in black. It was dated July 5th.

Dear Mike:

The lawyers are always telling me I need to formalize things, so here it is. Over the weekend you have become something of family to me. Which is not saying anything against Gray, of course. He's a fine young man, I'm proud of him, usually, but you know what I mean, I think.

In any event, circumstances have changed since we met, mine that is, and I find myself not so desperately in need of those funds for which you searched with such success and, if I may say, panache. Your magnificent leap was priceless on its own. It is in consequence my wish that you have $10,000 in compensation for your services. I am bestowing a like amount upon Liz Halloran for her role in the conclusion of this affair. It comes as something of a sadness that her engagement to Gray was no more than a fiction. Just as I could have wished to have you for a son, so too would I have claimed her as a daughter.

Perhaps you will humor a sentimental old man in this stipulation: Should you and Liz marry within the next year, I shall be pleased to make the award an annual event for the rest of my life. I leave it to the two of you. As you have demonstrated over the past several days, you know best.

Ever in your debt, I remain,

Barton T. Westfield

Mike reread the last section several times, running a finger under each word. He closed his eyes and let his mind spin down dizzy paths of imagined futures. A soft tapping brought him back to sunlight. The door swung open, and Liz poked her head around the corner.

"Any sign of the Terror?"

"Harassing other patients. She shouldn't be back this way for a while. Come on in. Although I have to warn you, the guards have fliers with your picture and orders to shoot."

She didn't move past the door. Her cheeks still glowed, even though there'd been plenty of time for her to catch her breath. "Oh, you got it." She glanced toward the letter in his hand, and her face grew pinker. "I suppose he offered you the same incentive."

"Yes." The rigid cast was unbearable. "I guess he did."

"And what do you . . . think about that?" She made eye contact.

A sense of weightlessness passed through him. He gripped the bed to keep from tumbling away. She stayed half-hidden behind the door. He pondered his answer, acutely aware, for once, that he was at a crossroads, now, at this moment. He struggled to loosen the sheets.

"Mr. Westfield doesn't know me well enough. It was never about money. And I couldn't do something like that, even if you wanted to. It wouldn't be fair to him. Or . . . to you." He held his breath.

She smiled. "Thank you." But he thought she slumped against the door.

Raspy breathing sawed through the flimsy curtain. He refolded the letter and set it on the bedside table. She ran her hand along the door.

"At least you found what you're good at."

"I did?" He wished it hadn't sounded so dense.

"Well, yes. Figuring out puzzles."

"But I've always been good at that."

"I believe you. And, with a few adjustments, you could try to make a living at it. I have to congratulate you. You're really something."

He didn't know where to look. Her eyes were on him as he scooched against the pillows, but there was a sparkle in them once more.

She came all the way into the room. "So . . ."

"So . . . ?" He caught sight of the clock and waved in the direction of the Caribbean. "I guess you'll need to be going, if you want to make that plane."

Shaking her head, she moved to the side of his bed. "Didn't I mention? There's been a slight change of plans. I won't be leaving for, oh, another month and a half."

"Really?" He sat straighter. "A month and a half? I'm supposed to be out of the cast around then. What a coincidence. You weren't thinking of nursing me back to health, were you?"

She gave just the hint of a laugh.

"I figured you could handle that on your own. I have some things I need to take care of in Vermont." In response to his ill-concealed disappointment, she continued in a more professional tone, "But I thought I might scope out office space for us."

The snoring beyond the curtain stopped.

"For us?"

"Hey, twenty thousand goes a long way toward setting up a business. You didn't imagine you could make it on your own, did you? And I happen to be available. Think about it. You'll need someone with a technical background to handle the electronic stuff." She raised a hand in anticipation of protest. "Okay, okay, I'll tell you what. Your name goes first on the door."

"Oh?" He couldn't keep from grinning. "You think so?"

"I do. I really do."

"Such generosity." He spread his arms, more in welcome than surrender. "How can I refuse?"

She moved closer. "I kind of counted on you not to. And there's another thing." She pressed her palms together. "Once your leg is healed, I thought you might like to see the Caribbean. I know this great island, practically deserted."

He wanted desperately, for once, to out-nonchalant her. "Caribbean, hey? You don't suppose they've sold the seat next to yours."

Her face clouded. "As a matter of fact, they have." From her purse, she pulled a couple of folders and spread them in a fan. "I just bought it."

"You are wonderful." And there was nothing else he could say.

"Now you tell me." She moved even closer. "If I remember right, you believe in bringing along a suitcase when the person you're visiting is in bed. Mine's in the hall."

He took her hand.

"I'm not promising anything," she said. "We'll just see if this works."

"I didn't ask for promises." He admired her a while longer. "All right. You seem to have all the answers. Where do we go from here?"

The dividing curtain billowed toward them with a resounding thwack. Across it fell the shadow of an uplifted crutch and a cranky voice filled the room. "Not too swift at figurin' things out, are you, kid?"

Good old Mr. Whiskerson. So sympathetic, so helpful.

WHISKERSON.

KISS HER. NOW.

Some answers weren't important. Some things didn't need to be planned.

"Oh." He touched a finger gently to her mouth. "I see. I understand."

Acknowledgements

My thanks to Pamela Goodfellow, for coaxing this story from me and pounding it into shape; to LaVerne Woods, for endless patience, support, and good humor; to Jeff Fairchild and Bruce Campbell, for the many pieces of Mike; to Eric Smith, Elizabeth Zobel, Ann Fry, Michael Brady, David Zobel, Jim Flint, and Deborah Wroth, for their extensive comments on earlier drafts; to Joanne Kuhns, for the music lesson; to Tom Bresaw, M.D., for the medical advice; to the Monday night crew, for listening, laughing and (when appropriate) pointing; to RCWG, for dozens of Wednesday nights; to Randall Thomas, for his generous support of Family Services; to Matt Buchman, for making it all look good; and to P.G. Wodehouse and Stephen Fry, for creating, respectively, *Leave It to Psmith* and *The Hippopotamus,* two books I really wish I could have written. Except for the scene with the horse.

Goodfellow Press

Novels from Goodfellow Press are smooth and seamless
with characters who live beyond the confines of the book covers.

Ivory Tower by May Taylor. Does the scent of lilacs herald a soft haunting?
ISBN 0-9639882-3-9 $12.99/$13.99 Canada.

Cookbook from Hell by Matthew Lieber Buchman. One part creation. Two parts software. Season lightly with a pair of love stories and roast until done.
ISBN 0-9639882-8-X $12.99/$13.99 Canada

The Inscription by Pam Binder. An immortal warrior has conquered death. Now he must conquer living.
ISBN 0-9639882-7-1 $12.99/$13.99 Canada.

Matutu by Sally Ash. To find healing and love, an English violinist and an American writer must explore a Maori legend.
ISBN 0-9639882-9-8 $12.99/$13.99 Canada.

Bear Dance by Kay Zimmer. A man betrayed and a woman escaping painful memories struggle to overcome the barriers keeping them apart.
ISBN 0-9639882-4-7 $9.99/$10.99 Canada.

White Powder by Mary Sharon Plowman. It's hard to fall in love when bullets are flying.
ISBN 0-9639882-6-3 $9.99/$10.99 Canada.

Glass Ceiling by CJ Wyckoff. Facing career and emotional upheaval, Jane Walker makes a bold choice to explore East Africa with an unorthodox man.
ISBN 0-9639882-2-0 $9.99/$10.99 Canada.

This Time by Mary Sharon Plowman. A man and a woman with differing expectations and lifestyles take a chance on love.
ISBN 0-9639882-1-2 $7.99/$8.99 Canada.

Hedge of Thorns by Sally Ash. A gentle story unfolding like a modern fairy tale, of painful yesterdays and trust reborn.
ISBN 0-9639882-0-4 $7.99/$8.99 Canada.

The Songs of Kalaran by Matthew Lieber Buchman. How should you treat your mother when she heads the interstellar mafia, and you don't remember her?
ISBN 1-891761-C4-8 (1999 Release)

Goodfellow Press
16625 Redmond Way, Ste M20
Redmond, WA 98052-4499
(425) 881-7699
Available from: Partners Publishers Group

Goodfellow Press
16625 Redmond Way #M20
Redmond, WA 98052-4499
(425) 881-7699

A Slight Change of Plans

1. How would you rate the following features? Please circle:

	Unfavorable				Favorable
Overall opinion of book	1	2	3	4	5
Character development	1	2	3	4	5
Conclusion/Ending	1	2	3	4	5
Plot/Story Line	1	2	3	4	5
Writing Style	1	2	3	4	5
Setting/Location	1	2	3	4	5
Appeal of Front Cover	1	2	3	4	5
Appeal of Back Cover	1	2	3	4	5
Print Size/Design	1	2	3	4	5

2. Approximately how many novels do you buy each month? ________
   How many do you read each month? ________

3. What is your education?
   High School or below _____ College Graduate _____
   Some College _____ Post Graduate _____

4. What is your age group?
   Under 25 _____ 36 - 45 _____
   26 - 35 _____ 46 - 55 _____ Over 55 _____

5. What types of fiction do you usually buy? (check all that apply)
   Historical _____ Western _____
   Science Fiction _____ Action/Adventure _____
   Romantic Suspense _____ General Fiction _____
   Mystery _____ Time Travel/Paranormal _____

6. Why did you buy this book? (check all that apply)
   Front Cover _____ Know the author _____
   Like the characters _____ Back Cover _____
   Like the ending _____ Heard of publisher _____
   Like the setting _____ Purchased at a book signing _____

For current Goodfellow Press updates:

Name ______________________________

Street ______________________________

City/State/Zip ________________________

We would like to hear from you. Please use the reverse side for your comments.